The Amasai Rising Quartet

STEVIE RAE CAUSEY

THE AMASAI RISING QUARTET

For information contact :

stevieraecausey.com

First Edition: February 2019

10 9 8 7 6 5 4 3 2 1

Book One

Anhedonia

PROLOGUE

THE DRAGON'S EYES DARTED OPEN. Though few others could hear the footsteps of the intruder, the sound of his leather boots fell heavily upon her ears. She turned her head to the cave mouth where a figure stood, cloaked in the shadows. He was no stranger to her. If she had not already identified him by the cadence of his gait, his scent would have given him away. He reeked of arrogance.

"You've some nerve disrupting my slumber, thief," she greeted him with a warning.

"Thief? Fiora, you wound me." The figure feigned insult. "Is that any way to greet an old friend?"

"A friend of mine, you have never been."

Tendrils of smoke swirled out her nostrils. Her ivory teeth clashed against one another as she spoke, setting off sparks. "State your business or be on your way."

"I've come for Anhedonia."

The dragon hissed, rising from her pile of treasure. Gold coins fell from her scales, clattering on the floor as she puffed out her chest in warning. The sound of her claws scraping against the stone echoed off the cavern walls. She smirked as she saw the figure shy away.

2

"Your arrogance has never surprised me, young prince, but I never took you for a fool."

"Does the old man still hold your loyalty? After all these years, I thought perhaps you've grown tired of being his guard dog."

Fiora let loose a stream of fire that lit up the cavern walls as it landed just before the figure's feet. Though the stone before him scorched, he did not flinch.

"Hear me out, Old One." His eyes scanned the beast's body language for any warning of an attack before continuing, "The wizard has long been dead. His rivals, imprisoned."

"You think them merely *his* rivals? They were a threat to us all, or have you forgotten?"

"A new enemy has risen in their place. One that only years ago, held you captive. Would you deny your desire to see *them* in chains?"

Fiora bared her teeth and let out a low growl as she approached the figure. As she slinked out of the shadow of her cave the moonlight bounced off her fiery red scales. Once a beautiful and fearsome beast, the light revealed flaws in her armored body—scars from where her captors had chained her.

"You have my attention."

CHAPTER ONE

KALA

I PAUSED AT THE EDGE OF THE CLEARING TO GATHER MY THOUGHTS, my eyes scanning the camp in front of me. The campfires had all dwindled and the only light came from the reflection of the moonlight dancing across the tops of the white canvas tents. The camp was silent. Its inhabitants had already turned in for the night. Still, I knew that at least two members of the Alliance would be awaiting my arrival.

I pulled the hood of my cloak away from my face and sighed before making my way to the center of the tent-city. Even before I approached the King's tent I knew that Eoma would be waiting for me. After all, she was the one who sent for me in my dreams.

I was growing tired of the constant invasions into my subconscious and, more than once, wished the enchantress would take the information she sought from my mind; rather than summoning me from my home. I suspected the distance limited her telepathic abilities. I had never summoned enough courage to ask.

Or perhaps my physical presence here was meant to serve as a morale boost for the rest of the camp. A reminder of the oath I took as I stood before their King all those years ago. The girl who would save their people. If that were the case, then why summon me in the dead of night?

I pulled back the thick fabric of the King's tent, ducking as I stepped inside. Lanterns hanging from the wooden frame cast a bright light. The air inside was warm and dry, amplifying. the damp weight of the cloak on my shoulders.

At the center of the tent sat King Charlezon, his back facing me. His head was tilted to the ground where the glowing embers of the evening fire flickered as he prodded them with a stick.

"Come, make yourself comfortable Kala." He did not need to face me to sense my presence. Indeed, facing me would've done little to aid his perspective. The king was blind.

"Thanks just the same, your majesty, but I won't be staying long."

The old man chuckled, and motioned to the seat beside him, "Humor an old man."

I obliged, removing my cloak before taking a seat beside him. The weight removed from my shoulders offered little comfort compared to the way it made me feel exposed. Though the King had always treated me like an old friend, in truth I was uncomfortable in his presence.

"Is he treating you well?"

"Of course he treats her well. You chose him for her yourself." I jumped as Eoma's voice flooded my mind. No. This time it was her physical voice.

The Priestess had snuck in behind me, a basket of bread in her arms. She placed a hand on Charlezon's shoulder to him to her position before placing a roll in his hand. His hand lingered over hers as he took it from her.

"Gareth is very patient. He treats us well."

"Speaking of him makes you uncomfortable," The King said.

My gaze darted to Eoma who took a seat across from me. I waited for the familiar tingling of the sorceress's consciousness prodding my thoughts. It did not come.

"'Tis not my place to pry into your personal affairs, child," she smirked.

"Would you have chosen a different partner?" the King inquired.

"Of course not," I sighed. Three years had passed since the death of Azlyn, the King's son. Though I was grateful to Gareth for taking me in, and to the King for making such arrangements, a part of me still mourned.

Especially as our daughter's face grew to take on more of her natural father's features.

My marriage had been a necessary arrangement, made shortly after I discovered that I was with child. Whispers of an unknown paternity and the attention garnered by an unwed mother in our culture would have made it impossible to conceal myself among my people. And yet, Gareth had never been anything but kind. Even when my daughter pitched herself onto the floor with all the force and despair of a toddler who felt themselves wronged, his manner had always been soothing, and his hand gentle.

A long-time member of the Alliance, Gareth was well-loved and trusted by the Royal Family. Though the arrangement was practical, Gareth's affections were not forced. He grew to love me over the years; and though I had worked hard to remain loyal to my first love, my affections for him had grown as well. Something for which I would always feel a twinge of guilt, especially in the presence of Azlyn's father.

"He would not fault you your affections, Kala," Charlezon's voice interrupted my thoughts softly. I nodded absentmindedly, avoiding any physical contact, though I was certain his intuition would tip him off to my demeanor, regardless.

"We are well enough," I said as if he hadn't spoken. It was the truth, and all I was willing to offer him.

"What of your duties?" Eoma changed the subject.

"My first duty is to my child," I reminded her, "As for my efforts for the Alliance..." My voice wavered, betraying my frustration. "I am not sure what other role I could play that would not conflict with my duty to protect her."

Though the Alliance had deemed my placement to be the most fitting, I found myself resenting them for it. There was no one among us with whom we could truly confide. I was isolated. Banished. A prisoner amongst my own kind.

"You still harbor resentment over your placement, even now?" Though he phrased it as a question, I knew the King was unsurprised.

"My people are ignorant and stubborn." I raised my chin high as a show of my indignation. "My placement among them remains an unbearable insult."

Eoma's eyes lit up. Whether from joy or anger, I could not tell. The King clicked his tongue softly the way one would do as they chided a child. I might have second-guessed my hasty words, had he not been smiling.

"A childhood spent sequestered has left you without empathy for your own kind."

"They do not deserve my empathy. I do not understand why I must remain among them. Have I not served you well?"

"Pity them, then," he ignored my question, "For they live a great tragedy."

"Tragedy?!" I was taken aback by the grace of the Elven King. I couldn't fathom how he could show such compassion to his son's murderers.

"The tragedy of your people is that the wisdom of your ancestors is snuffed out with their passing. Each generation must start anew. Thus, you find yourselves making the same mistakes again and again."

His people inherited a genetic memory. Prior knowledge acquired by their ancestors was passed on to their offspring at conception. It was true that my own people did not possess this advantage, but that did not excuse their loathsome acts.

"We have written records! Historical accounts are passed down. Yet they learn nothing."

"The written word is easily manipulated." The King countered. "Altered to fit one's view, or to further an agenda. 'Tis not the same as living a moment."

Eoma had moved from her spot beside us as we talked and now sat in front of a large loom. She plucked fiber from a basket, scrutinizing each piece before laying it across the frame and setting it. She paused between each row, analyzing the piece as if it held the answer to a critical inquiry. Her eyes held steady on her work as she spoke:

"You always had a soft spot for the mortals, Charles." It sounded like a reprimand, but I noticed the corners of the sorceress's lips turn upward ever so briefly when she said the King's name. I wondered how it had come to be that the Priestess would call the King by a pet name. I knew better than to ask.

"Perhaps this will not be their fate forever," he turned his attention back to me. "Tell me, how is my grandchild?"

It may have seemed like a reasonable question, but the way he led up to it struck a protective chord in me. I was aware that my daughter was destined to play a significant role in the Alliance. She was the first of her kind: a human-elf hybrid. Heir to the elven throne, and the first in line to ascend to a place of power should Mystics and humans unite.

Eoma and King Charlezon remained confident that she would grow into her role with the grace and poise of her father's people. I remained uncertain that my child would inherit the powers of her elven kin. For all intents and purposes, she appeared to be a normal human toddler. Secretly, and somewhat selfishly, a part of me hoped that she would remain as such.

"She is well." I turned to Eoma, "Is this what you have called me all this way for? To talk about the child?"

Eoma acted as if I had not spoken.

"Who does she take after? Is she curious...?" The King let the question hang unfinished in the air. Still, I understood its meaning. Is she curious about her lineage? Have I told her about them?

"She shows curiosity for the world around her," I strung my words together carefully, trying to hide the fear radiating like a hot iron from my core. "For all she knows, Gareth is her father. We have told her no differently, and she exhibits no signs that it isn't so."

"She is young yet." He muttered, more to himself than to me. "I should like to see her."

I felt my body stiffen. I was not surprised by the request. Indeed, it had been my greatest fear in coming here, that he would ask for her. I found myself at a loss for how to respond. My daughter was young and had no knowledge yet of her true heritage. My own contact with them was danger enough. Though I believed fiercely in the goals of the Alliance, becoming a Mother had softened me in many ways. It had given me something to fear for, outside of my own safety.

Simultaneously, my heart ached for the king. The child of his deceased son was a stranger to him. Would, perhaps, always be. Each time I met with him he would ask for her. Each time I would turn him down. It was too risky.

"She is... too young," I chose my words carefully. "Too young to be burdened with such dangerous secrets. Too young to grasp the gravity of the situation. One childlike slip of the tongue in front of the wrong person and all our lives would be in grave danger. You know this, Your Majesty."

"Perhaps you have become too comfortable in your new life," Eoma set aside her work to address me. "Perhaps you are allowing the illusion of security to keep her from her destiny. You cannot protect her forever, you know."

"She is only a child—"

"She is of elven descent, and the heir to the throne!" The force with which she spoke made me jump. I had never known Eoma to lose her composure, even in matters that dealt with fate. Especially in matters that dealt with fate.

"What have you seen, old woman?" I stepped toward the enchantress. Once upon a time, I may have feared her, but I was a child myself no longer. I did not appreciate being told what was best for my own offspring.

"Even I have not seen her fate."

So, there it was. Though she had always been protective of the king, it was not just his interests Eoma was protecting. She was, herself, left in the dark; just as we were. A breeze slipped through a crack in the tent door. I shivered and reached for my cloak, which was now warm and dry.

Eoma's eyes darted frantically between myself and Charlezon before she collected herself, setting her jaw in determination. I could not be certain, but I thought I saw it tremble ever so slightly before she spoke:

"There is no precedent. We cannot tell how her awakening will occur, nor when. We do not know if her human consciousness will accept it. If it will tolerate it at all. You cannot keep her from us forever Kala. It is unwise."

"I will not put my family in danger to placate your fears—"

"It is you who should be afraid, child, if you dare defy me—"

"Peace Eoma!" The King's voice rumbled over our own, silencing us both. In the heat of the moment, neither of us had noticed him making his way across the tent.

"But Charles," Eoma's sentence hung fragile in the air, unfinished.

"We have time," Charlezon placed a hand on her arm reassuringly.

A pained expression crossed the woman's face, and it seemed that her anger had gone as quickly as it had come. I sensed there was more to the matter than either of them would admit.

"I will tell her," I assured them both, "When she reaches the appropriate age." The words sounded hollow, even to me. I knew I could not avoid whatever fate awaited us, but that did not mean I wanted to hasten it along either. I bowed my head to the King and the sorceress and turned to leave.

"May I at least have her name?" Charlezon's plea did not carry the authority of his station. It was the request of a parent in mourning.

I stood with my back turned to them both. I did not have the strength to look his sorrow in the face.

"Azlana." I said softly, "Her name is Azlana." With that I squared my shoulders, steeling myself against my own heartache, and stepped through the doorway into the night air.

Chapter Two

Azlana

"**Y**OU CAN'T CATCH ME!" A voice taunted playfully behind me. I spun around just in time to see the figure of a boy disappear around the corner of my house, evading me again.

"No fair, Luka!" I cried out in exasperation before darting after him. When it came to speed, the advantage was mine. That is why he always waited until I was distracted.

"Weren't nobody said I hafta play fair, 'Lana!" he shouted back over his shoulder as he led the chase into town.

The soft grass gave way to a dusty road. Before I knew it, we were weaving through the throes of people who had come to the seasonal market. I cursed Luka under my breath. Every time!

The marketplace was abuzz with activity. Summer was ending, and farmers from all over the kingdom were rushing in to sell the last of their wares in the Capital's market. I tried to ignore the static hum of the people's voices as I made my way through the crowd, pushing myself even harder to catch up.

He knew I would best him in a straight race—no contest. That's why he played this game of cat and mouse; sneaking up on me when I was unprepared and forcing me into an environment where he knew I would struggle to maintain my focus.

I shook my head, willing myself to pay attention as I watched him slip down an alley way. You won't lose me that easily! I thought to myself, skirting the edge of a parallel building as I prepared to cut him off. The city of Aythia was like a labyrinth, though we'd both grown up on the outskirts, his father worked at its heart. A childhood spent in his shop meant Luka was more familiar with this part of the city. Another advantage he held over me.

My bare feet beat against the dirt as I turned another corner, picking up speed. I was just about to intercept him when a sound like a herd of stampeding animals overwhelmed me. The feeling stopped me in my tracks.

It was a group of Luka's friends. They had caught on to the game we were playing and flocked to us, hoping to join in on the fun. Not again. I held my breath and begged the Powers That Be to will them away.

"Catch me, 'Lana!" a boy darted across my path only inches from me. The rush of air caused by his movement took my breath away, making my head spin. Another girl snuck up behind me, tapping me on the shoulder before she hopped away giggling. Others zipped around me, all of them just out of my reach. Their voices washed over me like a riptide, dragging me down as I stumbled and spun in circles trying to decide what to do next.

My chest ached as if a weight had been thrust upon it. Like that time when I was five and fell from atop the counter that Mother warned me not to climb. I slipped, and hit the floor flat on my back, forcing all the air from my body. The shock of it made me believe that my lungs had collapsed in on themselves. Like I would never be able to draw air back in again.

There was too much happening at once.

"Come on Lana!" one of them called to me. I couldn't make out which one.

"What's wrong with her?" another voice muttered before becoming lost again in the chaos. The other children gathered to form a circle around me as they tittered back and forth to one another.

I felt my body start to curl in on itself. My knees made a soft thud as they hit the dirt. I covered my ears tightly with my hands, hoping to block out some of the excess noise. It didn't work.

"Come on, 'Lana!" another voice demanded. "Why do you always have to be so odd?"

"That's enough!" Luka pushed his way into the circle to my rescue. "Stop it, all of ya!" He placed his hands protectively around my shoulders, lifting me up.

Their voices fell silent, but I could still hear the rush of my pulse pounding relentlessly in my ears. My face burned and tears began to well up in the corners of my eyes. I bit the inside of my cheek, trying my best to hold them back.

"We were only trying to play," one of the younger of the girls offered, avoiding eye contact.

"Hush, Lily!" the voice came from the girl's older sister. The one who called me weird. "Tisn't our fault she can't play like a normal girl."

"Bite your tongue off Gertrude," Luka spat back, "Lana ain't done nuthin t'you!"

I tore away from Luka before anything else could be said, forcing my way through the throng of children and making my way back off into town. The tears I had tried to hold back rolled warmly down my cheeks, blurring my vision as I wove in and out of alley ways.

Why do I have to be so different? I chastised myself. No matter how hard I tried, I hadn't ever been able to fit in with the other children. They did not seem to share any of the challenges I faced with environmental noise. They did not need to run with bare feet to ground themselves.

They did not seem to hear the whispers in the trees.

And they had absolutely no interest in anyone who did not fit in.

Except for Luka. He was the only exception. My only friend. Sometimes, it was like I existed with a foot in both worlds. Mine, and the "normal" one. Meeting Luka had been like building a bridge between the two.

Luka was the son of a blacksmith. The first time I met him was in his father's shop. I was approaching my fourth summer, and it was my first trip with father into the heart of the city. I remember father lifting me up in one arm joyfully, showing me off.

"Well aren't ya a pretty little lass." The blacksmith's voice boomed over the clanking of hot iron. I buried my head in father's shoulder, overwhelmed. "You got yerself a shy one, eh? Count yer blessings, Gareth! My Luka'd talk yer ear off. Can't get a word in edgewise!" he said laughing. "OY! Luka! Get yer hide out front and say hi to Gareth's girl!"

He came tearing around the corner, covered head to toe in ash and sweat, sporting a devilish grin. By his size, I deemed him at least a season older than me. Father set me down to meet him.

"You ain't got no shoes on." He pointed out.

"Fine observation, coming from a boy who's covered in soot," his Pa scolded. "What do you care if she ain't got no shoes on?"

"Just weird for a girl is all." I clung to father's side as he looked me over before breaking out into another grin. "S'alright though. I'm weird too. More than a handful is what my Ma says. I figure we can be friends."

And just like that, we were.

I'd become so wrapped up in the memory that I lost track of where I was. But I didn't care. I just kept running until the clay walls of the buildings around me became a blur and the wind raced around my body, pushing the tendrils of dark hair that had come loose from my braid away from my face as I ran. I ran until I was free.

My thoughts were interrupted by a familiar voice.

"Whoa!" was all my mind was able to process before we collided. My body slammed into something. No... someone. I ricocheted hard off their soft frame. The force of the impact expelled the air from my body and I tumbled to the ground, dazed.

"Whoa there, girl!" An arm lifted me to my feet and brushed me off. It took me a moment to regain my bearings before I could make sense of the figure standing before me.

I was surprised, once my sight righted itself, to see a familiar face staring back at me. It was Brian, my Mother's father. It had been almost three seasons since I'd seen him last, and I nearly did not recognize him. He had let his hair grow out past his ears, and the beginnings of a beard framed his strong jaw.

"What has you in such a hurry, lass?" he asked.

I wiped the tears from my face, trying to collect myself before speaking. My hands, which had become smudged with dirt from my fall, did little to clean my cheeks. More likely it made a right mess of it instead. I hoped that the cold sweat clinging to my skin would mask the fact that I was crying.

My grandfather's eyebrows furrowed as he reached down and wiped away some of the dirt with his thumb, "Who are you running from, child?"

Though we did not see each other often, my grandfather understood me in a way that, at times, was quite eerie. On more than one occasion across my childhood, I had found him answering thoughts and questions I had only ever held inside of my head and never spoken out loud. Perhaps it was because he himself raised a half-breed. His son, Nykolas, the offspring of the Nymph Sapphire.

Still, I worried about what would happen if word of the day's events made their way back to Mother. Where other children of were beginning to gain more freedom as they aged; the older I had become the more protective Mother seemed to be. At times, the fervor with which she sought to protect me was suffocating, as if she was slowly squeezing the life out of me.

"No one," I squared my shoulders and held my grandfather's gaze. He eyed me suspiciously, tilting his head in such a way that I knew he did not believe me. Still, I knew he would not pry.

"How long have you been in town?" I asked, hoping to change the subject.

"I have only just arrived. Do you think I would dally long before coming to see you?"

"I have never known you to dally anywhere long," I countered.

"Aye, work does tend to keep me on the road." He smiled slyly, "I have come across some new...merchandise." He chose his words carefully and I did not ask for clarification.

Though Mother often felt the need to shelter me from the harsher realities of the world, I was old enough to figure out that, love him though I may, my grandfather was not exactly a man of what one would call upstanding character. I did not know the details of what he sold in the market, but I could venture to guess they were either forbidden items—Mystic artifacts and the like—or items which had been obtained by less than honest means.

Not theft, necessarily. More likely a wager artificially tipped in his favor. Which I suppose is more theft than not, I thought to myself. The line between right and wrong was still fluid for me. Much more than it seemed to be for Mother. I did not dwell on the matter. Besides, he was my grandfather. The only one I had, and I loved him, just the same.

"Does Mother know you are here?" I asked.

"I was just headed her way," He replied, holding out his hand. "Walk with me and tell me what could possibly be troubling my favorite granddaughter enough to send her crashing into old men on the street."

I placed my hand in his. It was warm and rough, like leather that had not been properly conditioned. The hand of a man who spent his life living off of the land.

"Papa, I am your only granddaughter!" It was a joke we'd had between us since I was little. I squeezed his hand gently, and he bent over, feigning weakness.

"Careful or you will surely shatter these old bones!"

I leaned into his side playfully knocking him off balance, "Oh, stop. You are not so old."

"Perhaps not." We took a few steps more before he continued. "So tell me, what was it you were running from?"

"'Twas nothing, really." I shrugged my shoulders, trying to seem nonchalant. "Just the other kids acting like fools again."

"Ah. I see."

We walked again in silence, both of us looking at the ground in front of us. My pale feet, covered in layers of earth were stark in contrast next to his untarnished black boots.

He must have ridden into town then, I thought to myself, but... where is his horse? My heart leapt with excitement as I looked around for any sign of it. I loved animals! Mother always said I was a natural with them, too. Most of the children my age moved too fast, and were too noisy for all but the most domesticated animals, but once when I was only eight I was able to coax a wild chipmunk to eat rice from my hand.

16

Grandfather misunderstood my behavior, "They are not following us if that is what you are looking for."

"Who?" I had become so wrapped up in my own thoughts that I had lost track of the conversation.

"The other children. They stayed behind."

"Oh." I looked over my shoulder again. It always amazed me how he could be so aware of the surrounding environment without having to even look. "Even Luka?"

"Even Luka."

I was surprised at my own disappointment. Though I truly wanted to be left alone, part of me still half expected him to come chasing after me. The way he used to when we were little. Back then I would have run home to find him in the back yard, waiting for me to run off my anger. I would storm into my room, still distraught, and he would be there, tapping on my window for me to let him in.

Maybe he is sick of being my keeper, I thought to myself. The thought hung heavy on my mind all the way home.

Smoke was billowing out of the chimney as we approached the house. Mother has dinner on early, I thought as I noted the position of the sun. As we walked in, I was also surprised to szee that father was home early. Well, that explains the early dinner then.

From time to time he and the other men in his company would be sent home for an early supper—usually, it meant they were to be sent on a mission later in the evening. I took note of the sword at his side. I did not know much of the details about his work, other than the fact that it was dangerous. He worked undercover for the Alliance as one of King Ludlum's soldiers. His station was not too prominent as leading the Elite drew too much attention. Attention was dangerous. The risk of leading an attack against your allies, let alone your friends, was too high. A cover like that would be nearly impossible to maintain.

Gareth was not my natural father. They had told me, together, shortly after my fifth birthday. They had spoken of it just that once, and never again. At least not in front of me. Even as they revealed to me that my heritage was one that was forbidden, they would tell me little about the man who had sired me. I didn't even know his name. Only that he had been a Mystic. Sometimes at night, I could hear them speaking in hushed tones and I wondered, were they talking about him? Or how my very existence put all our lives at risk? I tried not to let those thoughts linger. It was Gareth who had raised me since infancy. He was the only father I had ever known.

An outsider would never have guessed we were not related by blood as our bond was strong. He protected and loved me fiercely, and I loved and idolized him. I often found myself feeling a twinge of guilt knowing that he held a lesser station in life to protect me.

Maintaining a lower station was a challenge in and of itself. It meant holding back much of his skill—something a man of more pride would have found hard to accomplish.

My thoughts drifted back to the memory of a hunting trip he had taken me on the year before. I remembered how I watched in awe as he felled two wild birds with a single arrow. That kind of feat was not something he could allow himself to partake in very often. It was only in the solitude of those moments, away from the gaze of enemy eyes, that he could be himself.

I understood the feeling, to an extent, though I was not so good at blending in.

Gareth's laugh brought me back to the present. He stood with Mother, his arms around her shoulders. They often seemed to be in their own little world together, and this was one of those moments. I hated to disturb them, so I shut the door quietly behind us and gave grandfather a look. He smiled and put his fingers to his lips. He understood.

We watched them for a short while. I smiled as Mother's head tilted backward and her shoulders shook with laughter. I loved the way her entire face lit up when he made her laugh. It seemed to lift whatever weight she found herself carrying, even if it were only briefly.

Sometimes, secretly, I wondered if I would ever have someone that would make me laugh the same way.

"Mother?" I said softly. I hated to interrupt, to break the protective bubble of the moment they were having; but I also did not feel right intruding on that moment as a casual observer.

She turned around, obviously caught off-guard, "Oh! You are home." She looked me over, "Go to the well and wash up for dinner, love."

Then she saw grandfather. Her voice took on a different tone.

"What are you doing here?" She did not bother hiding her surprise, nor the touch of hostility that often found its way sharply out of her mouth when he was around.

They had a difficult relationship. Mama had looked up to him as a child, and she felt that he had abandoned her. He had been absent much of her childhood and she had thought him dead. When they were finally reunited, the hero she had mourned was not the man she had hoped that he would be. Even an unintentional deception can be a betrayal.

I thought, also, that Mother may have been disappointed that their reunion had yet to inspire him to live a straight laced, honorable lifestyle. It had not prompted him to become the hero she grew up believing he was. Though he was now more active in the Alliance, his adventures gallivanting and gambling struck a chord in Mother's heart, and that chord made a sour tone.

"I had just arrived in town on... business," Grandfather chose his words carefully, "When I ran into the girl." He looked at me out of the corner of his eye. I willed him silently not to go into detail about how exactly we had "run in" to one another.

I need not have worried, as he gave me a quick wink before looking back to Mother, "And here I am!"

"I see," she pursed her lips. I flashed her my best smile, hoping to ease the tension. It did not seem to work.

"How is my brother?" she asked grandfather. It was almost like she meant to make him uncomfortable. My uncle was kind of a family secret himself.

"He is well," Brian did not miss a beat. He was used to this game they played. "He sends his regards."

"Ooh is he here?" For a moment, I had forgotten myself in my excitement. It had been so long since I had been to visit my uncle.

"'Lana, sweetie, you know he cannot come here." Father reminded me gently. "It is not safe for him. For any of us."

"But whyyy" I whined, though I already knew the answer.

"Because he is a half-breed," my grandfather stated unabashedly. Nykolas only shared half of my Mother's heritage. Nykolas was the result of a controversial relationship between my grandfather and the nymph Sapphire. His existence was more than a bit of a scandal. I had met him a handful of times on various outings, our fall hunting trip being one of them. I had never seen his Mother, or any other Mystics for that matter.

Often, I imagined what it would be like to go on grand adventures with the Alliance like Mother had in the past, and her mother before her. Perhaps I would fit in there. I was sure I would.

"I am a half-breed!" I argued defiantly. Talk of my own paternity had become more frequent amongst the two of them over the past few years. They underestimated my keen hearing, thinking me asleep as they whispered to one another in the night. I had finally begun to feel that I would have the missing pieces of my ancestry given to me, but the talk had stopped shortly after my tenth birthday.

All of a sudden, things had gone back to their previous state, feigning as if I had always been nothing but a normal human girl. They wouldn't tell me why, but I could not help but think that perhaps there was something wrong with me. Something so horrible that it caused them to become silent on the matter. Still, I was determined that I could pry the information from them if only I pushed hard enough. Thus, outbursts such as this one began to happen more frequently. Each time I was sure I had backed them into a corner, but each time Mother would meet me at the line I had drawn. We would stand there, toe to toe, in a stalemate. This time was to be no different.

"'Tis not the same, Lana, and you know it," Mother sighed, "Nykolas would immediately be spotted for what he is. There is no way to hide him.

No way for him to blend in."

"There's no way for ME to blend in here!" I countered. "None of them like me. None of them understand me. YOU do not even understand me and you are my Mother!"

I stood with my fists clenched at my sides so tightly that my fingernails dug into the tender skin of my palms. The tears I had tried to hold back after running into my grandfather suddenly sprung back into my eyes, hot and angry. I let them spill over and roll down my face. The sound of them splattering against the wood floor briefly broke my concentration.

I seemed to be the only one affected by the noise. The others had all gone silent. Grandfather shifted his weight uncomfortably. I could tell he wanted to step in, but he waited for Mother to respond.

"Azlana... sweetheart—" My Mother's voice cut out. I wanted desperately to run to her and wrap myself up in her apron, the way I had done when I was very little and was sad or afraid. The scent of flowers and freshly made bread lingered on her skin, giving me an oasis, safe from the cruelty of the world beyond the soft cotton threads.

My anger kept my feet planted firmly where I stood.

"They think that I am stupid," I whispered.

"Why would they think that?" My grandfather took on a protective tone as he interjected himself into the argument. "Who said that to you?!"

"They all whisper it to one another. They think that I can't hear them, but I can."

I did not tell them why the children thought this. While children who were not of noble birth did not receive much formal education, everyone in the kingdom was well versed in one thing: the characteristics and weaknesses of the Mystic races. Information which was obtained during the First War when King Ludlum's soldiers had stumbled upon the writings of an old elven king. The journal was a bargaining chip made by the elven people. They hoped that by documenting their weaknesses, the dark breeds would be forced to join the Alliance. Vampires, ghouls, and other races who were otherwise unconcerned with the survival their ethically conscious counterparts. The Mystics had been at war with the dark breeds since long before Mother's people had come to lay claim on the land.

For reasons unknown to me, my parents chose to keep this knowledge from me and had forbidden me from seeking it myself. In its place, I learned Mystic folklore. Stories that they told to their children. At least, as much of it as Mother knew.

While I certainly saw the value in these studies, especially as someone who may potentially come to live among the other Mystic races, I saw no reason why I should not also be educated in the ways of my Mother's people—if only to blend in more successfully.

"This is exactly what they were afraid would happen," grandfather said to Mother.

They? They who? I wondered.

"They put her here for her own safety." Mother argued sternly. "Plenty of other children have trouble finding their place."

"They did not intend for her to be completely cut off from them, and you know it."

"Secluded from who?" I interrupted, "Who are they? Is it my fa—" I stopped myself short of the word, looking at Gareth apologetically.

My face grew warm with guilt. I would have used another word if I had known one. He smiled knowingly and put his hand on my shoulder. He was not offended.

"My father's family?" I continued.

"This is not a conversation to have in front of her." Mother chastised my grandfather, ignoring my question.

"It absolutely is a conversation to be had, not just in front of me, but WITH me," I demanded.

Mother shot me a look that on a normal day would have silenced me immediately. She was serious. Anger bubbled up from my stomach until it overwhelmed me. I clenched my fists at my side and lifted my chin higher.

"I am old enough to decide my own fate."

Mother glared at grandfather accusingly before turning her attention back to me.

"Lana," she started. She did not get the chance to say any more for my grandfather took it upon himself to silence our quarrel.

"Enough," He interrupted, "Lana, your Mother is right, in her own way. Now is not the time to discuss such matters." His face softened, "Besides, you have yet to see the gift I have brought you."

"A gift?" I will not be placated by trinkets, I thought to myself. That was before I saw the necklace he pulled from inside the pocket of his jacket.

From a thin, golden chain hung a polished emerald stone in a claw setting. A sparkling fog swirled beneath the stone's surface, mesmerizing me.

"'Tis beautiful, grandfather," I found myself murmuring. All the anger I had felt moments ago seemed to melt away as the gentle twirling of the fog hypnotized me.

"It is a gift far beyond her age," Mother protested.

"It has my initial on it," I pointed out. Mother leaned in to look. Sure enough, carved into the stone in calligraphy was the letter 'A'. Grandfather undid the clasp on the chain and hung the piece around my neck.

"Where did you find such a thing?" Mother asked suspiciously.

"It is an old family heirloom," Brian offered vaguely, "From the girl's other side."

Mother pursed her lips together so that they made a tight, thin line. The act almost made them disappear completely into her disapproving facial expression. She was silent a long while.

"Well," She said finally, "What is done, is done. Go on and wash up, Lana. Dinner will be finished soon." With that, she excused herself to the kitchen.

CHAPTER THREE

KALA

ITRIED TO IGNORE THE NAGGING FEELING IN THE PIT OF MY STOMACH. The one that always seemed to accompany Brian's visits. The fear I had felt grip my heart like an iron fist tightened its hold when I saw the emblem etched into the necklace he had brought Azlana.

Stressful though his visits were, they were not usually wrapped up in such discord. Indeed, this was the first time he had expressed an opinion concerning how my daughter had been brought up. It had thrown me off-guard, his disapproval. Nearly as much as my reaction to it.

"Why do you let it bother you?" Gareth's voice interrupted my thoughts.

"Hmm?" I tried my best to feign ignorance.

"They want what is best for her." He stood beside me, brushing my hair over my shoulder and away from my neck as I resumed chopping vegetables. They made a satisfying splash as I dropped them into the big stockpot that was simmering on the wood stove. I did not look up from my work, lest I reveal a moment of weakness. "I want what is best for her. I am her mother."

"And he was her father," Gareth glanced over his shoulder, speaking softly so that Azlana would not hear him. He had never before mentioned Azlyn in my presence. Though our union had been an arrangement made by the elven king, Gareth had never withheld his loyalty nor affections from either Azlana or myself.

Rather, he had fallen into his role as a husband and a father quite naturally. He had been a pillar of strength for me during my time of mourning. It had not been long before my own affection was no longer just a masquerade performed to protect my own identity.

It was a strange thing, to share my life with a man who was expected to love and accept the parts of me who had once loved someone else. And yet, it seemed so natural for him. He took it all in stride as easily as one takes to breathing.

Perhaps that was why talk of the past... of our daughter's true heritage... struck such a tender chord for me. The blending of my two lives had not come naturally to me. It was a skill I had built up over time. One that, even now, was not effortless. And it made me feel so very guilty. As if mentioning a memory from my past would somehow betray the man who stood now by my side.

"It is not his place to get involved," I tried to redirect the conversation. Though it was true that my father had taken on a more... active role in the Alliance since we had been reunited, our relationship was still an arduous one.

There remained a stark contrast between the man I had admired as a child and the one that I had come to know in my adult life. The two identities often found themselves competing with one another in my mind.

Azlyn had noticed that conflict as well when he had first told me that my father was still alive. He had, on more than one occasion, encouraged me to meet with him; but I had refused. The echo of his words still sprang to mind whenever my father and I found ourselves in conflict:

"Reach out to him Kala. True, he is not the man that you were expecting. He cannot undo the hurt he has caused, but deep down his intentions were good."

I realized then that he pitied my father. That perhaps he mourned the man he had hoped he would become as well. He had known my father before his fall from the Alliance's graces. I wondered, what manner of man had my father been, back then?

25

I watched the stew as it began to bubble, lost in my memories until Gareth's hand on my shoulder brought me back to the present. I gave him a half-hearted smile and looked briefly to the main room. Azlana, freshly washed, sat cross legged and enthralled as Brian told her tales of his adventures. The sound of my daughter's laughter danced through the house.

I turned my attention back to the stew, stirring it once more. The broth swirled, making a liquid cyclone that was both hypnotic and soothing.

"How long will you be in town?" I called over my shoulder.

"Not long," my father found his way back into the kitchen, running his fingers through his shaggy hair. "Actually, I should be departing soon. I have... other business to attend to."

"Mmm," I mumbled back, hoping that made it clear that the details of his business were not to be discussed in front of Azlana.

"So, you'll not be staying for dinner?"

"No, sadly, I will not." He gazed over his shoulder to where his granddaughter was sitting. "Perhaps it's best that I head out now, then." He made eye contact with Gareth, who cleared his throat.

"I shall walk you out." He offered. They made their way out silently, without even a goodbye. As the latch of the door closed, making a soft THUD. I realized that my father had even failed to say his farewells to Azlana.

"What was that about?" Azlana asked.

"What was what about?" I tried my best to keep a neutral face.

"The way they looked at one another. You think that I don't notice those sorts of things, but I do." Her eyes narrowed suspiciously, and she crinkled her nose. A face I found adorable when her scrutiny was not pointed in my direction.

"Why did you not see grandfather out? He is your father. And why did he not say goodbye?" She searched my face for any hint of validation for her suspicion, but found none. She nodded, content that I, too, had been left in the dark.

"'Tis just business between the two of them, Lana. Business you need not concern yourself with."

"You all brush me off as if I am still a child! As if I know nothing! 'Tis maddening!" Azlana threw her hands up in the air dramatically. "I know things, Mother! And things that I do not yet know I can venture to guess—better than you lot give me credit for."

I froze. I had spent so much time being selective about the information that I had given my daughter that I had foolishly underestimated her reasoning abilities. What did she mean, she knew things? Certainly, it couldn't mean... but no. She was well past the age of awakening.

The elven people begin the process of awakening at the age of ten. A birthday which had come and gone already, with little sign of her being anything but a human girl—save for the heightened senses that plagued her. How I wished I could wipe that burden from my child's life. Were it not for that challenge she would blend in beautifully.

It was not that I desired to withhold the truth from her. Some level of secrecy had been necessary to properly identify any changes in her behavior. Azlana was the first of her kind. We could not be sure how an awakening would present itself in the mind of a being with mortal blood.

Eoma had not seen how the child's fate would play itself out, but she had been certain that the knowledge would come to her. They all had. The Alliance, her father's people... everyone had been counting on her to grow into the destiny they had set before her. To use her genetic memory to force the dark breeds into the Alliance and to lead them, united, against the Elite.

That had been the plan since before she was born. I had always known this.

And yet, having an awareness that something shall come to pass and knowing it as one who is living it are two very different things. Looking into the face of a tiny child, one that I was sworn for all of my life to protect, made the knowledge of her destiny hang heavily on my heart. I had watched as my daughter had grown, wiser than her years certainly, but still so innocent. The thought of the road that lay ahead of her made my soul ache.

And then there was Gareth. He had given up so much when he had agreed to marry me. Indeed, with his talent and boisterous personality, he would be living a more lucrative lifestyle if it were not for our need to remain out of the eye of those who would do us harm. And still, every day he had risked his life to protect us. To protect the child that we had raised together.

Perhaps Eoma had been right. Perhaps I had grown too comfortable in my new life

"Very well," I conceded, "Perhaps you are old enough." I drew stew from the stock pot with a large wooden ladle, pouring it into two stone bowls and setting them on the table across from each other. Azlana took the cue and sat, watching the steam rise in swirls from her bowl.

"Be careful," I cautioned. "Tis quite hot."

Azlana blew softly over the lip of the bowl. The act made the stew swirl. The steam danced before dissipating in the air.

"You know that your grandfather is part of the Alliance," I began my explanation awkwardly.

"Aye. And father as well."

"Yes. Well, you see... It is your father's job to work within the ranks of the Elite soldiers and gather as much information as he can, secretly, about their plot against the Alliance." I paused to be sure she was following me.

Azlana nodded her head impatiently. This was not new information to her.

"Your grandfather brings Intel from the other side. He works from within the Alliance and brings crucial information to Gareth. Gareth is then able to influence, subtly, some of the movements of Ludlum's soldiers. For example, he might intentionally feed them false information, or mislead them through other channels to thwart their efforts. It is dangerous work, especially for one who must maintain a neutral presence.

Meanwhile, your grandfather takes the information given to him by Gareth and feeds it back to the leaders of the Alliance."

"I see." Azlana was silent a moment, mulling it over. "Grandfather's gift. What did he mean when he said it was a family heirloom? To whom did it belong before me?"

Azlana lifted the necklace for me to inspect, but I remained silent, lost in thought as I gazed out the window.

28

He had said it was a gift on her paternal side. My guess was that it had been a gift from Azlyn's father, Charlezon. Another bid to convince me to bring her to him. The emerald color was a mark of royalty among her elven line, and the 'A' etched into the stone suggested it had belonged to one who bore her same initial. That it had once been her father's. I did not reveal any of this to her.

"You really should be getting to bed now, love," I said, still gazing out the window. She did not argue as I had expected she would. I felt her lips brush lightly against my cheek.

"Night, Mama." She whispered, before disappearing down the hall.

CHAPTER FOUR

AZLANA

I GLANCED BACK AT MOTHER ONLY ONCE as I closed the door to my room softly, holding my breath as the heavy iron latch clicked shut. I slipped into my nightclothes and braided my hair before crawling between the linen blankets that lay on my bed. The sheets were cool against my skin, which was still somewhat clammy from my chase through the town.

I laid awake awhile, twirling the chain of the necklace that grandfather had given me as I agonized over what a fool Luka must think I was. Every time I felt my eyelids grow heavy it would play in my head again, taunting me. The other children's jeers echoed in my mind. How would I ever face them? I rolled over, facing the window that overlooked the back field. The day's light was still fading, and it cast an orange glow much like the reflection of fire.

My heart skipped a beat for no reason. Fire! Why did that seem important? There was an odd sensation. A tingling in the back of my head, like the answer was right there, dangling just outside my grasp. I wanted to hold the thought. To keep it from escaping. Before I could reach for it I felt myself drifting off.

I was surrounded by a milky fog, illuminated by a source I couldn't identify. Outside the fog was only darkness. The fog swirled all around me, but never touched me.

"The boy is of no concern to you" a voice snapped. I was being jostled about. Kind of like the time Luka had convinced me to climb into a barrel so he could roll me down a hill, but with less spinning. I couldn't see who was speaking, but his voice was close and overwhelming.

"He'll never turn against his own." Another voice argued. This one seemed further away.

"He is an opportunist, and she has softened his wit. We can make him see the light."

The fog spun around me fast and faster. The scene changed. The ground fell from beneath my feet and the fog drifted with me, melting into clouds. I was flying! Large wings beat against the atmosphere. My wings! I was in the body of a griffin! But how?

"Never mind that!" the griffin mind argued. It smelled something. Something new, yet familiar. Something delicious.

I circled a clearing and saw it! A rabbit tied to a tree. My mind tingled again. Why was it tied to the tree? The part of my mind that was my own warned me to stay away, but the griffin paid no attention, descending upon its prey.

Suddenly I was blinded by pain. Pain like nothing I had ever experienced. Something had struck my arm. No... my wing! Again, and again it struck, and we were spiraling to the ground. The griffin's mind panicked, fighting against my own.

As we fell, I caught sight of the source of our pain. Several arrows protruded from our right wing. They bore the mark of Ludlum's army.

Trap. A trap a trap a trap. I thought as we spun and fell. The ground came rushing up –

I bolted upright, chest heaving as I tried to catch my breath. A dream. It was just a dream. *Then why does my arm ache?* I wondered as I rubbed my shoulder. My fingers tingled as the circulation returned.

Must have slept on it funny, I reasoned with myself. I took in a breath and held it, willing my heart to stop pounding in my ears. *Thump, thump, thump.* Breathe out. *Thump, thump, thump,* breathe in.

Tap, tap, tap... no wait, that wasn't right. My eyes turned toward the window until they locked onto the source of the sound. Luka's eyes met mine through the glass pane, and he motioned for me to open the window.

I brushed back a strand of hair that had come loose from my braid. It was damp from sweat. Indeed, the rest of the hair that framed my face was plastered to it. Gross. For a moment I paused, self-conscious about my appearance.

But that was silly. Luka had been privy to much more unseemly sorts where I was concerned. Like the time we went chasing toads, and I'd fallen into the marsh. It had taken the whole evening just to comb the mud out of my hair.

I pushed aside my quilt and swung my legs over the edge of the bed, bouncing just a bit before tiptoeing to the window and undoing the latch. As he had done so many times before, Luka slithered over the windowsill silently and sat at the foot of my bed.

"I followed after ya, just so as ya know," he broke the silence but avoided eye contact. "I saw yer ran off with yer grandad an' I figured you wanted to be left alone."

So, he isn't sick of me yet, I thought with relief.

"Oh." I was unsure of what else to say.

"I was just sayin'," he continued somewhat awkwardly. "In case you might be thinkin' I had anythin' to do with how the others was actin'. Cuz I didn't."

"I didn't think you did." It wasn't quite a lie. I wanted to change the subject. "My grandfather brought me something." I showed him the necklace. "Isn't it lovely?"

"I s'pose." he shrugged, unimpressed. "If yer into girl stuff."

"I bet it's valuable," I offered, though I'm not sure why. Luka had never been impressed by fancy things, no matter what their value.

"Is that so?" he looked it over scrutinizing it, "What makes you think that?"

I wanted to tell him that it came from my family-from my father's side. From a land, far away. But I couldn't. It wasn't safe, for either of us. Mother had warned me of the dangers of confiding in someone, even someone you trusted. Even someone you loved. She had once been betrayed by such a person. Not just a friend, but her own kin.

"I just think it looks like it." I tucked the necklace back under my nightgown.

We sat in silence for a long while. One may think that would be awkward, but it wasn't for us. Even under the best of circumstances, we would often find ourselves passing the time silently, enjoying each other's company without the pressure to entertain one another. I wondered if all friendships felt this way. Alas, I had nothing to compare it to.

Suddenly there was a knock on the door. In a flash Luka was crouching on the windowsill, ready to jump out should the door open.

"Azlana love, time for breakfast."

"Aye Mother, I'm just getting up!" I called back.

"Meet me by the pond later?" Luka whispered.

"Yeah... sure. Soon as my chores are done." I shooed him out the window. "Now hurry up! I have to get dressed!"

He flashed one last smile before he jumped down from the windowsill. I latched the window quietly behind him and dressed, re-braiding my hair before walking out to the kitchen. Mother's face smiled, but her eyes were far away. I wondered if she'd slept at all the night before. On the table, she'd set out two bowls of porridge. I sat down, taking in its rich smell.

"Is Luka not staying for breakfast, then?"

It was no use playing daft. "How did you know he was here?"

"I'm your Mother, I know everything." She smiled wryly. "You have been friends a long while."

"Mmm," I said, my mouth full.

"And you are getting older." She was alluding to something, but I could not guess what might be significant in such context.

"Do you think you might fancy him, a bit?"

"Ew, Mother, no." I protested. "'Tis not like that at all. Luka is my friend and my only one at that. Why would I want to foul it all up with a stupid girlhood crush?"

"I just guessed the other girls might be jealous."

"Trust me Mother, no one is jealous of me." I searched for a way to change the subject. I didn't want to get into another fight. "Did father not come home last night?"

She stared at the front door, unblinking. Perhaps she hadn't heard me. I opened my mouth to repeat the question.

"No, no he didn't." She beat me to the punch. "They've gone on a raid."

That explained her haggard look. She'd probably been up all-night worrying. Raids were exceptionally dangerous for men who were playing on both sides of a war. I tried to hide my own concern. Mother didn't need another person to worry after.

"Luka asked me to the pond later. Is it alright?"

"Aye," she turned to me, but her eyes were almost looking through me. She caught herself and smiled as she reached across the table and placed her hand over my own. "You can go now if you want."

"What about my chores?"

"I can do them today. It will do me good to keep busy. Now go on before I change my mind."

Since I didn't have to do my chores, I beat Luka to the pond. It was early in the day and although it looked serene from a distance, up close it was a flurry of life. Water bugs skimmed the pond's surface, darting back and forth. Wild birds calling from the nests they'd hidden deep in the pond grass warned me to keep my distance.

Luka and I had met here as far back as I could remember. From an early age, we could be found wading knee-deep in the water chasing toads, or tearing apart the heads of cattails to stuff our pillows with.

Away from the bustle and expectation of society, this was the playground of my childhood. For some reason, today it felt foreign. I kicked off my slippers and laid down. I needed to be close to the earth. To feel the hum of its breath against my skin. In times of trouble that had always helped me find myself.

I gazed up at the wispy clouds drifting across the sky. They weren't quite fit for finding shapes, but I tried anyway. If I squinted really hard at one it looked kind of like a goat... no... a satyr.

Mother had told me the lore of the satyr. They were the children of Becha, the Goddess of summer. Often deemed to be a plague upon the nymphs, they had once been guardians.

It was after the Goddess Rohma had cast the nymphs down to the earth in a jealous rage, chaining their life force to their host tree. At first, the nymphs had rebelled. Hundreds of them traveled too far from their trees and died. Until Becha commanded her children to guard them. Over the years, the nymph's spirits had settled. Their minds had dulled, and they ceased their struggle. Still, the satyrs could be seen chasing them, keeping them close to their homes. Mama had said that it was both a blessing and a curse to them. I thought it was simply sad.

The cloud-satyr danced across the sky and a second figure joined him. It was tall and slender with long flowing hair. His nymph! They twirled in circles as he chased her across the sky. She turned to him, offering a goblet in exchange for a pause in the chase. No satyr was able to resist an offering of wine. He accepted, sipping from it greedily. Suddenly his arms flew to his chest and his body began to spasm. Poison!

I closed my eyes against the gruesome scene and darted upright, covered in sweat once again.

"Easy 'Lana!" a voice reassured me. I opened my eyes to find the sun was high in the sky and my friend kneeling beside me. I must have fallen asleep.

"It was just a dream," I gasped, trying to convince myself.

"*But was it, really?*" A voice that was mine-but-not-mine replied. I shook my head against it and stood up, brushing stray grass from my clothes. Luka stood with me, his face concerned.

"Tis nothing, I am fine," I lied.

"How long have ya been down here by yerself? He asked.

"Since this morning."

"How'd ya get out of doin' yer chores?"

I shrugged, "I think she felt bad about last night." I filled him in on the argument Mother and I had the night before.

"Lucky," He stuck his hands in his pockets and kicked the dirt, "All I get when Pa and I fight is a lashing."

"I guess," I didn't feel very lucky. I felt... heavy. Kind of like that time when I was 5 and tried on father's chain mail. The weight of it on my tiny shoulders had made it impossible to move. Except that was a physical weight. This one felt more... intangible. I had no idea what it was or where it was coming from, but I couldn't seem to shake it.

We walked along the edge of the pond as we had done so many times before. Now and then Luka would go nearer to the water and pull a cattail head from its stalk and twist it. I watched out of the corner of my eye as the breeze took hold of its fluff and carried it off into the air. It shot up into the air and spun, seeming to have a life of its own. The act reminded me too much of the cloud-satyr. I looked away.

You're being ridiculous, I chastised myself, *get ahold of yourself.*

"You sure you're okay 'Lana?" Luka asked. He was looking at me funny.

"Don't tell him," the voice warned. *"He will think you've gone mad."*

He will not! I countered. Luka and I had never kept secrets. He would never judge me.

"Unless you have, indeed, gone mad," the voice offered. It made a valid point. Whose mind would conjure up gruesome murders and see apparitions in the sky if not the mind of a mad person?

But they were only dreams, I feigned confidence. The voice that was mine-but-not-mine was silent.

"Yeah. I'm fine. Why?" I flashed him my best fake smile.

"You just seem... off... is all. Distracted-like."

"Father is out on a raid," I offered. "I'm worried about him, is all." It was at least half true. I couldn't tell Luka the real reason for my concern. That father was part of the Alliance and that every time he went on a raid Mother and I held our breath, wondering if he would be found out. I didn't need to though. Raids were dangerous enough, no matter what side you were on. The fear felt by the families left behind was palpable.

"Ah," he let the matter drop. He had no reason to disbelieve me. The wind picked up, and the sky darkened.

"Best be headed back," he looked upward, "I don't like the look of those

36

clouds."

I nodded, keeping my eyes cast down at my feet. There was no way I was looking at the sky again.

It was just a dream, I scolded myself. *Just a dream. Just a dream. Just a dream.*

And there was that voice again. The one that was mine-but-not-mine, *"But what if it isn't? What if it's you?"*

I didn't have an answer.

CHAPTER FIVE

KALA

I COUNTED THE DAYS SINCE WE HAD LAST SEEN GARETH. Four, five, six...more than two weeks later and we were still without word. It wasn't that it was particularly unusual to go this long without hearing from him. It was simply that every time was equally terrifying.

Azlana carried out her chores without complaint. Without much of a word about anything, really. We had not spoken much since the day she'd gone off to the pond with Luka. Her silence was not only reserved for me. She no longer hummed as she did her chores, didn't ask to go out, and had begun turning Luka away when he came calling for her.

The dark circles around her eyes told me she was not sleeping well, but anytime I mentioned it she would get defensive and retreat further into herself. I was starting to worry. I found myself at a loss as to how to reach her.

I wondered if my father may have been right. Maybe this was something her father's people experienced during their coming of age: The time at which the knowledge of their ancestors began to unlock itself from their minds. Perhaps I had kept her from them for too long.

I watched her silently as she swept the floor. The necklace around her neck caught the light briefly and for a moment it seemed to be glowing. Or perhaps, I thought to myself, perhaps I made the right choice after all.

It was not the gifting itself that bothered me. Brian often brought Azlana trinkets from his travels, mostly animals carved from wood. Never had he given her something so extravagant. My guess was that it was a gift from Azlyn's father, Charlezon. Another bid to convince me to bring her to him. The emerald color was a mark of royalty among her elven line, and the 'A' etched into the stone suggested it once belonged to her father.

Some might see the gesture as sweet. An attempt to reach out to the granddaughter he so fiercely wanted to meet. I saw it as manipulative, a sign of disrespect. The choices I made were for the love of her. It was for her own protection that I kept her away.

I told her none of this as she finished the floor and kissed my forehead before turning in for the night. One of the many mistakes I would add to the list of ways I failed her.

I sat by the hearth, staring into the fire as it dwindled. The house creaked as it settled but otherwise, I was surrounded by silence. Too much silence.

"I know you're there," I said calmly to the figure I was sure stood behind me. I rose, turning to face the intruder. "How dare you sneak into my home this way! You put all of our lives in danger."

"You know I would not have come unless it was of great importance Kala," Cazlyn said.

"What could be so urgent— "

"Charlezon is dead."

I heard a sound like someone choking on air. It took me a moment to realize the sound came from me.

"There was an attack on the camp. Somehow, they were alerted to our position."

"How many...?" the question hung unfinished in the air.

"Too many. Captured, mostly. A handful were killed."

"Eoma?"

"Escaped unharmed."

"How could this have happened? My father was only just here with news..." Of course, that had been weeks ago. Much could happen in that span of time.

"We have a traitor in our midst. 'Tis the only explanation."

"But who?"

"I do not know. The encampment had only just moved. Few would have an opportunity to expose our position." He paused a moment as if unsure how to word what he was thinking. "Kala, where is your husband?"

"Out," I replied tersely, "Surely you are not suggesting what I think you are?"

He opened his mouth to respond, then thought better.

"You know what this means Kala."

"What?"

"The girl. It is time for me to take her home"

"This is her home," my voice shook with anger.

"This is where she has lived, but these are not her people."

"These are my people and she is half mine"

"She is half ours too," He sighed, running his fingers through his hair. "You can no longer keep her hidden–from my people or yours. She is beyond the age of awakening already–"

"And nothing has happened," I insisted, "For all anyone knows, she is a normal human girl. Let her stay that way."

"I wish it were that easy, Kala, I really do. Even if your lives were not in danger, my grandfather's death requires an heir."

"Can you not take the crown in her stead?"

"Only until she has come of age," he explained, "My people will not accept me as their rightful ruler. My place on the throne, even temporarily, causes too much unrest."

"Surely they cannot still hold his actions against you."

"Lineage plays a key role in the transfer of power Kala. You are aware of this. Not only is my line without seniority, but it is tainted by scandal on the side of my Mother and treason on the side of my father."

"Cazlyn," My voice softened, "Scandal? Is that how they talk about her fate?" His Mother had been a victim of the Change. A fate that meant a mercy execution among his people.

But instead of accepting her fate, Cazlyn's father fled with her to the Uncharted Territories, where she could be among others of her kind. I had always considered the story to be romantic, in a tragic sort of way. Apparently, his people thought differently.

For a moment, his demeanor softened. He opened his mouth to respond but didn't get the chance. The thump of little feet parading down the hallway interrupted him.

Azlana came tearing down the hallway furiously, her nightgown billowing around her as she ran. When she caught sight of Cazlyn, she stopped in her tracks. Her eyes moved to me and back to him again, her mouth agape.

"What are you doing up?" I tried to hold my voice steady, hoping that if I behaved as if nothing was amiss she wouldn't notice we had company.

"How could you?!" Azlana raged. "How could you keep them from me all these years? How could you watch me struggle to fit in here when I had family on his side who would accept me? Family who wanted me!"

So, she had been listening in on our conversation. And she had heard Cazlyn's plea to bring her home. Dammit.

I knelt in front of her, placing my hands on either side of her face, "Oh, love."

My voice nearly failed me as I tried to come up with the words to ease her anger, "T'would not have worked that way."

"You don't know that! How could you know? You don't care what they wanted—what I may have wanted! You grew comfortable here and did not think how this would affect anyone but yourself!"

"Hush!" Cazlyn raised one hand to silence us, the other pressing a finger against his lips. "Someone is coming."

"I hear nothing," I whispered.

"No, he's right," Azlana argued, "I hear it too."

"Perhaps it is Gareth coming home," I offered. Looking out the window at the darkness I added, "He has been gone too long."

"No," Azlana squinted, trying to identify the sound, "The footsteps are too heavy to be him. I can't quite place it."

"Horses," Cazlyn said. "Ludlum's men coming back from battle."

In the distance, a trumpet sounded. It was a victory call, announcing the return of the King's men. Azlana and I went to the window as was the custom. All citizens within the city were to honor the soldiers upon their return from battle.

Cazlyn ducked back into the shadow of the hallway, out of sight of anyone who may happen to glance into the home. The sound of horses marching grew closer. Azlana put her hands over her ears as the trumpets sounded again. A group of men rode through the street holding torches calling out their victory over a rebel group of Mystics. Their uniforms were stained a deep crimson. Azlana closed her eyes tightly, but she dared not turn her head. To do so was considered a sign of disrespect to the king's men. A form of treason.

"Gareth is not with them," I let out the breath I had been holding in anticipation as the group moved on, deeper into the city.

"But, where is he?" Azlana asked. We both turned to face Cazlyn. If Ludlum's men were returning, there was no reason for my husband to be missing from their ranks. At least, I feared, no reason that would not end in tears.

"We cannot wait for him," Cazlyn urged, "We have to go."

"Go where?" Azlana asked.

"Somewhere safe," Cazlyn's voice softened in an attempt to reassure her.

I wanted to protest but Cazlyn did not give me the opportunity to speak, "Kala you know she will not be safe here. The very fact that they found the encampment means there is a traitor in our midst. How long do you think you can hide her? How long do you think you can hide before they know your own identity?"

I tugged at the sides of my pinafore nervously glancing over my shoulder. It was almost as if I could feel someone watching us. I shook my head to shed the thought from my mind.

"Very well," I conceded. And then to Azlana, "Pack a bag love, quickly."

CHAPTER SIX

AZLANA

IN AN INSTANT, EVERYTHING I KNEW CHANGED. I went from standing in my pajamas in front of a stranger to whom I was somehow related, to fully dressed and ready to leave my childhood home in mere moments.

Packing up my life had been strangely neutral. As I stood in my room, sorting through my belongings, I felt detached. It was if I was simply packing for another hunting trip, the way I had done a handful of times before. Nearly everything I put into the bag was practical. A change of clothes, a whittling knife, a wool blanket.

I paused a moment before adding a small pillow that Luka had made for me the previous summer. It was nothing fancy: a burlap sack sewn into the shape of a rabbit and stuffed with cattail fluff. Though Gareth had always stressed the importance of packing lightly—for survival, not for sentiment—I couldn't bring myself to leave it behind.

When it was all said and done, I shouldered my pack and sighed. Perhaps that is what those trips had been about. Had he been, all this time, preparing me for this moment? They had known. My whole life, they had known this moment would come. The thought threw me off kilter and for a moment rage rushed through me. I reviewed what I had overheard. Someone important had died. Someone from my natural father's side, and now they wanted me back. But what was the Awakening they spoke of? Who was the stranger in my living room? Someone of royal standing. And he wanted me back. They wanted me back. My father's people needed me to lead them.

How long had my father's family been waiting for me? It did not sound as if they wanted to stay away... More like Mother had forced them to. Why would she do that? Why would she watch as I struggled to fit in among her people when his were champing at the bit to get to me?

"Because she wanted you all to herself," The voice that was mine-but-not-mine did not fade with time as I had hoped. Rather, it had begun sneaking into the corners of my everyday thoughts much more frequently, casting doubt across event my most mundane thoughts. In an attempt to maintain sanity, I imagined it as a separate entity, though it existed within me. I named it The Darkness.

At times, I would argue with it, to assert that I was still the one in control. In control of what I was uncertain. Other times I just ignored it. Pushed it away, only to have it come back another time. This time I did the latter. Now was not the time to argue.

I stepped out of my room to find that mother had put out the lanterns. I shouldn't have been surprised. It only made sense to escape under the cloak of night. I blinked, waiting for my eyes to adjust. My ability to discern my surroundings would not be impeded by the lack of light, but Mother did not share the same advantage. I went to her, taking her hand. No one spoke.

The stranger led us around the back of the house and into the cellar. He placed his palm flat against the back wall and whispered something in a language I did not recognize. The wall swung open silently. The scent of wet earth washed over me and I froze, grasping Mother's hand tightly. She gave it a squeeze and started toward the door. I pulled my hand from hers and planted my feet.

"'Tis your father's side, that fear," the stranger said kindly. "Elves don't care to be kept underground. Nothing to be done about it." I couldn't be sure, but I got the feeling that he was as nervous about it as I was. He offered his hand to me and I took it. Together we stepped through the entry.

I hadn't known there were different kinds of darkness until the door shut behind us, choking out the glow of the night sky that I had always taken for granted. In the tunnel, I could barely make out the outline of my Mother in front of us. The stagnant air was musty and hung heavily around me, making it hard to breathe.

"You're going to suffocate," The Darkness taunted. *"The tunnel will cave in and crush you."*

Enough! I said back. It was silent.

The stranger squeezed my hand, as Mother had, and made a sound that reminded me of the rustling of leaves in the wind. Suddenly a soft light illuminated the tunnel, slithering down the passageway before us. I blinked as my eyes adjusted, searching for the light's source.

Roots. Gnarled tree roots sprang down from the top of the tunnel and wrapped themselves along its walls as if acting to support the weight of the earth that surrounded us. Their steady glow pulsed like a heartbeat.

"What is this place?" I whispered to myself in awe.

"Dwarves built these tunnels during the first war," Cazlyn said as we began walking. "They run beneath the entire city. The Alliance has used such routes for years, to make contact with our members inside the kingdom."

He paused as if waiting for a reply. I looked to Mother. She kept her eyes ahead of her and said nothing. Her lips formed a tense, straight line. I realized that none of this information was new to her. She had known the whole time.

"She kept it from you on purpose," The Darkness crept in from the corner of my mind. *"She wanted you to be human, and human alone. She would never have told you."* I pushed the thought aside and held my breath to slow my racing heart. Being rushed from home and confined underground would make anyone jittery.

"We've so much to teach you," Cazlyn's voice interrupted my thoughts.

"Perhaps not all at once," Mother finally spoke. "The girl was just torn from everything she has known. Do not overwhelm her."

"We are cousins, you know," he said to me as if Mother hadn't spoken. "Your father was my father's brother."

Cousins. I looked up at him and felt as if I was seeing him for the first time. He was tall and pale with icy eyes and wheat-colored hair pulled back into a braid. On his left ear hung a green diamond shaped earring on a short gold chain. It was the mark of the royal family. The colored stone resembled the same material as the necklace that hung beneath my tunic. I rested my hand on it absentmindedly.

At home, it had been necessary to keep it hidden. Indeed, Mother insisted I put it away somewhere out of sight. She had meant somewhere secret, where there was no chance of the other villagers seeing it. Instead, I chose to wear it under my clothing, an act of rebellion that seemed petty given our current situation. Still, I had kept it hidden, even if it was only by hiding myself. There was no need for such things now, but something willed me to keep it safe beneath my cotton gown. I lowered my hand.

"Your looks favor your Mother. What of your temperament, I wonder?" He looked at Mother, the tiniest hint of a smirk on his face. He was teasing her.

"She favors him in many ways." Mother's voice was terse. "She's taken on a bit of the man who raised her as well."

Gareth! In the chaos, I had forgotten he was not with us. My feet stopped moving suddenly without my telling them to. The reality of what was happening finally hit me.

The bag I had packed mere hours before seemed so inadequate for the road that lay ahead, and yet it hung heavily on my shoulders, as if in warning of the things yet to come.

"Mama—?" a lump in my throat cut my inquiry short.

She forgot her quarrel and knelt before me, brushing my hair from my face.

"Oh lovely, 'tis alright. This was not a day we hoped for, but 'tis one for which we planned well. When we settle, I will send word for him to meet us."

I could only nod in response, not trusting my voice.

"She's tired." Mother stood, facing Cazlyn. "Tis late and she needs rest. We should stop for the night."

46

"Absolutely not!" he protested, his eyes scanning the roots above our heads. "Elves do not sleep underground."

I found myself sharing his sentiment. "I'm fine. I can keep going," I insisted. I could tell that she didn't believe me. I couldn't blame her—even I didn't believe me.

"I'll carry her, then." He dropped to one knee and motioned for me to climb up on his back. Mother removed my pack from my back and shouldered it along with her own, dipping slightly under the added weight.

I clung to Cazlyn's shoulders, and he stood, grasping my legs behind my knees to support my weight. My body swayed gently side-to-side as he plodded on and it was not long before I drifted off to sleep.

Darkness lay before me, and the sound of something like metal scraping against stone.

"Without her, they have no hope," the voice speaking seemed familiar, and foreign at the same time. "It will drive her to the Dark One, and we will be waiting."

"What does this have to do with my revenge?" Another voice, more powerful than the first, replied.

"He will have a foothold in the girl-a taste for the human part of her mind."

"You're not suggesting..."

"We set him free. Let him do to the humans what he has done to your kind. To all the dark breeds." The scene changed suddenly, as if something was tearing my mind away and thrusting it into another. I had grown used to these dreams over the past weeks. They nearly almost followed the same pattern. First, a glimpse of something foreign. Something for which I had no context. Then something that felt vaguely familiar. I began to will myself to wake up before it came. Sometimes that worked. Other times it only made it worse. This time my resistance resulted in the latter.

I was in a cave, surrounded by shadows. They spoke to each other in languages I didn't understand, ignoring me. To one side was a small pool fed by a stream that ran into the cave from a waterfall at its mouth. In the pool was a shadow with a body that was half fish, half human. It swam frantically, its body convulsing as the water turned a deep purple. Someone was poisoning her water! But how? I looked around the cave in horror. The shadows fell silent and turned to me, circling around me angrily. I looked down at my hands. An inky substance covered them. Me. It was me. I was killing her!

I opened my mouth to scream, but no sound came out. Then everything around me fell into darkness.

CHAPTER SEVEN

KALA

'T WAS NOT LONG AFTER AZLANA DRIFTED OFF TO SLEEP that Cazlyn
spoke, "You've done well with her, Kala."

I choked on a mixture of emotion. The resulting sound was
almost a laugh. "She's done well with herself, that one. She's spirited, and
kind, and wise beyond her years."

"You didn't have to do it alone, you know," there was a twinge of blame
in his tone.

"We both know that's not true." I looked ahead at the tunnel before us.
"Besides, I wasn't alone. Not entirely."

"Gareth," he may as well have spat the name. He'd no reason to dislike
my husband, other than the feeling that he had taken Azlyn's place. Gareth
had not wronged him directly.

"You do him an injustice, judging him so."

Cazlyn grunted in response. It had been so many years since the death
of his uncle, I had assumed the grief would have dulled. It hadn't occurred
to me until now, how very young he still was among his people. The years
between my girlhood and the autumn of my life were fleeting when laid out
against his lifespan.

"'Twas not what I would have chosen," I spoke softly. Something I would never have said in the presence of my husband though we both knew it to be true.

"You know that. I would have stayed with your people. I fought to convince your grandfather..." I stopped myself there, not wanting to speak ill of the deceased.

Cazlyn sighed, "I know he called for her, Kala. For years, he called for her and you came and you denied him."

Charlezon's voice rang in my memory *"Peace Eoma, we have time."* The Priestess had insisted I bring Azlana. Had she seen the King's fate? That he would die having never known her?

I felt the familiar pang of regret. "It was too late by then, Cazlyn. She had roots here. She wouldn't have been safe, going back and forth."

"Were you protecting her, really?" his voice was sour. "Or were you punishing my grandfather for your perceived banishment?"

Probably a little of both, but I wasn't about to tell him that. "What's done is done. We cannot change what has already happened."

I looked at my daughter's sweet, sleeping face pressed against Cazyln's back. Her world was changed forever, and I could not protect her from that fact. Soon she would learn who she really was. At the tender age of 10 years old she would be burdened with the destiny her father's people had assigned her.

I remembered vividly the day I was sworn into the Alliance. I had stood before representatives of each of the participating Mystic races and declared my allegiance, "With full knowledge." I thought myself so wise and worldly at the time. I was sure I understood the weight of what I was doing. Why are we all such fools in our youth?

Cazlyn's father, Cain, had been vocal in his protest of my initiation.

"Does she even understand, Priestess, what you have committed her to?"

At the time, I had thought he was referring to the fact that I was committing treason. Betraying my own people. That perhaps they even knew what it would cost me in terms of my family.

Never in a million years would I have guessed he was talking about Azlana. That the "transfer of knowledge" Eoma had spoken of referred to the fact that I was carrying Azlyn's child. A child that would likely inherit the memories of his family line. That they had hoped she might inherit mine as well. Not only the memories I could recall, but the complete knowledge of my family line.

I knew nothing of that at the time. All I had known was my love for Azlyn. A love that had challenged everything I had known and had forced me into a beautiful and exciting new world. Though that world was at odds with my own, I was certain I could somehow merge them.

When Azlana was born, I realized how wrong I had been. They believed that she was the key to uniting our people. That the knowledge she would inherit would help them force the dark breeds into the Alliance, and that together the Mystics could overthrow Ludlum.

And since my family had ties to royalty in the old world, they believed that perhaps my people would accept someone from my line as their leader to avoid anarchy. Thus, they would use my child to unite humans and Mystics. To bring peace.

It was a shot in the dark. The last-ditch effort of a desperate people.

"Would you have changed anything, if you'd known?" It was as if Cazlyn read my thoughts. It wasn't as if I had not asked myself the same, over the years. Still, I was caught off-guard and paused a moment to measure my response.

"No," I replied with confidence. "Our paths shape us, Cazlyn. To change any fork in the road is to change our entire destiny." I was silent, ruminating on what I would say next.

"My time with Azlyn changed me in ways that are both wonderful and terribly painful. Both of which forced me to grow where I otherwise may have remained stagnant. I wouldn't have her."

"Or Gareth," he finished the thought I would have left unsaid.

"Or Gareth," I confirmed. "Cazlyn, know for you the pain is fresher. The passing of years does not feel the same to you."

"Your life is much shorter," he acknowledged.

"It doesn't mean I've forgotten him. He would not want me to spend the rest of my life mourning him. Charlezon knew that, and so do you."

Cazlyn nodded silently. I reached out and laid a hand on his arm. He placed his hand over mine briefly in reassurance. There would be no ill-will between us. For better or worse, Azlana's fate had caught up with her. Whatever that would mean, we would face it together.

"What will we do now?" I asked, more to the universe than to my travel companion. Still, it was he who answered.

"We are to rendezvous with your brother. He and Brian will take you somewhere safe."

"Where?"

"A place predetermined by the Priestess."

Of course. Cazlyn may have the formality of the crown, but Eoma had years of experience as the former King's advisor. The gift of sight didn't hurt either. If she truly had seen the King's demise, she would have spent much of the time between then and now making plans for the fallout that would inevitably occur.

I wondered, had that plan included my daughter? Perhaps her insistence that I bring Azlana to them wasn't just for the sentiment of it. Perhaps I had hindered a greater plan.

"Even I have not seen her fate." The Priestess's words rang in my memory. No, she had not known what would come to pass for Azlana, though she would likely have preferred to have the princess in her care.

What would she say now, I wondered? Without the King to calm her, would she take her grief out on me?

"Have you seen her, since...?" I let the question hang unfinished in the air. I could not bring myself to say it out loud.

"No," Cazlyn's voice was somber. "We were separated during the attack. We each led a group in opposite directions to maximize the survival rate. She sent word, but we have yet to meet face to face."

"I didn't realize you were there when..." I couldn't finish my sentence. That he had likely borne witness to the death of his grandfather, the last of his kin, save for Azlana. My heart broke for him.

He held his chin high, his face kept forward as if he hadn't heard me. Then he stopped in his tracks. We had reached the end of the tunnel. Before us was a tangle of large, gnarled roots intertwining with one another. Their woven shape formed what looked in the dim light like a ladder. I squinted and leaned forward to get a better look. A ladder is exactly what it was.

"You'd better wake the girl," a coy smile crept across his face. "She won't want to miss this."

CHAPTER EIGHT

AZLANA

IT WAS MOTHER'S VOICE THAT PULLED ME FROM THE DARKNESS.

"Wake up, love." Her hand laid softly on my back. It was my anchor. I leaned into it, willing myself into consciousness. My mind resisted. It was so tired, so heavy. How long had I been asleep?

My eyes fluttered open groggily. Mother reached under my arms, gently lowering me down from Cazlyn's back. I rolled the soreness from my shoulders and rubbed the sleep from my eyes. The tunnel had dead-ended. Gnarled tree roots formed a ladder leading up out of the tunnel.

"Think you can handle the climb?" Cazlyn teased. At first, I thought he was asking me since I had just woken up.

"I've not aged all that much," Mother replied.

"It will be darker at the top," Cazlyn warned her. Then to me, "You'll mind your Mother then? When we get to the top?"

The idea of being my Mother's keeper, even for the short climb, was more than a bit surreal. I nodded.

"Alright then. You go on ahead of us and lead the way," he instructed. "I'll come up last, in case she falls." I got the impression that the last part was said at least partially in jest. Mother said nothing in response.

I did my best to put on a brave face as I tested my weight on the first rung. It held. Slowly I climbed, pausing only once to confirm that Mother followed behind me. She sensed my hesitation.

"I'm here, love. Keep going."

At last, I reached the top. The gnarled roots extended up and across the floor of a dark room, offering a handhold for me to pull my body up and out of the tunnel. I sat down and got my bearings, then turned and waited for Mother. As I watched her hands search clumsily for a hold, I realized that Cazlyn may not have been teasing as much as I had thought. She really couldn't see. The realization stung. It was the first time I had experienced how different we were.

"Here," I offered, guiding her hands to the roots I'd used to pull myself up. After what seemed like an eternity, she pulled herself out of the tunnel. I barely had time to guide her away from the drop off before Cazlyn came bounding up behind her.

"Where are we?" I placed a hand on a nearby wall. It was cool and smooth.

"Portha," Cazlyn said, as he traced a symbol on one of the walls. "A gateway."

The symbol, a triangle tipped onto its side, began to glow green. The building shook. Mother pulled me in close as the wall in front of Cazlyn rolled away and sunlight flooded in.

Cazlyn grabbed my hand, pulling me away from Mother, "Come, see!"

I squinted, my hand over my brow as I took in my surroundings. The mid-morning sun was rising in the sky. We were surrounded by trees. Something behind me let out a low rumble. I spun around. Mother squeezed through the door just as it was rolling closed again. It wasn't a building at all, but a great giant tree! The same symbol Cazlyn had drawn inside was carved into its trunk, just above the doorway. It glowed green, as did the seam of the door before both disappeared completely.

"I bet you haven't seen anything quite like that," Cazlyn said.

I shook my head, in awe, "Have you, Mama?"

"No, my sweet. Even I have not seen everything the Alliance has up its sleeve."

"We've still some ways to go before it's safe," Cazlyn urged. "On we go."

"Cazlyn, we've walked all night."

I had forgotten that I was the only one who'd slept. Cazlyn and Mother had walked through the night, and into the day. Whatever strife was between them must have been at least partially resolved while I slumbered. He looked to her with pity.

"I know, Kala. Just a bit further, I promise."

"Aye, you'd not planned to walk her to death, had you, my friend?" a familiar voice called behind us. My feet flew out before me so quickly that they barely touched the ground.

"Nykolas!" I flung my body into him. He wrapped me in his arms and tossed me into the air gleefully, spinning once before setting me back down.

"Hello, brother," Mother greeted him warmly, though wearily. "It has been too long."

"Indeed, it has. I wish our meeting was under more joyful circumstance." He turned to Cazlyn, and the two clasped forearms in greeting, "I am sorry to learn of the loss of your grandfather. I cannot imagine."

I wondered if that last part was a formality, or if he meant it literally. Being half-nymph, Nykolas did not fully comprehend the intricacies of family relationships, though he had taken a liking to me. I guessed it was because I was very small when we met. Few sentient beings can resist the charms of a youngling.

A pained look flittered across Cazlyn's face. It was gone just as quickly as it had come. He nodded, clearing his throat. "There is little time to mourn one's losses in the midst of war," he said matter-of-factly. "We must keep moving."

"Yes, of course," Nykolas made a clicking noise over his shoulder. Behind him, three young mares stepped out of the shadow of the forest. As they stepped into the light their pearly coats shimmered. One walked right up to me, nudging me with her muzzle. I placed a hand on the side of her face. It was velvety soft, more like a rabbit than any horse I'd ever seen.

"Eoma's group met up with father and I after they escaped," he explained, "I'm to take you to them."

His words may as well have gone in one ear and out the other, so enamored was I with the creature that stood before me.

"What are you?" I whispered. If I hadn't known better, I'd have sworn she smiled in response.

Nykolas and Cazlyn had mounted their steeds. Mother climbed onto of the one I had already come to consider "mine". She reached out her hand and lifted me up in front of her. Though none of the horses wore saddles, we were secure on their backs, as if cradled by an outside force.

"You have marvelous horses, Uncle!"

Cazlyn started to speak, but Nykolas leaned over from his seat and nudged him playfully, "Let it be a surprise."

"Let what be a surprise?"

"You shall see, Little 'Lana," He smirked before guiding his horse to lead us through the forest.

We rode single file with Nykolas in the lead and Cazlyn riding in the rear. Though I'd ridden a few times before, this one was unlike any other. There were no trails in the forest, but although our steeds were forced to navigate through the underbrush, their hooves hardly made a sound. Nor did their bodies jostle ours the way I was used to. Indeed, I experienced little more than a gentle sway as I took in the changing scenery. It was like nothing I had ever seen. Of course, I had climbed trees back home, but never had I seen trees so close together. The forest was off limits to villagers. Only Ludlum's men dared enter. The trees back home paled in comparison. Here they stood taller than my eye could follow. Their branches reached out and up, toward the sun. Some of them intertwined with one another as if embracing a close friend.

Wispy moss clung to their limbs, draping like delicate lace. A gentle breeze rustled through the boughs, sending the occasional leaf or pine needle floating gently down. Some landed in my hair, and Mother plucked it out gently.

I looked up at her face. Fine lines crinkled in the corners of her eyes as she smiled back at me and kissed the top of my head. She had aged, it felt almost overnight. I wondered if my face would someday look the same.

Would I age more like a human or an elf? The mortality of my Mother's side frightened me, not just for myself, but for her. I tried to shake the thought from my mind, but it was replaced by one equally distressing.

"Mother, what about Gareth?" His name felt foreign in my mouth, but I wanted to be clear that I was speaking of him and not of my natural father.

Mother squeezed my shoulder gently, her eyes far away, "Don't you fret about that, love. Your father is a resourceful man, and we have long planned for a scenario like this one. As soon as he can break away from the King's men he will send word, and we will be together again."

I wanted to know more about the plan. How would he send word? Where would we meet? How would he know we had escaped and not been captured, or worse, killed? But the matter was not up for discussion. Whatever my heritage or role in what was happening, I was still a child in her eyes. I was too tired to argue.

Instead, I leaned into her. The comfort of her smell and the weight of her arms around me soothed me, and I soon found myself struggling to fight sleep. My dreams had not been kind of late, and I was in no hurry to return to them. Still, the gentle swaying of our horse soon began to lull me off into a peaceful trance. It was not long before I found myself unable to fight my fatigue.

I was surrounded by flames. Mother, the horses, they had all disappeared. A battle raged around me between men and Mystics. Arrows whistled as they were loosed from their bows. One struck a tree near my head. A black, tarry substance dripped from the arrowhead.

"Hydra's blood," said The Darkness.

It meant something. Something important, but I couldn't quite reach what.

I looked around, hoping to spot any of my travel companions. Instead, I was met with chaos. Dwarves, centaurs, men... all around me weapons clashed and bodies fell. In the distance, an elf called out as he was struck with a black-tipped arrow. His companion showed only a moment of remorse before beheading him.

"WE were there," whispered The Darkness. "Look at the beauty of our creation. Such chaos. Such loss. WE were so powerful."

I closed my eyes against the gruesome scene, refusing to watch. The world spun and everything was silent. I opened my eyes, hoping to find myself in my own bed. Hoping it was all a bad dream.

Instead, a different type of darkness greeted me. I was in a cave, but I was not alone. A tall figure stood at a stone table, mixing ash into several glass containers. He spoke, as if to a student:

"To kill a phoenix, displace the ashes in separate containers. Mix with water until dissolved." As he said this, he poured water into each container from a silver pitcher. The ash swirling in the water reminded me of the way the wind sometimes picked up stray leaves on the streets at home. "Beautiful, in its own way," The Darkness said. I recoiled in disgust. Slowly the ash turned the water black. It flowed from its container and rose up around me, enveloping me. Smothering me. Drowning me. I flung my arms outward against it, but it was no use. It overcame me.

I awoke to the sound of someone screaming. It took me longer than I would like to admit for me to realize that the sound came from my own mouth. I was still being smothered. I swung my arms out and kicked my legs against whatever was restraining me.

"'Lana STOP!" Mother's voice broke the spell. She had flung her body around mine to keep me on the horse. I went still, trying to catch my bearings. My wide eyes met the concerned gaze of Nykolas and Cazlyn, who had dismounted to help Mother. My face flushed with embarrassment.

"Sorry," I huffed between ragged breaths. My heart was still raging against my chest, "I had a nightmare."

Cazlyn's brow furrowed, "What type of nightmare?"

"They'll know you've gone mad," The Darkness warned.

"I...I don't remember," I lied.

Cazlyn and Mother exchanged worried glances. Nykolas held my gaze for a moment more than was comfortable, but none of the contested my story.

"I'm sorry. I feel better now," I didn't know why I felt the need to apologize. It wasn't as if I had wished for any of those thoughts to happen.

"*Then why do you let them?*" The Darkness taunted. "*Why do you know their weaknesses? Why do you conjure them again and again?*"

Stop it, I thought to myself. *That's ridiculous. I probably heard one of the village children recite it. It just manifested itself in a dream.*

"*Is that it, though?*'" The Darkness would not let up. "*Or is it because you really want it to happen?*"

I didn't justify the inquiry with a response. No use arguing with myself.

Chapter Nine

Kala

NYKOLAS EYED ME QUIZZICALLY as if asking me to confirm Azlana's excuse for her outburst. I pursed my lips and shook my head. I desperately wanted to confide my concerns in someone. Anyone. But not here. Not in front of her. I brushed her bangs back from her forehead and kissed the top of her head.

"Let's take a break, shall we? We've been riding too long for my old body, anyway."

Nykolas laughed, "You're not so old. Even for your kind."

"Yes well, I feel old, anyway," I dismounted, stretching my stiff muscles before helping Azlana down.

She seemed exhausted, despite having slept more than the rest of us combined. She leaned against our horse. The mare responded by leaning into her gently, almost as if it was reassuring her. A lifetime ago, I would have found the thought ridiculous. But I had long since learned better than to dismiss a creature simply because it could not express itself in a way that I understood.

It was one of the many lessons I had learned from Azlyn.

"Communication is a two-way interaction. The burden of understanding rests on the shoulders of the receiver. Too many people judge the value of an interaction on

whether it is easy for them to understand."

The memory made me smile though it was bittersweet. In so many ways it seemed like yesterday. At the same time, it was a lifetime ago.

The four of us sat silently in a circle as we ate lunch. Neither Nykolas nor Cazlyn tethered their horses. I found this odd, but did not have the energy to argue, and instead followed suit.

We sat in a circle and ate in silence. I looked upon the faces of my travel companions, one at a time. Each reflected similar emotion. Sorrow, fatigue. My heart ached for them. For myself.

I wouldn't have known we had been followed had Azlana not looked up from her meal.

"May as well join us, Brian," Cazlyn smirked.

"Bloody hell," My father came up behind him, pausing to catch his breath, "I've been tracking you lot all day."

"I know," Cazlyn's smirk grew into an all-out smile as he turned to face my father. "You're louder than a herd of Minotaur."

Father looked to Nykolas, his hands up in the air, "And you?"

My brother said nothing, but chuckled and winked mischievously at me. It was all a game to him. Something else he inherited from his mother's side.

Brian lifted his palms in defeat and sat beside me, catching his breath.

None of us said anything, but we all looked to him expectantly. Cazlyn passed Brian his water flask. He took a long swig, wiping the overflow from his beard before speaking.

"Your husband sends his regards, Kala."

I breathed a sigh of relief, surprised to find myself holding back tears. We were forced to leave so quickly that I hadn't been given much time to realize how scared I was for him. My focus was on getting Azlana to safety, and there was time for little else. Brian reached over and squeezed my hand. I took a deep breath and gathered my composure, worried that a moment of weakness would unravel me. *Not here*, I willed myself.

"He broke away from his troop just before they attacked the camp," he continued. "There was no way for him to maintain his cover this time." My father left the worst unsaid. There was no way for Gareth to maintain his cover without participating in the slaughter of his friends. My chest ached, and for a moment I wondered how many times one person's heart could break before it was unable to go on.

"Their lot nearly overcame us on their way back. We hid in the trees and I sent word for Nykolas to fetch you."

"How?" Azlana asked. I'd been so wrapped up in my father's tale that I had forgotten that she was listening. This world was new and, even under the circumstances, fascinating to her.

Brian smiled. He had always loved the girl's innocent curiosity, "Through the trees, of course." He looked at my brother, "A little trick I learned from your Mother, back in the day."

Nykolas shifted nervously. His parentage was still more than a bit of a scandal among the Mystics.

"Gareth stayed to look for survivors that may have been missed. I was to confirm you made it safely before rendezvousing with him."

"We are on our way to meet with Eoma," Cazlyn's voice was calculated. He was asserting his authority. "In the mountains."

The last part meant something to my father, for a look crossed his face that I could not put my finger on. He nodded, "Best be on our separate ways. Wouldn't want to keep the Priestess waiting." His gazed darted to Azlana, then back to Cazlyn. "She will be safe there?"

"The safest," Cazlyn assured him. "Gareth will, of course, be welcome. Any other survivors will be... well-tended."

"Aye." he nodded, then stood and brushed his legs awkwardly, "I'll see to it they get there."

I realized that Cazlyn's invitation subtly, and intentionally excluded Brian. It was not something that escaped my father's attention. His eyes met mine, and he confirmed my suspicion with a nod, but said nothing.

I wondered, what might have come between them that I was not aware of. In the past Cazlyn and my father had gotten on well enough. Technically, it was Cazlyn who had introduced me to my estranged father, all those years ago.

It was not exactly a tension between them so much as an... awkwardness.

Like something hung in the air that both were aware of but left unmentioned. It reminded me of the time my cousin Audri had baked bread for the first time. It was hard as a rock on the outside, and yet somehow not-quite-done in the middle.

Uncle John and I had sat at the table, silently trying to choke the meal down as Audri pushed her own dinner around her plate with her fork. All of us knew the truth: the bread was terrible. But none of us would say it aloud, for it wasn't polite to acknowledge such things.

Perhaps this was a similar situation.

"Do you have to go?" Azlana's voice cut my thoughts short.

"Do not worry, my pet. We shall see each other again soon, I am sure of it." My father wrapped her up in his arms and kissed the top of her head. "Now, you behave for your Mother. Listen to what she tells you and be brave."

"I'm always brave," my daughter squared her shoulders and for a moment I wondered how she had grown from infant to such a striking girl so quickly.

My father said his goodbyes to the rest of us as we mounted our horses and departed. We rode for what seemed like only a moment, but when I turned my head to wave one last time he was already out of view.

We rode on, racing the fading sunlight. Around me, the terrain changed from woodland to a bare, rocky field. In the distance, mountains loomed over us. The scenery began to blur, and I realized we had sped up. I couldn't be sure, but it seemed as if it was the horses setting the pace. Perhaps they were eager to be home.

Home. What must that be like? To Azlana, we had fled the only home she had ever known. My heart ached for her, and for myself. It's funny how the wounds of our children can unearth our own hurts, no matter how ancient they may be.

I shook the thought from my mind. No use drudging up the past now.

No time for it, either.

Suddenly we found ourselves at the foot of a mountain. Without speaking Nykolas led us up a steep, narrow path. Azlana clung tightly to the horse, and I to her. When it came to climbing the highest boughs of a tree, she had nary a concern, but riding on horseback up the side of a mountain was a different thing altogether!

After the third switchback, we came to a wall. In the fading light, it seemed that Nykolas' horse was unaware of the obstruction, for she continued to move. I opened my mouth to shout a warning before they collided—only to gasp as they disappeared into the mountain.

I gripped my horse's mane, tugging to signal her to stop. She obeyed, but not without letting out a disgruntled snort. I turned to Cazlyn, who sat tall and smiling upon his steed behind us.

"Go on, then," he urged.

I loosened my grip and my horse lurched forward. I closed my eyes, holding my breath as we approached the mountainside. It was an involuntary action. Something primal, in the back of my mind, felt as if there would be no air as we reached the other side. I needn't have worried.

"Open your eyes, Mama," Azlana urged. We were in a cavern. Easily, I guessed, the size of a great hall. A soft, blue light emanated from the walls far above our heads. Azlana looked up in awe. The phenomena was not new to me as it was to her. I had seen it once before, on the day her father died.

"Wisps," Cazlyn explained. He dismounted and led his horse to stand beside ours. In front of me, Nykolas followed Cazlyn's example. This is where we would stay. Whether it was for the night or for good, I dared not ask.

I slid from my saddle, surprised when my feet met not with cold stone, but with soft earth and grass. Azlana made the same observation as I helped her down.

"Look, Mother! Flowers!" And she was right. Little pink flowers sprouted here and there in clusters at our feet. Here, in the mountain where certainly no sun ever shone.

"Will wonders never cease?" I whispered to myself. Even here, in the land of Mystics and magic, I found surprises.

"Tis not the only one you'll find here, sister," Nykolas' eyes danced impishly. I knew better than to press him. He loved nothing more than a good surprise.

Cazlyn stroked the muzzle of each of our horses, whispering softly to them. They almost seemed to nod before trotting across the hall and into a small passageway I had somehow missed as we entered.

"What's all that, now?" I inquired. Talking to horses was not a new skill for Cazlyn, but letting our rides go their merry way without consulting the group did not sit well with me. Though I was among friends, I couldn't help but feel trapped.

"I released them. And asked them to summon—"

"Me," A familiar voice echoed in my mind. Azlana's hand darted for my own. Without asking, I knew that she, too, had heard it.

"Eoma," I greeted the High Priestess aloud.

She appeared, seemingly out of nowhere. There weren't any obvious entrances to where we stood, save the one our horses had entered. Such was her nature. She preferred an air of mystery. I wasn't sure if that was her own personality or more of an occupational hazard.

She hadn't changed much over the years. Her fiery hair showed no signs of gray. The only sign of age were small lines in the corners of her eyes that formed as she smiled, somewhat sadly, at Azlana.

She had not come alone. Two unicorns flanked either side of her. Her left hand rested on the side of one of them, not for physical support as much as emotional. The dark circles under her eyes told me two things. First, that she hadn't slept and second, she chose not to mask her appearance with magic. The latter was especially telling. She had chosen not to conceal her heartache.

But, why should she? She had just lost someone very dear to her.

Beside me, Azlana clung to my waist, placing my body in the path between her and Eoma. Her posture was that of a child afraid. Clinging to her mother for protection. It had been a long time since she had needed me in such a way. I smoothed her hair out and kissed the top of her head. This did not resolve the tension.

Then she saw the unicorns. What little girl has not dreamt of seeing a real unicorn? Her eyes lit up, and she stepped out from behind me cautiously, reaching out her hand. One of the unicorns stepped forward to meet her, but it did not get far before flinching and shying away. Azlana's face fell in disappointment.

"'Tis not personal," Eoma reassured her. "If you come to them alone, they will not shy away." Her eyes met my own. Of course. I had forgotten that unicorns could not mingle with the impure. Though I had not known it caused them physical pain.

"That is why father had to take his leave," Nykolas whispered beside me as if reading my thoughts. In terms of purity, there was no doubt of my father's failings. His presence among them would have been nearly unbearable. "Even the Deyanians are uncomfortable in his presence."

"The what?" I asked.

"Our horses," Azlana said. She had filled in the blanks on her own, my smart child.

"Deyanians are a... sort of sub-breed of unicorn," my brother filled in. "They have relinquished their horns, as well as their restrictions and immortality, in order to more fully aid in the efforts of the Alliance."

As he spoke, Azlana stepped away from me reaching out for the unicorn's muzzle. Her fingertips barely brushed it before she shied away and returned to my side. I wanted to ask her what had startled her, but I knew she would never confide in me with the others around. She wanted to put on a brave front, to prove to them she was not some child to be coddled. How I wanted to do just that. My sweet baby girl.

"You are safe here," Eoma's voice pulled me from my thoughts. "This place is a place of refuge, kept secret even from other Mystic breeds."

"Then how do you know about it?" Azlana inquired. I was relieved to see that her fear did not impede her curiosity.

"The unicorns are... old friends," I could tell there was more to the story than Eoma was willing to disclose just yet. She addressed me, "I have made arrangements for the child to stay here."

She made the announcement casually, as if she was doing us a great favor, and not uprooting a child from the only home she had ever known.

"For how long?"

"As long as it takes." She squared her shoulders in a show of authority. I waited for the familiar feel of her probing my mind but felt none. Whether it was from fatigue or overconfidence, I was uncertain.

I approached her, causing the unicorns to shrink back swiftly. I raised a hand in apology and leaned in to whisper, "She is only a child."

"She is the heir to the throne." It was said matter-of-factly. "She must lead her people, Kala."

"How, exactly, is she supposed to do that?" I pressed. "We are at war. Would you have a child-one who knows only the world of my people- lead you into battle?!"

"The knowledge will come," she insisted.

"No. The knowledge will not come." I hissed. "She has passed her tenth birthday already and shows no sign of Awakening. She is a child. A human child."

"Then she shall have to learn the human way. She may still know more than you suspect."

"What do you know, old woman?" I eyed her suspiciously. She glanced over my shoulder at Azlana as if in a daze.

"Her path is still beyond my grasp." She mumbled, suspiciously. "Something blocks me from her mind..."

She cleared her throat and held my gaze, "No matter. Where would you have her go? Where would she be safe if not here?"

I didn't have an answer. The Priestess' voice softened, and her hand rested on my shoulder, "We have lost too many already, Kala. Rest. Tend to your daughter. She has a great destiny, you cannot deny that. But let us talk more of it later. I must tend to the wounded and—" she fell silent, swallowing hard against the tears that formed in the corners of her eyes. I realized what she had left unsaid. There were dead to be buried.

Chapter Ten

Azlana

T HE WOMAN WITH THE RED HAIR FRIGHTENED ME. "High Priestess" they had called her. I could feel her power fill the room. It was overwhelming. I found myself clinging to Mother's side, the way I had done when I was very young.

"*Silly child,*" whispered The Darkness. I tried to shake it away. It wouldn't be shaken. "*You think you are so brave, do you pet? Then why do you cower before the witch?*"

The Darkness delighted in its use of the offensive term. I held my breath in anticipation, wondering if she could hear it. Beads of sweat formed on my forehead as I waited to be struck down. Nothing happened. I squinted my eyes shut.

"*She reads minds, you know. Maybe she will see what is inside yours and decide you are not worth saving.*" When the unicorn approached, the voice fell silent. I reached out to it like an oasis, but it shied away from me. I wondered if it could sense what was in my mind. Was it afraid of The Darkness as well?

"*Why would something so lovely have any interest in you?*" The Darkness taunted.

I was happy when the Priestess took her leave. I felt the tension lift from my body.

"Who was that?" I whispered to Nykolas. I did not want Mother to hear me asking questions. She did not seem in the mood for them.

"Eoma, High Priestess, and advisor to the King," he answered. "At least, she was..."

"Is that why she is so sad?" I had watched her talk with Mother. At first, she seemed angry, but her face quickly softened, weary and forlorn.

"Aye. She and the King were very close. As far back as anyone can remember, they were by each other's side. The best of friends since they were children." He let out a sigh, "You see, many believed that they would marry."

"But they didn't?"

He smiled at my ignorance. Not the way one does when they think that you are less, but in the way where they find you endearing.

"No, they never did." I wondered at how sad it must feel, to love someone for so many years only to lose them; without ever truly having them in the first place.

Perhaps it was something like discovering an entire family you knew nothing about.

Cazlyn led us down a cavern... well it was more like a hallway. The glowing blue lights made way to more natural light as we walked—almost as if the sun had found a way to shine through the mountain. I glanced up in search of its source. A dark blue sky greeted me, with tendrils of the impending sunset dancing at its edges and stars scattered all around.

"Tis not real," Cazlyn said, noticing my awe, "Just an illusion."

"Why is it here if it's not real?" It made no sense to live under a false sky when the real thing was just outside one's door.

"When you are hunted, you appreciate the small comforts, even if they lack authenticity."

I got the feeling that he knew from experience. Mother laid her hand gently on my arm, a reminder not to pry.

Before long we were led to a long hallway with a series of wooden doors. They were red, adorned with ornate golden hardware. Cazlyn stopped in front of one and whispered something I didn't understand. A rune appeared, glowing, on the door. It was the same rune we had seen on the tree earlier.

I knew what it meant now. It was a symbol for an entryway. Whether it was there to identify an entrance, or if it was some sort of magic that created them, I was unsure.

The door swung open, revealing a well-lit room. There was a bed and a chest of drawers. A faux window on the wall projected a distant sunset. Suddenly Cazlyn's words about being hunted felt too close for comfort.

"This will be your quarters," Cazlyn said to me. I looked to Mother for reassurance, clinging to her hand tightly. The room was nice enough, familiar in a weird way even, but something was missing.

"There is only one bed," I pointed out.

Cazlyn raised an eyebrow quizzically.

"It's just... I thought that Mother..." My face flushed with embarrassment. Of course, they would deem me old enough to room alone. I was nearly 11, after all, and had slept in my own room since I was a much younger girl. But that was a home where I was safe. Where I had felt safe, at least. With that illusion of safety removed I felt very much like a young child in the dark. I wanted my mom.

Mother raised a hand and brushed my bangs away from my face, letting her hand linger on my cheek.

"'Tis alright, Lana," her voice was soft, like the cooing of a dove. "You will be safe here. I promise."

"Your Mother will be in the next room over," Cazlyn reassured me. "Trust me, there will be times where you will relish the solitude."

I had no idea what he meant and turned to Mother for an explanation. She shrugged back at me.

"You have much to learn during your time here. Some of it will be—" he seemed to be searching for the appropriate word. "...overwhelming. You'll appreciate having your own space for contemplation."

I looked to Mother again for reassurance. She nodded, running her fingers through a lock of my hair. I wanted to sit with her, to climb into the comfort of her lap and fall asleep to the smell of her hair brushing the side of my face. But that was a comfort afforded only to children, and I was determined to prove that I was not just a silly child.

Still, I found myself looking over my shoulder as I stepped into my quarters.

"Tis alright," my Mother said again. "I'll come and say goodnight to you in a bit."

I managed a smile that I hoped was convincing and shut the door.

I set my bag on the bed wearily. I wasn't exactly sure what was expected of me, but unpacking seemed logical. Putting my clothes away took less time than I expected. I'd packed light, not fully realizing the gravity of the situation. That I may never step foot in my home again. I unpacked my stuffed rabbit, running my hand over it before setting it down next to a pillow made of a material that sparkled like the surface of the lake on a summer's day. The burlap material of Luka's pillow stuck out like a sore thumb, rugged in comparison. It was the only thing that felt like home.

I curled up on the bed, burying my face in the pillow, and wept.

I had only closed my eyes for a second, but when I opened them again, the scene in the faux window had changed. A dark sky, scattered with stars. The moon hung low, casting a warm glow on the foreground.

The scene was peaceful, but my mood was foul. Everything had happened so quickly that I hadn't had a chance to process it. The image of the Elite riding through town played in my head. Where was Gareth? Why wasn't he with us? Would I ever see Luka again? Or did today mark the end of everything?

"What is the end of one day, if not the beginning of the next?"

This voice was not any that I had heard before. Like The Darkness, it spoke in my mind, as if it were my own voice, and not at the same time. Still, it was familiar — like the kind of memory you want to wrap yourself in for comfort.

It was no memory of mine. I scanned the room for signs of intrusion but found none. I slipped beneath the weight of the quilt for comfort.

"Perhaps it is the witch playing tricks," The Darkness suggested. My breath

caught in my chest at the thought. I heard a creak as the door to my room opened. I bolted upright.

"Tis just me, love." The soft coo of Mother's voice soothed my fears. She crawled into bed beside me, kissing my forehead, like she had done so many times across my childhood. I curled up against her, trying as hard as I could to let my worries melt away as she stroked my hair.

"I know this is a lot to take in," She whispered. I nodded, afraid that my voice would betray me. My eyes stung with the threat of tears all over again. I closed them tight and pressed my head into her, taking in the scent of her hair. Fresh air and wilderness had replaced her familiar scent. Another reminder that everything had changed.

"Shhh," she whispered to me the same way she had when I was very small. It was as if she knew the chaos of my inner voice and sought to silence it. Her hand caressed my hair. For once, my mind was silent, and I drifted off into a dreamless sleep.

Chapter Eleven

Kala

I AWOKE TO FIND THE ROOM AWASH in the soft pink glow of an artificial sunrise. Azlana lay beside me, the gentle rise and fall of her chest let me know she was still asleep. I laid still a moment and watched her, the way I had when she was a baby. For the first time in weeks, her sleep seemed undisturbed.

I slid my arm out from under her and snuck away, stepping carefully so as not to wake her. The air in the corridor was cool and still, not unlike the morning air outside the mountain. It seemed I was the first among our party to wake. I made my way down the cavern, past my own quarters and into a great open space. Grass grew under foot and a blue sky projected overhead. One could almost forget that we were underground.

I caught sight of a herd of horses grazing in the far corner. The animals we had ridden here had been white, but in this group, a variety of coats were displayed. There were no unicorns in sight.

I observed the herd quietly for a while. One of them reminded me of a horse we owned when I was a girl, Sienna. I had wondered what had happened to her, all those years ago. I inched closer, wanting to get a better look. Their heads shot up, alert. Our eyes met. These were no ordinary horses.

"'They are not horses, at all."

The voice made me jump. The Priestess had caught me off-guard.

"I'd assumed your father would have told you. He always has delighted in impressing the girl."

"Azlana. She has a name." I ignored the slight against my father and made a mental note to ask Nykolas about the horses later.

"Yes. How clever of you, choosing the female form of her father's name."

"Enough with the games, Priestess; this is no game of cat and mouse. You did not come here to play with your prey, so out with it."

"Prey? Is that how you see yourself?" The corners of her lips turned upward impishly, "How amusing."

I rolled my eyes. "Whatever this mood of yours is, I do not have time for it." She grabbed hold of my arm as I tried to brush past her.

"*Tis no game, child,*" Her voice echoing in my mind was meant to remind me of her status. That I was not speaking to my equal. She was putting me in my place.

"Has the thought not crossed your mind that the ambush was not just some stroke of luck? That it was, indeed, a calculated attack? Our ranks have been compromised, Kala. Or have you become so wrapped up in yourself that you have forgotten all that is at stake?"

I did not try to deny it. The family I had created—that I had been forced into — had become the center of my world. Leaving my other duties to rot around the illusion of safety I had created. What a fool I had been. We were never safe. I thought of my husband and said a silent prayer to the Gods. *Please, let him be safe.*

"Where is he, this husband of yours?" I set my jaw in an attempt to restrain my words. I did not appreciate the intrusion into what should have been a private moment.

"I haven't seen him since—" I stopped myself before the fear of acknowledging all that had happened could choke off my sentence. As if somehow refusing to say it would save them. Clearing my throat, I tried again, "My father said he'd stayed near the camp to search for survivors. Brian was to rendezvous with him when we parted."

"There were no other survivors." Her voice was flat. "His troop made sure of it."

I felt the hair on the back of my neck stand up. Was she really suggesting what I thought she was?

"They are not his troop. Or have you forgotten that it was you who put him in this position, to begin with?"

Eoma's nostrils flared. It was obvious she was not accustomed to being argued with. "And he did not seem, even once, to be a tad overeager?"

"No. Not even once. Watch yourself, Eoma," I warned, "lest you let your grief lead you astray."

There was a time, when I was much younger, that going head to head with the Priestess would have never crossed my mind. A time when I was intimidated, nay, afraid of the woman who stood before me. But on this day, I did not see a woman worthy of my fear. I saw a woman in pain. One who was at risk of alienating her allies if she let that pain consume her. One who had crossed the line, questioning the loyalties of my husband.

"Gareth was loyal to the king. He has done nothing other than what was asked of him. He has put his life on the line countless times for your people." My argument began to lose steam. It was true, but it was not proof that he had not betrayed them.

It was not how he had earned my trust.

"He has been good to me. He has loved me and supported me. He took under his wing a child that was not of him and made her his own."

Eoma stood in quiet contemplation, digesting my words. Her focus shifted.

"Is she always so shy?" Her eyes locked with mine, betraying her. Her question was a mask for the information she was really seeking. *What is wrong with the girl?* That was her true inquiry.

"She has been... different, of late." Different was not an accurate description. Forlorn, shut off, distressed—all of those words would have been more accurate, but I was afraid to say them aloud. I remembered what it was like to be her age. To be torn between childhood and... something else from which there was no return. But this was something different altogether.

"What did you expect her reaction to be?" Had the Priestess been reading my thoughts or just my face?

"How would you feel in her place? Living life as an outcast—"

"You don't understand—"

"—only to find out the truth of her heritage when there remain none who can teach her rightful place?"

"There is one yet who might," I was losing patience. "Or have you forgotten who is leading?"

Eoma's eyes flashed red, then violet as she regained her composure. I couldn't help but feel the slightest amount of satisfaction. It seemed that I had struck a chord.

"I have not forgotten," Her nostrils flared as she spoke. I was treading on dangerous ground. There was a time when I would have chosen my words more carefully. Then again, I was young when I first met her, and much more naïve than I ever would have admitted.

Her voice lowered, and she spoke through gritted teeth, "I have not forgotten my place, but have you forgotten yours?"

"I have not forgotten my place or my oath. I have acted in everyone's interests — most of all Azlana's."

"You acted selfishly and overstepped your bounds! You are the mother to the heir — not queen."

"I have no desire to be queen," I assured her.

"Yet you thought it your right to keep her from him."

It was suddenly clear to me that we were not having the argument I thought we were. This wasn't about The Alliance, her kingdom, the throne. This was about Charlezon. About the pain of watching the love she could never have die before her eyes. Knowing that he did so having never met the person he'd wanted to most of all. Having never met his own granddaughter. My anger fell away.

"Eoma, I didn't know. I didn't know it would end this way. I always thought—"

"Stupid girl! You thought only of yourself! Don't you think he tried to tell you? That we both did? You are always so certain that you know best. You allow your illusion of superiority to blind you!"

The memory came rushing back to me. The force of the Priestess' intrusion was like a punch in the gut.

"*Peace Eoma! We have time,*" The memory of Charlezon's voice echoed in my mind. My stomach lurched, and the room began to spin. Eoma and I had fought on that day, too.

"*Even I have not seen her fate.*"

And then what? What had happened?

"We have time..." my own voice whispered and I put together the pieces of a puzzle I already wished I'd never known.

"You knew!" I met her eyes in horror. "You knew then, what would happen, didn't you?"

She squared her shoulders, raising her chin as a single tear fell down her cheek. It was the first—the only—time I saw the Priestess allow herself a moment of such weakness.

"We knew. The both of us. I couldn't keep it from him. The burden was too much."

I tried to imagine myself in her position. What would it be like to know how much time you have left with someone you love? To be able to savor every moment, to avoid the gut-wrenching shock of losing them suddenly. One may even consider it a blessing.

To count down the days. The hours. To have the shadow of their doom hang over your every moment together. One could say that was a curse.

And here she stood before me, the bearer of both the blessing and the curse, having lived it who-knows-how-many times in her mind, knowing she could do nothing to change it, before watching it come to pass before her very eyes.

My daughter's fate was not her doing. Nor was Charlezon's. But seeing her now, I wondered... how many times had she blamed herself for the things that she had seen?

"I'm sorry." It was all I knew to say.

"Aye." We stood in silence, a sign of respect for the dead. A ritual that mattered only to the living.

"Cazlyn has asked to stay with the girl," Eoma broke the silence.

I was not surprised. He had taken quickly to Azlana. In times of grief, we often turn to the next generation for hope. With her being the last of his blood-kin, it made sense that he would want to be the one to guide her through her transition into this new world.

"His leadership role is just a formality," Eoma answered my question before I could ask. "Something for the people to look to as proof that the empire still stands... Not that there are many left who would look for such an idol." Her face fell. Her eyes dimmed as they met mine. "We are a dying breed, Kala."

It was a plea, more than a statement. *Please. Help us.* I couldn't be certain whether the voice in my head was hers, or my own.

I let out the breath I hadn't realized I was holding, hoping the weight in my chest would go with it. It didn't.

"What do you need her to do?"

CHAPTER TWELVE

AZLANA

I AWOKE ALONE. It wasn't until I allowed my eyes to open, slowly, that the events of the previous day came flooding back to me. I wanted to shoot up in the bed and search for Mother, but my fear wouldn't let me.

I burrowed deep into the blankets that still held her smell. It reminded me of when I was a little girl and had a bad dream. In all the stories that the village children told, the monsters would sneak up on you in your sleep, attacking the hero once they bolted from the bed. So, I would lay still beneath my blankets, trying to slow my breath. Just in case the monster was waiting.

Except in this story, the monsters the children feared were just on the other side of my door. In this story, *I* was the monster. Or, at least, half-monster. Because to human children monster meant the enemy. It meant Mystic.

A knock at the door interrupted my thoughts.

"W-ho," I cleared the sleep from my throat. "Who is it?"

"'Tis time to greet the day, Your Highness," Eoma did not bother naming herself. "You'll find more appropriate clothing in the chest of drawers. Third one down."

More appropriate clothing? I thought. *What is wrong with MY clothing?*

When I did not respond, she added, "Do not leave me waiting, *girl*."

"*From 'Your Highness' to 'girl' in a matter of minutes,*" The Darkness sneered. "*I guess we know where you stand then, girl.*"

She has no real power over me, I thought to myself. They needed me for... something. I was sure of it. Regardless, I did not think it wise to drag my feet. I hurried to get dressed, only pausing a moment to wonder if the clean clothes had appeared by magic in the drawer, or if they had been placed by someone while I was sleeping. I wasn't sure which would be more unnerving.

Eoma said nothing as I stepped out into the hall. She looked me up and down, noticing that I had foregone footwear and nodded as if I had passed some test she hadn't expected me to. When she turned and walked away, I knew that I should be following, but my feet would not obey.

"Come on, then!" She barked without looking back. Suddenly my feet had a mind of their own, leaping to catch up.

We encountered no one as we walked together in silence. I wondered how big this place was, and what other creatures it might be hiding.

"This place is a sanctuary to those in need." Was she reading my mind, or simply making small talk? I hadn't felt anything. I figured I'd feel something, though I wasn't certain what. Better to play it safe and do things the old-fashioned way.

"Do many find themselves in need?"

She raised an eyebrow, gazing down at me from the corner of her eye. "Aye, at times. More so, of late." She paused. "Tell me, child, what do you know of your fate?"

I decided she couldn't have been reading my mind because if she had, she would know how little I understood of what was going on. She would know how scared I was. What would she do if I withheld the information? If I was non-compliant? Would she force her way into my mind? Could she, even? I didn't want to find out.

"What anyone knows about their fate, I suppose."

"Which is?"

"Not very much." My answer amused her, and I was sure I caught her stifling a laugh.

"What about you? You see the future and stuff, right?"

"In a sense." The Priestess tilted her head in quiet reflection before nodding. "I suppose you could say that."

"What do *you* know of my fate?" It seemed only fair to turn the question back on her. After all, it was I who was being forced into this new world. Whatever plans whether pre-fated or not, were hers to answer more than mine.

"Not very much." Her face was sly as she mimicked the cadence of my speech. This time I laughed.

Funny, how laughter can melt away fear. I looked at Eoma. She was certainly not less mysterious or powerful. And yet, that moment of honest interaction seemed to lift the veil of superiority from around her.

"Tell me of your life before, then. What was it like, growing up amongst your Mother's people?" Her eyes went somewhere far away, "Were you happy?"

"I never really fit in with the other kids," I admitted, surprised at the weight of the sadness saying those words out loud brought.

"Why is that?"

It was an odd feeling, being listened to. Eoma seemed genuinely interested—not like Mother who only seemed to listen so she could point out ways that what I said was wrong. She had wanted me to fit into her world so badly. At the time, I didn't understand why.

Now our family was separated. Who knew if I would see father again, or Luka. Maybe I should have tried harder to fit in.

"I can't play like they do. I get... overwhelmed."

"Overwhelmed in what way?" I almost felt as if she was guiding me toward an answer she already knew. The Darkness tugged at the corner of my mind.

"She'll never understand you. No one does."

My mouth had gone dry. I swallowed hard and took a deep breath.

"Well, for one thing, they're unbearably loud."

The Priestess threw her head back and laughed freely. The sound was mischievous, beauty dancing with danger. It brought to mind a memory of the first time Gareth had taken me shooting. He'd handed me one of his arrows—dark blue with a silver tip, it bore the emblem of King Irving. I had been so enthralled by the way it caught the light that I'd reached out and touched the point before he could stop me. The pain made me recoil, but it wasn't until I saw the crimson bead roll from my finger to the ground that I realized what I had done.

"That would be your father's side. We've a keen sense of hearing, and a nimble stride."

"I don't think I inherited the nimble part. Grandfather always said I have the grace of a baby ogre."

"Did he, now?" She raised an eyebrow.

I felt my face grow hot. I'd forgotten my grandfather's reputation was less than favorable here.

"'Tis better when I've bare feet," I offered, hoping to steer the conversation in a different direction.

"Interesting," she muttered. "Has it always been that way?"

"Long as I can remember." I tucked a lock of hair behind my ear, watching my bare feet move beneath me.

"Hmmm."

"What does that mean?" I demanded. I had hoped that opening up to her would reveal that I was more or less 'normal' on my father's side, but her reaction left me feeling deflated. Was I just some curiosity to her? Some mystery to be solved?

"It means I am thinking."

"*See?*" The Darkness snickered, "*You don't fit in here, either.*"

My heart sank. It was right, this voice in the back of my mind. I did not fit in anywhere. The familiar frustration at discovering that I was still an outcast bubbled in my chest. My fists clenched at my sides trying to keep it from breaking out into the howl it longed to become. It wasn't until Eoma stopped in her tracks that I realized I'd given myself away.

"Stop that," She commanded, kneeling to uncurl my fists. There were indents on my palms where my fingernails had dug into my skin. It stung, but in a way that was almost soothing.

That's not normal. This time the voice in my head was my own. Eoma's eyes locked on mine, and her brow furrowed.

"Something is keeping me out..." She said under her breath.

"What?" Her face snapped back to the moment, and I realized she hadn't meant for me to hear her. She ran her hands over my palms briefly before standing and smoothing out her dress.

"I guess we shall have to do this the old-fashioned way, then."

"Do what?"

"You know, you are the first of your kind," she said, ignoring my question. "A Human-Elf hybrid, that is. Born into one world, heir to another. It must be quite a burden already."

"I suppose," I wanted nothing more than to confess my sadness, loneliness, and fear. To her. To anyone, really. But something was holding me back.

"I, too, know what it is like to be two things at once."

"In what way do you mean?" I found it hard to believe that someone of her status could ever relate to the world I lived in.

"I was not always a Priestess, you know. Once, a very long time ago, I was a little girl."

I wondered at exactly how long ago that must have been. She appeared ageless, standing in front of me. And yet, she had counseled my grandfather, and, in a sense, raised my biological father through the position as his father's advisor. How old had he been, at the time of his death? Mother never did say.

"I was not much older than you when I was chosen by the Clave. Before that, I was just a normal elven girl."

"The Clave?"

"You'll learn about them in your studies. They are charged with identifying those with The Gift."

"Magic, you mean? Like a... witch?" I felt the word catch in my throat. I was testing her boundaries. For many that would be dangerous, but I was pretty sure that the heir to the throne might be able to get away with a thing or two that others could not.

Eoma's nostrils flared briefly, but she continued as if I hadn't spoken. I was right. She couldn't hurt me.

"*She doesn't have to like you either,*" The Darkness pointed out. "*She probably thinks you're a prat.*"

Does not! I shot back. *Why would she bother with me, then?*

"*Keep your enemies close,*" It mocked.

"Your Mother's kind calls it those things, yes." Eoma chose her words carefully.

"But not Mother!" I insisted, realizing my impudence would reflect poorly upon her. I had no desire to give Eoma more reason to dislike Mother.

The Priestess raised an eyebrow, feigning skepticism. I'd have been worried, had her eyes not given her away: I amused her.

"My grandmother had The Gift before me, though it does not necessarily run in bloodlines." She continued. "Indeed, I did not wish for it to be handed down to me."

"Who wouldn't want to see the future?" I thought of all the ways I could have avoided trouble if I possessed such a skill. Maybe I could have predicted the other children's moves. I'd have an advantage in their games. Maybe that would have made them like me.

The Priestess sighed, "Oh, to be young and naïve."

"*See?*" The Darkness chimed in. "*She thinks you are a fool.*"

"If someone near to you was doomed to death, would you want to know?"

I formed my thoughts carefully, bent on impressing her. "Well... If I knew it would give me the chance to say goodbye. To cherish whatever time we have left."

"Or it would tarnish those moments with an overwhelming darkness." she countered. "If you knew it to be unavoidable, at some vague point in the future." She fell silent, her eyes far away again. The words were meant more for herself than for me.

"What would you give up, for such a gift?" She asked.

I opened my mouth, but my voice faltered. I had only entertained the idea as a fantasy. A fantasy which held only benefits, not sacrifices.

"You see I, too, was taken from all that I knew. My family, my dearest friend. My duty to my people superseded my own needs, even as a child." She paused, facing me. Her expression was no longer one of superiority. It was one of sadness. The kind that goes so deep it can never be undone. She placed her hand on my shoulder.

"You see, child, I do understand."

A lump formed in my throat again. If she really understood, how could she force such a fate on someone else? Unless...

"Is that why you need me, then? Will I see the future?" Perhaps that was what made me so important to them.

Eoma looked taken aback. She had not been expecting such a question. "No, that is not the reason."

There can only be one living Priestess, the answer echoed in my mind. This time it was not the voice of The Darkness. Had the Priestess found her way into my mind? "There can only be one...?" I mumbled to myself.

"What? What did you say? Who told you that?"

"No one. I was just thinking." The change in her demeanor startled me. So, it hadn't been her in my mind. Then who?

"You, with the Gift?" The Darkness seemed to be laughing. *"What made you think you were so special?"*

"I... I should go." I stammered, turning to make my way back to my quarters. Eoma started after me, then thought better of it.

"Very well. I shall send someone for you when it is mealtime."

Chapter Thirteen

Kala

I T WAS DAYS BEFORE AZLANA WOULD SPEAK TO ME AGAIN. That first night that I had held her seemed a distant memory. The longer we stayed at this refuge, the more I felt her pulling away, isolating herself. I wondered how long it would be before it seemed less like a refuge and more like a prison.

Nykolas returned to be with my father, though we'd all bade him stay with us. Alas, he knew no other life than the life of a wanderer. Sidekick to a man who existed somewhere between outcast and hero. I felt it was an unfair burden on my half-brother, whose crime against the Mystics was only that he had been born. It did not seem fair that he should inherit the sins of our father. Then again, that seemed to be a recurring theme among all their peoples, that children would suffer the fate of their parent's reputation.

I thought how my own decisions might affect Azlana, in this new world she was destined to lead and cringed. I wondered how it was possible that my brother held less of a grudge toward our father than she did against me right now. Had he, at a younger age, also struggled against the authority of his parents? Or had he always accepted his fate?

Perhaps it was because my father had always accepted all parts of my brother. He had never insisted he repress what was half of his heritage.

There was no use in dwelling on my mistakes, I knew this; but it is the nature of all Mothers to do so, at least from time to time. Perhaps with the passing of time, we would find that I had made the right choice. That, somehow, my misguided over-protection had saved her life.

Tis no use, dwelling on the sins of our past.

The memory of Eoma's voice echoed in my mind. The memory tugged at something I'd buried. I did not try to push it away, but rather sat with it, letting it be. Sometimes that is the best approach when dealing with such pain. To simply acknowledge that it exists and letting that be okay. I did not know it at the time, but I was destined to sit with that sort of tragic nostalgia many times over the course of my life.

The Priestess, too, had taken her leave. With Cazlyn staying behind to tutor Azlana, someone of significant standing was needed to lead what was left of the Alliance.

She would be dropping in, from time to time, to check on the girl's progress, but for now, her presence was needed elsewhere. I begged her to take word to my husband, but she refused.

"None can know the whereabouts of the girl." She had argued. "In fact, it is best that none know she still lives."

"That wasn't the deal we made," I argued.

"Circumstances have changed."

"The King promised we'd not be separated."

"The King is dead," She spat back. "His foolish love for your people was his undoing."

"I pity you, High Priestess." My words elicited a physical response from Eoma. She froze in shock. Around us, the air crackled, the same way it does just before lightning strikes. I did not let her attempt at intimidation stop me. "I pity you, that you would ever consider love to be foolish."

"How well has it worked for you thus far, *child?* How many have you sacrificed, for the sake of love?"

Images flashed rapidly before my eyes. No, not just images... memories. The Priestess was in my mind again, manipulating it for her own benefit.

Me, as a child, sitting at the feet of my uncle as he read our bedtime story. A memory of my younger self, but I watched it unfold with a heaviness in my heart. The book he read had a happy ending. His own story, not so much.

The scene changes. I am in the treehouse with my cousin, Audri. She picks at the end of her braid nervously as we talk. I remember this day, and the story she is telling. It was the first time she'd mentioned her mother. The first time she had lied to me. As she is talking, time lapses. We are nearly grown. She ducks down, and I turn to peer out the window. It is the day I met Azlyn.

Azlyn. The scene changes again. Azlyn and I, walking in the forest. The sun shines down on us, reflecting off his wheaten hair. We are laughing. He leans in to kiss me and I feel something I haven't felt in a long time. The kind of regret you can only feel for your first love. The feeling took me by surprise.

Stop it! I willed my mind to look away. It felt wrong for me to relive those moments. Like I was somehow betraying Gareth.

The scene changes one last time. Gareth and I are in the kitchen. It is the day my father visited.

"Now then, that is not how you make a proper stew," he teases, drawing me close to him as I go about preparing the evening meal. The days that he is home for supper are few and far between. I cherish them. I lean into his embrace, taking it in.

"I wish you didn't have to go," I say aloud. He smiles sadly, brushing the hair from my face.

"Aye. You know I'd stay if I could." He kisses my forehead and then turns to tend to the vegetables. "Now this is how you make a stew!" he began adding ingredients without even measuring. His approach to cooking was the same as his approach to life—a beautiful chaos.

"Honestly my dear, it is as if you don't even carrot all," he held up a bunch of freshly washed carrots, from the garden. Despite his skills with both sword and arrow, I maintained the opinion that word play was his most powerful weapon. I shot my best exasperated look in his direction, but could not maintain the facade. I chuckled.

Here the scene deviated from my memory. Hoofbeats in the distance drew me to the window. The Elite, carrying torches, were marching through the town in blood-soaked uniforms. Their leader lifted his arm and his men roared their approval. In his hand was the head of the Elven King.

I choked on a scream, turning to Gareth for comfort, but he had disappeared. When I turned again to the window, I saw him atop his horse, jeering and clapping *with the rest of King Irving's men.*

No! I fought against the Priestess' influence on my mind. *No this isn't right. My husband is not a murderer.*

But how can you know, for certain? Her voice was not altogether taunting, nor was it friendly. It was the voice of someone with an agenda. Someone full of pain and anger, who was looking to soothe their hurt with vengeance.

My husband held secrets of his own, yes. But it was not out of any sort of ill-will. He wished to protect me. Whether it was the possibility of interrogation were he to be found out, or from the mental anguish of the acts he had to commit in order to maintain his cover I was not certain, but I would not let Eoma use my mind to incriminate him.

I lashed out with my mind and firmly as I could, forcing her from its recesses. The feeling was like ripping off a scab before it was healed. It left me reeling.

Or perhaps that was my anger.

"I expected more of you, Priestess. Your petty parlor tricks won't work on me. I will not be complacent to your witch hunt." I chose my words without malice, but with intent. Her actions had crossed the line. In her grief, she had come to behave the way my people had always feared someone of her power would.

My aim was true. My words landed hard, exactly as I had intended. She opened her mouth, as if to argue, then stopped herself. Her face fell.

"You are right. That is not the way that this is done." With that she turned from me and walked away, her footsteps echoing off the walls.

This would not be the end of the discussion, at least for me; but my efforts to convince Eoma were in vain. Though I vouched for Gareth many times, The Priestess forbade him from joining us.

It is amazing, the things that one can adapt to in order to survive. Despite my initial outrage, I began to grow weary of fighting as the time passed. It was not long before I found myself settling into our new home. The mountain had many secrets to discover. In addition to the bed chambers, we found other accommodations. A hot spring for bathing, fields for farming, and various halls for walking in quiet contemplation

A dining hall was made available as necessary, though I could not seem to locate it between meals. Every time I wandered the halls it seemed that they changed around me. I wondered if the other rooms behaved the same way. Could I find them, if the mountain did not sense a true need? I guessed not, and that guessing made me wonder at what else the mountain may be hiding.

On my insistence, we all met together for the evening meal. 'Twas one of the only parts of the day where I had a chance to see my daughter. Her studies had taken over, and most of her waking hours were spent with Cazlyn. When not engrossed in books of history, rune, and ancestry, she walled herself up in her quarters.

In the beginning, she would invite me to join her. There were several nights spent like the first, with me lying beside her as she slept. The mountain made strange noises as it shifted in the night. The sound was not unlike ones I had heard as a child. The creaks of an old house settling was a comfort I had come to miss. Living so close to the city, other noises drowned out the creaks and sighs of a building's rest. The sound was unfamiliar to Azlana.

"What is that?" She gasped.

"Tis just the mountain, settling."

"Mountain's don't settle," she'd argued. "They cave in. Mama, what if it buries us?"

"They'd not have brought us here if that were so," I reassured her, stroking her hair until she fell asleep.

It was an ancient magic that caused the mountain to shift, allowing it to change form to accommodate the needs of its inhabitants; which meant it would now change to accommodate us. In addition to the sleep chambers, it supplied us with a dining hall and various recreation areas-places for

swimming, resting, and play.

And then there was the study. This is where Azlana and Cazlyn spent most of their day. As a human, I was forbidden from entering. Nor was Azlana allowed to disclose what she saw or discussed during her studies.

I worried at the divide this caused between us. She was being led into a world where I could not follow her, not completely. While it was normal, as children grew, for them to begin letting go, I was finding the process nearly unbearable. She was still so young, in my eyes.

Yet she was changing so swiftly, right in front of me. Being among someone who could relate to her non-human half had given her renewed confidence. She no longer seemed bothered by loud noises or quick movements. Her cousin had taught her to rein in her elven instincts so that they could exist cohesively with the human part of her mind. For that, I could not have been more grateful.

I tried to make the best of the time we did have together, going out of my way to be near her whenever she was not with Cazlyn.

She had questions, at first. Questions about her natural father. About my parents. Things that were still painful to discuss. I tried my best not to keep anything from her, but she could sense my hesitation. It wasn't very long before she stopped coming to me for answers and went in search of her own. As time went on, she called me to her room less and less. One night as I passed her doorway I realized it had been nearly a fortnight since she had needed me beside her to fall asleep. The feeling was bittersweet.

Chapter Fourteen

Azlana

I T DID NOT TAKE ME LONG to become accustomed to my new routine. Eoma credited the human part of my mind. When faced with adversity, my mother's kind found ways to acclimate themselves; a skill necessary to their survival. To my survival. As much mental anguish as I'd suffered when torn from my home, it didn't seem that much time had passed before my new life became routine.

Much of my time was spent in the study. The room seemed to change depending on the day's lesson. The only permanent fixtures were the bookshelves carved into the cave walls. I could have read a book a day, every day of my life, and still only barely scratched the surface of the wisdom they contained.

"Eoma's library," Cazlyn answered my awestruck gasp on the first day. "'Tis the duty of the High Priestess to protect the records of all Mystic races in the Alliance."

The first lessons revolved around learning how to center myself. Teaching the human part of my brain to accept and translate the heightened senses I had inherited from the elven side. Cazlyn was sure that my struggles with my environment would improve over time.

He explained that it was almost as if I was two separate beings, speaking entirely different languages. What he called my "human mind" had to be taught to interpret the messages sent by my heightened senses. Over time I became more adept at filtering out the excess. I almost felt at peace in my own skin.

As I changed, so did The Darkness. Before, its voice had only been teasing. Much like the children back home. Tearing me down in small pieces, like it was a game. Now it began to meld with my identity. The voice became more and more my own, proud and defiant. Using anger as a bodyguard to protect my fear and sadness.

It wasn't long before my newfound arrogance began to get me in trouble. I grew tired of my cousin's monotonous lessons. So much time was wasted on the laws and customs of my people. A people that had no kingdom. What good were laws and customs without a homeland, anyway? I could not see how such things would help me achieve my destiny. How was I supposed to rule a people I did not understand? To lead an Alliance of creatures that I knew nothing about.

But whenever I inquired about other Mystic breeds, he would redirect me to the lesson at hand. It was as if what was happening outside the mountain's walls belonged to another world altogether. He would tell me nothing of the war raging between our people. Only of my duty to the crown.

When I was very little, I'd secretly dreamed that my father had been a king. Every little girl dreams of being a princess at some point. In my fantasy, he rode up on a silver horse and swept me away to freedom and adventure. The reality was stark in comparison. My royal status had turned out to feel more like a gilded cage.

Today's lesson was to be no different. Cazlyn began with an explanation of the laws concerning property. I wondered why he even bothered, given that his kingdom—our kingdom—had been reduced to near ruin in a previous battle. He sensed my disinterest in the subject, and to his credit, he was able to pinpoint the reason without explanation.

"It will not always be like this. We will not always be in hiding. Our people will rebuild." Whether he was trying to convince himself or me I was not certain. "And when we do, you will need to know this."

"Why?"

"Because our people will look to you to settle property disputes." He spoke as if that should have been obvious.

"Do we not have law-keepers to deal with those matters?" The contrast between my parents' cultures piqued my interests, if only for a moment.

"There are—were—record keepers and interpreters of law; however, in disputes where neither person is willing to settle, you will have the final word."

So, it wasn't as different as I had hoped, after all. I felt my interest start to wane.

"Tell me about vampires."

Cazlyn's hand froze over the text he had been referencing. This was not the first time I had attempted to guide him off-topic. And yet, I had still managed to catch him off-guard. This was the first time I'd asked him about a dark breed. Not just any dark breed, but one that I had a feeling he would have to address... though I couldn't pinpoint why.

"Lana, you know we cannot talk about the Others."

"But why?" I demanded. "Are they so terrible that you cannot even speak of them to me? How am I to lead our people if I do not understand the world outside of the mountain?"

"You know I cannot tell you. It must come naturally." I sighed. Genetic memory had been one of the first lessons he had taught me. While matters of law and custom could be taught, knowledge of the other Mystic breeds was the one thing they hoped would become clear on its own.

Why this was, no one would disclose to me, and as time went on, I felt the shadow of a responsibility I didn't understand looming over me. The pressure was almost unbearable.

"Just once can't really hurt, can it? I promise I won't tell the Priestess."

"Now is not the time to be rebellious," he held firm. "Not when so much is at stake."

"It seems the perfect time to act out of the expected norm," I countered. I would not let his fear-mongering sway my position this time. "Our people have fought this fight before, have they not? Each time with a similar result.

If we are to ever make progress, we must learn from the past and refrain from repeating the same mistakes simply because they make us comfortable."

"You have no idea what we are facing," he argued.

"He doesn't believe you," The Darkness whispered. *"None of them do. You won't ever be good enough in their mind. Half-breed. Intellectually you're as good to them as an infant."*

Shut up, shut up, shut up! I willed the voice to be silent.

"Since when has a **rebellion** sat patiently at the foot of its enemy?" I fought to hold my voice steady, hoping to mask my internal battle, "Inconvenience is exactly the point."

"But we aren't talking about inconvenience. We are talking about people's lives. Stepping out of line now will only divide us; cultivating a smoother path for our enemies to overtake us."

"And how is submitting to the lesser of two evils any better?" I countered. "It is when we have the most at stake that doing the right thing becomes a dire choice."

It no longer felt like I was speaking my own words. What place did I have to lecture him, several decades my senior, on his duty to our people?

"Who is to say that they know best?" The Darkness shot back. *"Are you not their leader? Why must they always push you around?"*

"Where did you hear that?" The eagerness in his voice surprised me. Excitement, and a hint of fear.

"Hear what?"

He stood from his seat and moved toward me.

"Having the most at stake is when doing the right thing becomes the most dire choice. Who told you that?"

"No one..." I said anxiously. "What does it matter?"

"He thinks you are daft," the Darkness fed on my insecurities. Its roots dug deeper into my subconscious. Of course, he didn't believe that I could come up with such wisdom on my own. I was no more than a silly girl in his eyes. I would not stand by and be insulted.

"You see that I am a child and half-mortal, and you underestimate me because of it. You think I have been sheltered from the dangers we will face." I held my chin up defiantly, locking eyes with him. "You think I am ignorant."

He opened his mouth to argue. I lifted a hand to silence him. "You are stubborn and set in old ways. You cannot even consider there may be another viable option... but I say to you that if fewer of us acted out of fear, and instead, took a bloody risk our numbers alone would be enough to elicit change. Tell me that I am wrong!" I dared him

"Tis not that I think you wrong 'Lana. Only naïve. Your hope and your valor would be such a prize if you had lived in a different time..." His voice faded and his eyes looked very far away. For a while, we were both silent.

"Would my father not have taken this same road?" I asked.

"Your father had a proper rearing," his words set a fire in my chest. How dare he question the validity of my upbringing, simply because it was different from his own! With all that I had learned, about my father's people, the war, and the efforts of the Alliance, there was absolutely no evidence that one's environment had any influence on the Awakening. It was more likely the result of my mixed genetics.

"*He will never see you as good enough, no matter what he says,*" The Darkness stirred. "*They seek to use your knowledge against the dark breeds. That is all they want. That is all you are good for. Half-breed. Half-blood. Half-as-good-as-he.*"

"And you think you've the right to deem me naïve?" I raised my voice to drown out the Darkness, "You think that because I am a half-breed, my memory will be incomplete. You are right that I have not unlocked all that would be available to me by this age if I had been born a full elf... but there is enough, tingling at the corners of my consciousness. Enough to know your heritage is also flawed!"

If he had been an animal, his hackles would have shot up, just a moment, before he gathered his composure. He leaned in closer and lowered his voice. "What do you know of it, then?"

I balked. I hadn't expected him to call my bluff. The truth was, I wasn't sure how much I knew. I'd heard things. Things said between him and Mother in hushed tones. Sometimes they acted as if she were alive. Other times, they spoke as if she was deceased. Always, there was a hint of bitterness in his voice. Like she had somehow betrayed him.

"Or been betrayed," The Darkness offered impishly. I was close to the answer, I felt it. It was just on the tip of my tongue.

"He's avoiding your question. Two can play that game. Say it."

"Tell me about vampires," It was not a request this time.

Cazlyn's eyes went wide. His voice caught in his throat. Somehow, the question struck a chord.

"That's enough for today, Lana," he said gruffly, standing to collect the books from the table. "You may return to your quarters."

I stood frozen in shock, waiting for him to return to the lesson. He turned his back to me, shelving the texts.

"You don't really matter to him at all, do you?" The Darkness struck another blow. Its aim was true. I stormed from the room, slamming the door behind me.

CHAPTER FIFTEEN

KALA

THE MOUNTAIN WAS HOME TO MANY WONDERS, but few could hold my attention for very long. I ached to return to the outside world. To escape this prison disguised as a sanctuary.

With little else for me to do but wait for my daughter to finish her studies, I found myself wandering the hallways, searching for something to occupy my time.

Though the mountain changed to accommodate its inhabitants, it seemed to have little interest in catering to my whims. It wasn't that I was neglected, by any stretch of the imagination. I was provided with dress, food, and a bathhouse; however, there wasn't much to be said for entertainment. Perhaps because the desire to be entertained was a human trait. Idleness was not a nuisance among the Mystic breeds.

I found myself wandering somewhat aimlessly, memorizing the walls of my new home, taking note of the small ways that it changed. The addition of a piece of art on the wall here or there. A faux window scene reflecting the varying weather. I wondered whether it changed to mirror the weather in the outside world. It had been weeks since I felt the rain on my face or a genuine breeze through my hair.

The little touches meant to give the atmosphere a more authentic feel may have been just fine for my companions, especially Eoma, who was able to come and go as she pleased. I, on the other hand, grew increasingly restless. And so, I took to walking the corridors, hoping that by keeping my body in motion I could fool my mind into believing it wasn't trapped.

On this day, I carried a book I had found in my chest of drawers on our first night here. It was a collection of legends I was familiar with. Stories my uncle had told me as a girl, of mystery and enchantment. They hadn't known about magic, back then. To them, it was all make-believe.

I thumbed through the pages. Stories of a princess who slept forever, a mermaid who lost her voice. Elves who made shoes. That one had been my favorite. I smiled to myself, wondering what the authors of such tales would think if they knew the truth.

I was so lost in thought that I didn't even see Azlana running down the hallway. A rush of air blew my skirt gently as she darted past without even acknowledging my presence. I took note of how quietly she moved. Whatever Cazlyn had been teaching her seemed to be working. I folded down a page corner, marking my place.

"Lana!" I called over my shoulder. She hesitated—the pause in her movement was brief. I doubted that anyone other than myself would have even noticed it. To anyone else it would seem as if she hadn't heard me, but the sound of her bare feet hitting the ground as she hesitated was a dead giveaway.

Something was wrong.

I found her in her quarters, curled around the pillow she'd brought from home. Some of the threading had come loose on one corner. She twirled it around her finger, the same way she had done to strands of hair when she was just a babe.

I tried to remember what it felt like, to be stuck in the place between youth and adulthood. I hadn't had to face nearly as many trials as she had by this age. Nor did I shoulder as much responsibility. My own youth felt like something just out of reach. A thing I knew to be true, but couldn't quite grasp. Still, I doubted that I had handled things as gracefully as she.

She made no indication that she knew I was there. I sat at the foot of the bed. "You were released from your studies early today." I received no response, save for a drawn-out sigh.

"Is something wrong, lovely?" I moved beside her, brushing the hair back gently from her face. Another sigh.

"I know 'tis hard, love. Leaving everything you've known. I can't even imagine what you must be feeling.

"Tis not that!" I was taken aback by the anger in her voice. "Not like I had any friends back home, anyhow."

"You had Luka."

She paused, untangling the pillow string from her finger and tossing it away from her before bolting upright.

"He underestimates me! You all do! Expect me to lead an entire people, and at the same time treat me like I am a child! Like I know nothing!"

Now I knew what was wrong. "You asked again, didn't you?"

She nodded, avoiding eye contact. "Why won't he tell me anything?"

I bit my lip. This was an argument Eoma and I had been over several times already. The Priestess was certain Azlana would eventually unlock the knowledge of her ancestors, despite the fact that she had passed the age of Awakening. While knowledge of her people's history and culture were well-established facts, there were some things that were half-knowns. Things that had never been revealed, or had been distorted over time to serve another agenda. Things concerning Mystic breeds, and the dark breeds, in particular, were to be off limits to her. The risk of bastardizing the truth was too great.

"It's complicated..." I felt helpless, unsure of what other comfort I could offer her.

"It's always complicated! UGH!" She flopped her body like a stranded fish, settling with her back to me.

"Which breed did you ask about, this time?" Perhaps I should have let the matter drop, but I was curious.

The mattress against her face muffled her response.

"Say again?"

"Vampires! I asked about vampires."

No wonder she had been sent from her studies early. Cazlyn wasn't one to lose his temper on a whim, and by now he was used to my daughter's persistent inquiries; but even he had his limits.

"You know he can't tell you..." I sighed. "and even if he could, I'm not certain that is a topic he would be open to."

"He questioned my upbringing." She grumbled.

So, there it was, the real issue. I couldn't fault her reaction, as I felt my own face grow hot with anger.

"He what?" I struggled to keep a steady tone.

"He said I've not had a proper upbringing." She turned to face me. She had tear streaks down her face. "He thinks I can't lead because of it, I know he does! He can sod off for all I care! But Mama I told him... I told him that his heritage is no better. I don't know why I said it, it just came out of my mouth and..." A sob choked off her speech and she curled up against me. "I just want to go home."

I wrapped my arm around her and kissed the top of her head. "Oh, my sweet lovely, so do I. So do I."

I rocked her, the way I had done when she was very young. We sat quietly together, not trying to solve anything, but wrapping ourselves in the solace of a joint pain. Sometimes there is nothing to do but sit with your sorrow. Accept it as it is before moving forward.

I couldn't fault my daughter her curiosity. She had always had a thirst for knowledge. A trait which came naturally to her. In my younger days, I had been much the same.

When I met her natural father, it seemed a whole new world had been revealed to me. I spent many an afternoon sitting at the foot of the forest learning anything and everything he was willing to teach me. His customs and history were fascinating, but my favorite had always been folklore. Of course, there were times when history and folklore bled together. This was the case when it came to the dark breeds.

"We weren't always at war with them," the memory of his voice echoed in my mind.

The Mystic breeds had been divided before he was born, but he spoke with the knowledge of those who had come before him.

"It was Anhedonia who fathered the dark breeds. Born of the darkness, he was the plaything of Nywa, goddess of the Spirit World. One day, Anhedonia tricked Nywa into opening his enclosure. Free from his prison, his wrath was unleashed upon the Earth. He corrupted many of the Mystic breeds, making them promises which he had no intention of keeping. With his brothers, he spread despair across the land, turning Mystics against one another and inciting chaos. The continent erupted into war.

It was not until a great Mage was able to capture Anhedonia that the fighting ceased. Anhedonia was hidden, never to be seen again. The dark breeds were exiled to the lands that Anhedonia had ravaged. A land that your people know as the Uncharted Territory."

I found it hard to believe that one sprite could have such an influence across such a large number of beings, but when pressed for more information it seemed that Azlyn had none to offer. At the time, I thought perhaps it was my heritage that prevented him from being entirely truthful. As I grew older, I began to understand that he had been trying to protect me. The same way I would protect our daughter.

Chapter Sixteen

Azlana

I STAYED IN MY ROOM AFTER MOTHER LEFT. I didn't want to chance having to face any of the others, especially my cousin. I refused to give him further reason to doubt my leadership abilities. To let him know I'd fallen apart so.

"*He doesn't trust you,*" The Darkness weaseled its way into the silence. "*None of them do. And, why should they? Look at you, hiding from them, but do they even care? None of them want you here.*"

"Sod off!" Lately, The Darkness had become more persistent. It wasn't enough to will it away anymore. It felt as if I had to physically fight it.

"*They all talk behind your back, you know.*"

I was too emotionally spent to argue. Rest, that is what I needed. Sleep would help. Or so I thought.

The mist swirled around me, an iridescent green bleeding into gray. When it cleared, I was standing outside what looked like a log cabin. It was dusk, but no light shone through the window. At the door, I saw the shadow of a man, hunched over a torch. The figure knocked. As the door opened, I felt drawn toward him. I blinked

and found myself at the window. I could see the figure more clearly now. He was tall, with honey colored hair. Before him, a woman stood with her back to us. Her hair was cropped short, shorter than the man's. The tops of her ears came to a point, protruding slightly from her straw-colored hair. Elves.

"Leora," The male reached out for her. She refused to face him.

"I haven't heard that name in a long time," her posture stiffened. "I am called Thana, now. Why are you here?"

The male flinched as if she had struck him. "I thought—"

"We have been through this before, I will not change you. If you seek to change elsewhere, I will not accept you. Your place is with our son."

"Cazlyn has forsaken me."

When she spun to face him, the light caught her eyes, but they reflected only darkness. Black, like spilled ink.

"What have you done?!" She hissed. The act made her teeth protrude from her mouth, overlapping her lips.

No, not teeth. Fangs. She was a vampire!

I was swept away from the scene, though I struggled to hold on to it. It wavered, like the surface of a still water disturbed, and for a second I could see something else. A cave. It felt important. I tried to bring it into focus, but something fought me.

Someone was screaming. No, something. A screech like the sound of a dying animal. Only it wasn't dying, it was angry.

I wasn't supposed to be here.

I covered my ears as the scene shattered before finally going dark.

When I sat up in the bed, my hands were still covering my ears. I lowered them slowly, afraid that the sound would return. Silence. My clothes clung to my sweat covered body. I wanted nothing more than to change them, but I was afraid to move. I pulled my knees up, resting my forehead on them and tried to catch my breath.

"Just a dream," I whispered to myself. "Just a dream. Not real."

"Or is it?" The Darkness answered. "Why else would he balk at your questions? Why does no one speak of her?"

"No," I said aloud. "It was just a dream. Something my mind created."

There was no argument, yet I felt uneasy. What if it was not the creation of my subconscious mind? What if there was, indeed, some truth to it? If Cazlyn's Mother really was one of the Changed, what did that say about his willingness to train me?

That he would work in line with the Alliance, knowing that they would use the weaknesses of the dark breeds against them. What did it say about him that he would betray his own Mother? If our places were switched, and the decision was mine to make, would I do the same?

"But the decision *is* yours," The Darkness cooed. "Ultimately the knowledge is yours to give or not. What would you choose, youngling?"

It was not like the voice to guide me to a path of morality. Then again, operating as another side of my own consciousness, it would make sense that it would want to protect those who shared its own darkness. I sighed. If only Nykolas were still here, I could confide in him. He had always been honest with me. If I only had the chance to ask, I knew he would give me a straight answer.

"He would, would he? Or is that just wishful thinking? Perhaps you overestimate his fondness for you, child. He too works within the Alliance, and they do not tolerate sympathizers of the enemy."

"I'm not a sympathizer!" I argued.

"Then what would you call it?" If The Darkness had a face, it would have smiled wickedly. "Perhaps you relate to them more than you care to admit."

"I do not!" I cradled my head in my hands. The voice was getting out of control.

"Going mad, my pet?"

The more I spiraled the more amused the voice became until I couldn't tell if I wanted to laugh or cry.

"How can you lead them like this? When you cannot even keep yourself sorted? What good is a clouded mind to them? You endanger them with your thoughts."

"Stop it."

"Or do you even want to help? Who are they, anyway, to decide the fate of the Others so callously?"

I couldn't take it any longer. I burst through the door to my room and down the hall, pumping my legs with as much force as I could muster. Running was the only thing that had ever silenced the voice. So, I ran.

The path before me grew longer as I ran. It was the mountain, shifting to accommodate me. This was not the first time. Each time I went out running it had created a new route for me so that I never knew where I would end up. It was a thrill really, and a comfort. The mountain always seemed to know what I needed.

The path turned one way, then another. Slowly the surrounding hall became less narrow the stone beneath my feet turned to grass. Increasingly it began to seem less like living quarters and more like an open field. But for the stagnant air, I almost would have believed that I was outside.

The path gave way to rolling hills. I was free to roam. I didn't let the incline of the first hill slow me down, but by the time I had crested the fourth I felt my legs start to give out. I bent over my knees, squeezing my eyes shut as I tried to ease the burning in my lungs. When I was sure the risk of collapsing was over, I stood up.

I had reached the last hill. Below me were only open fields as far as I could see. And horses... what had they called them? Deyanians. A whole herd of Deyanians. Most of them continued to graze, paying my intrusion no mind; but one seemed to have taken note of my position. I recognized her as the mare who had carried me here.

She tilted her head one way, and then the other before stomping her front hoof impatiently. Almost like she was waiting for me. I didn't care that it was impossible. I ran to her anyway, flinging my arms around her neck. Some measure of peace was found as I pressed my face against her mane and inhaled her earthy scent.

I couldn't say from experience, but I thought that maybe this is what it felt like to greet an old friend. For a moment, it felt as if I had someone to share my burden.

"I won't be part of it," I whispered. "I won't and they can't make me."

The beast leaned into me reassuringly. I stroked her muzzle and looked her in the eye. How much did she understand? I searched my mind for any hint of information on Deyanians, or even unicorns for that matter, but came up empty. It didn't matter. The less I knew, the less they would be able to use against me.

No...not me... them. The less they would be able to use against the Others.

The realization caught me off-guard. This wasn't just about me. There were whole races out there, somewhere, that would be affected. Why the dark breeds refused to join our fight may have been a mystery to me, but to force their hand? I was pretty sure that was wrong.

Especially if one of them was your kin.

I decided then and there that I would not be Eoma's pawn. Even if the knowledge came to me, I would not let her use it against the dark breeds. She would have to find another way to end this war.

The mare tilted her head curiously. Could she sense my thoughts? I had no way of knowing. I could only hope that, if she knew my true intent, she'd keep it to herself.

"I have to go now." I patted the side of her neck, trying to seem nonchalant. "Thank you."

She snorted in protest as I turned away, nudging my elbow. I rolled my shoulder, shrugging her off, but she persisted. We locked eyes. The rest of the herd acted as if we weren't even there.

Finally, I had to blink. I sighed.

"Alright!" I conceded. "Fine. You can come too."

CHAPTER SEVENTEEN

KALA

I CORNERED CAZLYN IN THE STUDY. He sat in an armchair in the far corner, lost in thought. How long he had been there, I was uncertain, but he was clearly not pleased with me interrupting his ponderings.

"Kala! You know you're not to set foot here." He did not get up from his seat.

"You will not tell me what I can and cannot do." I leaned over him, daring him to rise and challenge me. "How dare you speak to her the way that you did! How dare you question her raising!"

He raised his hands in a gesture of submission as he leaned back into his chair. "Peace, Kala. It wasn't how it sounds."

"Don't try to make it into something innocent, Cazlyn. You didn't have to see her. You take her from her home, lock her away in this room, day after day and for what? What purpose is it serving? She can't be what you want her to be. You can't force her to have something, to *become* something, just because you wish it were so."

"You cannot say she doesn't have it, Kala. You don't even know what to look for. You wouldn't see it."

"You don't see *her!*" I spat. "You see a tool. You don't care how she feels. You don't hold her when she cries. You don't see the burden she bears. The burden of an expectation she can never meet."

"But it is there, Kala. It *has* to be."

He rose from his seat, holding my gaze for a moment before he began pacing. His posture betrayed a mixture of desperation and euphoria.

"She asked me about her," His pacing quickened. At first, it had almost made me nostalgic. He reminded me so much of his uncle at times. Now it was making me dizzy. The air around us was electric. Full of power and danger at the same time. More than his mood was responsible, but I couldn't put my finger on what other element was at play. Not until I heard her voice bouncing off the cavern walls.

"The child has gone."

Her anger made the air crackle against my skin. I closed my eyes. Opened them. Drew in a breath. I could not let her see my weakness. Not now.

"What do you mean, she has gone?" Cazlyn rushed past me to greet the High Priestess.

"Exactly as I have said." She looked past him, locking eyes with me. "There are items missing from her quarters, and she is nowhere to be found. What have you done?!"

"What have *I* done?! I have done nothing but what I was instructed. All these years. I have given up everything—everyone—I have ever loved, and been at your beck and call, and for what? So that you can strip my child from me as well? So you can use her as your pawn?" I looked at Cazlyn accusingly "So you can treat her as if she is less than you, just because she is different."

Eoma's gaze fell upon Cazlyn. She raised an eyebrow.

"'twas not like that, your Highness."

"What was it like, then?" I spat. "What was it like when you told her she'd not had a proper upbringing?"

"Fool!" Eoma's eyes lit up like a flame. "That you would speak so insolently to your future queen! Do you know what is at stake? Your pride will be the end of us all!"

He cast his eyes to the ground, shrinking away as if a viper had bitten him; but no bite could have carried more venom than what she said next:

"The fruit cannot fall far from its tree."

I gasped. Angry though I was at the young prince, his actions did not warrant such admonishment. I remembered what he had said to me as we had traveled here, about his people placing the burden of his father's actions on his shoulders. Even Eoma was guilty of this, it seemed.

"That is enough," I whispered. The softness in my voice seemed to break whatever spell she was under. Her eyes dimmed, regaining their cat like appearance. Her shoulders sank and her face fell as she clutched a hand to her chest. She reached out apologetically, but the prince recoiled.

"I...I am sorry," she stuttered. "My anger caused me to speak falsely of you. Forgive me."

"It is not like you to let your anger loose your tongue so," Cazlyn agreed. "More so of late, I have noticed."

"I too, have sensed a shift in the burden I carry." They shared a look that made me feel that I was once again being kept in the dark.

"The girl has been under the weather for some time as well, has she not?" Eoma looked to me for confirmation.

"She has been through so much, in such a brief time. But she would never just run off. Not really. She's probably just blowing off steam."

The Priestess turned back to Cazlyn as if I hadn't spoken, "I believe she brought an Amasai with her into the mountain."

"But that is impossible. Surely the unicorns would have sensed it."

"Not if they were unable to get close enough," She looked at me and I remembered our first day here. When Azlana had reached out to one of the unicorns and it recoiled.

"But the other guardians... all the Amasai have been accounted for."

"Amasai? What's an Amasai?" I asked. If they weren't going to include me, I would have to include myself.

"The four burdens," Cazlyn said as if that explained everything.

"One of them has left the care of its guardian," Eoma insisted. "It is the only explanation. I've felt it, Cazlyn, reaching out to Imari, antagonizing his brother. At first, I thought it was my own failing. That I had let my grief weaken me, turning me back to a path of anger. But when I left the mountain the feelings ceased, and I was, again, myself." Now it was she who paced. "But which one, Cazlyn? Which one?"

Like a spell breaking, she rushed to me, having remembered my presence. She placed her hands on either side of my shoulders and looked me in the eye.

"Think carefully, Kala. Has anything changed? Before you came here, or perhaps on the journey. Was there any point at which she wandered off, or any strange artifact she carried with her? A key, perhaps? Or a piece of jewelry. It may even have been given to her by a playmate. Something they found in the city. Think!"

"We came with nearly nothing," I scanned my memory for any inkling of whatever it was she was looking for. "She keeps very few things, has very few friends. No one that would have..."

No. It couldn't be. I felt the blood run from my face. This whole time, it had been right under my nose. How could I have been so stupid?

"A necklace. Before we came, my father gave her a green necklace."

"Green!" Cazlyn exclaimed, "But that means—"

"It means," Eoma interrupted him. "That the girl carries Anhedonia."

She looked at me, this time with pity, "And we have found our traitor."

BOOK TWO

AMASAI

PROLOGUE

THE DRAGON'S TAIL TWITCHED IMPATIENTLY. The way it furled and unfurled reminded Cain of a cat just before it pounced. Gazing into the reflection of the beast's looking glass, he saw the girl challenge his son before storming down the hallway.

"Your plan has failed. You have doomed your kin for naught."

"It hasn't failed. She refuses to be their pawn. That is something. She will come, I know it."

Fiora snorted, "You'd bet your life on that, would you?"

"Don't tell me that you're still bitter about it."

"Stealing from a dragon is grounds for execution. You are lucky I was not hungry."

He knew better than to say any more. Though Fiora was considered tame compared to others of her kind, her patience had its limits. Taking the Amasai from her had been risky enough. Rubbing it in her face was like playing with the wrong end of a sword.

"Anhedonia will draw her to the Dark Lands," He assured her. "You know as well as anyone the way its whispers shape a wearer's will."

"Only those too weak to resist," smoke puffed out her nostrils in warning.

He ignored the subtle insult, "She is of the age to be easily swayed. She will come."

The image in the glass shimmered and changed. Azlana stood at the cave mouth with the Deyanian. She looked over her shoulder only once before stepping through the entryway into the night.

"And when she does, we will be waiting."

Part One

AZLANA

CHAPTER ONE

THREE DAYS. I had survived for three days in the forest on my own. Or at least, mostly on my own. The Deyanian provided heat and at times, transportation; but didn't contribute much in the way of shelter, food or conversation. So, I supposed, I could consider myself to be on my own.

In my haste to escape, I had not considered where I was running to—only what I was running away from. At first, I thought of going home, if I even had a home to go back to. That idea was quickly discarded as the memory of the Elite marching through the city filled my mind. There was nothing left there for me, save perhaps a swift death. No, it was better to leave such things in the past. Start anew, whatever that might mean. I tried to swallow the lump that rose in my throat at the thought of a life without Mother.

"What good was she, really?" The voice sneered at the tears that stung the corners of my eyes. *"You're better off. Safer. No one else can use you out here."*

But where was here, exactly?

The forest was far-reaching, dense, and ancient. Its canopy was marked by sequoia, larch, and yew, and had ample openings to let dancing beams of light through. Ferns reigned the stony grounds below. So different, this part of the world, from the forests that marked the edge of Ludlum's kingdom. What had once seemed dark and ominous to me was now teeming with life.

A mixture of sounds belonging mostly to prowling animals, echoed in the air, reminding me of how foolish it was to venture into the woods unprepared. Aside from food and water I had packed only a flint, the whittling knife I'd brought from home the night we had fled, and the pillow Luka had made me. I had made the mistake of letting my emotions rule over reason, and I was paying a hard price for it.

Not that I felt that leaving itself had been a mistake. At least, not during the daylight hours. Not if I kept moving. Night time was a different scene altogether. Curled up between the fire and the Deyanian when the sun had gone, and hunger pains became indistinguishable from homesickness, I had wondered more than once if I had made the wrong decision.

Perhaps I could have been more prepared, had I not left with such a hot head. *"Stupid girl,"* The Darkness argued, *"The only way to protect them is to stay away"*

Or was it my own voice? I had begun to find that it was getting harder to distinguish between the two as time went on. The Darkness' thoughts melded with my own to the point that I would not even bother to argue with it, most of the time.

The first night had been easy enough, with a full stomach and a fire; but by the third when my rations were sparse, and the weather turned I began to second-guess myself. Who was I to reject the decisions of my elders?

"Who are they to use you as their pawn? Their future Queen, indeed. You're nothing but a tool to them. A means to get what they most desire. Expendable. Disposable." The voice of the Darkness propelled me forward.

It was right. After all, if I was so important to them, why had they not come after me? I had hidden my tracks to the best of my ability, but surely the Priestess had other methods of tracking. So why had they not come for me?

"They think you are weak. That you will come crawling back."

Humph. I would show them! I'd learned enough to make it this far, hadn't I? I just needed to find a way to hunt, and some shelter, and all would be well again. I could do that. Father had taught me well.

Father. Where was he now? Mother and I had heard naught from him since before we fled to the safe hold. The only news we'd had was from grandfather, who had seen him after the Elite ambushed the Alliance. He was alive or at least he had been at the time. So why did he not meet us? Was it possible that it was he who tipped off Ludlum's soldiers? Could Gareth be the traitor Eoma had talked about?

The Deyanian leaned into me, nuzzling my arm reassuringly. She always seemed to sense what I was feeling. At times, I wondered if she could read my thoughts as well.

"*If that were the case she would know better than to befriend you. What Mystic would risk its life to become your travel companion if they knew what was inside your mind?*" The voice of the Darkness had become more persistent in the recent hours. The more I thought about turning back the more it crept in, reminding me of the danger I presented not only to myself, but to those around me.

And so, we pressed on. I spent much of the journey on foot, though there were times when the Deyanian insisted that I ride, not that she could say as much, exactly, but the more time that we spent together, the more it seemed like she was trying to communicate with me.

It made sense, of course. If she was descended from unicorns, who were self-aware, one would assume that she would share the same level of consciousness. Eoma had communicated with the unicorns, the first night that we had met. My cousin Cazlyn had whispered to the beasts as well. Could it be that my heritage would give me the same ability? I gazed into the animal's eyes, hoping for a straight answer, but received nothing more than the lingering feeling that I was on the right track.

On the fifth day we reached a river running down from the mountains. "This is a good spot for a rest," I said to the Deyanian, who snorted her approval, and began to graze on the foliage lining the riverbank. I envied her ability to sustain herself on what the forest provided. My stomach rumbled, reminding me that my own rations had run out the night before. I needed to find a way to hunt.

I knelt beside the river, careful not to submerge my water skin completely as it filled. Though late morning temperature was rising, the water was frigid as it ran over my fingers. I guessed the river's source must flow from the ice caps, high up in the mountains. Cold water was good—it had less chance of breeding disease. Warm, stagnant waters were dangerous. I did not know whether we would happen upon clean water like this again and wished that I had thought to bring more than one flask.

Sunlight danced over the running water, and for a second, I felt my mind wander to a place somewhere between sleep and waking. This place was familiar, somehow.

The sound of rushing water. The flash of light bouncing off blue scales. The murmur of a crowd surrounding me.

"Does she even understand, Priestess, what you have committed her to? You speak of acting with full knowledge, but she doesn't know yet, does she?"

It wasn't the voice of the Darkness this time, but a flash of something else. Like a memory, but less tangible. Like trying to find the right word for something that just barely escapes you but is on the tip of your tongue at the same time. I struggled to hold on to it, but it slipped away as quickly as it had come. The memory was not mine to hold on to. Not yet, anyway.

It hadn't taken me long, once I'd left the safe hold, to realize that some of what was occurring in my mind was inherited memory, a gift passed on to me from my natural father. At times, it was hard to tell what thoughts came from my ancestors, and which were my own. The voice of the Darkness often twisted them.

The voice had not come from my ancestors, of that I was almost certain, though I had not yet worked out its origin. Perhaps it was the result of my human side, fighting against the effects of my Mystic genes. Maybe the blending of memory from the two species at war put them at war with one another, even inside the confines of my mind.

Maybe it was putting me at war with myself.

I reckoned, either way, that it made me even more of a danger to all of them.

On the eighth day, I could stand it no longer. I had to find food. I'd resorted to riding more than walking at this point, and I didn't even feel guilty about it anymore. After all, the Deyanian wasn't the one who was starving.

We'd crossed the river, rather than following it up or downstream. The vision I'd had when I touched it had put me off that idea quickly. I was determined to avoid anything that felt even remotely familiar. I figured, if I ran toward the unknown, I had less of a chance of being found.

Unfortunately, it also meant less chance of survival. These woods were nothing like where I had hunted before, and the plant life was equally unfamiliar. Even if some of it had been edible, the chance of it being lethal was not one I was willing to take, yet.

Even so, I was so hungry that some of it had begun to look appealing. From the mushrooms that grew on the side of the nurse logs, to the purple berries that adorned the surrounding shrubbery. On one occasion a squirrel crossed our path, and I thought to myself I'd even eat that, had I any way of catching it.

And then, as if by magic, I saw it! In a clearing up ahead was a massive, lone tree. Its lower half was made of vines that extended outward, and then into the ground, almost as if they were extra roots. The high branches grew out and up toward the sun. Wispy strands of goat moss adorned its upper half. The resulting image was quite eerie. But, dangling from the top of its uppermost branches, there it was: food! A large basket of fruits and smoked meats hung, completely unattended.

I didn't even care that it was impossible. I dismounted and dashed into the clearing eagerly. The Deyanian whinnied behind me, obviously objecting to my lack of caution. Still she trotted along, following my lead.

I paused only long enough to plan the quickest way to the top before scrambling up the lowest branches. It was almost as if they had grown that way to encourage climbers. I had always been good at scaling trees, but even this was way too easy.

I was halfway up before the rumbling started. At first, I thought it was the earth shaking. I'd felt that once before, when I was very small. Mother had called to me to hide beneath the table with her, lest the pottery on the shelves fall onto our heads. But that was nothing like this. Rather than shaking from side to side, it felt as if the branches beneath me were twisting. I clung tightly to the tree's trunk, grasping the spaces in its rough bark with my bare toes, and looked down.

The lowest branches of the tree had pulled themselves out of the ground and flailed like the tentacles of a great sea-beast from fairytales that grandfather used to tell me, snapping like a whip at the Deyanian, who neighed and backed away.

The wood creaked and gave way as the branch beneath me shifted. A vine shot up from beneath it and wrapped itself around my ankle, lifting me up into the air.

I looked at where the basket had been. It was nowhere to be seen. In its place was a great cavernous hole, easily twice the size as the one where I'd found a family of squirrels living last fall. The hole expanded to reveal a set of petrified, jagged teeth.

The tree was sentient! More than that, it was hungry. And it looked like I was its next meal.

Chapter Two

I CLOSED MY EYES, bracing myself against an inevitable end, but it never came. Instead, I heard a sound that reminded me of the cry of a hawk. The tree creature froze, and slowly I was lowered to the ground.

It took me a moment to regain my bearings. The earth swam as I sat up, and I clenched my eyes shut, feeling as if I might vomit, had I anything in my stomach to empty. When my vision steadied I couldn't believe my eyes. A woman stood, clad in a skirt of moss which wrapped its way up and around her torso, covering only the essentials. Her white hair cascaded wildly down her shoulders. She approached the tree-beast with a finger raised, chittering in a language that I did not understand. Her green skin glowed with anger.

This was no ordinary woman. This was a nymph, and an angry one at that! In fact, it almost seemed as if she was chastising the tree-creature for almost eating me! I looked to the Deyanian for confirmation. She nodded and then tilted her head curiously. This was not normal behavior for a nymph.

Not just any nymph, I thought to myself. She glanced in my direction and for a moment as I gazed into her ruby eyes; she felt almost familiar.

"Sapphire?" What were the chances that I would run into her here?

Sapphire, mother to Nykolas, my mother's half-brother. She and grandfather had met sometime after the death of my grandmother. Mother hadn't wanted me to know the whole story, but I had worked out the important parts, with a little help from granddad. She wasn't like others of her kind. Naïve and a tad out of touch, Nymphs were more a danger to themselves than anyone else; but not Sapphire. Grandfather described her as sly, independent, genuinely affectionate when he'd known her.

Still, nymphs are not known for their maternal instincts. One day she showed up with Nykolas in tow and almost no explanation. Neither of them had seen her since. So, what was she doing here?

"*Perhaps she is a spy,*" The Darkness suggested. But that didn't make sense. Nymphs, even a smart one, would have very little interest in the politics of other species. Besides, if she had cared so little for her own offspring, why would she involve herself in my own fate?

The nymph finished her quarrel with the tree and, as if on cue, turned her attention to me.

"Just what do you think you were doing?" Her eyes narrowed as she approached me. "You could have ruined everything!"

"I'm sorry?" I sputtered.

"Mendarbore is on a strict diet. Quadrupeds only," She eyed the Deyanian. "That one would have been fine, but you?" She looked me up and down, her lip curling in disgust.

"I didn't mean to!" I shot back, "You think I wanted to be eaten by a... whatever that thing is?"

"Then you shouldn't have been climbing Mendarbore," She said as if the answer was obvious. "She is not a toy."

"She??" I looked at the massive conifer.

"Yes, she." The look on the nymph's face told me it was better not to press the issue.

"Well, I wasn't climbing her for fun, anyway. I was hungry."

"Mendarbore is not for eating," Sapphire wagged her finger at me, appalled. I wondered how it was, if she had no maternal instinct, that she was so good at such a maneuver.

"I wasn't going to eat her!" I threw my arms up in the air in frustration.

This was going nowhere. "Look, I—we've been traveling a long time. I saw a basket of meats hanging from a branch, and I went to fetch it. I really meant no harm."

A melodic sound caught my attention, like a crystal harp in the rain. I realized it was the nymph laughing.

"What is so funny?"

"Humans!" the laughter continued. "That is her hunting trick. She shows her prey what they most desire. That is what lures them close enough to eat.

"Why is that funny?"

"Mendarbore is still just a baby. Her trick should only work on feeble-minded things."

If eyes could shoot daggers, she'd have been felled right there. A sharp tongue would have to do instead, "You mean, like nymphs?"

The laughter stopped, and Sapphire blinked repeatedly. "Yes, I suppose, like nymphs."

"But she hasn't eaten you. Are you different?"

The nymph's head tilted one way, and then the next as she contemplated the question. "I... feel like I used to be. Perhaps that is why I was chosen to raise her."

"Raise her? But nymphs have no maternal instincts. They don't even raise their own young!"

"We are not...maternal. We are guardians. Were...guardians...I think," Her eye seemed far away. Nothing she was saying was making any sense. None of the lore that I had learned suggested that nymphs had ever been guardians of anything.

"No, you have guardians," I corrected her. Which reminded me, "Where is your satyr?"

"My satyr?" the nymph echoed absent-mindedly.

I looked around. There was no sign of either a satyr or her host tree. "You don't have a satyr? How is it that you're still alive?"

Nymphs had long ago been cursed by the Goddess Hannah. Their livelihoods were bound to their host tree and venturing too far from it would mean their death. And nymphs had a tendency to daydream and wander. Enter their satyrs. Originally intended to plague the nymphs with their affections, they soon became the creature's saving grace. Each day the nymph would wander, and each day the satyr would chase her back to her tree. Over the years it became like a game to the nymphs, seeing how far they could make it before being chased back. A game they didn't seem to understand meant life or death.

She tilted her head one way, and then the other, seemingly drifting in and out of her previous cognitive state.

"Someone else said that to me once...A long time ago."

"She's remembering something important," The Darkness warned. *She's not spoken to my grandfather in years,* I argued back. *She wouldn't even know how to find him.*

The wind picked up, dancing through the branches overhead. Could it be a warning? Or was it simply a dubiously timed shift in the weather?

The nymph looked up, squinting her eyes. "The trees whisper... something."

I decided to change the subject. "So, what exactly is Mendarbore?" Maybe if I could take her mind off whatever memory was tingling in the back of her mind, I could keep her focus off of who I was and why I was here.

"She is new." The nymph smiled. "So-few things are new nowadays. She is the first of her kind. Child of the Earth Goddess and a sea creature. A large one, with many arms."

"A Kraken," I whispered, wondering at how I had known the name. It wasn't a well-known creature, at least not among my mother's people. Her people had traveled across the seas where creatures such as this were nothing more than legends, but once they made their home here, there were few who ever returned to the shoreline. Surely even less than that would make it back to tell tales of such a creature.

The nymph tilted her head again, staring blankly at me. The name was not one she was familiar with.

"There you go drawing attention to yourself again. Foolish girl! Don't give her a reason to remember you." The Darkness warned.

"Ahem," I cleared my throat awkwardly. "Well, thank you for saving me from being eaten. We'll leave you to your guard work now." I motioned at the Deyanian to move out.

"You are going to the Darklands," I couldn't tell if it was an observation or a warning.

The wind rustled the leaves again.

"Be careful with that one," the nymph said wistfully. "You know from what line she branches."

I climbed atop the Deyanian's back hastily, turning only to be sure she hadn't followed behind us.

CHAPTER THREE

WE RODE ON ANOTHER DAY AND A HALF before I found any food. Completely by mistake, even. My fatigue got the best of me, and I tripped on an exposed root. I threw my hands out to catch myself, but failed, and fell onto the musty forest floor. I opened my eyes and found myself nose-to-gill with one of the largest milk caps I had ever seen.

I bolted upright, plucking the mushroom and its surrounding friends from the ground, not even bothering to protect my hands from staining. Milk caps were best fried with butter, but since I had neither butter nor a frying pan, I did the best I could with hot rocks stacked over hot embers.

It was hardly enough to satisfy me, but I found that riding the Deyanian provided some sense of relief from the ache of my stomach. Perhaps the constant contact exposed me to whatever residual magic her kind held.

It provided another advantage, one that I had not expected. As we traveled together I found that, not only did she seem to realize, intuitively, what I needed; but I began to reciprocate such intuition. It was almost as if we were able to speak to one another.

"Speak to a dumb animal? You must be going mad indeed." The Darkness scolded me. It seemed agitated by any chance that I might form a friendship.

It crept into the spaces between myself and those around me, creating a chasm I feared no one would be able to cross ever again.

And yet she defied it, this creature that had become my travel companion. Over time I began to realize that she was, indeed, trying to communicate with me. At first it was confusing, images flashed before me, created from my own memories. Sometimes things would get confused by differences between our two species. For example, the first few days she conjured the memory of me laying in the grass. I felt its soft blades beneath my hands, was overwhelmed by its aroma, almost as if I was actually back home near the pond. It took two days for me to realize that she was trying to ask if I was hungry. Of course, with little exposure to the human world she wouldn't know which images to conjure to express such things. The more time we spent together, the easier it was to understand what it was she was trying to tell me. I wasn't sure if that was because she was getting better at expressing herself, or if my mind was getting better at interpreting it. Either way, it seemed to work better when we were in physical contact, so I had taken to riding more often than walking, or to walking beside her with my hand placed on her neck.

"Do you miss home?" I asked her one day. I had worked out that, although she could not speak, she could understand spoken language just fine.

The image she projected back to me was not one I was ready for.

It was a memory from when I was very small. It was evening, and mother sat by the fire in her rocking chair, mending a quilt she held in her lap. Outside, I could hear the rain hitting the clay shingles of our home. Suddenly the clash of thunder shook the house. Across the house, I bolted out of bed, running for her. She dropped what she was doing to wrap me up in her arms, whispering reassurance as she kissed the top of my head and rocked me back to sleep.

The force of emotions evoked from the memory caught me off guard. I hadn't prepared myself for such a strong expression of the feeling of home. No, it was more than just home. The feeling was more specific than that.

My heart fell to my stomach as I realized what she was telling me. All this time I'd been leaning on her, trusting her presence to keep me safe and sane, but she was just a child herself.

"You miss your mother?" She nodded affirmation.

I was embarrassed to admit that the thought that she would have a family had not occurred to me. Back home, animals were beasts of burden, bred and sold to serve the needs of man. We raised them, cared for them, even named them sometimes, but I had never seen livestock kept in family groups.

That brought to mind another thing that I had overlooked.

"Do you have a name?"

This time the images overlapped with one another. Laying under the sky on a starry night, the campfire blazing beside me. In my mind, the flames lifted up into the night air, overlapping the stars until they became one.

"What is the end of one day, if not the beginning of another?" Again, the voice that manifested in my mind was familiar, yet foreign. Like a memory that belonged to someone else. And then it came to me. New star.

"Nova?" She snorted enthusiastically, pleased.

"Well, Nova," I said, happy to call her by name, "What have we gotten ourselves into?"

Scene after scene flashed through my mind, overlapping one another. Our first night on our own, wild animals calling in the background, the gaping mouth of the tree creature Mendarbore, my conversation with the nymph. Darkness. Cold. Loneliness.

"Trouble," the mind-pictures folded themselves into one word.

"Yes," I agreed, "Trouble, indeed."

We wandered aimlessly another day, or maybe it was two. They were all starting to bleed together. Sunrise, sunset. More hunger. And then one day the sun didn't rise. Or rather, we couldn't see it through the fog. Storm clouds rolled in above us, blotting out the light and making it even more impossible to measure time. Rain began to fall, lightly at first, then more fiercely until my clothes were soaked all the way through.

"We need to find shelter," I said to Nova. She blinked her eyes against the rain and nodded in agreement. The image of a fire-lit cavern filled my mind.

"Well why didn't you say so before this all started?" I demanded. "Your lot may be just fine in the rain, but I'm soaked-through and freezing!"

She only snorted in response.

"I am not being dramatic!"

The cavern was large and, much to my disappointment, did not come with a pre-lit fire. I had half-hoped that Nova had friends around here somewhere, and that those friends had a fire. The surrounding forest was too damp to burn properly now.

I reached into my bag, knowing what needed to be done, but dreading it just the same. The black button eyes of Luka's rabbit stared blankly back at me. I wondered about him now, for the first time in what felt like forever. I wondered if he ever thought about me. I would not blame him if he didn't. After all, I had done quite a good job of shutting him out, even before we'd been forced to flee. Ruddy awful friend I was.

"And a traitor to the crown to boot," The Darkness reminded me. As if I needed reminding. *"He probably counts himself lucky that he no longer had an association with you. He'd be a pariah at best, having a friend who committed treason. Beheaded at the worst."*

Perhaps in a way, my cruelty had saved him.

"Don't go trying to play the hero in this, little lass," The Darkness scolded. *"You'd no noble intention when you shut the boy out. And after all that he had done for you, too. Probably broke his little heart that one. He was sweet on you."*

The hell he was! I shot back. Moments like this reminded me, no matter how it may masquerade as my own, the voice of the Darkness did not belong to me.

"Then who do I belong to, poppet? What creation could I be if not your own?"

I did not answer this time, mostly because I did not know. Instead, I pulled out my knife, using the tip of the blade to loosen a stitch near the bottom of the stuffed rabbit. I reasoned to myself that I could always patch it up again at a later date. Still, I cringed as the blade tore out the stitching, like I was slicing through the threads of my own childhood.

I stuffed the cattail fluff between the wood that I had gathered. The fire sprung to life, warming my bones, but not my heavy heart.

A scraping sound tore me from my dreams. The last smoke of the cooling embers from the fire dissipated in the air. I sat up, careful not to wake Nova, who was snoring beside me. She'd taken to sleeping right up against me as the weather had turned. Whether it was for survival or emotional comfort I was not certain, nor was I complaining. It was nice to think that, even in the darkest of hours, at least I had one friend left in the world.

I looked about as my eyes adjusted to the lack of light, glad that I had inherited my father's ability to see in low-light. The cover of the cave walls made it a bit more challenging, but eventually my vision returned.

So did the noise. *Screee!* The sound made me flinch. I covered my ears, but it did little good to protect me from feeling as if lightning were rattling my bones.

Nova's ears flicked back and forth. She'd heard it as well. We held our breaths, waiting to see if it was just some sort of fluke.

Our hopes were met with the rumble of a low growl.

"Did you hear that?" my voice squeaked more than I would have liked.

The sound grew closer. Suddenly the storm did not look so threatening. I began to back away slowly. Nova followed my example.

"Not so fast, young one," The voice vibrated off the stone walls so forcefully that I could not tell whether it was that, or the thunder roaring outside that caused the walls to shake.

My eyes darted to the exit, trying to calculate how long it would take me to reach it. *Too long.*

"No use running," the voice laughed. A monstrous figure rose from the shadows, accompanied by the sound of chain-mail clanking.

No. Not chain mail. Scales.

"*Foolish girl,*" The Darkness chided angrily. "*Dead girl, more than likely. What have you done?*"

How could I have been such an idiot?

The beast approached us, letting loose a stream of flame into the air. Its light bounced off her armor, blinding me. I stumbled back, trying to regain my bearings.

We had stumbled into the lair of a dragon.

Chapter Four

"COME CLOSER, THEN. Let me see you in the light," The beast let loose another stream of flame, bringing my meager fire back to life.

Fear made my mind go blank, but my survival instinct kicked in. I knew better than to argue with something that could swallow me whole. I stepped closer until the warmth of the fire was hot on my face. Nova followed suite.

"What a funny little creature," the dragon's head poked out from the shadows and I gasped in spite of myself. She was beautiful.

"And this one." Her emerald eyes blinked rapidly as she appraised us both. "Tasty looking horse. Perhaps I shall eat her?"

"You will do nothing of the sort!" I shouted, waving a finger at her the way I had seen the children back home do when scolding the street dogs. A ridiculous reaction, given the circumstances. The dragon agreed, and her lips curled upward, revealing a set of sparkling, spear-like teeth. I swallowed hard, bracing myself against my inevitable end, but it did not come. Instead, I was met with a low chortle. The dragon was laughing!

"She's a spitfire! More guts than the likes of you, it seems." As the creature turned her head over her shoulder, I thought again of running, but my legs would not move. I felt my own pulse beating like drums in my ears as I wiped my sweaty palms. The dragon had called me brave, but I was frozen by fear.

"Youthful idiocy often masquerades as bravery," a voice answered. Its owner stepped out of the shadows, smirking. His wheat colored hair was pulled back, revealing his pointed ears. An elf!

His eyes danced impishly in the firelight's glow as he approached. Eyes that I had seen before, on someone else's face. So familiar...but I couldn't put my finger on why.

"I told you she would come," he said to the dragon.

"You are lucky she did," the dragon replied. "I've half a mind to fry you up, just for the trouble of it all."

"Now, now, Fiora. We both know you better than that. You've never had a taste for bipeds."

What is with these beasts and special diets? Apparently, a diet of strictly quadrupeds was more common than I'd thought.

"A promise she made to someone a long time ago," the elf said, as if he had read my mind. "The only way they'd let him keep her." His explanation was met with a hiss.

"Tread carefully," she warned him. "Your status will not protect you from death, only consumption."

Fiora turned her attentions my way once more. "You've got something that belongs to me." She leaned forward until the heat from her breath rushed over me. I braced myself against what I was sure would be an unpleasant smell and was surprised it was more like my wood stove back home that any beast's breath.

The thought made my heart drop, and for the first time in a long time I realized exactly how homesick I really was.

"Can you miss a thing that never truly was?" The Darkness countered.

Yes. I whispered in my mind. *Yes, it seems I can.*

"What does The Darkness say to you, child?"

"W-what?" I stuttered, snapped back to reality by Fiora's voice.

"It speaks to you now, does it not? The voice that is yours, but not yours." She tilted her head, leaning in even closer than before.

A jolt of pain rushed over my body as she approached, and a high screech pierced my being. I fell to my knees, my hands covering my ears in an attempt to block it out, but it was no use. The sound did not have an outside source. It was the Darkness' reaction to Fiora.

"Get back!" The voice of the elf was muted and far away. The noise had stopped, but it had taken with it some of my ability to hear. I looked up at my captors, their figures blurred and flickered before my eyes as if I was looking at their reflection on the surface of a pond.

No. Like I was looking from beneath the surface. I felt myself sink farther and farther away from them. They spoke amongst themselves, their voices nothing but wordless whispers in the distance.

The velvety touch of Nova's muzzle against my cheek was the last thing I felt before the world went dark.

When I opened my eyes, I was laying in the grass by the pond. White, puffy clouds danced across the sky. The same clouds that had given me the vision of the poisoned satyr. Had it all been a dream? I sat up, half-expecting to see Luka come bounding through the tall grass. Instead I was met with the shadow of a woman dancing in the distance. Her violet hair fell down to her ankles, surrounding her body as she spun out of the cover of the woods. I looked on, mesmerized by her dance as she bounded further and further from the trees.

Too far! My mind screamed. "Go Back!" but when I opened my mouth to warn the nymph, no sound came out. I stared on in horror as she fell to the ground. Without her satyr to chase her to safety, the nymph had wandered too far from her host tree. She had danced to her death.

The scene spiraled back into darkness before a flash of light blinded me. Warmth surrounded me, like nothing I had ever experienced. I felt myself lean into it as a voice whispered:

"Dark days are coming, my friend."

I awoke with a start, bolting upright. I regretted it immediately. Drums pounded in my head, and my vision swam. I held my head tightly between my palms, scrunching my eyes shut against the pain.

"She wakes." A voice greeted me.

I opened my eyes slowly. I gathered that I was still in Fiora's cave, but as I looked around, there was no sign of the cave's entrance. A dim blue light emanated from the cave's ceiling, not unlike it had done back at the safe hold.

The dragon laid against a pile of treasure in the farthest corner, her back facing the cave wall. Her massive tail curled around her body, making a clinking sound as her scales caressed the gold coins around her. There was no sign of the others.

"I was dreaming," I said groggily, hoping to stall as I gathered my bearings.

"No," she replied. "Not dreaming. Remembering."

"Remembering?" I mumbled, more to myself than anything.

"Yes, memories that span across the generations of your ancestors, and more."

The Awakening, I thought to myself. It had finally come. But —

"The memories, they aren't all yours."

I balked. Could she read my mind?

"You talk in your sleep." Fiora smirked at my concern. "*Dark times are ahead, my friend.* That memory is not yours."

"That is how it works, isn't it? Someone else's memories, in my head. I thought that was how it worked?"

"Not with those who came before you, no. At any rate that particular memory belongs to someone outside of your bloodline entirely."

"How do you know?"

"Because, child, that memory was mine."

CHAPTER FIVE

"**B**UT HOW IS THAT EVEN POSSIBLE?"

"Now that is the question, isn't it," Fiora's lips curled upward, revealing the tips of her spear-like teeth, and I was suddenly reminded who I was speaking to. I got the feeling that she was being mysterious on purpose. That perhaps this was somewhat of a game to her. Like a cat, playing with its food before it eats it. I gulped. I did not want to be her next meal.

"Where are my manners? You must be famished." If I hadn't known better, I'd think she had been reading my mind. When was the last time I'd eaten? My stomach rumbled, betraying me.

She opened her great claws, revealing a pile of meat from a beast I couldn't identify. My heart leapt into my throat.

"Never fear, young one. 'Tis no beast that you knew. Your travel companion is safe," Fiora seemed to read my thoughts. "Merely out feeding. The elf is with her to make sure she doesn't make any...hasty decisions."

"*To keep her from escaping. Stupid girl, you've doomed us all,*" The Darkness muttered.

Fiora speared the meat with one of her claws and let out a thin stream of flame, effectively roasting it before taking a bite.

"I didn't know that dragons cooked their food," I said. *Might as well make conversation.* I thought to myself. *After all, she can't eat me if she's talking.*

"*Ever heard of talking with your mouth full?*" The Darkness teased. I ignored it.

The dragon chortled. "Silly child. Who do you think taught the bipeds to heat their meat? Fools were falling left and right from disease before my kind showed up."

"But I thought the dragons were..." I caught myself before I could say it out loud.

"Go on then," Fiora raised an eyebrow, goading me on.

"It's just that... I didn't think they mingled with other species."

"Perhaps not anymore. At least, not most of them." Her emerald eyes were distant, and I could tell that her thoughts had drifted. She spoke of her own kind forlornly, as if they were separate from her. Could it be that she, too, was an outcast?

"So, it's true then, the story of the Dark breeds? Of how they came to be?"

She made a gurgling sound deep in her throat and her nostrils flared as she puffed smoke out her nose. The smoke formed a pair of rings which floated toward the cave's ceiling, first linking, and then merging completely before dissipating.

"I suppose," she crowed, "that it would depend on what story you have heard."

My destiny hung frozen in the silence. No matter how tame she seemed now, I understood the risks of offending a dragon. I decided the truth was my best shot at surviving...whatever this was.

"The story of Anhedonia."

"You tell me, half-breed." She reached out, offering me a piece of meat she'd impaled. I accepted cautiously and was rewarded with the return of the shrieking noise that had immobilized me before. I fought the urge to recoil as my hunger fought the pain that was piercing my skull. Hunger won, and I retreated to the nearest corner with my prize, tearing into it as I waited for the ringing in my ears to subside.

"Do you believe in the tale of the burden you bear?"

"What do you mean?"

"The jewel you wear is no ordinary trinket."

Without thinking I raised my hand to cover the necklace, protecting it from her. "It was a gift."

"It is his prison, and it belongs to me."

"She just wants it for herself," The Darkness warned. *"Never trust a dragon with treasure. Thieves and hoarders, all of them."*

"His voice speaks to you now, doesn't it?"

"I don't know what you're talking about." I lied.

"You've carried him long enough. If I recall correctly, over time the voice becomes very much like your own. All of them do if you aren't careful."

"Who?"

"The Amasai." The dragon tossed her meal up into her massive jaws, gulping it down in one bite. "The Four Burdens. Of course, you wouldn't have heard of them. Not with your upbringing."

"She's no different from the others." The Darkness scoffed. *"Thinking she's better than you."*

This time I didn't answer, but still Fiora seemed to know what was happening. Perhaps it was the sideways glare I gave her, or something about the way I smelled. Like rage. Or maybe she could read my mind. I didn't know enough about dragons to say for sure.

She simply nodded knowingly. "Yes. There it is."

"You don't know anything about me, or my upbringing!" I countered. The way she acted as if she understood me was infuriating though I couldn't put my hand on why.

"Mmm." It wasn't really a response. She scratched the side of her jaw with her front claws, lost in thought.

"You're mistaken," I insisted, clutching the jewel against my chest once more. "Grandfather gave me this necklace, and he would never do anything to hurt me."

The dragon raised a brow suspiciously, "Is that right?" her snake-like tongue darted over her razor teeth as she spoke, dragging her words out. "It would seem that it is you who know very little about your upbringing, child. Your grandfather may not have known the details of the gift he was giving, but he knew it was of Mystic origin."

"He said it was a family heirloom," I did my best to keep the doubt out of my voice. "It was no secret that he'd gotten it from the Mystics."

"So, he knew that much, did he? He's even more of a fool than I thought if he would accept such a gift from the traitor."

"Don't trust her," The Darkness warned. *"She'd eat you just as soon as look at you."*

"He will play with your head like that, if you let him," Fiora acted as if she, too could hear the voice of the Darkness. But that was impossible. I was pretty sure that dragons did not possess any kind of telepathy.

"What do you mean? What traitor?" I decided the best plan of action was to ignore her reference to the Darkness and focus instead on gathering as much information from her as I could.

"Interesting," Smoke rings puffed from Fiora's nose as she mulled over my response. "Do you not recognize your own uncle?"

Uncle? But that would mean..."

"Cazlyn's father!" I knew I recognized those eyes from somewhere. Apparently, my cousin had inherited them from his paternal side.

"Indeed."

Pain shot through my head once more, making my eyes water. My vision blurred, and I squinted them shut, trying to clear the tears from my eyes. Instead of being met with darkness, a series of visions invaded my mind rapidly.

A younger version of mother's face, her hands bound behind her back.

Flash

Cazlyn on a bedroll in the woods. He looks ill

Flash

A cave, not unlike this one, full of magical creatures. Eoma stands before them, but I can't hear her words, only someone else's:

"You would use her as your pawn?"

Flash

I stand over the body of a man, an arrow protruding from his chest. In the distance I hear footsteps. I turn, and my eyes meet those of the killer. Eyes I have seen before, on someone else's face.

"What is it that he shows you, child?" Fiora's voice was distant, hardly an echo in the chaos of scenes that swirled before my eyes.

In the distance I heard the sound of horses marching. Images of the night we fled home flashed before my eyes. Human men in uniforms. And blood. So much blood.

And then, out of nowhere, there was a bright light, and warmth. I was lying in a field, staring up at the stars.

"What is the end of one day, if not the beginning of another?" The voice was both comforting and foreign. I felt the warmth of someone's breath on the side of my face, and a familiar weight on my shoulder. Nova leaned into me, grounding me. Bringing me back to the present.

I drew in a deep breath, filling my lungs with the musty cave air. My hands found the cave floor. *You are here. Nowhere else.* I couldn't tell whether the thoughts came from Nova or myself, but at the moment, it didn't really matter. Slowly, my heartbeat stabilized, and I opened my eyes.

"Interesting." Fiora's eyes narrowed, and she extended her neck toward Nova, looking her over with scrutiny. "You are more than the steed you appear to be. Perhaps it is good that I did not eat you."

The two stood, eyes locked. Though they said nothing, I got the feeling that they were communicating in some way or other. The dragon nodded, "Yes. This will do."

She turned her attention back to me. "Now, youngling. It is time you knew what destiny awaits you."

CHAPTER SIX

"**M**ANY HAVE HEARD THE TALE OF ANHEDONIA," she began. "But few, today, know the true history of the Amasai."

"Amasai?" I had never heard the word before. Nova snorted softly. Neither had she.

"Amasai," Fiora repeated. "The Four Burdens. Sprite-like creatures that spread fear, anger, greed, and despair across the land. The original instigators of the First War. Their names are: Metuza, Imari, Avadari, and Anhedonia." With her claw she drew a circle in the stone before her. As she named the Amasai, she drew a notch in each side of the circle. It looked oddly familiar.

"King Irving's family crest." I whispered to myself. With a few modifications removed—embellishments really—the symbols were the same. On the crest, each dot was a different colored jewel. Red, yellow, green, and black. A line was drawn vertically, which flared at bottom, and another crossed it, curling inward at opposite ends, like a double-headed serpent.

The crest was something adopted not long after my people first settled here, though no one seemed to know why. Some of the elders said it paid homage to the religion of the Old World. Others claimed it was reminiscent of a hydra—the source of our greatest defense—being run through with a sword. A warning to the Mystics.

Maybe it was a bit of both. I looked again at the symbol Fiora had carved into the stone. Maybe it was something more. Fiora's cat-like eyes held mine solemnly and I wondered if she sensed my thoughts. If she did, she didn't say.

"Playthings of the Goddess Nywa who kept them safely locked away. Until, one day her curiosity got the best of her. Anhedonia called to her that he was so lonely. His lamentation echoed her own loneliness, preying on the Goddess' weakness. She released Anhedonia from his prison, and he in turn released the others. That was the beginning of the First War."

"We were there, in the beginning," The memory of words echoed in a dream floated to the surface of my mind. A dream Anhedonia had given me. No. Not a dream. Something remembered, from generations ago.

"They are more powerful together." I realized aloud.

"Yes. Fear may be conquered on its own, or anger, sorrow, even greed. But when combined, the four become too powerful for most to overcome."

"Then how did the war end?"

"The Professor," she said, as if I should know who that was. "Humans called him Mage, I believe. He found them, one by one, and imprisoned them. However; as I am sure you have experienced, he found that even while imprisoned they retained their power to influence those around them."

"Only the weak ones," The Darkness used the opportunity to pull my attention from Fiora's tale, *"Like you."*

Fiora paused as if waiting for something. How did she know when the Darkness spoke?

"Dragons read body language." I startled. I was certain I hadn't spoken the question aloud. "As do all the great hunters."

"You are just prey to her, then. Tread lightly, silly girl."

I swallowed hard, my eyes glancing from the dragon's claws to her massive jaw. She could crush me in one bite. The thought made me shiver.

"I am familiar enough, with the voice of Anhedonia. His patterns have not changed, even after all these years. When he speaks to you I see it in your face. In your posture. I can smell your doubts and fears."

There was no use denying it. "You speak as if you've heard the voice yourself."

"Anhedonia and I have spent many years together, for I have been his guardian."

My heart fell down to my feet, and I felt my face flush. I tried to steady myself, to will myself to smell less like fear. "You protect him?"

"Be still, child," Fiora commanded. "I protect the world from him. Or, at least, that was the task I was given."

"By the Professor?"

"Indeed. Each of the Amasai were assigned a guardian. Someone who knew them well enough already. That was, in my mind, both his wisest choice and greatest mistake."

"How can it be both?"

"Only those who are familiar with the Four Burdens can truly comprehend the dangers they represent. In that way, we were the only ones who would respect their power enough to keep it hidden."

"So how was it a mistake?"

"By choosing us the way he did, he was asking us each to face our greatest weakness, every day. And to fight it."

She didn't need to say anymore. In the short amount of time that I'd experienced the voice of the Darkness, I could already feel that it had changed me. Constantly fighting against its criticism, even when I was certain it only existed inside myself, brought on a weariness beyond anything I'd ever thought possible.

"If it truly belongs to you, I could just give it back."

"And then you wouldn't have to eat me," This time, the thought belonged to me.

"I'm afraid that won't do any good. Not now."

"W-why?" I cleared my throat in an attempt to distract from my stammering. Getting emotional wasn't going to help me now."

"Because Anhedonia has found something in you. Something new. And he has latched onto it, intertwining his consciousness with your own. He will not let go of it willingly."

"You said something...about my dream. That the memory was yours. Is that what you mean?"

"The Amasai collect memories from those who carry them. It gives them power. Sometimes, they will pull a memory just to taint it and use it against you." She paused, and for a moment I wondered if dragons could shed tears, for it looked like she was holding them back. "The words you called out in your sleep—"

"Dark days are coming, my friend." I repeated the words from my dream.

"That memory was one of mine, from long ago, before I had even hatched. Before I was tasked with guarding him." Her tone turned sour, "It is a memory he plucked from my mind and has used over and over throughout our years together."

Fiora unfurled her wings slightly and snarled, baring her teeth in my direction. "The Amasai do not share the memories of others. Not willingly. Somehow, you have been granted access to Anhedonia's mind."

"I don't mean to!" I squeaked. The dragon's lips uncurled, and her wings folded against her back, satisfied that I was not cooperating with Anhedonia. "I see things, sometimes," I admitted. It was a relief to say it out loud to someone; even if it was a dragon. "Horrible things. Thoughts that feel like my own but aren't. Not really."

"Such as?"

"Deaths, mostly, or murders, I'm not sure what to call them, but they are awful."

"Whose deaths? Do you remember? It is important, child." Fiora's eyes betrayed her. I'd caught her off guard with my confession.

"M-mystics, mostly," I stammered. "A nymph, a phoenix, a satyr...there are more," I struggled to recall without recounting, shaking my head to rid myself of the images swimming in my mind.

"The Awakening. He is trying to force it from you. Melding his awareness with your own. That is why they manifest in the way they do."

So, I was partially right. It was the Awakening. If Anhedonia was forcing his own memories on me, that meant it wasn't something wrong with me after all!

"She didn't say that, stupid." The Darkness countered, *"I'm simply giving*

you the power your human mind suppressed. Without me you would be nothing. A misfit among both your people." I tried to block out Anhedonia's lies, but it was hard to tell when to ignore the thoughts and when to give them credence. Either way, that one stung.

"Can you stop it?" It was a plea more than a question.

"Given your reaction when I approach, I fear for your life if I were to take it. As it is, you're at risk just by being here."

"Then why give it to me in the first place?!"

"I didn't. It was stolen from me. And, as you so vehemently insisted, your grandfather was the one who gave it to you."

"He would never have done so of his own accord," I insisted. "He wouldn't hurt me. He loves me!"

"The two are not mutually exclusive. It is often those we love that we hurt the most; whether we mean to or not." Her eyes softened, and I got the feeling that she spoke from experience.

"Whether your grandfather knew what it was he possessed, I cannot say. As for the thief who sold it to him, that I can answer not only the who, but the why. That is, if you care to know it."

"It has to do with what you said earlier, about my destiny, doesn't it?"

She nodded, flicking her tail in unison.

"Then I suppose you'll tell me whether I care to know or not," I replied curtly. I was growing tired of this back and forth, and my irritation only fed my suspicion that I was being toyed with.

"Like a game of cat and mouse," The Darkness—Anhedonia—whatever it was, affirmed my suspicions. The dragon was merely playing with her food. Perhaps I could run — The sound of one of Nova's hoof stomping against the stone floor brought me back to my senses. Without knowing, I had stood up as if to leave. The beast leaned into me, preventing me from making a choice that would have surely ended in my own demise.

"You have to fight it, or you will surely perish," Fiora warned. "I cannot take his burden from you and spare your life. Nor can I chance releasing you under his control. Anhedonia cannot be set free."

There it was then, the truth. The dragon was biding her time, deciding whether I could fulfill whatever purpose she had yet to reveal to me. If I failed her test, I would die. But if I passed, then what? What kind of quest would await me? What doom had I marched myself into? I said nothing, as I sat back down. The Deyanian laid beside me and rested her head in my lap. The voice of the Darkness was still. I ran my hands absentmindedly through her mane as I waited to hear my fate.

CHAPTER SEVEN

"**T**HE ELVEN PRINCE CAME TO ME, not long before you approached the age of Awakening, seeking Anhedonia." She began. "I cannot say that I was not tempted, at first." She stretched her wings and adjusted the way her weight was distributed on her pile of treasure. Gold coins clinked against her scales as she did so, and more than a handful rolled down the massive pile. I watched her eye them as they landed between us. Smoke rose from her nostrils and the tip of her spear-headed tail flicking back and forth, curling in on itself and then out again like a whip.

"Not all Mystics get along" a voice echoed in my mind. This time it was not painful, nor tainted with the voice of Anhedonia. It was a more like a passing thought, something I knew meant more, but that I couldn't hold on to. It fluttered away as quickly as it came.

I knew better than to reach for the gold.

"Tempted to seek my revenge. It wasn't that long ago, after all, that your ancestors held me captive. Used me to do their bidding. Shackled and beat me."

So that is where her scars came from. I looked her over solemnly. Around her neck, ankles, and tail the scales were dull and grey. Part of me ached for her, nearly as much as it feared her. At least my captors had been kind. At least in their mind, they were doing what was best for me. For all of us.

And how had I responded to their kindness? I had lashed out in anger and run away. It would probably serve me right if the dragon ate me.

"But even the promise of revenge was not enough to make me forget my oath," Fiora continued. "I was sworn to guard Anhedonia until the end of his days—or mine. Whichever comes first." She chuckled to herself. "Ah. But we both know who it will be. I am no 'spring chicken' as they say."

I wondered who exactly "they" were. I had certainly never heard the saying myself. Fiora seemed to have retreated into herself, and she was quiet a long while. Puffing smoke rings out her nostrils once more. I sat silently until I couldn't stand it any longer.

"To whom did you make such an oath? Was it the Professor? Why would a dragon swear allegiance to an elf?"

"That, is a story for another day." She said. It was a warning. "What matters is that the oath was made, and I had no intention of breaking it. But he is not easily dismissed; that one."

"You mean Cazlyn's father?"

Fiora nodded, "Cain. He is stubborn, and quick to anger. It has gotten him, and those he loved, into a lot of trouble."

"Why did he want Anhedonia?"

"Because he was sure that The Darkness would stop you."

"Stop me?" From what? My mind swam as it tried to piece things together. There were too many layers to sift through on my own.

"It is no secret, I think, that your father's people have their own plans for you." The way she said it made it sound much more sinister. I shuddered.

"T-they want me to rule, someday." I tried to keep my voice steady.

"They want more than that, child, and we both know it." She leaned in slowly, watching me. The shrill noise filled my ears slowly as if in warning. If she moved any closer, I was sure I would pass out again. Still, I did my best not to flinch, locking eyes with her instead. She held my gaze for what felt like an eternity.

"They want what's in your head," she nodded slightly before pulling away. I had passed the test. "Knowledge they have long forgotten. Secrets that were intentionally hidden from them."

"Hidden?"

"Surely you're familiar with what Ludlum took from the elves?"

I had heard the story. All children had. Just when my mother's people were ready to surrender, the journal of an old elven ruler containing information about the Mystic races had been found. It was the foundation of their education system.

"I have not been schooled in the way of my mother's people."

"Aye. It doesn't mean you don't carry it just the same."

Of course. If I had gone through the Awakening on schedule, they'd have had access to the journal through the passing of memory on my human side. That is, if I inherited those memories. It was a big if. No one could be sure how it would work in a hybrid. Something still didn't sit right.

"Why would they go to such trouble over me, when Mother could give them the same information?"

"Isn't it obvious?"

I shook my head.

"Because she can't. None of them can. None of them have the true story." She laughed, "Do you honestly think Ludlum would allow his people that sort of knowledge? That much power? No, he gave just enough of the truth to be convincing, and a lot of lies which have cost many lives."

"Then how would they expect me to help them at all?!"

"This is not the first time that they have meddled in the affairs of your family. The knowledge they seek was not from the stolen journal, but information gathered by your grandmother when she worked for the Alliance."

I gasped. I didn't know much about my grandmother. Only that she had died when Mother was very young. I suppose it wasn't too much of a stretch to think that she would be part of the Alliance herself. After all, grandfather was.

Grandfather!

"Why would grandfather give me this?" I demanded, holding the necklace away from my chest by its chain. I was done listening to stories. I wanted answers.

"Because he is a fool, of course!" Fiora's teeth clashed together as she spoke, setting off sparks. "The idiot Prince stole it from me and sold it to him. Heaven knows what he got in exchange. Something equally dangerous, I fear."

What Cazlyn's father got in exchange was of little concern to me right now.

"It doesn't make sense," I said. "Why would Cain care about what the Alliance was planning?"

"They intended to use you to expose the weaknesses of the Dark Breeds," she said as if that should make everything fall into place.

"So? That seems like something you'd be more concerned with."

Nova snorted at me in warning. I was treading dangerous ground.

"Yes, well. You know what they say about those who assume?" Fiora raised an eyebrow.

I swallowed hard, shaking my head.

"That they are feeble-minded."

My face grew hot. *Feeble-minded my behind!*

A rush of imagery filled my mind. Stars on a clear night, the smell of grass after the rain. *"Calm. Be still."* Nova was right. The last thing either of us needed was for me to lose my temper and get us both roasted.

"I was not raised with the rest of my flight." She let out a heavy sigh. "I was hand-raised, from a whelp, by the Professor. He had hopes that they would take me in, once I was strong enough, but..." she left the rest unsaid. "Naturally I have little care for those that I have never known."

More like those who cast her out, I thought better than to say so out loud.

"The elf, on the other hand. He has a stake in what happens to the Dark breeds because of her."

I blinked and found myself somewhere else. A dark room. A woman stood in its center. When she turned around...

"Thana," I said aloud, opening my eyes. I was back in the cave. Or rather, I had never left. It was an odd feeling, recalling something on my own. I wasn't quite sure how I had summoned the memory. Perhaps it was because it was one I had seen before. One that Anhedonia had shown me.

"So, you know of her, then?"

"Yes." I said. "And no. I've seen her, once. In a memory. One the Darkness showed me."

"Thana. Previously Leora, Wife of Cain."

"She is one of the Changed," I beat Fiora to the punch. She bowed her head in affirmation.

It was true, then. The vision I had was not just a dream, but a memory. Cazlyn's heritage was flawed, just as much as mine. I couldn't help but feel slightly vindicated. The thought made my face flush with shame.

"The Alliance plans to force the hand of the Dark Breeds. Make them fight against their will. Naturally the Prince has no desire to put his beloved through more trauma."

"But why won't they fight? If everyone's way of life is threatened, what does it matter that you're not exactly on the same side? The enemy of my enemy is my friend, and the like?"

"It is less about what is between the Alliance and the Dark breeds, and more about fear," The dragon said solemnly. "The Alliance fears the unknown—whether they could stand against Ludlum's men on their own. But the others, they fear what they already know. A thing that other Mystics cannot understand."

"What do you mean?"

"Remember that the Amasai are four. Four burdens, and four guardians. The one you bear—"

"Anhedonia. What of the others?" It was as if pieces to a puzzle were falling into place in my mind.

"Imari. Anger. Guarded by the Professor's best pupil. I believe you know her as High Priestess."

Eoma. Memories of the Priestess flashed through my mind. The way she flinched sometimes when we spoke. The flash of red in her eyes. If Anhedonia was able to affect me from within his prison, then it made sense that the Priestess would also feel the effects of the burden she carried.

Suddenly her brazenness made sense. I wondered if that was why she was so revered, so feared, among her people. Not only was she in possession of The Gift, and advisor to the King, but she held in her possession one of the most dangerous weapons known to her people.

"Avadari. Greed. The professors most foolish placement, if you ask me," Fiora continued. "That one, was placed into the care of the human king."

"King Ludlum?" I demanded. "Was he mad?! Who in their right mind would give him that sort of power?"

"Remember, your mother's people were not always at odds with Mystics. Your ancestors came bearing the mantle of peace, at least at first. The Professor underestimated Ludlum's weakness. It was not long before greed overtook him."

"So, the war was his fault then, the Professors?"

"In a way, you could say that. Many blamed him after the fact. He sought to make amends for his misdeed, but it only solidified the fate of all our people, in the end."

"How so?"

"The fourth burden. Fear. That one, the Professor placed in the care of his brother. Some might say that in doing so he sealed the fate of the Kingdoms."

I was no expert in dragon facial expressions, but I had been watching her long enough to detect the sorrow in her eyes. Whether it was for love of the Professor, or the burden of guarding the embodiment of sorrow itself I wasn't sure. Perhaps a mixture of both.

"You see the Professor's brother was the King. Your great-grandfather."

"The one who made the journal?" I asked, in awe. The Burdens were woven more deeply in history than I could have ever imagined.

"The very same. It is easy, in retrospect, to see how foolish it was. How it put the entire kingdom at risk. Some might even argue that, without Metuza's influence the journal would never have been." She waved a claw dismissively, "Not that such musings change anything."

"Ludlum's men got ahold of his journal," I finished the story for her. "The records he kept of all the races."

"Yes," her voice was deep. It seemed to have aged in the short amount of time we had been sitting together. "But that was not all. Hidden with the records was the fourth Amasai. Haven't you wondered why death has not claimed him? He has lived far beyond the norm for your people."

"They say he is favored by the Gods," I said.

"Preserved by their pets is more like it."

"Because of the King."

"He left his burden unguarded, though in truth he had little choice."

I knew better than to contradict her but couldn't help but wonder at the hypocrisy of it all. She must have sensed my doubt because she answered the question that I hadn't dared to ask.

"He was dying. He had no choice. Knowing his own kind were preparing his execution...there was no one left that he could trust."

"What about you?! Or Eoma? Any of the others could have taken it and then we wouldn't be in this mess!"

"How powerful it must feel, to see life through the eyes of youthful ignorance." It was not a compliment. "Surely you know by now the Amasai must remain separated. Even within their prisons, they feed off one another. No, there was no one else who could have taken it." The last part was spoken more to herself than to me.

"But if Eoma carries one..."

"Then they surely set each other off. Played off of your weaknesses. For her it would masquerade as anger. And for you." She waved a claw dismissively. "You can't say you didn't feel the effects. After all, you ran away, didn't you?"

I wanted to believe that I had fled of my own free will. That there was something inside me that had drawn a line between right and wrong and refused to cross it. But I couldn't. At least, not with any certainty.

Foolish girl. My eyes stung with tears. It may have been the memory of the Darkness's voice echoing in my mind, but this time the thought was my own. I ducked my head down to hide my shame and ran my fingers through Nova's mane.

Fiora's voice softened, "It is a lot to ask of any child, to bear such a burden." I got the feeling that I wasn't the only one she was referring to. How old had she been when the Professor decided her fate? I had more sense than to ask.

Nova whinnied. I patted her head, reassuring her, but it wasn't me she was addressing.

"Yes, you're right," Fiora answered. "That is more than enough for today. The Prince will be back before long with a new kill. I suggest you get some rest. Tomorrow we start your new training."

"Training for what?"

"My dear I thought you'd have guessed it by now," There was a glimmer in her eye that was almost mischievous. "Training to save the world."

CHAPTER EIGHT

O DDLY ENOUGH, I slept better that night than I had since leaving my home. Nova remained close, and the warmth of her body against mine brought comfort, chasing away the visions brought on by Anhedonia. Instead, as I slept, I dreamt of becoming a hero. I reckon that every lonely outcast child dreams of someday becoming something great. I was near enough to the age of outgrowing such fantasies that the idea terrified me, but not so near that I wasn't also intrigued.

I'd expected to be trained in combat, like a great warrior. I envisioned myself clad in leather armor, sword and shield in hand as I worked my way through an obstacle course in the woods, leaping through fire and dodging arrows. Nova ran at my side, warning me of upcoming dangers as her mane billowed in the wind behind her.

The reality was not nearly as glamorous.

I woke reluctantly, fighting off the heavy feeling that told me to roll over and go back to sleep. Harsh whispers from the back of the cave convinced me otherwise.

"—rescue the boy, or all will be lost."

"Playing with the Master's toys again? I thought only those with the gift could see the future in the stone. I don't recall it being a gift bestowed upon lizards."

"This is the way it will be Cain, or so help me—"

"Fine. Have it your way. But it will be nothing but trouble, and when the time comes, know that I will do what is necessary with or without your blessing."

Cain was back! I fought to keep my breath steady so as not to give myself away. I couldn't be certain what they were fighting over, but I suspected it had something to do with me, and I was sure that talk would cease if they knew I'd awoken.

"What would she think if she saw you now? If she saw what you have let your grief become?"

"I could say the same for you, and your old master," Cain shot back. His response was met by a soft growl from Fiora, and I sensed that things were about to become more serious than I was prepared for.

"Now or never," Nova's consciousness prodded mine forward. It seemed my act hadn't fooled everyone. I sat up, yawning loudly as I rolled the soreness of a night on a stone floor from my shoulders. The arguing ceased.

"She wakes," Fiora stated, just as she had done the day before. She would say it many more times before we would part ways.

The cave was well lit, with sunlight streaming in from around the corner behind me. The cave was not as deep as I had thought. Fiora sat perched atop a ledge on the cave wall, looming over Cain in a way that would make even the bravest of knights nervous.

Cain's fists were clenched at his side, and his jaw set tensely. He looked up at Fiora, and then at me before rolling his eyes and scoffing.

"Come with me," he demanded gruffly as he brushed by. He did not wait to see if I followed. I stood quickly, stumbling a bit before looking to Fiora for confirmation. I'd decided that, between the two of them, I most feared being on her bad side. When in doubt about a possible enemy, always choose the side of the one big enough to eat you.

She nodded her approval, and I turned to leave. Nova rose to follow me.

"Just the girl," Fiora instructed. Nova lowered her head apologetically. It made sense that they would want to keep us separate. They couldn't be sure yet of my intentions any more than I was of theirs and I couldn't make a run for it without the Deyanian. Still, I couldn't help but feel somewhat betrayed as I made my way out of the cave.

I'd figured out by now that something about Nova's presence helped keep the Darkness in check, and I was sure that Fiora had come to the same conclusion. If she had been a guardian as long as she claimed then I reasoned she must understand what it would be like to find some measure of relief, only to have it stripped from you, even if it was just for a short while.

"Stop feeling sorry for yourself and pay attention," Cain said. "The snake has her reasons for wanting things the way that they are."

Could he read my mind? I gulped. He looked down at me from the corner of his eyes and smirked. "All your years among the humans have ruined you. You've picked up their habits, absorbed their reactions. You're as good as dead out there on your own."

I had no idea what he meant. If I had absorbed their manners so well why had I always been an outcast? And besides, it wasn't like I hadn't had any exposure to my own kind.

"Cazlyn was teaching me, before I ran away." A pained expression crossed Cain's face when I said his son's name. It was gone as soon as it had come.

"Either you are a poor student, or my son is an inadequate tutor. The latter seems unlikely." He looked down his nose at me and sneered.

"That's not fair! It wasn't like we had very long, not really! And so much of that was wasted on culture and customs. You can't expect me to pick up everything in a matter of months!"

"Apparently not considering your maternal side. That pesky human blood, inhibiting your potential."

My face flushed with anger. "How dare you speak of her that way!"

"Even the traitor knows you're no-good, just like her." Anhedonia's voice in my mind was an unwelcome reminder of what was ahead. Painful, but oddly comforting in its familiarity.

Cain raised a hand to silence me. "My opinion on the way things are no longer matter. For better or worse, you hold the destiny of all on that chain around your neck, and if Fiora is about to convince you to do what I fear, then you have little chance of surviving unless you listen carefully."

We came to a stop at the edge of the clearing and he picked up a hatchet that was leaning against a tree stump. It was obvious the tool had been neglected and left out in the weather. The metal was dull and tarnished, the wooden handle was in danger of rotting. Cain didn't seem phased by its appearance as he placed a log the size of my torso atop the stump and handed me the ax. I flinched as the grimy wood settled into my palms.

"Split the wood." The glimmer in his eye danced and his lips curled upward. "Silently."

I tried to restrain myself from scoffing visibly. What he was asking was impossible, even for a Mystic! Even if I had been given a proper tool— something well-tended and recently sharpened, there was no way that a girl my size could cut through a piece of wood as large as what he'd placed before me. Let alone, silently. Still, it seemed as if I had no choice but to attempt this impossible task.

I approached the piece of wood. Sitting atop the stump it was nearly as tall as I was. I swung the ax around my shoulder and slammed it down with all my might, bracing myself against the impact. I closed my eyes as metal hit wood, half expecting the handle to shatter. Much to my surprise it held. I opened my eyes slowly, sighing inwardly as I saw that, as I'd expected, the dull blade had barely made a notch in the wood. Not only that, but it had been decidedly un-silent, announcing itself with a loud *THUNK*.

Cain said nothing, but raised an eyebrow and folded his arms, waiting to see what I would do next. I pushed the tip of my foot against the stump, giving myself enough leverage to pull the ax out of the log before trying again. And again. Each time I was met with the same *THUNK*. Each time I made a tiny notch in the log. Half the time I couldn't even hit the same spot more than once, so rather than making progress in splitting the wood, I succeeded only in creating a series of crisscrossed notches along the top.

"Not up to the task, silly girl?" Anhedonia taunted me as I worked. It still sounded a lot like my own voice, but now that I knew the truth it was

easier to distinguish what thoughts were my own, and what ones belonged to The Darkness. That didn't make them any easier to ignore though. *"Not elf enough. He wants to see you fall into oblivion. He wants you to fail, so he can have the power for himself."*

Finally, I'd had enough. Exhausted, sore, and drenched in sweat, I charged the log. A guttural noise emanated from the core of my being, and before I could stop myself I had kicked the log off its pedestal, screaming and hacking away at it all the while.

"Interesting," Cain said once I had stopped. "Not what I expected."

I could feel the weight of the ax in my palms long after he took it. My hands were shaking, my arms felt like wet noodles, and my back ached. I wasn't sure if my legs could carry me back to the cave on their own or if they would give out under my weight. Maybe that was the point—to exhaust me so that I couldn't run.

Cain lifted the log back onto the stump, placed the ax against the tree, and motioned back toward Fiora's cave.

"We will try again tomorrow."

He was silent the whole way back.

Fiora did not speak much when we returned but exchanged a look with Cain. He shook his head solemnly before leaving once again.

I had failed his test, or so I thought. Fiora neither confirmed nor denied my suspicions. We ate in silence. Even Nova had nothing to say to me the rest of the day.

Every morning Cain would return and give me the same task. Every afternoon he would return me with the same results. It became normal to me over time, even mundane. I was fed well, protected from the elements. Fiora even gave me access to roam the area on my own. She said it was to find a place to bathe because I was fumigating the cave, but I suspected it was because she knew I was bored. Still, she was no fool, and neither Nova nor myself were permitted to leave the cave without leaving the other behind.

I was certain that Nova could have made it on her own. That she knew where home was and could safely have traveled through the forest relatively unhindered. Yet she stayed.

"She is a prisoner because of you," Anhedonia would often remind me. Some days it weighed heavy around my neck, and on my heart. Other times it was easier to brush away.

And though Anhedonia was correct in saying that we were technically captive, it wasn't at all how one would imagine captivity to be.

I couldn't say that either of our captors had become friendly. Cain maintained his air of superiority and smug satisfaction at my failure. And Fiora? Well she was mulling something over. What it was, she would not say, Indeed, she had seemed to retreat into herself the further I got into my "training".

Finally, I could stand the silence no longer.

"What is the point of all of this?" I demanded one afternoon after Cain had left. It felt like I had been hacking away at that piece of wood forever. I was making almost no progress, though I had become more accurate, hitting the same notch up to four times in a row before missing.

The dragon looked up from her work. Stuck supervising us, she had taken to menial tasks like sorting her treasure and carving intricate designs into the cave walls. It seemed we weren't the only ones who had become prisoners.

At times she would retreat to the ledge at the back of the cave. It was there that she spent the most time. I wondered what could occupy so much of her time. Whatever it was, it was hidden from my view. All I could see was the end of her tail as it swung back and forth.

The ledge is where she sat now as I shouted at her from the cave floor.

"I go out every morning, knowing I will fail again. You must know by now that whatever test you are giving me, I will never pass!" My body and mind exhausted, I unleashed my rage with my voice, soaking up the echo of my words against the cave walls.

"You might as well just roast me now, serpent! Because I will not go back out there and attempt his impossible task one more day. I just won't!"

I sounded much like toddler throwing a fit, but I didn't care. My body ached, my soul was lonely. I was through feeling like a failure.

Fiora's tail disappeared from sight. I held my breath. Having expelled most of my frustration, I realized that I didn't actually wish to be roasted. I hoped the dragon had enough sense to know I was being dramatic, not literal.

Her head appeared over the edge, tilting curiously.

"Is that what you think this is?"

My voice failed me. I nodded silently. The dragon sighed.

"It is not so much a test for you," she explained. "As it is a test of Anhedonia's power over you."

"I don't understand."

"Anhedonia has embedded himself in your mind, so deeply that any attempt to take him from you may prove fatal."

She wasn't telling me anything I didn't already know. Even after all this time, Fiora had to keep her distance from me. Any attempt to get close resulted in the same piercing pain as the first day we'd met. We had tried a few more times but had the sense not to push it so far that I passed out again. For that I was grateful. It was not an experience I was eager to repeat.

"We—Cain, myself, the Professor—none of us have ever encountered such a phenomenon. We needed to know...if he is so rooted in your psyche, does he have full control over it? Over you? And so, we put him to the test."

I stared, slack jawed. My mind couldn't put together the pieces. How was wood cutting going to test The Darkness?

"Anhedonia convinced you to run from those who would protect you," she pointed out. "And so, we knew there was some influence on your behavior. Young minds, after all, are not difficult to sway."

I resisted the urge to argue. Setting aside the perceived insult. Which only made me want to point out that I had done so and therefore was not as prone to the nature of children my age. The irony escaped me, at the moment.

"We assigned you an impossible task and waited. How would you react? Even a dull blade can become a weapon."

"You didn't think that I'd—"

She didn't let me finish.

"Desperate people will do many things when they feel trapped. We had to be sure that Anhedonia would not sway you into violence."

I stood slack-jawed as her words sank in, "You mean this whole time you've held me here I've near killed myself trying to complete a task that you knew was impossible? And you just sat there atop your pile of treasure, fat and happy serpent that you are, and let him treat me like garbage? For no reason?"

Fiora's nostrils flared. My flippant words had me standing on dangerous ground. I knew it, even as I let them fly out of my mouth, and I wouldn't let fear take them back.

"*How dare she! Who does she think she is?*" Nova's muzzle against my shoulder melted my rage, until it was less of a rising flame and more of a dying ember: present, painful to the touch, but not an immediate danger.

Fiora rose from her seat and approached me, stopping just short of the distance that would cause me pain. She'd measured it, more than once since I arrived. She bowed her head until we were almost eye-level—or as close as we could come with our size difference, anyway.

"The time has come for you to leave us, half-breed," Her voice was soft and solemn, and her breath reminded me of the warm ash of the dying campfire. It was not a threat nor a punishment, but a statement of fact. One that she announced somewhat forlornly. And for the third time in my short life, everything was about to change.

CHAPTER NINE

THE FOREST ON THE OTHER SIDE OF FIORA'S CAVE was no different in terms of foliage than the terrain we had encountered before. And yet it felt denser, darker...more ominous. Perhaps it was a matter of perception, the knowledge that my movements carried the weight of my people's salvation, that made it seem that way. Or perhaps it was because we were skirting the borders of the Uncharted Territories. Either way, I had no desire to dawdle and instead urged Nova to pick up the pace.

Her hooves made soft crunching noises on the forest floor. My body swayed atop the ornate saddle Fiora had insisted we take to make the journey easier. Nova had not been a fan, puffing out her belly to keep me from tightening it appropriately until I threw my hands in the air and declared her no better than the common horse. It wasn't until Fiora pointed out that the saddle would provide a measure of safety for me that she finally conceded, and we were on our way.

Exactly where we were going was a mystery. Fiora had not given much guidance on the matter, only caution. As much as she eluded to the workings of fate, my departure was premature.

"There is so much more that I wanted to teach you before this moment," she'd said, as if we were old friends rather than a girl that had been captured by

a dragon.

"Alas, the young prince has forced my hand, and it is no longer safe for you here. His time with Anhedonia has not left him unchanged, and your life is in danger. He thinks that I cannot see what is in his heart. How he has let the Darkness feed his hatred."

"I don't understand," I'd said. It seemed as if she were speaking to someone else. As if she had forgotten about me entirely. Her eyes were sad and far away.

"There is a traitor in our midst," Fiora echoed the words I'd first heard on the night I left home. But how could that be?

"Of course, the blame will fall upon another," She swung her great neck around, locking eyes with me. "But there is naught you can do for him now."

"But where will I go?"

Fiora let out a forlorn sigh. "That is a decision that must be your own. Where will you go, little one? Will you become the leader the Alliance seeks to shape you into, or the savior of all the Mystic races?"

I wasn't sure how she expected me to be anyone's savior. But then again, I didn't see myself leading the elven people either.

Fiora's head shot up, her body hunched like a cat about to pounce. Someone was coming. "Our time together is at an end, child. You must take Anhedonia and flee, now. I will deal with the Wayward Prince."

The further into the Darklands we got, the more ominous things felt. It wasn't that the forest was naturally dark. In fact, I was surprised to find that my predeterminations about the scenery were so wrong. The moss hung off the tree branches like gnarled lace. More than once I had to reach up and brush it out of our path. Back home I had learned to navigate by where the moss grew, but in the Uncharted Territories it cloaked the trees all around, overtaking them.

Foliage covered most of the forest floor. Everything from ferns to fungi carpeted our path, and soon Nova's hoofbeats became muffled by its softness. But aside from the dankness, the forest felt rather benign. At times the sun would break through and it seemed beautiful, in its own way.

I hadn't thought about what we would do when we reached Thana. Fiora had said only that she would know what to do next. Though marching into the land of the Dark breeds seemed like a huge risk to me, Fiora was insistent that she was the only one who could protect me from Cain.

Why had she thought that Cain's wife could protect me from him? I had asked the same thing. Other than the fear of the Alliance using me to force the dark breed into submission, which she was sure would secure the fate of all Mystics by forcing Irving to unleash his Amasai and doom us all, she also feared for my life because of what she called the traitor in our midst.

I remembered Eoma using those same words to describe whoever had tipped off the elite, leading to the death of the elven king, but I hadn't given much thought to it since I had run away. I supposed, based on what I knew now, that everyone would blame grandfather. After all, he had given me the necklace which housed Anhedonia. But I believed in him. I didn't think that, just because he was guilty of smuggling goods, even if he did know who they came from, that it meant he would betray his friends.

Certainly, he wouldn't have given the information to the enemy on purpose

"Are you sure of that?" The Darkness questioned. *"Can you be sure of anything, really?"* I leaned in to Nova, pushing the voice away. I was getting better at ignoring Anhedonia's attempt to bait me. I knew what it was now: a liar. But it didn't mean that his words couldn't take a toll on me. The amount of mental and emotional labor that went into keeping the voice in check was exhausting. Add it to the anxieties of going on what may have been the most dangerous adventure of my life, and I was downright exhausted. Luckily Nova didn't seem to need me to guide her. She floated effortlessly through the woods, seemingly unhindered by the fact that we were treading on enemy territory.

"Wish I could do the same," I muttered under my breath. Nova triggered a memory of me running through the streets of Aythia. I could almost hear the sound of my bare feet beating against the dirt.

Then another one. I was guiding one of Luka's horses through the crowded streets of the market. It whinnied, bucked, and nearly threw its cart. I whispered softly to her, caressing her muzzle, and she settled, her ears still turned back slightly as we continued through the throngs of people.

"*Born into different worlds,*" Though her messages still came in visual form, my mind had begun to translate them more quickly the longer we were together. Now it was almost as if she said them aloud.

She was right, again. Though my ability to navigate the city market was hardly comparable to what we were doing now, and truth be told I'd felt just like the horse had. Frightened, trapped. I'd only kept my cool because she needed me to lead her.

Oh.

I patted Nova's neck softly. "Thanks, pal."

She whinnied and pressed on, picking up speed. I couldn't tell how much ground we had covered since the morning, but by the way the trees began to blur around us I knew that it had to be quite the distance. Beads of sweat began to gather on Nova's back, and her nostrils flared with the effort of drawing air into her lungs as she bore me deeper into the forest.

Confident as she was, and as benign as the woods seemed compared to my imagination, neither of us was eager to spend the night here.

Still, I was worried she'd ride herself to death. I'd seen it happen to one of the king's horses once. It had been a messenger coming with news of a resistance, who had ridden the beast all night without stopping. The poor thing barely made it past Luka's house before collapsing in the street, dead.

His rider, consumed with his mission, had simply dismounted as the horse fell, leaving his steed behind in favor of completing his task.

I remembered being appalled that someone could do that to another living thing. To treat its life with such little respect. To force it to sacrifice itself for something its rider considered the greater good. The thought made my stomach churn. I'd run home, tears streaking down my face and barely made it to the front yard before retching in the bushes.

The memory was so powerful that I found myself tugging at Nova's mane, urging her to slow down so I could dismount. She slowed her pace, but refused to stop, sensing what I was thinking.

"*Too dangerous,*" her thoughts filled my mind "*Must keep going.*"

She was right, of course, even at my fastest speed I couldn't match her pace. Trailing behind her on my own legs would only slow her down, putting us both at risk.

I was jolted from my thoughts by a blur of motion up ahead. I tapped the side of Nova's neck, pointing to where I had seen it. She paused, her body tensed in high alert. Nothing. And then, just as she was ready to move on, I saw it again. A large bobcat darted between the trees. I followed its movements with my eyes. It was stalking a large white hart.

The two seemed to be aware of each other, bounding from one tree to the other, almost as if playing a game. It was natural, and out of place at the same time. Then, just as the bobcat caught up to the deer, it leapt behind a bush and disappeared, replaced by a small girl in a tattered white tunic. Her skin was pale, and her stark white hair glittered in the rays of sunlight that broke through the overhead foliage. Her bare feet barely touched the forest floor as she darted away from the big cat. Her laughter sounded more like music than a human voice. The bobcat picked up speed before leaping into the air. A gasp caught in my throat as the air around it shimmered. The bobcat shifted, and the body of a boy wrapped his arms around the girl's shoulders, both of them laughing as they tumbled to the ground.

"*Fairy folk!*" a voice in my head said. "*Shapeshifters, imposters, and instigators of trouble and chaos.*"

The children rose from the ground, their laughter caught in their throats as the realized they were being watched.

For a moment we locked eyes, uncertain of what to do next.

"Wait up, you guys!" A familiar voice called from the depths of the forest.

No. It couldn't be.

"Luka?" He had grown taller since we last saw one another, and his shaggy hair had been whitened by the sun. His tunic matched those of his companions. His mouth hung agape, matching mine, for what felt like an eternity.

The other two chittered to one another before taking off into the wilderness. The girl paused only a moment to let out what sounded like a bird call. The sound caught Luka's attention, and he seemed torn.

"Luka!" I called, "It's me, Lana!" I wasn't sure how he had gotten so far from home. Had he been looking for me all this time?

He bit his bottom lip, his eyes shifting between his companions and myself. *C'mon Luka!* I crept closer, holding out my hand as if he were a frightened animal.

Wrong move. He flinched, locking eyes with mine. They were different from the eyes I had grown up with. Wild in a way that I had never seen. I was frozen, as if in a trance. All I could do was watch as he and his companions disappeared into the forest.

Part Two

LUKA

CHAPTER TEN

"**S**TOP IT, LUKA! GET OFF!**" Philip struggled to push me off him, but it was no use. I had a good hold on his collar, and my legs wrapped tight around his torso, pinning him down good. It reminded me of the Fall Festival, how we used to wrestle pigs. 'Cept no pig ever squealed as much as Philip was now. He flailed and carried on as if I'd already hit him, the big baby. He choked on the dust he was kicking up, and milked it for everything it was worth, hacking extra pitiful-like so I'd go easy on him.

I pulled my right hand back and clenched it into a fist.

"Take it back," I said through my teeth.

"NO!"

That was his first mistake. By now the other children had circled 'round us, gawking. It wasn't often that they got to see a good fight. Not anymore, anyway.

"Leave him alone, Luka!" A familiar voice shouted from the crowd. *Not her again. Why can't she just stay out of it?*

"Shut up, Gertrude!" I shot back. "This is none of yer business!"

Philip took advantage of the distraction, swinging his body out from under mine. It happened so quick that I hardly had time to brace myself against the fall. Before I could get up, Philip grabbed my shoulder with one hand and swung with the other, hard. The punch landed square on my jaw, making my eyes water and my mouth taste like copper as blood pooled in my mouth. He wasn't gonna get the best of me. I smiled impishly before spitting in his face. Not the reaction he was hoping for.

"Ugh, gross," He jumped back, wiping his face with the sleeve of his gray tunic. It bloomed red as my blood seeped into the fabric. His Ma would have a fit over the stain. Another win for me.

That feeling only lasted for a second.

"You're just as much of a freak as she was!"

That was his second mistake.

I dove hard for his knees, locking my arms around them and taking him to the ground. He kicked at me a few times, barely missing my head, before I saw my opening. I dodged and sank my teeth into his calf.

"Aieeee!" he yelped, stumbling back and reaching for the wound. I let go, satisfied that I had made my point, and spat another mouthful of blood into the dust for good measure.

"That'll teach ya to run yer stupid mouth!"

The other kids stood, wide-eyed and slack mouthed. No one said a word. Not even dumb Gertrude.

"And let that be an example t'all of ya!" I kicked up a pile of dust.

"Philips just saying what we all know," leave it to Gertrude to ignore my warning. She could never resist a chance to stick her big nose where it didn't belong. "She was a freak. She's probably a dead freak, now."

My whole body went stiff. It took everything in me not to throttle her too.

"Don't think yer safe just 'cause yer a girl, Gertrude. The only reason yer not getting a lashing right now is 'cause I don't want to upset Lily." Her baby sister shied away, clinging to Gertrude's skirt. She'd always been the quiet sort, but today the look on her face was different than any I had seen before. She was scared. *Scared of me.* I sighed. "Get on then, ya'll aren't worth it anyway. Bunch of idiots." I glared at Philip one last time, delighting in the way he flinched, before bolting off into the city.

Pa was busy with a customer when I stormed into the shop. I kept my head down so as to hide the fist-shaped bruise I felt forming on my face, but there was no fooling my old man. I felt his eyes hot on my back as I made my way past the storefront, through the main living quarters and up the stairs to my room.

Normally the tiny space felt more like a prison to me than a home, but today it was my sanctuary. Away from the jeers and whispers of the other kids. Away from the whispers and rumors. The only one I had to answer to here was me. *And Pa*, I reminded myself. My stomach flopped. I shut the door behind me, knowing it was only a matter of time before he followed.

I flopped down on my cot, pausing to grab something from the table beside my bed before laying down on my back. An old toy mother had made me when I was still small. She called it a ball, but really it was little more than a leather sack stuffed with rice and sewn together with twill. I tossed it in the air angrily with one hand, catching it just before it hit my face. A game I had played since I was small, when my anger got too much to handle.

"Sometimes people, even very little ones like you, have very big feelings," she'd said brushing the hair back from my face to examine a black eye that I'd earned in a brawl with the boy down the street. It wasn't my first. By the time I turned five I was known as the town hellion. People would click their tongues when I ran by, pityin' Ma for the burden of tryin' to raise me right.

It didn't seem to bother her none, but it drove Pa mad. Every time I crossed the line he'd gain a new gray hair. He wanted to whoop me good, but Ma wouldn't have it.

"He's gonna have to learn, Alison!" he'd said.

"You don't learn self-control by being scared into it," she'd insisted.

Later, she'd come to my room carrying a bag of rice she'd stitched together. We practiced tossing it against the wall, into a bucket, and then just tossing and catching it over and over. It was soothing, doing the same thing over and over, and before long I felt my anger give way to exhaustion.

I never got into another fist fight again.

Not until today, anyway.

I sighed, wonderin' what Ma would think if she could see me now. "'Prally best that she can't" I muttered to myself. The ball landed hard in my palm and a piece of rice fell from it. I examined the stitching, which had begun to fray over the years. It was strained and coming loose in sections. A reminder of how long Ma had been gone.

"Come here, boy," Pa's voice rumbled over my thoughts, drowning them out. I sighed. *No use prolongin' the inevitable.* I slid off my bed reluctantly, letting my feet hang a moment before making a dramatic 'thunk' against the wood floor. The weight of anticipation made it feel as if I'd gained a stone, and I had to force my legs to propel me forward as I shuffled off to meet my fate.

Pa was waitin' for me at the storefront entrance with his arms crossed. His stern expression was no surprise. The door was shut and latched, and the 'closed' sign hung in the front window. I gulped. He'd never closed shop early, not once in my whole life.

We stood in silence as he looked me over. I tried my best not to squirm under his gaze, but I couldn't help but wipe my sweaty palms against the side of my tunic. He frowned.

Then, surprisingly, his face softened. "They were talking about her again, weren't they?" He took a step forward and lifting my chin with his hand, assessing the damage.

"I tried to avoid trouble Pa, I really did!" I plead. "I warned 'em plenty!"

"You can't change their minds with your fists, Luka. You know that." His voice was more sad than angry. Maybe I wouldn't get a lashing after all. "How does the other guy look? Am I gonna have trouble with his parents?"

I shook my head, "Nah. He's roughed up some, but I got the worst of it for sure."

"I see." I felt his disappointment sink into me.

"Pa," my voice was hoarse, nearly a whisper. "They called her a freak."

"Son, we've been over this."

"She isn't a freak dad. I mean, yeah, she's different. Hard to understand sometimes. Most times. But—"

"But she's your friend, and you're worried about her."

The lump in my throat choked off my speech, and I could only nod. It had been months since 'Lana and her Ma had gone missing. Or run off. I wasn't sure which it had been.

'Lana had been distant leading up to it. At first it was just with the other kids, and I couldn't blame her none for that either, the way they treated her. Eventually she started turning me away too. I wondered if I had done something wrong. If maybe she felt I hadn't done a good enough job standing up for her when the other kids got riled up.

Her Ma had tried to make me feel better. Said it wasn't my fault that she'd gone into hiding; but I couldn't see whose fault it could have been if not mine. Maybe if I hadn't been trying so hard to lay low with the other kids, she wouldn't have given up on me too. Why had it been so important for me to fit in with them anyway? Looking back, it seemed like a fool's game.

But the thing about games, and pride? I always wanted to win. After a while I stopped coming around altogether.

Until the night the Elite came home. It was late when the horns rung out announcing their arrival, and I'd had to shimmy out of the covers right-quick to make it to the front of the shop in time for them to pass. As the men rode into the city, the torchlight cast an eerie glow on the uniforms. Uniforms that were stained with blood. My eyes scanned their ranks as they rode past, an act every citizen had become accustomed to doing. The whole town was still with anticipation as loved ones held their breaths, hoping to see a familiar face within the crowd. I remember I held my breath, too. 'Lana's father did not ride home that night. The Elite didn't even bring back his body, which could only mean either capture or treason. When a soldier betrayed his comrades, his body was left for the animals. There was no doubt in my mind that Gareth was an honorable man, but rumors would spread through the town like wildfire by morning.

I had wanted to run to her right then, but Pa made me wait until morning. Sneaking out past curfew was risky, and business couldn't afford another scandal on my part. Luka the troublemaker. I tossed the whole night, waiting for the sun to rise. The second it did I hopped out of bed, not even bothering to change into my day clothes, and tore through the town as fast as my feet would carry me.

I was met with an empty house. There was no sign of 'Lana, or her Ma.

It was not long until others in the city took notice of the vacancy. Grown-ups whispered to each other, saying 'Lana's dad had committed some sort of act against the crown. There were things said about her Ma too. Things Pa said I was too young to understand. Things like 'Lana not being Gareth's natural kin.

The other kids, who had always had it out for 'Lana anyway, came up with their own tales. Tales about 'Lana's family being Mystic sympathizers, and that she must have been some sort of half-breed. Mutt, they'd call her, when they thought I wasn't listening. As if she was no better than a street dog. As time went on, they felt less like a group of kids and more like an angry mob and, well, I'd had enough of all of 'em anyway.

Rumors being what they are, word about 'Lana got back to my Pa faster than I did, and I'm pretty fast. But rumors aren't burdened with the weight of truth, and so they fly faster than a hawk on the hunt. When I got home, Pa sat me down. He made me promise not to start nuthin' with the other kids. He didn't want me drawing any more attention to us than we were already bound to get, me bein' friends with 'Lana and all.

"It's not like they haven't run their mouths about us before," I argued. "Gertrude and her flock have always had it out for both of us."

"This is different, Luka," Pa warned. "I mean it! No matter what they say about 'Lana or her Ma you keep your head down and keep your fists to yourself, you got it?"

"But that ain't fair! 'Lana would stand up for me; and her Pa for you and you know it!" I couldn't believe he expected me to sit back and let them slander the one family who had stuck by us after Ma left.

"There is more at stake here than their honor!" He leaned forward, putting his hand on my shoulder. I swallowed, knowing what he was going to say next and wishing I was wrong.

"Gareth committed treason. They all did. They were part of the Alliance," the way the words rushed out of him reminded me of the way a bellow deflated as it blew air into the hearth. It had the same affect, as I felt something a lot like fire rise up inside of me. The Alliance was a group of rebels working to overthrow King Irving and renew the treaty between humans and Mystics. Befriending a traitor to the crown made you a traitor by association. We couldn't afford to draw attention to ourselves, because it could mean death. And because of what Pa said next:

"And so am I." There was that feeling again. The rising fire. It was different from the kind I had felt before, that came from anger. This one made my skin break out in goosebumps. This one came from pride. No wonder Gareth and Pa had been such good friends all these years. They'd both had their hand in the same pot, stirrin' it. All those years he'd been hollerin' at me to lay low and fall in line had been for my own protection.

And I was proud of him for it, though I couldn't really say why. Maybe it was 'cause I'd always thought somethin' about taking people's land and then killing them for retaliating didn't make any sense. Or maybe I figured if people could be as cruel to a sweet girl like 'Lana, that maybe we were on the wrong side of things. Especially if she really was half-something-else. Maybe, just maybe, they were all wrong about the Mystics.

And besides, weren't nobody else on the face of the earth who had more honor than my Pa. None that I had met, anyway. So that was that. If he was a traitor, then I was too. I promised to keep my head down and stay out of trouble. A promise I'd actually managed to keep, until now.

"The kids believe what they were raised to, just like their parents before them," Pa continued. "Most of 'em aren't even old enough to remember a life before the War. Most of them act out of ignorance rather than malice. Especially the children."

"They act that way because they're rotten!" I argued. "Gertrude always had it out for 'Lana and you know it! No reason for it, neither. Besides, I wasn't raised no different than the rest of them, not really, and I like 'Lana just fine."

"Yeah, well," for the first time it felt like my smart-mouth had got the best of him. "You're different than that lot, Luka. Always have been, always will be." Something about the way he said it sent a shiver down my spine.

A knock at the door stole his attention.

"Go clean yourself up," he barked. Then, looking me over, "And stay in the back. Standing out is the last thing we need right now, you hear?" With that he turned to answer the door.

Don't have to tell me twice. I shuffled to the back, relieved that our visitor seemed to have gotten me off the hook with a warning. I was almost all the way to my room when I heard a voice booming behind me.

"Closing up shop early today, Robert?" The voice was familiar, but I couldn't put my finger on why. It wasn't any of Pa's regular customers, I was sure of that. Yet, the tone with which he greeted him suggested that they'd known each other a long time. I crept closer, pressing my ear against the wall so I could hear better.

"Might it have something to do with the boy's scuffle this morning?"

My heart raced. I made a mental note to pummel Philip harder next time, so he couldn't go wagging his tongue around town, the little snitch.

"Maybe it does, and maybe it doesn't," Pa said gruffly. "What's it to you?"

"I thought we'd agreed he was to keep his head down."

"Is that why you're here, Brian? To keep tabs on the boy? Don't you have your own family to look after?"

I knew well enough to know them was fightin' words. *Brian?* Why did that name sound so familiar?

"You know I have more important matters to deal with than your son's temper tantrums."

"Watch yourself, old man," Pa warned. "Just because Kala vouched for you doesn't mean the rest of us have to like you. Let alone trust you any farther than we can kick you. Now tell me, what business do you have here?"

I held my breath, afraid that the force of it leaving my lungs might drown out the man's reply.

"It's the girl, Robert. She's taken off."

CHAPTER ELEVEN

"**Y**OU LOST HER?!" Pa was tryin' to keep his voice down, but he never was very good about keepin' quiet once he got riled up. Instead what came out of his mouth was half-whisper, half-hiss. I was glad I wasn't the one on the receivin' end of it. I wondered who was.

"She ran off, Robert, left the safehold. Word only got to me three days ago now. I was hoping I might find her here."

By now I was certain they were talkin' about 'Lana. What with there bein' talk of a safehold. And the stranger's voice? I was sure I had heard it before, and more than once. I held my breath, tryin' to avoid drawing attention to myself as I nudged open the door that separated the shop from our living space. *Maybe if I could just get a little look at the visitor...*

I let out my breath slowly, careful that my relief didn't rush out and give me away. Pa's back was turned away, which was just fine except for the fact that he was also blocking my view. Drat.

"We've seen no sign of her 'round these parts." Pa said. "I hope she's got enough sense to keep it that way, for everyone's sake"

"Aye, that's what I was hoping as well. Are you sure she hasn't contacted the boy?"

"He'd have told me, if she had."

"Mind if I ask him myself?" He didn't wait for Pa to answer. "Come on out, boy."

My heart froze in my chest. I'd gotten off easy for my scuffle with Philip, but eavesdroppin' would get me a lashin' for sure.

"S'alright boy, I won't hurt you," The stranger mistook my hesitation for fear of him.

I swallowed hard and squared my shoulders, hopin' that I looked braver than I felt as I stepped through the doorway. Pa shot me a look that could curdle milk straight out of the cow, before wavin' me over to join him. I knew better than to keep him waiting.

The first thing I noticed about our visitor was the smell. He had the stench of a man who had been long on the road with little care. A vagrant, perhaps? Or a trader with no home to return to.

The second thing I noticed as I examined his disheveled clothes, wild hair, and overgrown beard, was that he wasn't a stranger at all. Indeed, I had seen him in the city on more than a handful of occasions.

"Yer 'Lana's granddad," I said, matter-a-fact-like.

"So I am," the corners of the man's eyes wrinkled as a smirk ran across his face. "And you, youngling, were her best friend."

"Damn right I was! Still am!"

"Language, son!" Pa smacked my shoulder, but Lana's grandad laughed.

"I take no offense, Robert. I like the boy's spirit. Always have." He spoke as if we'd known each other my whole life, but I had no such recollection of him. I scanned the lines of his leathery face, waiting for something beyond a vague recognition to come to me. Nothin'

"I told you to stay in the back, Luka," Pa turned to me, a brow raised in disapproval. I cast my eyes to the ground sheepishly.

"I know, I just... I heard you two talkin' and it seemed like maybe it was about her and...I couldn't help but find out for sure."

"Go easy on him, Robert. You can't fault the boy his affection."

Affection? "Ew, no!" I slammed both my hands over my mouth, tryin' to trap the words before they made it all the way out, but I was too late. "I mean...no offense or nothin', but 'Lana and I, we're just friends. An' she's been missin' with no word and...well I'm just worried about her is all. Got nothin' to do with 'affections'."

The man threw back his head, laughin' heartily. "Ah, to be young again!" He clapped a hand on my shoulder. "Boy, affections come in all forms, as I'm sure you'll soon learn. One does not have to have a romantic interest in order to hold someone dear." The corners of his lips turned upward, shifting his tangled beard around it. "Although, as the years go on, you may find your mind changes where romance is concerned."

"That's enough, Brian." Pa nodded his head toward the back of the shop. "Back to your room with ya, Luka. Let us finish our talk."

"Now wait just a minute," Brian argued. "He has a right to know what's happening just as much as anyone else does."

"He's too young."

"He's older than my 'Lana, and none thought twice before putting her in the position she's in."

"That is an entirely different situation, and you know it!"

"'Tis not so much, considering the boy's heritage."

"STOP!" Pa's voice shook the room, causin' me to jump clear outta my skin. I hadn't heard him raise his voice to no one but me in...I didn't know how long.

The two men locked eyes, jaws set stubbornly. Pa's soot-covered hands curled into fists. Brian's eyes got as big as saucers. Not from fear. I got the feelin' watchin' the two of them that he would have been happy to scuffle with Pa, if it came down to it. Nah, the look on his face weren't scared at all. It came from an idea—an understandin' of some sort. I wished they would let me in on whatever secret they were sharin'.

"You mean you still haven't told him?"

"I said enough, Brian." He hissed like a kettle about to boil.

"He has a right to know, Robert. Especially now."

"It's nobody's business what I tell my son. Least of all, yours!"

Lana's grandad ran a hand through his hair, lookin' down at his feet. Pat had struck a chord, for sure; but instead of respondin' in anger, Brian seemed ashamed.

"Pa, what's he talkin' about?" The words were out of my mouth before I could talk myself out of them.

"Nothing that you need concern yourself with, son." His words were chosen carefully, and his jaw set in a way that told me the matter was not up for discussion. It only made the desire to know burn more fiercely in my chest.

"Sounds more like exactly the sort of thing I should be concernin' myself with." I felt only a twinge of regret as the words left my mouth. I couldn't remember the last time I talked back to Pa. Still, I squared my shoulders as he locked eyes with me, and raised my head high, determined to stand my ground the way a man would. Maybe if he thought of me less like a child, just maybe then he would see fit to let me in on whatever secret he was keepin'.

"Is it about Ma?" I asked. "Does it have somethin' to do with her leavin'? Is that why you don't want to talk about it?" I was sure I'd earn myself a lashin', but I didn't care anymore. I was sick of pretendin' she never left.

"Her leaving had nothing to do with you, and everything to do with herself," Pa's voice was firm to shield the hurt that Ma's memory brought to the corners of his eyes. He turned his attention back to Brian.

"See what you've started, old man?"

"You knew this day would come, Robert. We both did. I tried to warn you—"

"And I'll say it again: The boy is none of your concern!"

"You can't keep it from him forever, you know. One of these days he'll find out, whether it's from you or from one of *them*."

One of who? "Pa, what's he talkin' about?"

His eyes were locked with Brian, and he acted as if I hadn't spoke, "Go to your room, Luka."

My eyes moved between the two men, unsure of what to do. Brian looked nervous, like an animal that's caught sight of a hunter as they try to figure out whether they can run before they're felled. Pa stared him down, shoulders squared like he was daring him to run. Like he'd have run him down and caught him.

Except it would have been better if he'd taken off, rather than what happened next. Pa snapped his fingers at me, keeping his eyes on Lana's granddad as he waved me off. As I turned to go, Brian's voice followed me.

"Robert's not your real Pa."

Pa had Brian up against the wall before I could blink.

"You hold your tongue you dirty—"

"This is bigger than you, Robert! Bigger than either of us, or our egos. The boy has to know, and he has to know NOW!" Brian held his hands up, refusing to fight back.

"Pa?" My voice came out raspy, on account of my mouth goin' dry. I licked my lips, willing myself to raise my voice above a whisper, "Is it true?"

Pa hung his head and sighed before turnin' to me. I held my breath, waiting for reassurance. Surely Brian was mistaken? Maybe he'd been out in the sun too long, or maybe he'd been hittin' the bottle. I just knew that Pa would say the man had gone mad. He had to!

Pa laid a hand on my shoulder, motioning to a wooden stool by the door where customers would wait for their orders. "Sit down, boy." I obeyed.

"Well, old man," he said to Brian. "It seems you've started a thing that can't be undone." A chill went through my body, making my hands and feet tingle.

"He'll want to hear it from you, Philip."

"Ruddy figures you'd chicken out, you damned fool." Pa sighed and knelt down in front of me.

"Luka, whatever comes after this moment I want you to know this: I am and always will be your Pa. Whether you're my flesh and blood or not."

"I-I don't understand," I stammered, gripping the edge of the stool so I wouldn't melt right off of it.

"Luka," Brian's voice softened, and he placed a hand on Pa's shoulder in solidarity. "You're a Changeling."

Chapter Twelve

"I'M A WHAT?" I stood with my mouth agape like some fool.

"A changeling," Brian repeated. "A child of the fairy-folk."

It wasn't that I was havin' trouble understandin' what he'd said. The words were clear as day. I knew what fairy-folk were. Heck, I'd even heard the term Changeling once or twice growing up, though it wasn't somethin' we learnt about in our teachings about Mystics.

"This is some joke, right?" *Either that or Pa's gone off his rocker,* I thought. Maybe all those years of dealin' with my shenanigans had finally got to him, and now he was tryin' to make off like I was adopted.

"No son, it's no joke." Pa's voice was dead serious. "You see, Alison had just given birth, not two weeks before." His voice cracked. I'd not heard him speak about Ma in ages, and never did he use her name that way.

"She and the babe both fell ill. The city doc did what he could, but—" he blinked, eyes glistening. *Was Pa crying?* Pa didn't cry. Weren't no reason to, neither. Ma and I had both turned out just fine, hadn't we?

"The babe was too new," Brian took over for Pa. "Too weak. The doc told your parents there was no way it would survive."

Pa's mind came back from wherever it had drifted off to. "And then, one morn' I went to the babe's cot to...a miracle. There he was; fresh, strong.

It was as if the sickness never took hold of him."

I didn't know what kind of miracle could have saved me from Death's grasp, or why Pa was still so torn up about a thing that had happened a lifetime ago, but a sinking in my stomach told me I shouldn't have pressed so hard for him to tell me.

"I knew it, then," Pa continued. "I knew, but I would not—could not—accept it. What parent in their right mind could question the fates? We'd been given our boy back." He looked to me as if asking for absolution. As if, somehow, I was the only one who could grant it.

"Alison had her suspicions, of course. A mother knows her own son. But the illness, and her grief...I think it was too much. Over time, she accepted it too."

"Accepted what?" I squeaked. He continued as if I hadn't spoken.

"And then came the colic. You were up all hours, screamin' your little head off. Some said it was normal, a result of the illness even. But I knew better, I just did. So I removed all the iron from the house, and the screaming stopped."

"But, I don't—?"

"Our son, our baby boy. They'd taken him. Switched him out. Replaced him with one of their own young."

My mind swam as I tried to make sense of what he was saying. *Me, some impish freak-type?* I mean, sure I was a handful, but surely Pa couldn't have gone that far over the edge.

"Pa?" I said hesitantly, "You haven't been into the ale this mornin', have ya?" It wasn't often that he would take to the bottle, but now and again, if he were really missin' Ma, I'd seen him have a swig or two durin' the daytime.

"What?" he looked at me, as if he was seein' me for the first time. "Luka, I'm being serious!"

"Alright then," I held my arms up in exasperation, "If I am some sort of fairy folk, then where are my wings?"

Brian threw his head back and guffawed, "oh, this is the age, isn't it? Where they think they know all there is to know about everything!"

Pa just shook his head.

"'Course you don't have wings, you ninny," Brian continued. "A Changeling is meant to blend in. 'Tis part of the magic. If you don't fit in, you can't stay hidden, and then they have to switch you out again. It's a banishment, not a death sentence, after all!"

"Is that what 'Lana was, then? A changeling?" The laughter stopped. I guessed that meant no.

Something else occurred to me. "How can I be here then, if I'm really a changeling?" I motioned to the tools that surrounded us. "Iron, all of it. Why aren't I writhing in agony? How could I be the blacksmith's son?"

"Your father was not always a blacksmith, boy."

I looked at Pa. *Not always a blacksmith?* What had he been, before me? I had never known him to be anything other than what he was.

"When I was sure," Pa answered my thoughts before I could turn them into words. "Absolutely certain that you were what I suspected...it was too late. You were my son, as much as the other babe had been. I could not bear to lose another child. As soon as you weaned from your mother we went away, just the two of us, when you were still a wee thing. Slowly, I began building your tolerance to iron. It was slow going, and painful for both of us. You screeched like a banshee those first few days. Sometimes you'd retreat to the corner, refusing to let me come near you. It broke my heart to hurt you. Shattered it to pieces. But it had to be done, to protect you."

"Protect me? How?" I couldn't fathom how torturing a small child in such a way—human or not—could have been for its own protection. I looked upon the man that I called Pa with wide, horrified eyes. My mind didn't want to accept a thing that he was saying, but neither could it resist hearin' the whole story.

"Eventually you were able to tolerate the presence of iron, and even salt in small servings. You came home to your Ma a new child. You no longer shied away when people came to visit. You functioned like every other human child, save for your temper, and love of mischief and sweets."

I shook my head. It couldn't be true. I would know, if I were really somethin' that different. I would remember. *Wouldn't I?*

"Alison—your Ma—she never knew, if that is what you're wonderin'. To her you were always her son. Always."

I got the feelin' he was tryin' to reassure me. It almost worked, too.

"But then she left." I said flatly, "Was it because of me?" I couldn't bear to say what I was really thinking. *Was it because you told her I wasn't her real son?*

"Your Ma leaving wasn't your fault," Pa's face was stern. "Don't you believe otherwise, not even for a second. It was her own weakness. She couldn't...well, it doesn't matter right now, does it? She left, and I stayed and here we are, and you are safe, as long as we are here together, you hear me?"

I nodded, swallowing a lump in my throat. "S-so you built my tolerance to iron, and then you became a blacksmith. But why?"

"To protect you, boy!" Brian pitched in, "The Fae don't always leave their youngin's forever. Some, maybe, if they don't fit in for some reason or other, or if they're a danger to the Hollow. Others they leave just to the age of weaning, letting them grow strong on the human mother's milk before they take 'em back. No way to know which one you were."

"But why not just let them take me then? Wouldn't you want your own child back?"

"Weren't never a changeling changed back," said Brian. "Not without some sort of trickery involved. They do away with 'em, or keep them as slaves, they say. Some even say—" He stopped himself, noting Pa's reaction.

Pa licked his lips like you do when your mouths been scared dry, "Some say they only take the ones that are bound to die anyway." He finished. "It doesn't matter now." He put his hand firmly on my shoulder. "You are my boy. You have always been my boy. You got that?"

He pulled me into his arms for the first time in I don't know how long. I sniffed, blinking back a hot feeling in the corners of my eyes. When I was younger the other kids used to tease that I looked nothin' like Pa. That I must have been some street urchin he'd picked up somewhere. I'd laughed it off back then. It wasn't so funny, now.

"Your Pa left everything he'd known and took on a new trade. Surrounded you in an iron fortress so that they could not take you back." Brian's voice jarred me back to the present. "And neither of you have dared leave it, until now."

"No, Brian. Absolutely not." Pa released his hold on me and stood to face Lana's grandad.

"She's gone, Robert. Alone. Into a wilderness she does not understand. You know what is at stake," he ran his hand through his shaggy hair nervously. "There is not a single one of us she trusts now, except the boy."

"What have you done, old man?" Pa's eyes narrowed suspiciously, and I saw the man with new eyes. Lana's grandad acted as if he and Pa were friends, but Pa didn't seem to trust him as far as he could kick him.

"The things that have been done were done out of necessity," Brian skirted around the question. "She has a destiny that she cannot run from. One that affects us all."

Destiny? What on earth were they talking about? She was just a kid, not much younger than me, but they made her sound like she had a duty greater than a king. I had so many questions, none of which seemed like they would be answered this day.

"Doesn't seem like she wants much to do with her destiny," Pa said wryly.

Brian shook his head, "She acts not of her own will."

"Then why did she leave?"

"They believe she is under the influence of an Amasai."

"An Amasai?" The way Pa said it sent a shiver up my spine. I'd never heard of him bein' afraid of nothin' in my whole life, not the way he did when he said those words. "Then there's no one this side of the boundary that can help her, and you know it."

Brain said nothin', but his eyes shot in my direction real quick-like, "We have to try, Robert."

"Why don't you go after her then, she's your kin."

"I doubt that she would come with me, even if I could track her. The trees, they whisper now and then, but most have gone silent since she left. I'm not welcome, for one reason or another."

"A good reason, if I know you at all," Pa's voice was sour. "Why not run off on your own then? Go hide somewhere, protect your own hide. That's what you're best at, isn't it?

Brian spoke as if Pa hadn't said anything, "Something is afoot, Robert. Something bigger than both of us. The Priestess, she'll listen to you; and 'Lana will listen to the boy. It's our only shot."

"No," Pa shook his head, his voice firm. "That wasn't the agreement, Brian. 'No fieldwork.' That's what I said when I took my pledge. I'll not risk my kin."

I wanted to interrupt them. To shout at Pa that it was not just some stranger we were bein' asked to save. It was my best friend—might as well be kin herself! I wanted to take her grandad's hand and pledge my allegiance to whoever it was that was lookin' for her. The Priestess, Brian had said. Whoever that was. I'd swear to her that I'd find 'Lana, and make her come back, if only she would be safe.

But I didn't do any of those things. I stood there, frozen and unable to process what was happening around me. I failed her.

"We will keep an eye out, and an ear," Pa offered, his voice softening. "Though if she's any sense left at all, she will steer clear from here."

"And if you have any love for her at all, you *will* find her," he faced Pa, but he glanced at me again quickly and I got the feeling that last part had been meant for me. He turned without another word and left the shop, flipping the sign on the door from 'Closed' to 'Open" before disappearing into the crowd.

That night I laid awake tossing my leather ball from one hand to the other as I reflected on the day's events. 'Lana was alive, but in danger. She'd run off. Why? What could make her abandon her kin? Brian had said she was under the influence of ... something. Pa seemed to act as if it were somehow Brian's fault. Why would her grandfather put her in danger? I didn't have an answer.

And then there was the matter of my own ancestry. If what Pa said was true, then I was a Mystic. Not just half, like 'Lana. Full-blown Fae. A wolf in sheep's clothes, masqueradin' as one of their own. Maybe that's why I'd stuck out so much as a youngin'. And why 'Lana and I had gotten on so well, even from the beginning. Maybe, deep down, I had realized that we were the same.

But this is my home, I reminded myself. This is where I'd grown up. Here, I was safe. Here I had a man who would call me son. But here, she could never be again. Dangers aside, I couldn't stand the thought of never seein' her again.

What would happen to me, if I left the safety of these walls? Would my true kin really come looking for me, even after all these years? What interest could they have in me now, a boy raised among human men? Surely they couldn't still be searchin' for me.

I struggled with my thoughts until it was nearly dawn. The moon had sunk behind the trees, but it was not yet first light. The world was in transition. *Seems as good a time as any.* I slipped out of bed, holding my breath to keep the floor board from creakin' as I went about gettin' dressed. Pa's snores echoed through the shop, almost drownin' out my own thoughts.

I packed light. I was no fool, sneakin' off without the proper supplies. A day and a half's worth of food could last me three if I rationed it right. A flask of water and a long iron knife hung from my belt. I figured even if the fairy-folk weren't lookin' for me, there were plenty of other threats to be wary of. I hesitated a moment as my eyes fell on the leather pouch sittin' on my bed. I reached out, but my hand hovered over it, hesitating. I knew better than to pack extra weight, especially since it wouldn't be long 'til Pa started chasin' after me. What good was it, anyway—a reminder of someone who hadn't seen fit to stay? I sighed heavily and shoved it into my coat pocket, holding my breath as I tip-toed through the shop.

It was only after the door shut silently behind me that I let out my breath. "I'm sorry Pa," I whispered to its wooden planks. "I can't leave her alone out there."

Around me the city still slept, but it wouldn't be long before the market sprang to life. There was no time to lose. I shouldered my pack, blending into the shadows as I made my way toward the border.

I didn't look back.

Chapter Thirteen

S NEAKIN' OUT OF THE CITY WAS THE EASY PART. Coverin' my tracks was harder. The grasslands that formed the boundary between our land and the Mystics marred easily, making it obvious when someone passed through. I didn't want to tip Pa off if he came lookin for me, but I knew I couldn't just take the same path the Elite had on their last excursion either. I reckoned they'd have been smart enough to cut through the same way every time, so as to make it obvious if any other travelers had come this way from the other side. Which meant it was probably pretty well traveled, and I had no desire to run into one of the soldiers on my way out.

"Step lightly," A voice behind me made me jump clean out of my own skin. I turned, holding my hand to my chest to keep my heart from burstin' through it.

"Brian!" My shoulders sank in relief.

"Took you long enough," he chuckled. "I've been tracking you ever since you left the city."

"How did you know I'd come?"

"I didn't, not for sure. I hoped, though." He ran his hand over his scraggily beard. "Glad I was right."

"So where are we going?" I asked.

"We? We aren't going anywhere," He scanned the horizon. "I have... other business to attend to. I'm just here to see you off right-quick. I figured this part of the journey might be tricky for you."

A tuggin' in my gut said he knew more than he was tellin' me, but I couldn't put my finger on why. I didn't trust him, not entirely. But I did need to cross the field without leavin' any tracks, and I was runnin' out of time. There wasn't much choice.

"Alright," I said. "What do you suggest?"

"Follow me," He motioned with his hand as he turned parallel to the field, not bothering to wait and see if I would follow. I hung back a moment, hesitating. Nope, he wasn't gonna wait for me. I took off so as to catch up before he left me behind.

"So, you travel back and forth, then?" I looked over my shoulder, unable to shake the feelin' that we were bein' watched.

He kept his eyes on the path before us, "Aye, when it suits me."

Not much of a talker now, is he? I thought to myself. For someone who was so eager to share his knowledge just hours before, he'd sure clammed up fast. *Suspicious.*

We walked in silence a few minutes, until we came to a pathway through the field. *You've got to be kidding me!* "Hey old man, I didn't follow you just to get snatched up by the Elite. What kind of fool do you take me for, leadin' me to the one way I'm almost guaranteed to get caught?" I backed away, scanning the area for any sign of trouble.

"Peace, Luka," Brian held up a hand to silence me. "Sometimes the safest way to avoid the enemy is to hide right under their noses."

"This is the path you travel, then?"

"It is, and it isn't." He turned down the pathway where years of tramplin' by the king's horses had worn away the grass. The dust kicked up by his feet as he made his way across the field was different from any I had seen before, and it took me a moment to realize why: The dirt was tinted red, just like the grass that grew from it. The realization made me shiver.

I shifted from one foot to the other, tryin' to decide the best course of action, before sighing and taking off after him for a second time. *Sure doesn't waste time, that one.* I thought to myself. Considerin' he was sendin' me on a wild goose chase after his kin, you'd have thought he'd be more accommodating.

I caught up with him just as the fields ended and the forest began. I leaned over my knees tryin' to catch my breath. My legs were stained red from the knee down. I brushed them vigorously, hopin' to wipe the dust from my pants. No such luck.

"The Mark of the Intruder," Brian nodded at my shins. He didn't seem to have the same trouble as I. His clothes were free from staining. "It takes them time to accept newcomers. Never you mind."

"Them?"

"The spirits of the forest." He said, as if that explained everything.

"How come you've got no markings?"

"I've spent much of my life here," he said. "I may not be well-liked amongst Mystic kind, but I am no threat either. Nor am I a stranger to the forest."

I glanced back at the path we'd taken. Only one set of footprints. Mine.

"How is this supposed to make it harder for 'em to find me?" I demanded, suddenly regrettin' trusting him. In fact, I was beginnin' to regret leavin' home altogether.

"Patience," he said, walking up to the nearest tree. He leaned in, whisperin' something I couldn't quite make out. "Ah, yes." He said as if the tree had answered him. He patted its trunk, much like some farmers did to the flanks of their horses. It was an odd sight to behold: This wild and disheveled man bestowin' an act of affection to an inanimate thing.

Perhaps he is mad. I tried to force the thought away, but it would not be set aside. What if he was just some beggar who'd attached himself to 'Lana? What if he was no relation to her at all? Or maybe her absence had driven him mad. Either way, I began to scan the landscape for an exit.

Brian laughed. "Yes, he is a tad jumpy, isn't he?"

The tree. He's talkin' to the tree! He raised a hand, tracin' a shape on the trunk that was foreign, yet not. Like a memory from a dream. The shape he traced marked the bark of the tree, though he'd used his bare hands and not any sort of knife. The marking glowed brightly, and the tree began to shake. I raised my arms to my face, turning my head and squinting against the light.

When all had settled, the tree stood, split in half. But instead of seeing the forest on the other side, there was a...room? Cave? Meadow? The images wavered and shifted. I blinked, trying to force my eyes to settle on one image.

"What witchcraft is this?!" I demanded.

"Aye, there is some magic to it," he laughed at my astonishment. "Though the Priestess has little to none to do with it. No, this is magic of another sort. One that isn't remembered by many."

"How do you know it, then?"

"Once upon a time, there was a lass...Well, that's a story for another time." He stopped his tale before he'd started proper. "Some of the others—dwarves and elves and such—They made pathways similar to this one. 'Tis how 'Lana and her mom escaped the night the Elite came home."

So that explained how they'd left without a trace.

"This isn't the one she took, then?"

"No. The one she took, it's not friendly for folk like us. Lets out too close to the Safehold."

"Safehold?"

"The place they took her. Retracin' her steps won't tell you where she's gone, only where she's been."

"If you know where she's gone, why don't you go after her yourself?"

"You've got a lot of questions for a boy who's running out of time," he pointed out. The sun had broken across the horizon. Pa would soon be waking. I didn't have much choice.

"Where will it take me?"

"Somewhere safer than here, though I wouldn't count on it stayin' that way for long." He said. "You going or not?"

I'd come this far already, and I figured whatever was on the other side of the portal he'd created couldn't be as bad as bein' caught by one of the king's soldiers. Or worse yet, the lashin' I'd get from Pa if he caught me first.

I nodded and took a deep breath, holdin' it in as I stepped into the portal.

As soon as I stepped through the entryway it zipped shut. and darkness surrounded me. In a panic I thrust my hands against the wall where the opening had been, but there was no sign of it. Not even a crack or crevice to indicate what had been there only moments before.

Where was the cave? The room? The images I had seen before were nowhere to be found.

The air became stale and I was sure that I would suffocate. My palms grew sweaty and I felt panic overtake me. It was a trap!

There was a rumbling sound and the earth shook, causing me to stumble and nearly lose my footing. I was tossed this way and that, catching myself against the smooth walls of my prison. And then it stopped, just as quickly as it had started. The entryway unzipped before me again. Without a second thought I bolted out into the open glad to inhale fresh air once more as I leaned over my knees, gathering my wits.

When I finally caught my breath and stood up, I noticed that it was near dark. Going from pitch black to the current amount of light didn't require the same amount of adjustment as going from one extreme to the other would, but it still took me a moment to get my bearings.

But...this wasn't right at all. I scanned the sky as best I could through the treetops. The sun had just been creepin' over the horizon when I'd left Brian. Yet, somehow it was just starting to set.

How much time had I lost?! Or had I been sent to the other ends of the earth, instead of just beyond the border?

"Time's a bit different in these parts," A voice made me jump.

I looked around me, tryin' to locate the source. My eyes couldn't see it.

Perhaps my mind's gone loopy, I thought.

"Nuthin' wrong with your mind, youngin','" the voice said again.

"'Aye! Who's there?" I demanded, spinning around frantically. My hand settled on the hilt of my blade instinctively.

"Now, now, no need to go usin' that." The voice tsk'd. From the shadow of the forest appeared a figure, small at first, then larger as my eyes settled on him. *Was it a trick of the light, or something else?*

"A bit of both, I suppose," the man said. His scrawny body was covered in moss and twig such that if he'd crouched I was sure to lose sight of him against the forest floor. His beard hung down past his knees, indicating that he was aged, yet he barely came up to my own shoulders in height. Wispy grey curls poked out from under the red cap that sat atop his head.

"Who are you?" I demanded, stepping forward to show that I wasn't afraid of him. He leaped against the trunk of a nearby tree, rebounding to another, and yet another until he reached the lowest branch of the mighty cedar.

"We are as we are suited to be," he said, dancing from one branch to another playfully.

I kept my eye on him, knowing better than to turn my back on one of the Fae without knowing which family it was from. While some were said to be charitable sorts, others were known for their dubious nature. Imps, for example, were known for their harmful pranks. And since they could disguise themselves at will, there was no guarantee that what I saw was who I was speaking to.

He found my diligence amusing, and chuckled to himself, "Like ye've never seen a forest gnome before!"

I didn't find the situation funny. "Where are you from?"

"We walk in the twilight realm, where only fae may go." He snapped his fingers, and a set of small pipes strung together appeared out of thin air. He blew into them gently, as if testing them. The sound was sweet, even soothing in a way. My hand returned to my blade and the noise stopped.

"You keep saying 'we'" I said. "Who else is with you?" I scanned the woods briefly before locking eyes on the figure once more.

"Interesting," he mumbled as he lowered the pipes. He hopped down from the tree and looked me up and down.

"What is?" I demanded.

He crept closer until, raising a hand when I began to unsheathe my sword. "Steady," he cautioned me as if I were some wild horse. He raised the pipes to his lips and blew into them. Nothing. He tried again, harder this time. The instrument was silent. He tried once more, blowing into them until he was red in the face before giving up.

"Unaffected," he whispered in awe. "But how?"

I unsheathed my sword, tired of his games. He shrieked and jumped back "Ah! Ah!" he said jumping up and down in a mixture of excitement and fear. "That be it! The iron, it hurts us!"

I waved the blade in warning "Who is 'us'?" I called. "Where are your friends? Are they here?"

"We walk in the twilight realm, where only fae may go."

"Is that where she went?" I asked. Maybe Brian knew what he was doing after all.

"He seeks the girl!" The creature responded, obviously pleased. "Yes, yes that is where she went! I can take you, follow me!" and with that he took off into the forest, with hardly a glance over his shoulder to see if I'd followed behind.

Chapter Fourteen

EEPING UP WITH THE GNOME proved trickier than I thought, for instead of running on the ground he bounced from tree to tree, almost as if he were weightless. I chased him until my lungs burned, and then I chased him more out of spite. Just when I was sure my legs would give out he paused and smiled over my shoulder.

"Iron bites and iron anchors!" he tittered, "Best to leave it behind."

If that old bitty thinks I'm followin' him unarmed he's got another thing comin'! I'd have said it out loud had I not been too busy struggling to catch my breath.

"Suit yourself then, slowpoke." He shot me an impish grin before boundin' off at double speed.

I'm gonna kill 'Lana's grandad next time I set eyes on him. I thought *That is, if I don't get run to death first!* I cursed myself under my breath as I came to a halt. I wiped the sweat from my brow and resisted the urge to retch. I needed water.

I dropped my pack onto the ground and pulled the flask out, but before I could get the cap undone someone snatched it from my hands.

"Why are ya takin' my water? Off with ya, ya pesky thing!" I swatted at him.

He jumped back and laughed at me as my hand whooshed by him, missing by inches. *Fast for such a little thing.* Determined to catch him, I threw my whole body his way and he darted up another a tree before danglin' my flask out in front of him.

"Off with that iron and I'll trade you," he said.

"What kind of a fool do you take me for?"

"You can't go any further without it. Simple as that." He crossed his arms. "So, what'll it be?"

I stared at him defiantly. The long knife was my only defense against... whatever was out in this wilderness. Leaving it behind would leave me completely vulnerable; but I had been foolish in exerting myself so early on. My muscles screamed at me, threatenin' to cramp if I took another step. I swallowed. It felt like swallowing sand.

The gnome shook the flask gently near his ear. "Sounds delightful, doesn't it?" he taunted, raisin' an eyebrow as he waited for my response.

I shook my head, but I knew that he could tell I was lyin'.

"Stubborn, are ya? Hmm. Maybe the Stanford clan," he mumbled to himself. He held the flask out to me again. "That's you're final answer then? You sure?"

I nodded. This had to be some sort of test, or a trick. I wasn't going to fall for it.

"Well, I wouldn't exactly put it that way." The gnome chuckled as he yanked on a nearby branch that gave way like a lever. I had hardly a moment to realize that the ground beneath me had disappeared before I realized I was falling.

I woke to pitch black and a sore head. Wherever I'd landed must have been underground, because I couldn't find a light source, and everything around me was pitch black. I sat up, testing my arms and legs for signs of injury, and found none. *Odd.*

"Fairy dust." I jumped. The voice was foreign but sounded female.

"They treat all outsiders to a heavy dose on the way down. Part of why the trap works. You should get your sight back shortly."

What?! I rubbed my eyes as if doing so might clear away the darkness.

"No, not like that silly." The voice said again. "That just makes it worse. No, *blink* it away, soft-like." I felt a rush of air on my face and realize it was her breath. I recoiled slightly, blinking as she said. Sure enough, the light broke through, and I began to make out the blurry shape of the person in front of me. She looked human enough. About my age, if not a tad older, and clad in clothes that would be considered normal back home.

"Your head will start feeling better soon too." She promised. "The transition is harder for some than others though."

I looked around us. Nothing looked familiar. In fact, it looked downright odd. Too bright for indoors, for one thing. Three walls were white, and the fourth was a set of curved ivory bars imbedded into the stone floor. The girl stood on the other side.

"What is your name?" I asked.

She tilted her head curiously, as if she didn't understand the question.

"You know, your name?"

"Name?" It was almost a whisper. "Yes, I think I had one once. It was... Well I don't remember, exactly."

"How can you not remember your own name?"

"It happens after a while, I suppose. When you've been here long enough, things like that start to fade."

"How long have you been here?"

She blinked rapidly before answering. "Time moves...differently here. It's hard to tell."

Perfect. How long had I been here then? How much time had I wasted? No use getting caught in that spiral before I even knew what I was up against.

"Who are you?" I thought maybe, if I phrased it in another way I might get something more out of her.

"I am a servant of the Fae," she said, as if that should have been obvious.

"You're one of those human kids they trade for their own, then?" My eyes went wide. If she was near my age could that mean...No, I reminded myself. Pa's babe had been a male. This couldn't be his rightful kin.

"No. Or yes. Or, not exactly." She trailed off again. "I don't suppose it matters much anyhow."

"What do you mean, it doesn't matter! They've taken you from your rightful home—from your Ma and Pa!"

She shrugged, "I don't recall a life other than what I know now; and tis not like they are unkind. Not if you follow the rules, anyhow."

"Well I've not got time to sit here and rot and forget my own name! I've got someone I'm supposed to be lookin' after and I ain't about to be no one's slave!"

"It's not so bad," she shrugged nonchalantly. "We're well cared for: fed and kept warm."

"How would you know if you were bein' mistreated when you can't even remember your own name?" The thought was absurd.

"They can't touch you while you wear that, anyway" she motioned to my hip. "And besides I don't think they're keen on having you as a servant. You're too old."

Too old? The idea seemed absurd. We were nearly the same age! Maybe she meant since they'd not had me as a wee babe I was too old to be tamable. I was about to prove them right.

I looked around the room. A pallet in a corner covered in moss and hay was obviously meant to be my bed. On the other side was a small table with eating utensils, and on the far end hung a privacy curtain—the kind where you could see a person's shadow but not much else.

"For washing up and other private business," She confirmed.

I felt myself blush. I'd never worried about what was and wasn't proper to discuss with a lady before, but I was pretty certain my bathroom habits fell into the category of improper.

"Let me go," I changed the subject. Whatever it was that moss-covered little imp wanted with me, it looked like he was prepared to wait me out, and I didn't have time for that.

"Well that's not for me to decide," she said, puzzled.

Enough of this. I stood and pulled the long-knife from my belt, slamming it into the cage bars. The act jarred my arm somethin' awful. I tried my best not to flinch in front of the girl, but I couldn't help but cradle my shoulder in hopes that my bones would stop vibratin' from the impact.

"Silly boy," she tsk'd. "Them's dragon teeth. Ain't nothin' can cut through them. Not even iron."

"*Dragon's teeth!*" I exclaimed. The bars had to be at least ten times my height. "I ain't never heard of a dragon as big as that!"

The girl giggled. "Of course not, you ninny! You've been shrunk!"

"Shrunk?"

"Of course! How else would you have fit in the Hollow?"

"But that's impossible," I stammered. "I can't be in the Hollow. Not unless..."

What was it the forest gnome had said? "*We walk in the twilight realm...*"

It wasn't just any pathway Brian has sent me into. He'd sent me directly into the land of the Fae.

Chapter Fifteen

THE GIRL WAS RIGHT ABOUT ONE THING. Time did move differently in the twilight realm. Light came and went inside my enclosure, though its source was a mystery to me. I counted three cycles before she returned.

"Long time no see," I gave her a half-hearted smile.

She tilted her head curiously, "Has it been long?"

"Well...I'm not exactly sure," I admitted. The light cycle indicated that it had been 3 days, and yet I'd only just begun to use up the rations in my bag. Maybe it hadn't been as long as I'd thought. I shrugged.

"Have you come back to free me?" Fat chance, but you can't blame a guy for tryin'.

"I told you before, it's not up to me."

"But if it were, you would?" Pressin' the issue was risky, but the possibility of findin' an ally in a land that was foreign to me seemed worth the gamble.

She looked at the ground, coverin' her face with her hair. "S'not wise to cross the Fae." She mumbled, glancing up at me through strands of blonde hair, producing a pair of spin tops from the pockets of her apron. "But I can keep you company." She sat, sliding one of the toys to me. They were just small enough that if spun just right, it could slide through the bars. We took

206

turns sending them back and forth to each other until they crashed into one another. This sparked a new game in which we spun them through the bars, trying to clash with our opponent and throw their spinner out of an imagined arena. Before long we were both laughin' so hard we could hardly breathe. I fell back, clutchin my sides, exhausted.

A small consolation. Or was it? I hadn't found an ally, not really. But perhaps I had found a friend.

She came to visit in regular intervals. She was always shy at first, almost as if she was stuck in a loop. She didn't have much to talk about, so we mostly just played the game.

Then there was a lull in her visits. She hadn't mentioned havin' to stay away, and I began to worry that somethin' had happened to her.

I'd just lost count of the light cycles when she appeared again. Just in time. I was starving. My rations had run out...well I wasn't sure how long ago it was but the ache in my gut said it was plenty long enough.

In place of the usual spin tops, she carried a set of very small wooden bowls on a tray and was silent as she slid them through the bars. I surveyed them suspiciously. The first two were filled with berries and tree nuts, and the third a warm spiced water. "Rosemary tea," she explained when I sniffed it. "Safe to drink."

I wasn't convinced. There were tales back home that warned against eating things offered by the Fae, for fear of becoming trapped in their realm forever.

"We're not that type of Fae." It was the voice of the gnome I had followed into the forest. He'd appeared, seemingly out of nowhere, while I was busy scrutinizin' breakfast. "You're thinking of fairies, most likely. Lure humans and the like to their hollows now and again. Most are catch and release, but a few of 'em grow attached and," he shrugged. "Well they're determined to keep them somehow, and that's as good a way as any. We gnomes have no need of such trickery."

I took a berry from the bowl, inspecting it. It was a deep red, slightly unusual for the season back home, but not overly suspicious. I sniffed it. Smelled normal. Tentatively, I took a bite. It was delicious.

The gnome nodded his approval, then waved a hand in the girl's direction. "You're excused."

She nodded, avoiding eye contact, and left without even a glance in my direction, though how she made her exit I couldn't be certain. She simply faded from existence as she walked away. My eyes lingered where she had been, and the gnome smiled.

"Nice lass, that one. A bit older than we usually take in, but obedient."

There it was again. She couldn't have been much older than me, and he seemed plenty interested in taking me in, for whatever reason.

He waited for me to respond and seemed disappointed when I had nothing to say. "Not one of ours, unfortunately. Too bad, too. We'd have made you a fair trade. It would make things so much easier if she hadn't wandered to the fairy hollow first."

I wrinkled my nose. This guy wasn't makin' any sense, and even if he was I wasn't sure why I should care one way or the other. I mean don't get me wrong, I felt bad for the girl, but I had other things to worry about. Like gettin' outta here, for one. And findin' 'Lana for another.

The gnomes head tilted curiously. "So she's not the one you're lookin' for. My mistake!"

I was gettin' fed up with his tricks. "Get outta my head, those thoughts are mine!"

He smiled, "You could keep me out, if you really wanted to. Just give up the knife."

The damn knife again. "If you've spent half as much time in my head as I think you have, you know I'll do nothing of the sort!"

"A shame. I'd have very much liked to show you around. I'm sure she'd have liked it too, though she won't remember why." He turned to leave, having suddenly lost interest in me.

"Wait!" I trusted him about as far as I could throw him, but that didn't mean I was eager to be left alone again. Pa used to say that too much solitude was bad for one's mind. I hadn't understood why until now. "Who did you think I was lookin' for?"

"Why, the girl of course!" He turned back to face me, his interest reignited.

"What would I want her for? I've never even met her before."

"Or have you?" He raised an eyebrow. "Did you ask her for her name?"

"She didn't remember it."

"Ah, yes that happens sometimes, especially with the older ones." His tone was soft, almost apologetic, "The fairies are foolish in that way, thinking that they are giving a gift when they bestow eternal youth. But it muddles the minds of mortals to do so."

"I don't understand."

"She doesn't remember her true name, or her true self. But she remembers you, I think. After all, you are the reason she is trapped here, in the twilight realm."

"What do you mean, I'm the reason why? I ain't done nothin' to her, or you, or anyone this side of the boundary, ever!" I didn't like where this was going.

"But you have, even if you don't realize it. Even if you don't remember. You see Luka, she had a family, and a name. That name, was Allison."

No. It couldn't be true. I refused to believe it. *It's just a trick. It can't be real.*

"And yet you know it is," he said. "She felt familiar to you, did she not? Though it's been quite a while since you've seen her, judging by your human age."

"Human age?"

"Oh surely they've told you what you really are. If they hadn't you'd never have been granted passage. In fact, I was right when I pegged you for a Stanford, though I'd forgotten the details. Always stubborn, that line. It gets them in trouble from time to time. No wonder they'd wind up with a babe that needed switching."

"Switchin'," I repeated. *Nice job, Luka* I scolded, *A regular old parrot you are.*

"Aye. Seems he'd tangled with some of the fairy lasses from time to time, though he knew better. Gnome blood doesn't mix well with Fae who bare singletons."

He studied my face, noted my confusion, and continued. "Gnomes are born in pairs, you see. Better that way. We may look small, but we are powerful, and big eaters!" He nodded to the wooden bowls which had long been empty. "Twins split the magic, and the appetite. Make it more manageable for everyone. But a singleton—and a mixed one at that—well there was little chance of your own survival. And fairies are but fickle things, no mother has it in her to starve her own child. You had to be switched."

My head swam. So it really was true. Pa hadn't gone mad. *But that meant that Ma—*

"Yes, she did leave because of you. In search of you, in a way. She came to find the real Luka."

I felt my eyes go wide and my heart leapt up into my throat. I gripped my blade instinctively, as if it could protect me from the truth.

"I see you integrated well," his voice was almost empathetic. "I forget how attached some humans become to their offspring. It seems the feelings go both ways, do they not?"

No use denying it. I nodded.

"Then it must pain you to realize her fate."

My mind hadn't even made it that far. I was still gutted over the reason she'd left. "She knew, then?"

"A mother knows her own son, or so I'm told."

"Did she ever find him? The boy I was switched for?"

He shook his head, "The babe was not long for this world when the switch was made. Not even magic can change that."

I half-expected to be relieved knowing that Pa had been right. That there was none alive who could take my place; but instead I just felt sick.

"She came lookin' for him," I whispered to myself. I thought of the way she looked at me as she tended my bruises after a fight. The way she brushed my hair back from my face to kiss my forehead when she'd tucked me in. My hand found its way to my forehead, as if trying to capture the memory.

I hadn't been enough. It was the ultimate betrayal.

"It pains you," the gnome observed. "The intricacies of humanity astound me."

"But I'm not human," I said, wiping my face with my sleeve.

"You've walked among them long enough to take on some of their features, it seems. Perhaps you are more human than you think." He waved a hand in the direction of my own, which still clung tightly to my knife. "Down to using their tools against your true kin."

"I don't want to hurt nobody," I argued. "It's for my own protection, is all."

"Aye, just as those bars you stand behind are for mine. I can't have you wanderin' the realm with such a thing."

It seemed we were at a stalemate.

"I can't very well hand it off, can I? Then what would keep your like from holdin' me here forever."

"Not us you should be worryin' about. We're not the ones who came lookin' for you."

"But my Pa said—"

"He would have, wouldn't he? Wouldn't want you finding out your true powers."

"Powers?"

"Iron bites and iron anchors," he repeated the words he'd used out in the woods. "The human you call Pa may have you believe your prison is protectin' you, rather than holdin' you back from your true potential."

I stared blankly, tryin' to make sense of what was bein' said. *Don't let him get in your head.* I willed myself.

"Try it, if you don't believe me. Leave the blade behind, and you'll find your true potential in the realm. Those bars won't hold you. You'll walk free, and we won't stop you. Even let you take the one you would call Ma, if that is your choosing."

"But won't the fairies notice her missing?" There had to be a catch.

"Of course they would! There is a bit of politics involved in it all. Funny creatures, fairies. Though they relinquished you to our care, they considered the trade their own. Don't like to get their hands dirty, you see. When the human babe... let's just say that they felt cheated out of something they felt was theirs."

He must have noticed the look of disgust on my face, for he paused there.

"Suffice to say they would happily have had you re-switched, had the one you call Pa not surrounded you in a cage of iron."

"And now? Would they still re-switch me?"

"No need for it now, not for you. You were only switched to keep you from wastin' away. The moment you weaned they could have taken you back if they wanted." He rolled his eyes, "Don't like getting' their hands dirty, no, but they have no problem reapin' the reward once the job is done."

"And you?" I asked. What part did they play in all of this?

He waved a hand, "We'd have welcomed you with open arms if that is why you'd come. Indeed, that was my hope when I first saw you. But we've no interest in takin' folk that don't want to be here."

"And yet you had no qualms in trappin' me!"

"I offered you a choice, if you remember. You're the one who walked into my home armed."

He made a solid point, though I hated to admit it.

"So now what?"

"Now, I'm going to send in the girl, and I'm going to walk away. Whatever happens after that is up to you." He turned to go, pausing just a moment to call over his shoulder. "But I warn you, whatever decision you make, be quick about it. Once they find their trade missing, they will come for you, and you may very well find yourself wanting them to."

"Fat chance!" I yelled after him, but if he heard me he gave no indication. Unperturbed, he walked away, disappearing into the light.

Chapter Sixteen

I DIDN'T HAVE TO WAIT VERY LONG before the girl returned, this time empty handed.

"I was told to keep you company," she said simply, sitting on the floor outside of my enclosure.

I looked at her more closely this time. She was dressed simply in an off-white dress without frills or embellishments. Her blonde hair was only half tied-back, with bangs that just barely brushed the tops of her eyebrows, a style reserved for girls who were still young to not be entirely proper. And yet, there was something about her eyes. Something comforting and familiar, like the smell of your own bed after nights of sleepin' somewhere else. It was there only a moment before it faded again, replaced once more with an almost vacant look.

"Ma?" I whispered in spite of myself.

"I'd imagine she's here somewhere," she said, mistakin' my intent. "Though you're not likely to find much comfort I'm afraid. Few Fae raise their own young in the way you're used to. It's a cruelty really, to expect one who was switched to reintegrate."

"So ya've a mind of yer own after all," I breathed a sigh of relief. "Allison."

"What?"

"Allison. That was yer name, before." *Best tread carefully.* I thought to myself. I had no idea the extent of the fairy's control over her, and givin' her too much information at once could be dangerous. I figured it was best for me too, thinkin' of her as a person aside from the one who had raised me. Mother and son weren't our roles anymore, at least not right now, and muddyin' that up with sentiment and wishes would only make what I was about to do more dangerous.

"Do ya ever wonder what yer life was like before?" I asked. "Ya must have..." suddenly my heart was racing. I wiped my hands on my tunic, suddenly aware they'd gone clammy. "Ya must have a family."

"I must have," she said, as if she were only just realizin' it was true. "I mean, I suppose we all do, in one way or another. I hadn't thought of it, really. Not in a long time, anyway."

"And if ya have a family, it stands to reason that they'd miss ya." I continued.

"Aye, I suppose they would, if they were a good one. Some aren't, I hear."

"I'm sure yers were plenty good," I replied a little too quickly. "Err, but either way, don't ya think they'd want to know what happened to ya?"

"Perhaps?" she didn't seem to follow, and I was gettin' frustrated with beatin' around the bush.

"Allison, have ya ever thought of leavin' here?"

"Certainly, I must have, in the beginning," her voice was shaky and uncertain. "But humans cannot pass between the realms. Not of their own will, anyway."

"But if ya were at the will of one of the Fae, then ya could, couldn't ya?" Her face lit up with understanding. "You mean, if you were to take me?"

I'd expected her to be more excited. After all, I was offering her freedom! If I were her I'd be jumpin' at the thought of freedom, yet she seemed uncertain. Maybe if I could jog her memory a bit she'd be more enthusiastic.

"Don't ya remember anything? At all?" I leaned in, both eager and afraid to hear her answer.

214

She bit her lip. The silence seemed to stretch on forever, and I began to wonder if there was a time limit on the gnome's offer to let us walk free. Finally, she spoke:

"I...I think I remember looking for something. Or someone." She looked at me apologetically, shrugging.

"What if it was me?" I offered. It was true enough, in a way. Or was it just what I wished were true?

The statement piqued her interest. "You?"

"Yes! What if ya were sent to look for me?" I was grasping at straws trying to fill in the blanks in a way that might make sense.

She leaned in, examining my face closely. "You do seem familiar, somehow."

"Great! It's settled then! Do ya know how to get out of here?"

"Out of the gnome's hollow? Yes. Servants are able to travel within the twilight realm as needed, just not out of it."

That brought up another issue: Could I get us out of here? Even if I found the portal Brian had sent me through, could it be used both ways? And for that matter, wouldn't it just send me back home? *One problem at a time*, I reminded myself, takin' in a deep breath. I removed my long knife from my belt and set it down beside me. I felt suddenly lighter, as if I'd been carryin' an invisible weight on my shoulders I'd not realized. I stood nervously, waitin' to see if it was a trick and the fae folk were just waitin' out of sight to snatch me up. Nothing happened. At least, that's what I thought until I heard Allison gasp.

I looked up at her face—wait, up? Yes! Either she'd grown a good two feet or I'd shrunk. Lookin' around the room I guessed the latter. The wooden bowls that had carried my breakfast were near big enough to wear as head coverin's, and that wasn't all! The spacing between the bars of my enclosure seemed infinitely wider. If I turned just right, maybe I could squeeze through.

Allison let out a quiet squeal as I tested my theory and found it successful. I was free!

"But now you're tiny!" she exclaimed, as if I hadn't noticed. I felt my face flush in irritation and before I knew what was happening I met her eye to eye. The world shifted and my head spun, causin' me to stumble. I was me-sized again!

"Whoa." Allison said, wide-eyed. "I've never seen anyone do THAT before!"

"Do what, exactly?"

"Change size without changin' shape."

"Huh?"

"The Fae can shapeshift some, mostly out of a need to camouflage in the day-and-night realms. Some are better at it than others; but I've never seen one that could shift size and stay their own shape before."

I decided it wasn't the best time to tell her I'd not done it on purpose. I found myself glancing longingly over my shoulder and wonderin' if I could reach through the bars and grab my knife after all, but it seemed to have disappeared into thin air. My stomach sank. No goin' back now.

"Alright then, c'mon," I said, taking her hand. "How do we get out of here?"

"Oh, that's easy," she said, walkin' toward the far wall. "Through here!"

"Through where?" It looked like an ordinary wall. Stark white, but solid as any other wall I'd ever seen.

"Just think of the light," she explained as if it were obvious, "But not too much light. Wouldn't wanna over-shoot.

I didn't have time to ask any more questions. She stepped forward, and a light appeared. I barely had time to will myself through with thoughts of light as she pulled me along. *But not too much light!* I added, hoping that was enough.

I don't know what I'd expected when the light faded, but whatever it was was nothing like what lay before us. Instead of open forest, we appeared to be in a large ballroom. At least, as much as I knew what that looked like, and that wasn't much. Most of what I knew was based on stories that Pa used to tell when I was little, about the great parties the King used to throw, and how would he know about that, anyway?

Whatever the room we were in was, I knew it was important. The floor was ivory with symbols painted in a spiral in different shades of green and blue. The walls appeared to be made of wood, carved with fancy forest scenes. A fawn and its mum, guarded by a man in the distance covered the wall on one side. A sleeping dragon being watched by a great bird on the other...no. Its body was that of a bird, but it bore a woman's likeness from the chest up. The pairing was nothing short of horrifying.

"A Harpy," Allison explained. "Representations of the day-and-night-realms. We are in the in-between."

"The in-between?" I repeated. Seemed I was about as a good as a common parrot lately.

"The twilight realm," she said, as if it were obvious. "The place in between day," she motioned to the picture of the fawn with one hand. "And night." With the other hand she pointed to the harpy.

"Ya mean, like the boundary to the Darklands?"

She tilted her head and squinted her eyes as if tryin' to solve a puzzle.

"Precisely like the boundary to the Darklands," A voice rang like bells all around us. I spun, trying to find its source. I found none.

"We exist in the in-between," The voice echoed off the walls around us, making its source impossible to pinpoint "Where the outside world sees good and evil, we see shades of grey."

"Who's there?" I looked to Allison for an explanation.

"I'm sorry," she mouthed silently, folding her arms against herself in shame.

I looked up and was blinded by a white light. I blinked against it, finally able to make out the shape of a woman. She had long flowing hair that wrapped around her like a gown. She floated down on us, her green iridescent wings flitterin' swiftly to keep her aloft. I felt my jaw go slack in awe as her bare feet landed silently beside us. She touched Allison's hair gently, the way a mother might to a child. Allison flinched, shrinking away from her touch. I decided, whoever this creature was, she was not to be trusted.

A decision that was validated when the fairy spoke:

"Such a good little servant," she cooed. "You've brought me my son."

CHAPTER SEVENTEEN

"**Y**-YOUR WHAT?" I stammered. The sight of her had taken the breath out of my lungs, so that my statement was nothing more than a whisper.

"I'm sorry!" Allison moved toward me, but the fairy thrust her arm out, blocking her.

"That's quite enough, Allison. You are dismissed."

She looked as if she'd been struck across the face. Still she sighed and turned obediently, walking down a corridor that I was sure hadn't been there before.

"Wait!" I called out after her. "Ma-Allison" in my haste to keep her from disappearin' from my sight I forgot myself. If she'd heard me, she gave no indication.

"Now, now, boy," the fairy said. "That's quite enough of that. We've much to catch up on, you and I." She wrapped an arm around my shoulder warmly and guided me toward the carving of the deer.

"Lovely, isn't it? So bright, so innocent," her crystal eyes locked on mine and she smiled sadly. "So easily tainted by mankind." She waved toward the outline of the man in the distance. I hadn't noticed it before, but he carried a bow and a sliver of arrows: A hunter.

"Not unlike you." Her voice was sweet, comfortin' in a way. I felt my mind start to slip away, like the feelin' you get right before you fall asleep. She squeezed my shoulder reassuringly, guiding me to the carving on the other side of the wall. This one felt more ominous. The harpy flew against a dark purple sky, claws extended as if to attack.

"Look again," the fairy leaned in and I saw what I had missed. I had been thrown off guard by the beast's appearance that I hadn't seen the harpy's true aim: A branch holding a nest of hatchlings.

"Strange," I murmured, for it felt as if both scenes had changed as I had looked at them.

"Or perhaps it was you who changed," the fairy suggested. I was beginning to resent the Fae's mind reading abilities. I closed my eyes, tryin' to will her outta my head.

"Oftentimes the things we believe to be matters of right and wrong actually exist in shades of grey," she went on, ignoring my attempts to block her out.

"Take you, for instance. You who were not supposed to be. Not supposed to survive. And yet, here you are. Fierce, and strong. More so than any other offspring I've ever borne." She put her hand under my chin and lifted my head one way, then the other, examinin' me.

"A bit of your father's looks, no doubt. Maybe even some of his powers. We shall see."

"We shall do nothin' of the sort!" I shot back, yanking my mind out of the fog she'd laid over it. "I'll not fall for this—this—whatever you're doin'!" I shrugged her arm off my shoulders. "I want no part of it. Bring Allison back! Bring back my Ma!"

"Silly thing," her wings fluttered, lifting her feet from the stone. "I am your mother. There is no other."

"Maybe you bore me, but you're no mother to me!" I spat back.

"You'd take the one who abandoned you in my stead?"

"Better than someone who would keep a human as a slave!"

"Allison is a thief and a cheat. She is serving her sentence according to the law of the Fae."

I felt my face flush with anger as I balled my hands into fists at my sides. My body was so tense it shook as I tried to talk myself off the ledge. Actin' on my anger would only be satisfyin' for a minute and could have dire consequences. Better to wait until I had a better idea of what was happenin'. My nostrils flared as I forced myself to take in a breath and hold it. The air chilled my lungs, makin' them burn somethin' fierce.

The Fae woman watched with interest as I let the breath out, slowly.

"See?" she said, "Much like the carvings on the wall, you change the closer I look." She was pleased.

"Do I?" I chose my words carefully, "Or is it just that ya don't really know me in the first place?"

"Oh, I know that temper well," she laughed. "I'd bet anything your childhood was full of royal tantrums."

The way she said it made me uneasy. "I got in my share of scuffles. 'Til Ma' taught me how to control it."

She glared at me from the corner of her eye and I thought I caught the hint of a grimace on her face when I said the word 'Ma'. But it didn't come from a place of hurt, not in the way it was supposed to. It was more from offense, as if she was put off havin' been replaced by a mortal woman.

I decided she could take offense all she liked. I was no trophy to be won.

"Ya said -Ma—," I used the term intentionally this time, delightin' in the way she tried to hide her displeasure. "Ya said she was a cheat. That she was bein' punished. Tell me more about that."

"Oh well, that. It was some time ago. A boring story." She waved a hand dismissively. "We've so much more important things to catch up on."

"Tell me now or I turn around and leave." I was bluffin' but I hoped she couldn't tell. I stayed my mind on the idea of walkin' back through the wall, to the place where I'd left my iron knife. I held onto that thought as hard as I could and looked her square in the eye.

It worked.

"Very well," she sighed. "It was, as I said, some time ago. The girl you call Allison came to us here in the twilight realm."

"I thought mortals couldn't enter on their own. Not without an invite or such." The details were a bit foggy, but I was pretty sure the gnome had said somethin' along those lines.

"Who said she travelled alone?" She raised an eyebrow. "We are creatures of the in-between, the Fae. Most of us keep to our own, but we have a few rogues that fall here and there on either side of things." She looked at the picture of the doe "The one who came with her was from the Alliance. Thought she was helping the poor lass. Little did anyone know the girl had come to steal from us."

"Steal?!" My mind couldn't conjure a reason that Ma would seek the wrath of the Fae in such a way.

"You see, she'd come for the child. *Her* child," she held my gaze for emphasis. "Of course, such things do happen now and again. Depending on why a changeling was switched we do occasionally trade back. Those who do not pose a threat to the Hollow are welcomed back with open arm. Such would have been the case for you."

Ma had known. She'd found out, some way or another, and done exactly what Pa was afraid she would do. She came lookin' for her own child. No wonder he was so sore about her leavin'. It hadn't just been a betrayal to him, but to our whole family.

And yet, could he really blame her? Could I? If you'd come to find that the child you'd borne was switched out for another, would you not want to at least make sure it was well cared for? Could you live with not knowin'? My mind bounced back and forth between anger and forgiveness. The fairy seemed to enjoy this, for she looked on silently a long while. I felt as if my thoughts had shattered into a million pieces, and I was strugglin' to pick them back up. I shook my head, tryin' to clear it.

"She thought she could have you both." The tension melted from my shoulders as her words echoed in the cavern. "Though we'd made a deal to trade, it soon became clear that her plan was to take the human child and run, with no plan to return my own. When she found that the babe hadn't survived, she rescinded her deal and tried to escape. Obviously, we couldn't let that happen. She'd promised me my son! I could hardly let her walk free.

And so here she stays, my humble servant. I figured perhaps someday you would come searching for her yourself. If not...well her service would have to do."

Her face lit up as she finished the tale, "And now, here you are. The best of both options!"

"Take me in her stead!" I suggested, forgettin' why I'd even come in the first place. It had been important, the reason. *Surely it was for Ma*, the thought filled my mind until it became as good as memory.

*Yes! That's it. They sent me to rescue her! I've got to rescue...*The thought slipped from my mind like sand through my fingers. I stared at my hands, and then up again.

I have to...take me instead of...

"Ma?"

A face greeted me, basked in warm light. She brushed the hair from my face, folding her wings behind her as she smiled.

"Yes, son," she cooed, wrapping her arm around my shoulder. "Welcome back."

BOOK THREE

ABSOLUTION

PROLOGUE

A FIGURE STOOD IN THE ENTRY OF HER CAVE. She studied it, surprised to find it was not the one she had been expecting. The silhouette was broad-shouldered and filled out. Nothing like the wisp of a figure the prince had become during his life on the run.

"Reveal yourself," the dragon called. It was a warning. One wrong move and her new visitor would find himself in quite the predicament. She wasn't supposed to eat bipeds, but she was betting he didn't know that. She was also betting that no one else would know if she just took a little nibble.

"Peace, Fiora," a voice called as he stepped into the light. "I come in peace."

"The Vagabond. The Prodigal Son." It wasn't a compliment. "What brings you here? Hiding out from those who hunt you? How quaint." Fiora polished a fang with her tongue nonchalantly. One couldn't help but get the feeling she was the kind to taunt her prey before a kill.

"Never did quite understand that last one," Grandfather remarked as he brushed his hair back from his face. A clear sign that he was nervous. "But it seems to have stuck around a while, hasn't it? I take it I'm not the visitor you were expecting. What have you been up to, Dragon?"

"I could ask the same of you, Wanderer. State your business. Could it be you've come here seeking refuge from those who hunt you?"

"I've done as you asked." Brian ignored her question. His current relationship with his own kind was none of her business. Especially not when the fate of everyone else was at stake. "The boy will follow her."

Fiora smirked, pleased with herself.

"Do not think this absolves you of your sins," she cautioned.

"You know as well as anyone I wouldn't have given her that confounded thing if I'd known what it was!"

"And yet, many are dead due to your carelessness."

"I'm not the one who called on the Elite," he protested. "Cain betrayed his own, not I!"

"And how did he happen upon their location?"

Brian avoided eye contact out of shame rather than fear. "I didn't know he was under the influence of an Amasai. He simply gave me a gift for my granddaughter and asked about his son. He betrayed me too!"

"Are you so starved for absolution that you let yourself believe he was capable of redemption?" He thought he detected a hint of pity in her tone. He lifted his chin high.

"I have no use for pity, and no need for forgiveness."

"And yet, there is blood on your hands."

He couldn't help but stare at his palms, as if expecting the accusation to take on a physical manifestation. He took note of their leathery appearance as he curled them into fists. The act irritated his joints more than he would like to admit. He was too old to have this argument with the dragon. Too old to be begging others for their approval. He decided to change the subject instead.

"Why the boy?"

Fiora lifted an eyebrow but let the matter drop. "He has his part to play, as do we all."

"You've been playing with the Professor's looking glass again."

"I have a duty to fulfill." Her voice was a low growl as she pulled herself up from her pile of treasure. Brian held his hands up in submission, only lowering them when the beast settled.

"Few can boast the loyalty of a dragon," he offered. "'Tis no skin off my back, as long as my 'Lana is safe."

"She will be, as long as she fulfills her role." The dragon's demeanor softened. "We all seek absolution, Brian. Don't let your pride put your loved ones in more danger than it has already."

It was both a commiseration and a warning.

"Aye." He ran his fingers over his beard and sighed. "And what will you do, then?"

"I shall seek council with the Priestess, before moving forward," Fiora said.

"Eoma? What do you want with the likes of her?"

"The Priestess and I are old ... friends." The beast smiled. "It's past time I paid her a visit."

CHAPTER ONE

I JUMPED AS A BRANCH SNAPPED UNDER MY FEET, startling me in the dark. The further we had ventured into the Uncharted Territories, the thicker the foliage overhead had become. It was almost as if it were intentional. Like the branches of the trees had drawn toward one another in an attempt to sabotage our efforts. Even with my half-elf sight, I struggled to make heads or tails of our surroundings. The forest was no longer friendly.

"*Dark Lands.*" The echo of Nova's voice in my mind made me shiver. Whether she was taking note of our proximity to the dark breeds, or simply making an observation about the lack of light, I wasn't certain. Either way, it was as good a name as any, and I wasn't really in the mood to clarify.

"*Stupid horse,*" the Darkness muttered as Nova tugged at her harness, protesting my lack of response.

I tugged back. "Knock it off, Nova. I'm trying to concentrate."

As if on cue, I stubbed my toe on a root I could have sworn hadn't been there a minute ago. My whole body tensed as I suppressed my desire to scream. Something about staying silent through the pain multiplied its intensity.

Nova snorted. It translated into something like, *I told you so.*

"Well maybe if you did a better job at guiding me I could focus!" I shoved her with my shoulder before stomping away, only to find myself not a minute later, splayed out on the forest floor with a mouthful of dirt.

The Darkness laughed.

I stood slowly, assessing the damage. Nothing hurt except for my pride. *Serves me right*, I thought to myself. The Darkness didn't argue.

Behind me, Nova pressed her nose against my side reassuringly. I sighed. It wasn't her fault we were in this mess. I was the one who had veered us off course. I was the one who insisted I would track Luka better on foot. A lot of good that had done. Even in the proper light there had been no trace of his presence in the woods. In fact, there was no trace of anyone at all. The forest floor was completely undisturbed, save for the path Nova and I had created.

Nova chose not to respond to my frustration. After two days of tracking we were both exhausted. Maybe she figured that excused my behavior, or maybe she was too fatigued to argue. Either way, I felt a wave of guilt wash over me as my words settled in my mind.

"I'm sorry," I offered, scratching her neck affectionately. She turned her head and pushed her muzzle into my shoulder reassuringly. "I'm tired and scared for my friend."

Nova nickered quietly. *"I'm scared too."*

I leaned into her, taking in her comforting smell as I stroked her forehead. "I know. It's okay. We'll get through this together, all right?" I had spent so much time depending on her for guidance that I had lost sight of the fact that she, too, was still little more than a child. For a moment we stood there, absorbing the enormity of the situation we found ourselves in. Chasing Luka had veered us off our original path and I feared that, even with Nova, we may not find our way back again. Not only were we vulnerable to the creatures banished to this part of the forest, but we had no way of knowing if Cain was still in pursuit of us.

"You're doomed no matter what you do, foolish child," Anhedonia seemed to grow stronger the deeper we made it into the forest, and I was beginning to once again have trouble distinguishing between my own self-doubt and the Amasai's influence, even in Nova's presence.

"We should find shelter," I decided. It was no use trying to track a trail that didn't exist, especially if we were both exhausted. She snorted loudly, pulling away and tossing her head back and forth in protest. I didn't have to wait for the gesture to translate, I already knew what she was thinking. Our last search for shelter hadn't exactly gone as planned. Instead of escaping the elements we'd found ourselves captives of the dragon, Fiora.

"What other choice do we have?"

She pulled to the side, back the way we had come. While the way before us was dark and overgrown, a dim light appeared in the distance along the path we had blazed through the woods, as if the forest were lighting our way back.

Like it wants us to leave. I bit my lip, taking note of how obvious the trail we'd created was. Cain would have no trouble tracking us, especially considering his familiarity with the terrain. He was no stranger to the Dark Lands.

"I'm not leaving Luka," I said.

"Not. Safe." Nova insisted, accentuating every thought-word.

He certainly had no problem leaving you, the Darkness countered.

That settled it.

"Anhedonia wants us to turn back. As far as I'm concerned, whatever the Amasai wants, we do the opposite."

Nova's ears twitched. She wasn't convinced.

"He's getting louder," I confessed. "The further into the Dark Lands we get. I think he's afraid too."

"Afraid," Nova echoed. *"All afraid."* Again, she pulled away, shuffling her hooves in trepidation.

A searing pain behind my eyes had me doubled over before I could reassure her. Much like the feeling I'd gotten when Fiora tried to take Anhedonia from me, pain shot through my skull. But this time, it came with something else. Images of a forest, the feeling of being on horseback, and a voice that was both strange and eerily familiar at the same time.

"The trees have no need to hide the light from friends."

The image faded into white light, and the pain subsided. I drew in several gasping breaths before standing and wiping the sweat from my brow.

Nova tossed her head, leaning into me while I regained my bearings

"*What was that?*"

I rubbed my eyes, blinking away the white orbs that lingered.

"I ... I think it was a memory," I stammered, trying to make sense of what I'd just experienced.

"*Not yours,*" she replied matter-of-factly.

"No, not mine," Anhedonia's voice was no longer the only one invading my mind. Other thoughts—some familiar and some foreign—had begun to make themselves known. Among the elven people this was known as the Awakening. The process by which all the knowledge of our bloodlines is unlocked. For most it occurred at a younger age, somewhere around ten. But it seemed I was a late bloomer. Not surprising, given my half-human heritage.

It was an odd feeling, this acquiring of memories that weren't mine. Sometimes it came to me as if I were recalling a previous school lesson. Other times it came like this one had: In a flash of visual and auditory input.

But it had never been accompanied by pain. No, that had to have come from somewhere else.

Or someone else.

"A memory the Darkness doesn't want me to have," I murmured. Nova stared at me quizzically, stamping a hoof. She still wanted to turn back.

"Okay," I said, taking another breath. "Okay, I hear you but wait. I want to try something."

I stumbled my way through the dark until my hands pressed against the trunk of the nearest tree. With everything in me I willed it to believe I was friend, not foe. How does one convince a tree of this? I had no idea, and frankly I wasn't too keen on trying, considering my last encounter with a tree had almost gotten me killed.

"*Not just killed,*" Anhedonia reminded me. "*Eaten. Prey, even to the plants out here. Best turn back before it's too late.*"

It was hard to argue with the voice, not because it was louder, but because it made a good point. Every decision I'd made up to this point had only led us into more danger. If I had known what had awaited me when I ran away, would I have made the same choices? I looked over my shoulder to Nova, who stared expectantly but said nothing. If she could change her decision to follow me into this wilderness, would she? When I'd agreed to take her along I'd hoped only for a steed, and maybe a companion. If I had known the depth of her intelligence, let alone how young she was, I never would have let her come.

Or would I? This time the thought was my own. I'd been so lost in myself, felt so alone, that I'd have settled for any measure of comfort I could find, and Nova had provided more than enough of that.

And where would you have me go, anyway? I asked the Darkness. *After all, it was you who willed me to leave in the first place.*

"No one forced your hand, child." His voice was hypnotic. "I merely brought forward the fears I found within. You wanted to leave."

We could play this game forever. The game of what came first. Was the darkness inside my mind something planted by an outside force, or merely a part of me brought to the surface by Anhedonia's presence?

"It doesn't matter." I blushed as I realized the words in my heart had spilled from my lips, hoping my shame wasn't visible to Nova in the low light.

Wait, could it be? I scanned the treetops for confirmation. Tiny beams of light had begun to shine through their foliage in small patches. A wave of apprehension shot through me, much like when I'd dip my toe in the pond before the first summer swim, testing the waters.

It was only after I removed my hand from the tree that I realized the feeling was not my own: It belonged to the forest. Tentatively, I ran my fingers along the rough bark of the tree once more. The feeling returned. My head filled with a sound that was somewhere between a buzz and a hum, not unlike what I experienced when Nova spoke to me.

I looked over my shoulder at her. "Can you hear that?" The sound grew louder, drowning out her response, but I could guess what she was thinking from the way she tossed her head. *Hear what?* I closed my eyes, concentrating on the noise. It became less like a buzz and more like a hum. Or rather, several hums. As I homed in on the sensation, pulling it into the front of my mind, it became more apparent that what I was hearing was not one voice, but several. I couldn't make out what they were saying, or whom they were saying it to, but I was able to pick up the tone of it. Some of the voices sang a light, but cautious harmony. The notes were high and airy, like wind chimes.

The responding song, in contrast, was bold and low. The bass of it filled my skull, vibrating my bones from my head down to my toes.

The two went back and forth a few times, one pausing for the other's response, each with an increasing sense of urgency.

"The trees are arguing," I realized aloud, opening my eyes. I half expected Nova to provide a snarky reply. After all, it sounded crazy. Instead she blinked, as if surprised I hadn't figured it out sooner.

"Hey, give me a break! How was I supposed to know trees could talk, let alone argue?"

I think if she could have rolled her eyes at me she would have. The new light revealed a patch of dandelions at her feet. Her tail twitched, obviously conflicted. On the one hand we didn't seem to be in immediate danger, but that didn't mean we were safe. I nodded my permission and her stomach won her over. She grazed contentedly as I turned my attention back to the trees.

During my lessons with Cazlyn I'd learned that elves were gifted in the area of language, which was part of why they'd made such great ambassadors during the times before the wars. Such was a gift I seemed to be lacking, whether from lack of exposure, or my human heritage, I was uncertain. I knew the trees were talking amongst themselves, but I had no idea what they were saying. I was sure it had something to do with us, though. Or, at least, with me. Why else would their limbs have parted to let the light in?

I looked overhead as my hand rested against the rough bark of the tree once more. It was tall, but not as tall as some of the others, and its trunk was narrow in comparison to the others. Yet, it had leaned away to make way for the sun, I was almost positive. I closed my eyes, focusing on the tree and trying to identify its individual "voice". It took me awhile to untangle it from the other, but eventually I was successful. I still couldn't make out any words, but the sound had a unique pitch, one in a higher octave than those who responded to it.

They're arguing with the elders! My heart skipped a beat at the thought. I'd reasoned that the higher-pitched hums must belong to the forest's youth. The lower sounds carried more authority, and the higher seemed timorous in their replies. The humming intensified, the sounds overlapping one another.

"I wonder what they're talking about," I mumbled to myself.

"They're talking about you." I nearly jumped out of my own skin. I knew that voice! I spun excitedly.

"Nykolas!"

Chapter Two

I RAN INTO HIS OPEN ARMS with enough force to make him lose his footing. He stumbled backwards, nearly falling to the ground as I clung to him.

"It's been too long," he said, placing a hand atop my head affectionately as he leaned down to embrace me. I buried my face in his shoulder. His tunic smelled faintly of oak and sunshine. It felt like home. Suddenly I was overcome with homesickness. I swallowed hard, trying to choke the feeling down before it could escape from me. Like flipping a switch, the feeling was gone. I pulled myself out of his embrace, having regained my composure.

"What are you doing here?" I asked.

"Funny, I was about to ask you the same thing." His tone was soft, but not without authority as he pulled back to look me over. I dropped my gaze to the ground, hoping he couldn't hear the sound of my heart trying to burst through my ribcage. Did he know I'd run away?

"How did you find me?"

He motioned skyward as if it should be obvious. "The trees, of course. You've created quite the conflict among them, I'm afraid." He winked playfully, the way he used to do when I was little and in trouble with Mother. It was his way of saying, *It's okay, I've got this.*

"You can hear them too?"

He grinned. "Having a wood nymph for a mother has its advantages."

Sapphire. I'd almost forgotten my encounter with her. It felt like a lifetime ago. I looked up at my uncle, whose red eyes met mine with just a hint of mischief.

"The forest speaks of many things," he said, answering the question I hadn't dared to ask. "Did you think no one would notice a young elven girl sneaking across the boundary?"

"We didn't mean to!" It wasn't entirely true, but I was hoping he didn't know that. "I mean ... it's complicated. I—"

"Ran away," he finished the sentence with an admission I hadn't planned on offering freely. So, he did know. I looked at the ground, ashamed.

"'Lana." He knelt beside me, placing a hand on my shoulder. "What were you thinking, taking off on your own?"

Nova whinnied behind me. *"She wasn't alone!"*

"Aye, not entirely." I gasped. He could hear her too! I stared at him in shock.

"There is much you do not know." He seemed to read my own thoughts as well.

"Yeah, so I've noticed. Our family sure loves hiding things from me." I crossed my arms, knowing I was acting childish and yet not really caring. Though I was long past the age of childish outbursts, in that moment I wanted nothing more than to stomp my feet in protest and wail.

"Yes, well." He rubbed the back of his neck as he tried to gather the words that would best appease me. Being half-nymph, the intricacies of human relationships often escaped him. Nymphs did not raise their own young, and so a tantruming girl in the woods would be a situation for which he had no context.

"He was in on it," the Darkness sneered. *"He's no better than the rest of them."*

"There was really no helping much of it, 'Lana," Nykolas admitted.

He was right. I knew he was, and yet my anger still boiled beneath the surface, forcing the words out of me the way a tea kettle forces steam out its spout. "You knew this would happen. That they would come for me. Didn't you?"

Nykolas sighed. "Keeping the truth from you was for your own protection. One slip of the tongue and you'd have doomed not only yourself, but those closest to you."

I scoffed. *Those closest to me indeed.* Even as I thought the words I realized I was focusing on the wrong issues. Seeing Nykolas had brought up old wounds and I'd almost forgotten about—

"Luka!" I exclaimed, snapping out of it. "That's why I'm here. I mean, I ran away and all, but Luka is why we crossed the boundary. Except not really, but—" Nykolas placed a finger on my lips to silence me. Though his touch was gentle, it disoriented me. I felt myself sway on my feet, just a little. It was enough to give me away.

"She needs water." Nykolas' eyes narrowed as he turned to Nova, who looked up from her grazing momentarily. Her ears twitched defensively. Being half-nymph, my uncle did not experience the emotions that came from family ties quite the way other beings did. Indeed, Mother had often marveled at how he fretted over me when I was a babe. They locked eyes a long while, and I grew uncomfortable. It was almost as if they were arguing, yet they were silent. I didn't appreciate being shut out.

"Leave her be," I demanded. "She's barely more than a foal herself!" At this Nova snorted indignantly. I pretended not to notice.

His attention returned to me and he sighed. "Very well."

He turned to the nearest tree and placed his hand against it, making a soft whooshing sound. The trees rustled in response, though I felt no wind. Without even looking at me, he turned and walked further into the forest, a path in the foliage parting before his feet.

"Come," he commanded.

I shot Nova an apologetic look before darting after him.

My lungs burned as I trailed after him, careful to stay close so as to take advantage of the trail the forest made for him. Briefly I had glanced back to see the foliage zip back into place silently behind us. Clearly the forest only meant to let him through. I pushed aside my exhaustion and forced myself to keep pace as Nova trotted beside me.

"Easier if you rode," her mind reached out to mine alone.

I shook my head. *"Not right now!"*

Still, I found myself leaning into her as we followed.

"Where are we going?" I gasped. What I really meant was *How much farther?* My legs were beginning to buckle under me as I ran.

"To my home." He was short in his reply. "We're almost there," he added as an afterthought, no doubt trying to sound encouraging. The attempt fell short.

I'd never considered that he might have a home. Not a proper one, anyway. Our time together had been limited to places the eyes of King Ludlum did not wander—which didn't leave too many options. I tried to imagine my uncle in a cottage somewhere in the Darklands. Would it be made of stone, or wood? Would it have a thatched roof? The idea seemed absurd, though I couldn't put my finger on why.

Then we came to the clearing. It was small, maybe the size of my old bedroom twice over. In the center stood a single tree. The bark was a smooth reddish-brown and was adorned by a crown of spear-shaped leaves.

"Bay Laurel," I whispered in awe. A rare tree in Irving's Kingdom, the leaf of a Bay Laurel had several medicinal uses. I'd never seen one in person, but I recognized the aroma released from the leaves as the wind rustled them.

"Yes, well." Nykolas scratched the back of his head sheepishly. "Mother is a Daphnaeae, so..." he trailed off.

Of course. The Daphnaeae were nymphs who lived in Laurels. But that meant—

"You have a host tree?!"

"Of sorts, yes." He avoided eye contact. His matronage was a source of embarrassment for him still, but I could not have been more honored to share his secret. I crept toward it cautiously, hesitating as my uncle drew nearer. He made eye contact briefly, nodding. I pressed my hand against its trunk, expecting it to be cool as the other tree had. I was surprised to find the opposite was true. This tree was warm and full of life like none I had ever encountered before.

"It was from this tree that I was born," he said reverently. His shoulders relaxed, and he placed his hand against its trunk, like he was greeting an old friend. "Though, unlike my mother, my mortality is not chained to it, I am dependent on the shelter of my tree for rejuvenation from time to time. The tree provides all I need. Which reminds me." He whispered to the tree, whose branches rustled in response. The tree creaked, and a hollow appeared where I was certain none had been only moments before. Nykolas reached his hand inside and retrieved a clear orb.

"Careful," he warned, handing it to me gently. "It's fragile in this form."

"Water?" I marveled at how it held its shape.

"Encased in resin," Nykolas explained as he pulled another orb from the tree, pinching the resin softly to create a spout. The orb shrunk as he drank from it but held its shape. I followed his example. The water was cool and slightly sweet, like nothing I'd ever tasted before. It wasn't long until my strength was renewed.

"Now, little 'Lana." Nykolas motioned for me to sit and I obliged. The grass was soft like eider down beneath me. I leaned against the Laurel and its warmth enveloped me. Suddenly a wave of exhaustion washed over my body. "Why did you run?"

Sometimes we spend so much of our energy masking our true feelings to push through the thing we are trying to survive, that we forget they even exist until they come pouring out of us. Tears rolled down my cheeks as I recounted the events that had led me to flee the safehold. Nykolas listened patiently without interjection as I unloaded my every fear and sorrow, all the way up to my vision of Luka in the woods. When it was over, he pulled me close, kissing the top of my head gently.

"Sleep," he whispered, and the world went dark.

CHAPTER THREE

OR THE FIRST TIME IN A LONG WHILE, my sleep was dreamless, though I did sense the deep hum of the tree. It lulled me deeper, like a lullaby. When I awoke my body felt renewed in a way I hadn't experienced since before the days of Anhedonia.

I looked around for signs of my travel companions. I did not have to search very far. Nova was grazing at my feet. She looked up. *"Awake, finally."* She sighed.

"Where is Nykolas?" I stood, stretching the sleep from my body. It felt glorious.

Nova snorted softly, nodding in the direction of the Laurel. *"Still sleeping,"* she answered shortly.

I wondered how much more talking had gone on between the two of them while I'd slept.His mother's side did not live in family groups or raise their own young. Yet he had always had a soft spot where I was concerned. Mother said there was something about little ones that brought out the softness in him. He had, from the beginning, been my protector.

I hoped he had not been too hard on Nova on my behalf. I also secretly hoped our bond would mean he'd help me in my endeavor to save Luka, rather than turning me in to Eoma and the rest of the Alliance.

"Like they'd have you now anyway," Anhedonia reared its ugly head again. I didn't argue. The worst part about the burden of the Darkness was that not all that was said was fabrication. The doubt it seeded in my mind was often based in truths, or at least half-truths. It made it harder to sort out what was worth worrying over, and what to discard.

Before I could dwell on it further, the Laurel creaked. I turned in time to see the trunk split right down the middle. A pair of hands emerged, parting the tree's bark like a set of curtains. My heart leapt into my throat, and for a moment I forgot myself. I was frozen somewhere between a crouching position and a run when Nykolas emerged, looking more at peace than I'd seen in a long time. Like me, he stretched, tilting his face toward the sun. For a moment I could have sworn he was more tree than human.

It wasn't until he smiled at me that I realized I'd held my fleeing stance. My face flushed as I relaxed my posture. The tree mended itself behind him, leaving no trace that it had even been disturbed.

"'Tis an odd sight, I'm sure." He chuckled. "Especially the first time." I shrugged, unsure of how to respond.

"Did you sleep well?"

I nodded. "Better than I have in ... I can't remember how long."

"Good. We'll leave after breakfast then." He busied himself with the satchel around his shoulder and produced a meal of nuts and berries, as well as a small amount of smoked meats.

My heart sank. I was certain he'd understood why I wouldn't go back. Why I couldn't. Didn't he care about Luka? Maybe not. After all, the two had never met. And with Nykolas' heritage, forming emotional bonds to family was hard enough, as nymphs, by nature, were not known for their interpersonal relationships. Let alone forming bonds with a stranger. Still, he should have cared enough about me to at least have entertained the idea of his rescue.

"No," I refused, my fists curling at my sides.

Nykolas looked up from the crouching position he'd taken as he set out the morning's meal.

"No, you don't want to eat?" He seemed confused. "I'm afraid I must

242

insist. You'll need your strength, 'Lana."

Against my will, tears began to well up in my eyes. I hated crying when I was angry. It made his face soften. Not the effect I wanted. I wanted him to shrink away from my rage. To realize his mistake.

"I'm not. Leaving. Luka." I spat the words at him. It was all I could manage without breaking down into hysterical sobs again.

His brow furrowed. "I should certainly hope not, else you would not be the lass I've watched grow all these years."

Now it was my turn to be confused. "But, I thought—"

"The Alliance has good reason for wanting you in their care." He eyed the jewel around my neck. "But there are larger forces at work here, and I fear their judgement may be clouded." I began to ask why he felt this way, but he gave me a curt shake of the head. "It is not for me to say, not yet. But I have a feeling your Luka is part of the greater scheme. And if you say you must rescue him, what kind of uncle would I be to tell you otherwise?"

I couldn't restrain myself any longer. I ran to him, wrapping my arms around his neck in an embrace that nearly sent us both tumbling to the ground. Many things in my life had changed, but he had not.

We did not dawdle over our meal. Nor did we speak until it was over. There was not much else to be said. Nykolas took me on the same path he had used to get to the clearing. At least, it felt the same. The forest still moved before his feet, adjusting to accommodate us as we traveled. Perhaps it was that any direction he led us would lead to where we needed to go.

We stopped just short of the tree he had met me at, the one who had argued with the elders. It turned out to be the only one who would agree to transport me, though it had never done so before. "Not all trees have such powers," Nykolas explained. "And those who do aren't always willing to use them.

"You'll have to go alone," he added, casting an apologetic glance in Nova's direction. "'Tis the only hope she has to travel unnoticed."

Nova whinnied in protest, and Nykolas reached a hand to her muzzle in comfort. "Peace, my friend. We will be waiting when she returns." He took my pack from Nova's saddle removing my knife before handing it to me. "Iron is a powerful weapon against fairy folk. They would sense it in their realm and identify you as a threat. If you are detected, you will want to maintain an illusion of innocence. Best to leave it behind."

"But how will I protect myself?" I protested. I had no idea of the world I was walking into and did not fancy the idea of going in unarmed.

"With this." He reached into his satchel, pulling out a pan flute. He'd taught me to play some when I very young. Not more than a few notes, which I would play in random order. I knew I was no good, but still he would dance about as if my song were the most beautiful he'd heard. Soon Mother would join in, spinning me as I played. It always ended with the two of us falling to the grass breathless from laughing. The memory made my heart ache.

"Fairies can't resist a good song." My uncle winked. I placed my bottom lip against the longest reed of the instrument and blew softly. A deep sound reverberated from the pipe. Nykolas nodded his approval.

"And this." He placed a woven necklace over my head. I grasped it cautiously, afraid it might unravel in my hands. Flowers were woven into a material that I had assumed was leather. Upon further inspection, I noted it was too smooth, too cold, and too sweet-smelling to have come from the hide of any animal I'd encountered. But the flowers, those I recognized.

"Daisies," I said softly to myself, tracing their petals gently with my fingers. Daisies grew abundant in the yards of all Aythians—a popular flower for children. Now I knew why.

"And Rowan bark." Nykolas laid a hand on my shoulder. "To protect against fairy charms and glamour."

I ran my fingers over the Rowan threads once before letting the necklace fall against my chest. The act covered Anhedonia's prison, concealing it from prying eyes. I felt the Darkness recoil, shying away from the protective weave. It seemed the necklace would serve more than one purpose.

I squared my shoulders trying to look brave as I let out a long breath.

"I'm ready."

And so, he whispered to the tree, whose great intertwining arms unraveled into a portal that cast a bright light. I shielded my eyes with my arm, turning my head as I stepped through the entryway and let the tree swallow me whole.

I blinked as the light faded, eager for the glowing orbs that overwhelmed my vision to disappear. Stepping into the unknown was bad enough, reaching the other end blind was terrifying. I held my breath.

CHAPTER FOUR

OR A LONG TIME, THERE WAS ONLY DARKNESS. My lungs burned, and panic welled up inside me as I realized I would not be able to hold in my breath much longer. I held onto it like a lifeline, afraid I would suffocate. I sensed something in response, almost like a laugh. *The tree!* I realized. My breath rushed out without my permission, partially because my lungs had reached their limit, and partially due to surprise. Traveling through the tree was another form of physical contact, giving us a stronger connection to communicate with.

Tentatively I inhaled, and relief washed over me. My aching muscles thanked me for it. *See?* the tree seemed to say. *Nothing to worry about.*

"I wouldn't go that far," I murmured in response. As if on cue, a light split the darkness in half as the trunk parted before me. I was here. *Wherever here is,* I thought.

Be careful, the tree cautioned. *There is much danger here.*

Didn't have to tell me twice. I crept through the exit, keeping my body low to the ground in hopes that it would make my entrance less obvious.

The first thing I noticed as my eyes adjusted to the new light, was just how little light there actually was. I glanced overhead, expecting that the foliage was blocking out the light, and was surprised to find the sky was virtually free of obstruction. Mighty pines rose up and into the sky farther than my eye could follow. Though their branches reached toward one another, none of them seemed to touch. Backlit by a magenta sky scattered with unfamiliar stars, I guessed it to be dusk. Or maybe dawn? I wasn't certain. How much time had passed? I couldn't be sure.

"Well," I whispered to myself, "On we go."

Unlike the Dark Lands, this new place was easy to navigate. Rather than clamoring over ferns, roots, and shrubs, I stepped effortlessly across the moss that covered nearly every inch of the forest floor. My joints seemed to sigh in relief as I walked, thankful for the cushion it provided. Something else was different. Though I should have been on high alert, I felt more at peace. *The Darkness*, I realized. It was silent. But why? My hand flew to my neck fearing I'd lost it somehow during the transition and I was confused when the first thing I came in contact with felt foreign. I looked down and chided myself for losing my wit. Anhedonia was where it had always been. Hidden beneath the wreath of Rowan and Daisies. *Perhaps it doesn't only affect the Fae*, I mused. No one answered. I decided it would be best not to let my guard down, just in case. It could be that Anhedonia was simply lying in wait. Even when I was free of the Darkness, I could never truly be at peace.

I continued through the forest, marveling at how uniform everything seemed to be. I was surrounded by sameness. I began to worry that I was going in circles, when a movement caught my eye. I spun in the direction it had come from, rubbing my eyes in disbelief. In a spot I was certain had been empty only a moment before stood a large stump covered in moss of varying colors. Near the top was a hollow no more than ten inches tall outlined with intersecting twigs. From the hollow, a series of mushrooms formed a spiral staircase. This was no ordinary tree!

The movement I'd caught from the corner of my eye was a small girl descending down the staircase. She had sandy hair and bare feet and with each step down the stairs she gained height, until she was nearly the same size as me. She carried a silver tray of cakes and berries on one hand, steadying it with the other as she made her descent. I watched the ordeal dumbfounded, not just at what had transpired before my eyes, but by the fact that she didn't seem to see me at all. Even as she moved within an arm's length of me she paid me no mind.

I scanned her once more. No wings, nor pointy ears. She was human, as far as I could tell. But what was she doing here? I waved a hand in front of her eyes. "Excuse me?"

She started and let out a little squeal that sounded more mouse than girl-like. "Oh!" She blinked several times as she gazed in my direction, as if she were trying to get her eyes to focus on something not-quite-there.

"So sorry," she added. "I must have been day-dreaming again."

"Does it happen often?" I asked, hoping to keep her talking. I had no clue what business a human would have in the realm of the Fae, but I figured she was my best bet in figuring out how things were run around here. Maybe she'd seen Luka!

"At times. More so since..." Her voice trailed off and her eyes went somewhere far away.

"Hey! Hey, stay with me!" I put my hand on her shoulder shaking just enough to bring her back to the present. It was the clinking of glasses on her tray that really did it, though.

"Oh!" she exclaimed as she took inventory of the food she was carrying. "Musn't drop the Master's gift!" She swatted my hand away protectively.

"The Master?"

"Aye, sweet on the fairy-queen he is. Bit of a scandal, back in the day. Not so much now, I think?"

"I don't follow."

The girl blushed. "You're not from around here, are ye? Won't get me in any more trouble!" Quicker than I could blink she darted around me and off into the woods.

"No, wait!" I reached out to stop her, but she was too quick. Soon as I caught sight of her she'd disappear again, as if by some enchantment. It was no use. I'd never catch up to her.

"Please!" I called after her in desperation. This could be my only chance. "I'm looking for my friend, Luka!"

She stopped dead in her tracks, nearly tipping her tray in the process.

"The boy?" She didn't turn around.

"Yes, yes the boy!" I tried to keep my voice level as I crept closer so as not to spook her. A feat made more difficult by the fact that my lungs still burned from the chase. This was harder than trying to herd a flock of wild chickens to the coop!

"I liked the boy. He was nice. They don't let me see him anymore." My heart skipped more than a few beats.

"You've seen Luka? He's alive?"

"Of course he's alive. She'd never kill her own son. Well, probably never." She turned to face me once more, the fog gone from her eyes. For a moment I had the strangest feeling that we'd met before. *Perhaps in another life,* I thought.

"Her son?" My heart sank. Luka's mom had run off more than a few seasons ago, but she'd never been anything other than human—I was sure of it.

"Their son, really," she continued her story, oblivious to my disappointment. "She fancied my Master, once upon a time. But the babe couldn't stay, he had to be switched. They say the Fae don't care much for their offspring, but I'm not so sure that's true. Anyway, he came back a wanderin' in the Twilight Realm lookin' for his friend, and my Master captured him right-quick. A gift for his love." She motioned toward the tray of sweets. "Still hoping to woo her, he is."

"And her son? What would that make him then?"

"Oh, he'd be Fae as well as the rest of them. Or at least he'll think he is, now that she's got her glamour on him."

"A glamour?"

"To keep him from remembering his life outside the Mound," she stated, as if it should be obvious. "Most changelings don't come back, but the ones that are returned are usually infants on the outside, toddlers at the most. This one was older. Too human in his thinking. He wouldn't have stayed on his own."

"How much older? Older like me?"

The girl glanced nervously one way, and then the other before nodding.

"Aye, like you. Maybe a tad older."

It had to be Luka, I was sure of it! But that meant...

"Luka's a Mystic!"

The girl tilted her head at my exclamation. Of course, to her it would be obvious. I didn't bother explaining myself, and she didn't ask for an explanation.

"Where did you see him?" I asked.

"Where I left him, of course. In the hollow." She shifted her weight from one leg to the other, glancing over her shoulder in the direction she'd been running when I stopped her.

"Is someone waiting for you?" My eyes followed her gaze, but I saw nothing.

"Waiting..." Her eyes glazed over. "I had a family waiting..." She snapped out of the haze suddenly. "I'll be missed if I don't get back to the Master soon. I could show you the way, but..." She bit her lip and looked at me once more. "You must do exactly as I say. Go nowhere else, trust no one, and most importantly, let neither food nor drink pass your lips, no matter what. They'll have you forever if you do."

Chapter Five

WHETHER BY LUCK, OR FATE, it was a good thing I'd run into the girl in the woods. I couldn't have made it through the Realm without her. From where I stood, everything looked the same. The trees were spaced evenly, almost as if they'd been measured to a specific distance as seeds. They reached up and out, their branches weaving in and out of a magenta haze.

"Fog." The word tugged at the corner of my mind. It didn't seem to be toxic, but still it sent shivers down my spine as it slithered through the tree branches. Something told me I didn't want to catch myself stuck in it, should it venture any closer to the forest floor. Not a single leaf laid on the forest floor, which was coated in moss that cast a teal glow on my ankles. There was an eerie immortality to it all, but the feeling that loomed over me was not one of wisdom or awe, but a hollowness I couldn't quite put my finger on.

We walked for an eternity, and for only a minute. Time passed in an odd way in the Twilight Realm and everything was both foreign and familiar, like a dream.

The girl's hand on my shoulder brought me back to the present.

"We're here," she whispered, motioning toward a change in the horizon.

"The Mound."

A formation of stones stacked upon one another in an arch, with a bare spot in the front. Lichen cascaded down its sides like lace. At first it seemed no taller than my knee, but as we crept closer my perspective changed. It was the size of a small cottage, at least! It should have stuck out like a sore thumb in the background of the forest of sameness. Yet I hadn't noticed it until she'd pointed it out to me.

"Part of the magic. Its size increases as you grow closer. Or you grow smaller. I'm never really certain which."

I recalled the way she'd grown as she walked away from the gnome's hollow only minutes before. Or was it hours? "We shrink," I said, more to myself than to her. She shrugged.

"The Queen will be distracted, at least for a while." She nodded to the plate of sweets. "Especially if she accepts the Master's offering. Through the main hall there is a staircase. Take it down as far as it will go. There you'll find the fairy waters. If he's any chance at all of escaping—of remembering who he is, he must bathe in the water. He'll not come with you otherwise, and even if he does, he'd never be the same."

"How will I find him?"

"The Mound is like a moving maze, always changing." She eyed the Rowan necklace. "It won't trick you, I don't think. There's a bit of fairy glamour to it. Meant to trick outsiders."

"What about you?"

"I'm a servant of her Majesty. I move unhindered, as is her will."

"Can't you take me then?" I didn't like the idea of wandering into enemy territory alone. Especially if it was likely to change. What if I couldn't find Luka? Or worse yet, what if I couldn't find my way back out?

She shook her head. "Best if I don't. It'll draw more attention if there's two of us. Plus, I'm your best bet at keeping her off your tail." My face must have betrayed me, because she quickly added, "I'll meet you at the fountain, if I'm able. To make sure you find your way out. Count before you follow me in. I'll need a..." She pressed the thumb of her free hand to each of her fingers as she counted. "At least a ten-minute lead from this side."

Just before she disappeared through the entrance I stopped her. "Why are you helping me?" Her eyes met mine with clarity for the first time, causing the hair on the back of my neck to stand on end. Her eyes felt familiar somehow, in a way I couldn't place.

"He was my friend too, I think," she said, and a fog fell over her eyes once more. "In another life, maybe."

With that she ducked beneath the archway and disappeared.

Chapter Six

W HO KNEW TEN MINUTES COULD FEEL LIKE ETERNITY? I paced back
and forth, counting my steps as they fell. I figured that was a
good enough measurement of time. I never had been much
good at waiting. My anxiety caused me to fidget as I walked, and before
long, my steps were falling faster than the seconds were passing. I lost count
somewhere in the thousands and realized how much energy I was using up
for no good reason. I stopped to catch my breath, leaning against a nearby
tree as I sat on the mossy floor. I closed my eyes and drew air into my lungs,
hoping to battle the pounding in my temples as blood rushed through my
veins. Suddenly this all seemed like a terrible idea. What was I thinking,
sneaking into a fairy mound on my own? I could hardly hold my own in the
forest, what made me think I could rescue Luka?

My hand hovered over Anhedonia's prison. It sat cold against my skin,
lifeless. No, these doubts were my own. I sighed. I didn't know what was
worse—having an outside source taking over the corners of my mind, or the
fact that it had rooted itself deeply enough that I was now fighting myself
as well.

"Enough of this," I declared aloud as I stood, hoping the words falling
on my own ears were stern enough to propel me forward. I brushed my

hands against my legs and braced myself for the unknown before running through the dark archway.

I don't know what I had expected, exactly. Based on the stone structure on the outside perhaps darkness, and a dusky smell. I was met with neither. Instead, I found myself blinking against the light and surprised to find a breeze brush against my skin. The air was fresh and sweet, though I couldn't figure out exactly where it came from.

As I gathered my wits my eyes darted around my surroundings, afraid I may have rushed in too quickly. No one seemed to be around. I sighed with relief and took in the environment with more appreciation.

The ground was blanketed with grass, as if I was still outside. In contrast, walls of stone rose in high arches, decorated by ornate carvings of various creatures. Some I recognized as common wildlife: squirrels, butterflies, and robins. Others were unfamiliar to me but seemed magical in nature. When I looked harder, it seemed as if they were telling a story. Like the statues might move, if I concentrated hard enough.

The thought sent a shiver down my spine. I didn't fancy sentient architecture, especially when I was supposed to be moving through the hollow in secret.

I kept moving, trying to shake off the feeling that I was being watched. A little paranoia keeps one safe, but too much puts one in harm's way.

The hall came to a T, with a corridor on each side. I wasn't certain how I was supposed to choose which path to take. Darn that girl and her vague directions. I'd never thought to ask her where Luka may be hiding, let alone how to get to such a place.

"*The Mound is like a moving maze, always changing,*" her voice echoed in my mind. "*I move freely, as is the Queen's will.*"

The Queen's will. Maybe the girl couldn't navigate on her own, but only down the paths the Fairy Queen wanted her to. That's why she wanted me to wait.

This plan was looking more and more foolish by the minute.

I looked to the left hall, then the right. They were nearly identical, with only one difference. The right seemed to have more light cast across it. The left was darker. I surveyed the window arches. If the right side had light, it stood to reason it was on the same level at least. The left being darker ... perhaps that meant it led to a lower level?

The girl had said something about a staircase leading down to the fairy waters. Even if I wasn't lucky enough to find Luka on my way to the fountain, it couldn't hurt to know for sure where it was, right?

I chose the left.

The light dimmed almost immediately, and the temperature dropped. My arms broke out in goosebumps as I made my way silently down the hall. I looked back where I'd come from to find the way blocked off by a stone wall—as if it had never been there to begin with. *No going back now.*

I wrapped my arms around my shoulders, trying to shake off the growing feeling of dread in my stomach, but it was no use. What if I'd chosen wrong? Or worse, what if I'd chosen correctly, but couldn't get back to the exit? If my surroundings changed as I passed through them, did that mean I was susceptible to the fairy glamour?

I looked around. While the architecture was nice, it wasn't exactly what I'd call spectacular. Really, it was plain at best. Not what I'd expect from some mystic being who lived between worlds. That settled it then, no fairy glamour. Still, I vowed to keep my senses about me, and not believe my eyes when it came to temptation, whether it be beautiful objects, grand parties, or food.

Food. She'd warned me not to eat here. That wouldn't be a problem, if I were in and out as quickly as I hoped. But I had something else to consider. All that blasted pacing outside the mound had sapped my hydration. I was parched. And of course I'd not packed anything. Suddenly I was aware of how dry my mouth was.

Stupid girl, I chided myself internally. The thought stopped me in my tracks. It seemed Anhedonia had left its mark on my mind. Even without its voice whispering in my subconscious I was starting to hear its words in my own voice. No time to worry about that now. I ran my tongue over my parched lips, hoping it would give me some relief. The results were mixed, but it gave me something else to focus on besides the fact that I'd gotten myself trapped in the Fairy Realm.

As I suspected the hallway led to a lower level. The smooth floor gave way to a stairway of stone so subtly that the shift was almost indistinguishable. As it was, I was halfway down the spiral staircase before I noticed.

Was I so focused on my task that I'd become oblivious to my surroundings? The idea made me nervous. What if I'd been spotted? Would I have snapped back to reality in time to escape?

Or was it things were shifting around me? What if I hadn't actually descended the staircase, but rather, the staircase had formed itself around me?

I wasn't sure which idea I liked least, but I decided to put it to the test. This time I kept my head up and my wits about me as I made my way down the spiral staircase. I pressed a hand on either side, dragging my palms along the cool stone walls. I walked like this until my knees became sore from the weight of my body shifting down each stair. I took note of my position. I could have been walking in place for all I knew. There was no end in sight.

"Alright then. Time for plan B." I let my arms rest at my sides and my aching shoulders thanked me. I closed my eyes and imagined Luka's face. The way his sandy hair sometimes fell over his eyes. How his impish grin made his right cheek dimple. I thought of every time he'd stood up for me against the other kids when they made fun, and how he'd sneak into my room after to make sure I was okay.

"Please," I whispered to the powers that be. "I want my friend back."

When I opened my eyes, I was in an entryway framed by hawthorn trees. A quick glance over my shoulder revealed the bottom of the staircase. The image wavered, stuck in an in-between as it waited for me to cross the threshold. It worked! Or at least, I was pretty sure it did. I stepped through the entryway and looked back once again. The staircase was gone, replaced by another wall.

I surveyed my surroundings. If walls had not surrounded me I'd have thought I were outside. A blanket of moss carpeted the floor. The hawthorn branches that had framed the entryway spread out and around, framing the ceiling. In the far corner a boy sat propped up on a pile of silken pillows, plucking wool from a wicker basket and feeding it into the spinning wheel in front of him. His right foot pressed the pedal in perfect rhythm and for a moment I was mesmerized from the way the wheel spun.

Luka!

CHAPTER SEVEN

I WANTED TO RUN TO HIM AND WRAP MY ARMS AROUND HIM, but the memory of how he looked at me in the woods made me pause. He didn't remember me, and I didn't want to scare him off. Instead, I approached him slowly, careful to stay within his line of sight. He was so engrossed in the task of spinning that he didn't even acknowledge me as I approached.

"Hello," I said softly. He hardly looked up from his work.

"Oh. Did they send you to help?" He motioned to a pillow beside him. "Sit." I didn't argue, but sat beside my friend, picking wool from the pile and handing it to him.

"Do you remember me?" I asked. I knew it was a long shot, but I couldn't help myself.

He looked up from his work, studying my face before shaking his head unapologetically. "There are lots of human girls here, like you. From the outside." The face of a mortal would be of little consequence to the Fae, unless they'd done something to vex them. I shouldn't take it personally. I swallowed the lump in my throat.

Better to maintain a facade. "Yes, there are many of us. I suppose it would be easy to forge." I tried to sound nonchalant. He nodded, returning to his work.

"I was sent by another. Someone you may remember. A little human girl with blonde hair?"

This piqued his interest. "The girl that brought me here."

"Yes, that one. She sent me ... to take you somewhere else."

"We don't get to talk anymore. Mother makes her stay away."

"Yes..." I was at a loss for what to say next. If he remembered enough to know he couldn't talk to her, I wasn't sure how else to reach him.

"I forgot, it wasn't the servant girl. It was your mother that wanted you to come with me. The girl was the messenger."

He plucked more fiber from my hands, examining it as if it may have been tainted by my touch.

"No," he argued casually. "I'm to stay here. Mother's orders. My punishment for playing too close to the boundary."

There went that idea. I sighed, scanning the room for anything I could use to my advantage, and coming up blank. Some flowers sprouted here and there beneath the moss, but for the most part the room was plain. I shifted on my pillow. Something was suddenly uncomfortable. I reached underneath and retrieved a simple lute.

That's it!

"Hey Luka, do you play?"

That got his attention. His eyes lit up and the corners of his mouth curled into the mischievous grin I knew so well. "'Course I do. Weren't a fairy this side of the Realm that doesn't know how to work a flute!" He snatched it from my hands eagerly and put it to his lips.

I retrieved the pan pipe from my pouch and pressed it to my lips hoping against hope that I was good enough to make this work. I played the first tune that came to mind—something Nykolas had taught me when I was young. It was lighthearted and playful. Luka began to dance joyfully, following along on his lute. It pleased me to see the smile on his face. It felt good to be with him again. So much so that I almost forgot the situation that was responsible for reuniting us. I took a step back, curious what would happen. Luka, still in full dance, shadowed my movements. I laughed, twirling around the room forgetting myself for a moment.

Every which way I went he followed.

The tune changed, picking up tempo. Luka's dance changed to match it. *This is it*, I thought to myself, *now or never.*

As I played I imagined the words Allison had said to me when describing the fairy falls. Before me the wall shimmered, creating an opening where once there had been none. On the other side of the doorway the stairs appeared, descending once more.

I twirled around Luka and toward the stairs, careful to maintain my carefree façade. If Luka saw that I moved with intent, it might tip him off.

I inched down the stairs, keeping my eyes on Luka. I made sure to act surprised at the first step, stumbling briefly as I descended. It worked, and Luka paused only long enough to giggle at the face I made as I caught myself on the third step.

Down we went in circles as the stone steps spiraled. Every now and then I'd twirl cautiously, hoping to catch sight of the stairway's end.

Come on, I thought to myself, as I began yet another tune. "Where is it?" My mouth was beginning to dry out from playing so long. Beads of sweat rolled down my face. Finally, my feet met even ground.

I stopped, mid spin, lowering the flute from my mouth, which had gone slack in awe. The fairy waters were beyond anything I could have imagined. The pristine waters glimmered. Wavy teal light danced on the cavern wall. From a hole in the roof of a cavern water danced down to the pool elegantly. Instead of the rushing sound most waterfalls make, this one sounded like wind chimes. I wanted nothing more than to bury my face in the pond and drink. In fact, I'd have done exactly that, if it weren't for Luka who, oblivious to his surroundings, had run full force into my back.

As it were, the impact nearly sent me tumbling into the water anyway. If the servant girl hadn't caught hold of my tunic when she did, well, I'd have been a right mess.

"Where did you come from?" I gasped. I could have sworn we'd come in the only entrance.

She shook her head. "No time for that now. Her Majesty shall be missing me before long." She turned to Luka, who had come to a stop after our collision and stood eyeing the two of us with skepticism. "Step into the water, Luka."

But he would not be coaxed. "I don't fancy a swim right now. Come on, let's play!" He pressed his flute to his lips and tugged on my sleeve expectantly. I shook my head. He stomped his foot in frustration. The act made him seem like a young child. I looked to the servant girl, who was beginning to fidget nervously.

"We need to get him in the water, and quick."

Suddenly, doubt overwhelmed me. I couldn't force him into the water, couldn't take away his free will. All of my own frustration at having my choice stripped from me bubbled to the surface, laying on the shoulders of my friend like an invisible cloak. "No," I insisted. "He has to make the choice himself."

"He isn't capable," she argued. "Look at him! The Fae have already taken his choice from him. The boy that stands before you is not the boy who entered the Realm. That is not my friend. Tisn't yours, either."

I looked at Luka, who had lowered his flute. His large eyes looked to the girl and back to me in confusion. No, this was not my Luka. Still, I could not force him into the water.

She was done waiting. In one fluid movement, she moved past me and grabbed hold of Luka's hand. Surprised, Luka resisted, but it was too late. The pair stumbled over one another, nearly colliding with me in the process. I jumped out of the way, turning just in time to see them tumble head first into the fairy waters.

I ran to the edge of the pool, waiting with baited breath for them to resurface. Luka came up first, scrambling for his flute, which had bobbed to the surface and was swiftly floating out of his reach. He pulled himself back onto shore, his brow furrowed in irritation as he drained the water from his lute.

"What'd ya do that for?!" he demanded, glaring at the servant girl who had come sputtering to the surface and stood, staring at Luka expectantly. "I told ya I didn't want to swim!"

My heart sank. The water hadn't restored his memory. If it had, he no longer cared for life outside the Realm. I wasn't sure which was worse.

"Oh, Luka," she whispered, her eyes filling with tears. The waters had changed her. She stood taller, able to wade through the waters with less effort. Her face, too, had changed, shedding its youth. She climbed back onto the shore. On land she was nearly a foot taller than me. She knelt and placed a hand on Luka's face tenderly. It was no child who stood before us. It was—

"Luka's Ma," I whispered in disbelief. I may as well have been invisible as far as she was concerned. Every fiber of her being was focused on her son.

"Oh, my sweet boy. I'm so sorry." A tear trailed down her face.

"You should be sorry! You nearly ruined my lute!" He pushed past her without so much as a second glance. My breath caught in my chest. He didn't recognize her!

"Why didn't it work?" The question broke through her grief and drew her attention back to the matter at hand. "It ... cured you." I wasn't sure that was the right term for what I had just seen. "Why didn't it restore his memory?"

"I don't know," she whispered.

"Because he is Fae," a voice boomed above us. My gaze flew upward, and I was met with a sight that was both beautiful and frightening.

She stood easily twice Allison's height, her golden hair cascading down her shoulders in waves. Light illuminated her iridescent wings, which were extended to their full length in a show of power. Whether this was her natural stature or a fairy trick, I was uncertain, but the way she loomed over us, even in the distance, made the blood drain from my face.

"Did you really think that your silly trick would work on the son of the Fairy Queen? That he was not already his true self? You mortals are even dumber than I thought."

Allison stood with her fists clenched at her sides. "He's no son of yours, you rotten Fae. I am the one who held him when he had the colic. I wiped his tears from the time he was a tot to the time he grew into the boy you see now. Your lot abandoned him. You're no mother to him."

I braced myself against the smiting I was certain was imminent, but none came. Instead, the Queen tossed her head back and laughed. I'd heard that fairy laughter sounded like the tinkling of wind chimes, but this laugh was more like shattered glass. Beautiful, but dangerous.

"How precious, that you think you hold any power here. Don't you see?" She moved closer, motioning to the water. "You've been restored to your true self. You just traded him for your own freedom."

Allison drew Luka to her side protectively, her eyes wide in horror. "No," her voice came out little more than a whisper.

"Yes," the queen replied gleefully. "Now you and your little elf friend may be on your way, but the boy is coming with me." She reached her hand out to Luka. "Come here, son."

Luka pried Allison's fingers from his shoulder, moving toward the Fairy Queen as if in a trance. I threw myself between them, holding my arms out to keep Luka from moving around me. The Queen smirked in response and reached a hand toward me. I closed my eyes, preparing myself for whatever was to befall me, but was met instead with a gasp. Confused, I opened one eye cautiously. The Queen had recoiled, holding her arm to her chest as if in pain. Her eyes homed in on the ring of rowen and daisies around my neck.

And then I had an idea. I braced myself, knowing what I was about to do would likely unleash Anhedonia's voice upon my mind once again. There was no other choice. I took hold of the daisy chain and slipped it over my head, planting it around Luka's neck in one hurried movement.

The change was instant. Light returned to Luka's eyes. He let out a long breath, and for a moment I was certain I saw a shimmery mist escape from his mouth. The spell was broken.

Unfortunately for me, that meant Anhedonia was free to wreak havoc on my mind once more. A series of dark thoughts flooded my mind all at once, like a series of voices calling over one another. My hands flew to my head as pain pulsed through my entire body. I was relieved when I felt Luka's arm wrap around me just as my legs grew weak. *"Might as well end it here,"* the Darkness cooed. Its voice was heavy, yet soothing. Funny how familiarity can be a comfort, even when it brings pain.

"No." I fought back against it, though all I wanted in that moment was to fall into it. To accept things as they were—as I was sure they would always be—and let myself rest.

"You'll pay for what you've done!" Allison's voice rang out behind me.

The Fairy Queen looked down on me with a new understanding, then turned to Allison. She raised her hands above her head and lightning crackled from her fingertips. "No, dearies. It is you who will pay!"

Allison grabbed us both by the hand, pulling us out of the Queen's line of fire. "RUN!"

CHAPTER EIGHT

W E SCRAMBLED UP THE STAIRS, pulled along by Allison. My vision blurred, and I stumbled more than once, scraping my knees along the way. At first, Allison was in the lead, but as the stairs wound up endlessly before us it became clear she was no longer able to navigate in the Realm. I wondered whether it was the result of her contact with the Fairy waters, or a trick played by the Fairy Queen. After all, if we were lost, she wouldn't have to chase us.

Anhedonia's voice sent piercing pains through my body in waves. Half the time I thought its goal was to bring me to my knees, and it almost succeeded. At the same time, the feeling was driving me forward, as if in a panic. Something about the Twilight Realm frightened it.

Luka pulled to the front, holding me by the shoulders gently as he handed me off to his Ma. "Keep her moving, she's in bad sorts," he instructed, before addressing the pathway before us. I stole a glance at Allison, who was staring in awe and adoration at her son. When she had left he had still been a boy, but somewhere in her absence his boyhood had been stripped away. As he led us through the shifting architecture and out of the mound I, too, saw him with new eyes. It was then I realized we had both reached a time of transition, hovering somewhere between the childhood we'd left behind and the journey into adulthood that lay before us.

It felt a bit like being cheated. Like this moment we had waited for had been stolen from us. Mine because of my time in the Alliance, and his because of his time in the Mound.

It was not long before we clambered out of the fairy mound. At this point I was doubled over in pain, fighting internally with Anhedonia. Leaving the mound brought a small measure of relief which in my current state I failed to question.

"Come on," Luka urged. "We can't stop now."

Allison stood still, waiting for something we couldn't understand.

"Come on, Ma!" Luka insisted. Tears welled up in her eyes.

"Oh Luka," she whispered. "I can't."

Luka shook his head as the realization dawned on him. "No. No, no, no, YOU CAN'T!" he shouted angrily at her, his eyes wet with the threat of tears.

"Oh honey." She opened her arms and he catapulted into them, falling to his knees and burying his face in her tunic. She wrapped her arms around him, kissing the top of his head and taking in the smell of him. Her son. This would be the last time she would ever take in the scent of the child she'd raised.

"The Fae will not stand for being cheated. We have to even the score. You know this."

Though I'd not had the same education as Luka and the other children of Aythia had growing up, I knew she was right. I knew it intuitively, the way you can smell rain on the air just before a storm. We had to go, and she had to stay. A trade, to appease the Fairy Queen. It was the only way to save Luka.

"I won't do it," he sobbed, refusing to meet her gaze.

"Luka, look at me." She put her hand under his chin, guiding his eyes to hers. "You have to take her to safety." He looked over his shoulder and I tried to put on a brave face, to make them believe we had time before the Darkness ravaged what was left of my mind. A white-hot, searing pain overtook me and I bit the inside of my mouth so hard it bled, trying to keep my face from showing it, but it was no use. Luka knew me better than anyone—better than I knew myself most days.

"I am so, so proud of you," Allison praised, kissing the top of his head one last time. "Remember that, okay?"

Luka pulled away slowly, wiping his cheek with the sleeve of his tunic before standing. He nodded. "Yeah. I'll remember. I love you, Ma."

"I love you too, son." She squeezed his hand, trying to reassure him. "It's going to be okay, I promise. Now go."

My heart ached for Luka. For his Ma. For his Pa who waited at home who may never know what had become of the love of his life. I wanted to reach out to Luka, to comfort him even though I knew there was no comfort to be had. What could I possibly hope to offer, that could fill the void of losing a mother?

Another wave of pain coursed through my body, causing me to tense as if lightning were coursing through me. Luka lifted me into his arms and moved through the forest with new resolve.

The last thing I remembered was the feeling of his warm tears falling softly onto my face.

And then the world went black.

I opened my eyes. The galaxy swirled around me in hues of vibrant pink and dark purples that faded to black with scatterings of stars unlike anything I had ever seen. The scene rotated, spinning until I lost my bearings. Somewhere, someone brushed the hair away from my face. The feeling was familiar, and yet foreign at the same time.

"*Luka!*" I tried to call out, but my voice was lost in the wind. I tried again. "*Luka!*" Even as the words left my throat I heard them go silent.

The stars grew brighter, expanding just before they burst into a series of brilliant white lights.

Light. A rush of warm air on my face that smelled of apples and decomposing grass. Something soft nuzzled my hair.

"Come on, 'Lana, fight it." The voice was gruff and far away. It seemed familiar, and strangely foreign.

"She's coming to!" I recognized Luka's voice, but that couldn't be right. It didn't match the feeling of warm velvet pressed against my face.

"*Open*," something in my mind told me, but the voice was not my own and I didn't know what it wanted. *Go away*, I thought back. I was tired. So tired, and the pain was gone now. All I wanted to do was sleep.

"*OPEN*," the voice demanded again, but with more authority. My eyelids fluttered. They were heavy, and the light was harsh. Whatever had been brushing against my face was losing patience, and pressed against the side of my cheek, rotating my head against my will.

"Okay, OKAY," I relented, pushing it away as I sat up, blinking against the light until my vision cleared.

Nova stood poised beside me, her ears flitting back and forth with worry.

"It's about time," a familiar voice said. "We were starting to worry." A tall figure pushed its way past Nova, pausing to pat her muzzle appreciatively. "Good girl."

I couldn't believe my eyes. "Grandfather?"

Chapter Nine

MY FIRST FEW CONSCIOUS MOMENTS WERE CHAOS, as everyone vied for my attention. Nova nuzzled me until I stood up, leaning against me as I swayed. Movement still made me nauseous. Luka handed me a flask of water. I didn't bother to ask where it came from, or how long I'd been out. My thirst was too strong to care. The water was still cold, soothing the fire in my throat. For a moment the sensation of relief was the only thing on my mind.

"I told him you'd be okay," Grandfather's voice rose over the chaos, shattering the moment. "You're a fighter, like your mom."

I stood in limbo. Part of me wanted to run to him. To feel his arms wrap around me and hold me, safe at last. But Fiora's words of caution tugged at the back of my mind. The burden I bore was his doing, whether intentional or not. I'd nearly died a handful of times because of Anhedonia. Its influence was the reason I'd run away, and the reason I could never go back. How could I possibly rule my father's people, if I couldn't even trust my own mind?

It was an uncomfortable feeling, to look at my idol removed from his pedestal. Like a bit of the magic of my childhood had died away.

He saw my hesitation for what it was. "I suppose I have some explaining to do." He rubbed the back of his neck nervously.

"No time for that right now!" Luka interrupted. "We have to go back and save Ma!" He grabbed hold of my wrist.

"She is in no condition to travel right now!" Grandfather's booming voice carried an authority I'd never heard from him before. Luka froze, eyes wide.

Grandfather's face softened. "You can't go back, son. Not now, not ever."

Luka furrowed his brow. The words didn't seem to sink in. "No, I can do it. I can make a portal and go back. You don't understand, I have these powers—"

"I know, boy. You forget who came to your Pa the night you left. You can't go back, Luka. Not without sacrificing yourself. The Fae have to accept her sacrifice as trade. If you go back the deal is null and they will keep you both. It would be an insult to her sacrifice to let them have you."

Luka gulped. "It was you. You knew I would look for her." His gaze fell on me and I felt suddenly self-conscious. Because of me, Luka had lost his mother a second time.

"Aye, I did. Though I wasn't sure how it would come about. I wouldn't have sent you in there, to the Realm, not on purpose. Just like I wouldn't have saddled 'Lana with the burden she bears." It was an apology of sorts. Not a good one, but then he never was very good at making amends. I didn't know how to respond, so I turned to Luka instead.

"You mean you remember being..." *Fae? Kidnapped? Brainwashed?* I couldn't decide on the right word. I didn't have to.

"I remember every minute of it! 'Cept it feels like a dream." He looked over his shoulder, presumably in the direction we'd come from. The dream wasn't over. Not for him. After a moment he snapped out of it, returning to the present.

"What happened to you in there?" he asked. "I thought you were a goner for sure!"

"I don't know," I said, leaning into Nova. "But it was awful. Like my mind was being ripped from my body."

"The Amasai was afraid," Grandfather's voice startled us both. "It was trying to take control."

"Amasai?" Luka was confused. They were a thing of legend, not part of the curriculum taught to children in Aythia. Perhaps he'd heard rumors, a whisper here and there or something lurking in a dark corner. The source of all mortal suffering reduced to a fairy tale.

"One of the four burdens responsible for corrupting the Dark Breeds: Greed, Fear, Anger, and Despair," I explained. "Avadari, Metuza, Imari—"

"And she carries the last, Anhedonia," Grandfather finished.

Luka's eyes fell on me as he processed what he had been told. "You mean to tell me you..." I nodded, holding the jewel around my neck up for him to inspect.

"Unbelievable," he muttered. "Does it hurt?"

"Not usually." It wasn't quite a lie. More like stretching the truth. "I mean, except for what you saw."

Luka's eyes changed. A fire rose up from behind them, one I'd never seen before. He turned to Grandfather. "And you're responsible for it, aren't you, you ... you dolt! That's what Pa and you were fightin' about the night that I left!" He started toward my grandfather with clenched fists.

"Luka, don't!" I reached out to stop him, but Grandfather lifted a hand in my direction.

"Let the boy be." I couldn't be sure, but I thought I saw the corners of his lips curl upward. A hint of smile, gone as quickly as it came. Luka marched up to my grandfather, drawing himself up as tall as he could. Grandfather didn't even flinch, nor did he move to defend himself.

"Go ahead, boy," he said. His voice was even. He wasn't taunting Luka, he was giving him permission. Luka froze, uncertain what to do next. His fists shook with rage, but he didn't strike.

"How could you hurt her?" He clenched his jaw, fighting back the urge to let loose a rage that had been building in him his whole life. This wasn't just about me. It was about every loss that had accumulated in his life leading up into this moment. In a moment of clarity, I realized Luka's actions weren't about his anger. They never had been. Every fight he'd ever been in, every time he'd raged, it was all just a façade to protect him from his own grief. A grief that had never been more powerful than in this moment. And in that grief, I saw his transformation. He was at an age where it was no longer appropriate to use anger as a bodyguard.

"It was never my intention, Luka." His tone melted away my own anger as well as Luka's. "Sometimes our actions have consequences we never imagined." He looked at me sadly. "Terrible ones that hurt the people we love. I can't change what's been done."

"So, she's trapped with this ... this Amasai ... forever?" Luka's voice cracked, strained raw from earlier tears.

"I didn't say that," Grandfather reassured him. "But she is in danger."

"It can kill her, can't it? That's what it was doing in the Realm."

"To understand the Amasai, you have to know their history. I don't believe that Anhedonia meant to end her life. It was merely desperate to leave the Realm before it could be recognized for what it was."

"But what is it, exactly?" I hoped a shift in subject would help ease the tension. "I mean, I know what it is, sort of. A plaything for Nywa, which she released onto the earth without knowing the consequences. I know they played a part in the first war..."

"Aye, that's all most know nowadays. Even if you were to have full access to your inherited memories, you'd not find a touch more than what you've been told. Only the Dark Breeds knew the truth of the Amasai's origins, as they were the first to fall under their influence. The touch of the Amasai left a permanent mark their kinds carries from one generation to the next, and so the story has survived and been handed down.

You see, long ago, the Amasai lived among the Fae, each banished from their prospective hollows due to an inability to control their fatal flaws."

"Anger, greed, fear, and despair," Luka recalled as he mulled over my grandfather's words. "Everyone feels those things."

"Aye, everyone does, in one way or another." Grandfather nodded. "But the Amasai felt little outside of their flaw and had no desire to change that. Some say that they acted out of revenge for their banishment. Others speculate that their greatest desire is to be understood."

"It certainly doesn't feel like Anhedonia wants to be understood," I countered.

"Maybe not. But what would you do, if you truly felt you were the only one who experienced life in such a way?" He looked at Luka, and then at myself. "You lot had one another. You were drawn to the other like you. But what if there was none? Some think the Amasai wreak havoc in hopes of creating others like themselves. Of making their own community."

"A community full of fear, greed, anger, and despair." I shuddered at the thought. "It sounds terrible."

"Aye, it can be." The way my grandfather responded was cryptic enough to make me raise an eyebrow.

"Finally, the Gods had to intervene. They collected the Amasai and gave to Nywa for safe keeping."

"And she released them," I finished. "But why?"

Grandfather shrugged. "Who can venture a guess as to why the Gods do as they do."

"Wait a minute," Luka chimed in as he processed. "You're saying Anhedonia was trying to get out of Azlana? To escape the Twilight Realm?"

"That's my theory, yes."

"But it nearly killed her in the process!"

"It did." Grandfather's voice was solemn.

"So, you mean, it can't leave, even if it wants to?" My heart sank in desperation. I'd never be free of the Darkness.

"Not while you're living," the familiar tendrils of Anhedonia's voice slithered from the corner of my mind, taking center stage. I bit my lip, afraid to confirm what was being implied out loud.

"Which is why, Luka, no matter what, she can't go back. Neither of you can."

We were all silent a while, suspended in the reverence of a moment that changed all our lives forever.

"Now what?" My voice was almost a whisper. I looked from Luka, who had come so far, sacrificed so much to find me, to my grandfather who had doomed me to a life of misery whether intentional or not.

"Now, my little 'Lana," my grandfather chose his words carefully, "you learn your true destiny."

Chapter Ten

"Y OU MEAN TO TAKE HER BACK, THEN?" Luka's voice was sharp and sour. My heart skipped a beat. I had no desire to become a pawn of the Alliance once again. Nor did I think I could successfully lead my father's people while carrying the burden of the Amasai.

No way was I going back.

"Easy, boy," my grandfather's deep voice urged, with just a hint of a chuckle in its undertone. "I'm not here to take her back."

"Then what *are* you here for?" Luka demanded.

"I'm here to tell her the truth." At this, his gaze fell on me, and his eyes grew sad. "I know I have a lot of explaining to do. A lot of wrongs to make up for. There are blemishes on my reputation I can no longer outrun." He sighed wearily. "But I need you to believe in me, the way you always have. I'm trying to do the right thing."

I stood silent, trapped by my own trepidation. Even Anhedonia had nothing to say, though in the corner of my mind I could feel its curiosity pique.

"All right," I said. "What do you have to say for yourself."

"I know you thought that what the Alliance was doing was a mistake. That there is a better way to unite the Mystics."

"Blackmailing the Dark Breeds is wrong," I objected firmly.

He nodded. "You're not the only one who feels that way. A group of us—small, secret, and mostly outcasts ourselves—have been working together with some of the leaders of the Dark Breeds to forge a treaty."

"Fiora." My mind tingled as I put the pieces together. "She said she'd had a plan for me, before she sent me away."

"To Thana," Grandfather said. "I know. Thana has been acting as an ambassador for the Dark Breeds. It has had the unfortunate side effect of attracting Cain's attention."

"Yes, he was there too!"

This came as no surprise to my grandfather. "The dragon placed her faith in the wrong person," he said sourly.

"Friend of yours, is she?" Luka piped in, eager to challenge my grandfather again. "Sounds like she's a sucker for outcasts."

I knew he didn't mean it the way it came out, but I couldn't help but flinch at the reminder of my own status. It must have shown in my face, because Luka was quick to acknowledge the foot he'd just shoved in his mouth.

"Oh, 'Lana I didn't mean—"

"It's fine. Just let him finish." Luka recoiled like a slapped puppy but nodded and shut his mouth.

"We made a deal with the Dark Breeds. One I wasn't sure we'd be able to keep, but the dragon ... well that's a story for another time. The important thing is what comes next."

I was torn somewhere between fear and curiosity. As usual, curiosity won. "And that is?"

"The Dark Breeds are bound by the laws of the Amasai. They cannot attack one who wields any of the four burdens."

"Irving has two," I thought aloud.

"Aye, that he does. And as long as he has them, the Dark Breeds won't set foot in his kingdom."

"You mean to send her after them!" It was an accusation more than a question.

My grandfather ignored his outburst and continued, "We promised we'd find a way to remove them from his possession before the Autumn Festival."

"Waitin' 'til the last moment, are ya?" Luka motioned to the changing leaves.

"It looks that way, doesn't it?" He gazed up at the hues of red and orange that surrounded us. "Almost like it's ablaze," he murmured to himself, lost in some far-off memory. After a moment his mind returned to the present, and he brushed the hair from my face. "I never imagined it would be you."

"What would be her? What are you not telling us, old man?" Luka's eyes darted between the two of us desperately as he tried to piece it together.

"It has to be me, doesn't it?"

Luka froze. My heart raced. Somewhere a leaf fell softly on the forest floor, its rustling the only thing that cut through the silence.

"No!" Luka started for my grandfather, pushing him away from me. "You have to find someone else!"

"There is no one else!" Grandfather's shout startled Luka into silence. "Everyone else who has tried has failed."

"And by failed you mean...?" Anhedonia already knew the answer, but I needed to hear it for myself.

"The Amasai are powerful beings. They have a will of their own and are drawn to positions of power. Wielding one of them is dangerous enough— that's why they were separated to begin with. We sent three others. None survived."

"Don't do it, 'Lana," Luka begged. "Please." He knew me well enough to know I'd already made up my mind.

"But you think I'm different. Why?"

"The Dragon has her reasons, though they're best left in her own head." I couldn't tell whether his answer meant he didn't know, or simply that he wouldn't say.

"And when I claim the Amasai, and the Dark Breeds are free to advance, what is to keep them from ravaging all of Aythia?"

"The only way we have out of the situation we are in is to trust our allies. There will always be risks, but we have to believe the reward is worth that risk."

I pondered this a moment. The chance to unite not only the Dark Breeds with the other Mystics, but to unite them with humans as well. For both sides of my heritage to live in harmony. What was my life worth, when stacked against that possibility?

"Okay," I agreed. "I'll do it."

"But how can we even hope to get into the castle?" Luka folded his arms. "'Cuz I'm goin' with her, ya know."

Grandfather's eyes danced. I got the feeling he'd have expected nothing less of my childhood protector. He smiled mischievously. "For that, I'll be calling on an old friend."

Chapter Eleven

"T HE ALLIANCE HAS HAD EYES behind enemy lines for a very long time," my grandfather began. "Including those in the King's own court." He turned to Luka. "Your father was once the King's scribe. One held in high regard, part of the group assigned to look after the translation of the elven King's journal."

Luka's eyes grew wide. "I didn't know Pa could read."

"No one in his new life knows," Grandfather said. "From the moment he chose to raise you as his own his life was in danger. He went into hiding. But he still holds many memories from his time spent in the castle."

"So that's how he knew what a changeling was," Luka thought aloud. "Even though it wasn't somethin' we learned in school."

"Aye, there are many things King Ludlum has chosen to keep to himself," Grandfather said sourly. "Not everything in the journal made it into Aythia's curriculum."

"But why not?" Luka was hanging on every word.

"An educated people are harder to control, but most people won't stand for being left completely in the dark. If you give them just enough information to demonize your enemy, they become afraid. Frightened people are easy to control."

"So even though my mother knew more than the Alliance, she couldn't have told them everything in the journal anyway." I began to put the pieces together. The Alliance's plan had been faulty from the start. Grandfather gave me a moment to process before continuing.

"It will be your father, Luka, who we turn to next. He knows the castle like the back of his hand and may well still have friends on the inside." He looked to the sky, and then to me once more. "The Autumn Festival is in less than a week."

"We'll never make it in time," I worried. I couldn't say for sure how far we were from Aythia. Maybe a week as the crow flies but traveling by foot through unfamiliar terrain would make it impossible.

"We can," Luka countered, "If I make another portal."

A strange look fell over my grandfather's face, like he was watching the pieces of a puzzle fall into place. "Aye, it would have to be the right portal, but..."

"But it is possible, I knew it!" Luka exclaimed. "I can travel other ways—not just to the Twilight Realm."

"It poses its own kind of danger," Grandfather cautioned. "You won't be traveling to the Twilight Realm per se, but in a way you will be passing through it. It is possible you'd be detected by the Queen. Best to leave it as a last resort. Besides." He nodded at Nova. "You'd have to leave this one behind."

Nova's displeasure flooded my mind, amplifying my own. "Absolutely not! No way, I'm not leaving her!" I couldn't tell whether the words I uttered were my own but sharing the sentiment, I had no problem hearing her words in my own voice. Memories of my time before my equine companion played in my mind, and most were full of Darkness.

"You've traveled without her before," Grandfather reminded me.

"And almost died in the process!" My heart beat against my ribcage as I recalled the pain that ripped through my body as Anhedonia tried to escape. "And I'm meant to collect the other Amasai. To walk right into the enemy's castle with this thing in my head! And for what? To be stuck there when the Kingdom falls under attack?"

I locked eyes with my grandfather's pained expression, daring him to look away. He did not, but a single tear made its way down his cheek as his eyes stared back into mine.

"I would never ask you to put yourself in harm's way. Not if there were another choice."

I believed him. Of the many flaws my grandfather possessed, sacrificing someone he cared for was not one of them. Not intentionally, anyway. I wondered at the kind of man it took to sacrifice his own kin for a chance at peace.

I also wondered what kind of person it would make me if I refused. What would I do with my life, then? Knowing I'd turned down a chance to create a world where it was okay for people like myself to simply be. I looked at Luka and could tell he was wondering the same. He took my hand and squeezed it gently.

"You know I'll stand with ya, whatever you do."

Nova tossed her head before moving to press her forehead against mine. At first our emotions mingled and the conflict inside of me rose over itself like crashing waves. After a moment the feeling subsided, and I was at peace.

"You'll need to prepare yourselves for the journey. Nova knows the way," he said.

"How would she?" Our travels had taken us every which way through forests that may have well been labyrinths. How could she possibly tell which way my home was from here?

"You forget, she's much more familiar with Mystic lands than the likes of you. Besides," Grandfather added, "She's been that way before."

I recalled being spirited away from my home. It was true that Nova had been one of steeds to accompany me from the edges of Aythia to the safehold in the mountains. At the time, I hadn't realized how sentient she really was. The thought that she'd have known the way without my grandfather's guidance had never occurred to me before now. It seemed fitting that she would carry me back to my homeland, possibly for the last time.

"*More like probably,*" the Darkness sneered. Nova sensed Anhedonia's voice and moved in closer, leaning against me softly until the words faded from my mind.

"Trust each other," my grandfather advised, looking first to Luka and then to me. "And trust yourselves. It is the only way you'll make it through this."

"And what will you do?" Luka asked. "Where do you fit into all of this?"

"I have my own demons to face," Grandfather replied. "And a relative of the girl's to keep at bay."

"Cain." My heart sank. In all the chaos I had almost forgotten the risk my uncle's pursuit posed on the mission—on our lives.

"Aye, none other but the Wayward Prince." Something about the way he said it sparked a memory at the edge of my mind. One I couldn't quite put my finger on. Someone else had used that term in reference to Cain, I just knew it. Before I could put the pieces together Grandfather continued.

"You can't judge him too harshly, though his actions are indeed inexcusable," he said. "They come from a place turned dark by a great pain, but that pain once started as love. Learn from his example: refuse to let your love be corrupted in such a way."

My heart leapt into my throat and I wondered how much my grandfather knew about the Darkness that had made its home inside my mind. Was this merely the ranting of a man who was uncertain he'd see his granddaughter alive again? Or was it a wisdom passed down on to me by someone who knew the Darkness personally? I was too afraid to ask.

We made camp for the evening. Grandfather decided it would be best for Luka and me to start our journey well-rested. Grandfather had come to us prepared with rations and water as well as some rope and canvas to make a small shelter. Items I didn't recall him having the day before.

"Where'd the likes of you happen upon such things?" Luka's brow furrowed as he secured a flask to Nova's saddle.

"An old man has his ways," Grandfather chortled, cinching up the last of the load. "Which reminds me." He grinned over his shoulder at me. "I forgot to tell you Gareth sends his regards."

My breath caught in my throat. I'd long wondered what fate had befallen the man I called Father after he escaped from one of King Ludlum's raids on the Mystics. My eyes welled up with bittersweet tears as I remembered how much I missed him. Mother too.

"He's okay then?" My voice cracked. "Mother too?"

"Aye, they're both safe." He said, "And they miss you fiercely. Though you'll not have heard it from me, when you get about to seeing them again." At this he winked slyly. "I'm still not quite welcome among Eoma and her lot."

"They think you're a traitor," I recalled aloud. When the Alliance had fallen under attack, my grandfather had been the one blamed for leading King Ludlum's soldiers to their previous safehold. I was one of the few who knew the truth: My grandfather hadn't given up the Alliance's location to the enemy, Cain had.

"Can't say I blame them, to be honest." He tried to keep his tone casual, but his eyes were sad. "I don't exactly have the best track record."

My grandfather had done many things in his life some would believe worthy of punishment. And though he had been the one to invite Cain back into the fold, I couldn't see how an error in judgement could be punished the same way as an intentional betrayal was. How could anyone learn to do better if their community cast them out so easily? It didn't seem fair. I made a mental note to change whatever ordinance supported such punishments when I took the throne.

That is, if I lived long enough to see my coronation.

"But it wasn't you who betrayed the Alliance! Cain led the army to the safehold."

"But it was by own ignorance he came upon that information to begin with," Grandfather argued. "My heart ached for the man I once considered a friend. When he reached out to me, I was too eager to welcome him back into the fold, even knowing his friendship had become like a poison. I thought, since we'd both known the same loss, that it made our hearts the same."

"What loss is that, eh?" Luka stood with his arms folded, less than impressed by my grandfather's heartfelt confession.

"His mate may be still be considered living by some twisted Mystic standard, but he has lost her." I looked at Luka. I had no idea what it was like to lose a mate, only a friend. And even that had been a pain I wouldn't have wished on anyone else. Grandfather continued, "He is alone in the world."

"He has a son," I pointed out. My cousin Cazlyn and I had spent much time together before I'd fled from the Safehold. I didn't know him well, but I was certain he'd have welcomed his father with open arms if given the chance.

"That he does. Having a child who feels..." Grandfather chose his words carefully, "conflicted about your character. That is another burden the two of us share. In my eagerness to consult with someone who could truly understand me, I let slip information that led to the death of my friend. It is not something I can ever atone for."

"If this works, I'll tell them!" I promised. "I'll tell them it was your idea, and they'll have to take you back."

He gave me a sad smile. "I hope you do. And I hope they will, some day. Though I don't guess it will come easily."

Not much was said between any of us after that. As the sun disappeared below the horizon Luka built a fire to keep us warm. I stared into it silently as it burned, its smoke dancing as it rose up to join the stars.

I wondered if that was what death would feel like. If somehow our souls were simply tendrils of smoke made by the slow burn of our lifetimes.

Chapter Twelve

I T SEEMED LIKE I'D ONLY CLOSED MY EYES FOR A MOMENT—barely more than a blink—but when I opened them the early morning sun cast a light over my face. Grandfather was gone, the only sign he'd been with us was a set of footprints in the dewy grass leading away from our camp.

Luka was already awake, sitting next to Nova as she grazed making soft clicking sounds. She glanced up at him from time to time, nickering softly. I felt a twinge of jealousy as I realized Luka was able to talk to her in a way that I couldn't, and I had no idea what they were saying to one another.

"She's awake!" Luka exclaimed as he caught sight of my bedraggled frame. I was hit with a wave of self-consciousness that had me frantically picking the twigs from my hair as he smiled in my direction. "I was afraid I was gonna have to do this by myself!" he teased.

I laughed awkwardly as I pulled apart my braid and reset it. Nova nickered, and I held my breath, hoping he couldn't understand what she'd said. *"Flirt,"* she teased.

I wasn't sure how she could mistake my nervousness for flirting. It definitely wasn't the reaction I was going for. Even if I'd wanted to, I would have failed miserably. I was too busy trying to work out why I suddenly found myself feeling so insecure in the presence of my best friend. Perhaps it was because we'd been separated for so long. I had changed so much, and I imagined he had as well. What if he didn't like the new me, or vice versa? Then I'd be alone out here, friendless once again.

I could feel Anhedonia smirk, soaking up every bit of my insecurity like roots taking up water after a long drought.

Nonsense, I tried to force the growing doubt from my mind. *There is nothing in this world, or the next, that could tear us apart.*

"*And besides,*" Nova chimed in, tickling the edge of my consciousness. "*He's not your only friend anymore.*" I walked up to her and scratched her behind the ear.

"Thanks for the reminder, friend," I said. "Ready to go?"

She whinnied, stomping a foot in affirmation and we set off.

I'd expected us to trace our way back the way I'd come and was surprised to find that I didn't recognize our route at all. Nova knew the forest better than I, and she led us in the safest and most direct route. As we traveled I was surprised to find I no longer feared this forest. What had once been a mystery—one that had filled my nightmares, I now knew it for what it was: A home to many fantastical creatures. Some more dangerous than others, but all working toward the same goal of survival.

Luka walked beside me, darting ahead from time to time, bouncing off the trunks of trees gleefully. He'd always moved with more grace than I, but this was different. He was at home here, in a way he had never been back in Aythia. I realized that, in another life, he too would have been part of the forest. In another life, so would I.

Watching him frolic through the forest it was easy to forget for a moment that we were no longer children. His energy was familiar, even comforting, but his tall, lanky frame was foreign to me. I wondered if he looked at me with the same awe and confusion.

"*Fancy yourself grown, do you?*" the Darkness smirked. "*Best not to let him know. He's sure to point out your every failing. No matter how different you may be you'll never be more than a silly, scared child in his eyes.*"

I had nothing to say in response. I leaned harder into Nova, but it didn't relieve me of my lingering sense of despair. It wasn't just Luka I was worried about, it was everyone, the whole Kingdom. Even if our quest was successful I feared that no one would ever accept me as more than the frightened and confused child that had been spirited away from my home.

"Only to abandon your people in their time of need," the Darkness fanned the flames of my self-doubt.

No, I insisted. *Even if I had stayed, their plan to unite the Kingdoms would never have worked. This was the only way to save them.*

"Not that you knew that when you fled," Anhedonia reminded me. *"Don't pretend to be a hero, silly girl. You were nothing more than a selfish prat, running from her destiny."*

"Will you talk to me?" I asked Luka. He stopped his frolicking and looked me over seriously. My tone must have given me away.

"I ... I need a distraction," I stumbled, unable to come up with a convincing excuse.

His brow furrowed. "It's that thing, isn't it?" he said, motioning to the chain around my neck.

I nodded.

"Does it hurt?" He moved toward me cautiously, as if he were afraid he could set it off by moving to quickly.

"Yes ... and no," I was uncertain how to describe it. "Not physically. Not all the time, but." I sighed, frustrated with my inability to make him understand. How could he, if he'd never experienced it himself? "It's just ... it's easier to not think about it if I'm focused on something else."

"It's okay," he said. "You don't have to have all the words. I don't have to understand it to want to help." He was trying to be reassuring, I knew. To tell me I wasn't alone in this, even though it was a battle he couldn't see. I should have been relieved, but I found myself fighting back tears instead. I was alone in this, even though he was right here.

"I wish you could understand," I lamented.

Luka gave me a look I could only interpret as helplessness. He didn't know how to respond. How could he possibly understand the burden I bore, having never experienced such a thing himself? My frustration boiled into anger at the thought. I knew it wasn't something he could control. I even knew that, given the choice, he would take my place. But that didn't matter to the Darkness.

"*He's talking down to you,*" Anhedonia's whispers were escalating. "*How dare he think he can relate to your pain.*"

Another voice spoke over the Darkness. It was Nova's. "*He, too, has experienced loss.*"

The statement startled me, not just because I'd forgotten how good Nova had become at reading my thoughts, but because I had all but forgotten Luka's struggles, I was so wrapped up in my own. I suppressed the urge to argue that my loss had been greater, ashamed that such a thing had become a knee-jerk reaction in my mind. Instead, I forced myself to take inventory of all that Luka had endured: The loss of not one mother, but two. Banished from the kingdom of his birth, and facing the destruction of the home he was raised in.

It's a lot easier to confide your pain in someone when you know they can relate. Trying to explain myself to someone who had never felt pain this deep was like talking to a blank canvas: You can paint your story across them this way and that, and maybe end up with an okay picture, but its meaning would be lost on the casual observer. Talking to Luka would be more like telling my story to a looking-glass. Someone who can reflect the pain back in a way that lets you know you're not alone.

Though a darkness traveled with us, not all of our journey was spent brooding over the task that loomed before us. There were playful parts as well.

"I can't believe you're meant to be a queen," Luka said at one point. "Imagine, the girl I used to chase barefoot through the city!"

"You're no better," I replied, recalling the bedraggled boy who used to climb in through my bedroom window. We'd both changed a lot over the years. The sandy-haired, disheveled boy had grown into a handsome young man with a strong jaw and bright eyes. We wondered as we walked, which of his features came from each half of his heritage.

His golden skin was no doubt from his father's side. Gnomes tanned beneath the sun. His hair, in contrast, bleached almost white in the summertime. That, we decided, had come from his mother. That wasn't all he'd inherited from her either. During our time apart, he'd learned to fade or camouflage when in danger, and even shift his form to that of a small woodland creature, as I'd seen him do before when he and the other fairy folk had fled in the Dark Lands. It took a lot of effort and wasn't something he took lightly. He'd not had the opportunity to learn the full extent of his powers, and now he never would.

"But it's still pretty neat, don't ya think?" he asked after his first demonstration.

My experience had been different. I shared with him some of my family history, as well as what I'd learned about the Alliance, the first war, and of course the dragon Fiora. His jaw went slack with awe as I recounted my time with her.

"You've got to be the bravest girl I've ever known."

I felt my face flush, a feeling I was eager to be rid of. "Yeah well, the girls you've known don't provide much in the way of comparison," I said a little too sourly as I thought of children who'd tormented me back in Aythia. And then, "Nothing is ever going to be the same for us, is it?"

The depth of my statement hit Luka hard, and for a long time he was silent. "No. No, I don't suppose it ever will be," he said. "But at least we're doing it together?" It came out more like a question than a statement as he slipped his hand into mine.

"Yeah, at least there's that." My stomach lurched at his touch, almost causing me to recoil. The sensation startled me, but I thought better than to mention it to him. I didn't want to ruin the moment.

Chapter Thirteen

As time went on I found myself more familiar with my surroundings. The forest was a lot quieter than I expected, and we encountered very little in the way of trouble. It was almost as if the forest understood our goal and was clearing a path for us to succeed. When we needed water, it was easily found. When we needed shelter from the rain the tree branches knit themselves tightly together to protect us. I wish I'd had more time to wonder at the beauty of what I was experiencing in that moment, but I was too busy fearing the danger waiting for us at the other end.

At the beginning of our journey I kept track of the days, carving a notch into a stick I'd picked up on our first night. As time went on, Anhedonia grew louder, dulling my motivations. If it hadn't been for the obvious rising and setting of the sun, I wouldn't have been able to distinguish night from day, let alone one day from the rest.

Luka began to notice this difference in me, and I could feel his concern mounting. Though he said nothing, he was often lost in thought.

One night he sat on a log by the fire, whittling away at a stray piece of wood he'd saved from the fire used to warm our evening meal. After awhile it began to take a familiar shape, and I realized he was carving it in the image of a creature. It was a new skill for him, and yet he was quite adept.

"It's less about carving the shape, and more about finding the right piece of wood," he explained when I'd been staring for a while. "I'm not shaping it from my will so much as helping it to realize its true form."

I took a seat next to him and he paused to blow away some of the shavings. "See?" he tilted the shape in my direction and I realized what form he'd modeled it after. It was a small rabbit, not unlike the stuffed one he'd given me when we were children.

"I found the leftovers in your pack when we were loading up." He handed the figure to me. "Thought you could use a new one."

I cringed inwardly, embarrassed that he'd not only seen something so childish still in my possession, but that he also knew I'd destroyed his gift. "I ... um, well you see—"

"S'all right. I'm surprised that old thing lasted so long as it did. This one is much more durable. That is, unless you burn it."

For a moment I was afraid I'd offended him, but he couldn't maintain his composure for long before the corners of his mouth curled upward. He was teasing me! I pushed him playfully with my shoulder.

"Hey!" he exclaimed, shoving back. "You nearly knocked me out of my seat!"

"What do you think we will do after this?" I looked up at the night sky framed by tree tops. So many stars glittered in the heavens. It made me feel small.

"I don't know," he admitted. "I guess I haven't given much thought to the possibility of there being an after, really."

His confession shocked me. Of the two of us, he'd always been known as the optimistic one.

"That's odd, I was sure you'd have your whole life planned out by now." I tried to keep my tone light, but the effort fell flat. "What great things will Luka do when the war is over?"

He said nothing but looked away. Finally, it hit me. *How could I be such a dolt?* "You're afraid to see your Pa again, aren't you?"

He nodded, swallowing hard. "He ... he doesn't know about my Ma.

My real Ma, who raised me. Not the freaky-odd one who birthed me and abandoned me to the Fates. I haven't worked out what I'll say to him yet."

"Why not the truth? That she sacrificed herself for you. I can't think of a braver thing than that." I figured it would ease his mind, to know that there was still a chance to redeem her in his Pa's eyes. To let him know she hadn't abandoned them. Maybe then he could let go of his anger and move on.

"I've thought for awhile about that," he said. "Whether it would make a difference if he knew. If he'd be able to let go of his anger if he knew the truth. That she hadn't abandoned us on purpose. That she meant to come back with..."

"With their true-born child," I finished the sentence for him. "But she didn't, and besides you're his rightful child. You're the one he raised."

"It's not just that." Luka's eyes shimmered, brimming with tears he tried to bite back. "It's that I don't think I can stand seein' his face when he realizes she's gone for good because of me. What if he hates me, too?"

"Oh, Luka." I wanted to reassure him. To tell him of course his Pa wouldn't hate him. How could he? I wanted to shower him with praise—to make him see how wonderful he was. But the words died in my throat, and all I could do was reach over and squeeze his hand gently.

Luka's eyes turned to the sky. The last rays of the setting sun cast a violet light on the forest. "We're almost there," he declared, more to himself than to me. He knew the forest better than I, having frolicked with the other Fae during his time as a fairy prince.

He's not the only one dreading what tomorrow brings, the Darkness brought my fears forward in my mind. I looked at Nova, who was grazing a few feet away, her ears flicking this way and that as she took in the sounds of the forest at twilight.

This would be our last night together, we all knew it, but only Luka was brave enough to point it out. I didn't know what I would do without Nova. My loyal steed. My companion. My friend. She'd seen me through more Darkness than most. I tried not to dwell on it, this idea of a final goodbye, but my dreams that night were filled with images of what may lay before us.

Swords clashing, the city aflame. Death. War. My friends, caught in the middle. I awoke at dawn's first light, my face wet with a mixture of salt and morning dew. Luka was snoring away a few feet away, with his sleeping pack pulled all the way up to his ears.

Nova was restless, trotting a circle around the camp.

"Easy, girl," I soothed as I made my way to her, scratching her forehead between her eyes. "Easy."

"*Scared.*" The thought filled my mind, overwhelming me. Where would Nova go once we'd parted ways?

"It will be okay," I said. "You know how to get home from here." She stamped her hoof in irritation, a sign that I had misunderstood.

"*Scared for you,*" she clarified. "*I want to come!*"

The weight of my own sadness was enough, I couldn't stand to bear hers as well. "Oh Nova," I cooed, kissing her face. "How I have come to love you. And it is because I love you, that I can't take you with me. It isn't safe. Besides." My eyes wandered back to the sleeping pile of Luka. "Even if it were safe for you to go, there isn't time."

"*I can run fast!*" she insisted.

"I don't doubt that, my friend. But there is more at stake than you or me. It is about everyone, in every Kingdom. So we might live in harmony one day." I said the words I knew were right for the moment, but they were passionless, rote repetitions of phrases I'd heard from others, pasted into a sentence that I hoped would appease her. "We can't risk a late arrival."

She snorted, obviously displeased, but she didn't argue. "*I will find you,*" she promised.

The three of us said little to each other as we packed our things, leaving behind anything too heavy for us to carry. The sleeping packs and cookware my grandfather had gifted were loaded onto Nova's back to be returned home. Luka kept one small pack of smoked meats and dried fruit.

"Just in case," he said, and I hid a smile. Luka had never been one to miss a meal, even as a young tot.

"See that it doesn't slow you down too much," I teased, though I knew he'd not packed more than a day's rations.

"*Won't need it anyway,*" the Darkness taunted. "*Can't eat when you're dead.*" Its laughter filled the recesses of my mind, filling me with dread. I didn't even bother fighting it. I needed my energy for other things.

"It's time," Luka said, moving to a path that had been cut in the forest by a company on horseback. The tracks were fresh enough to give me pause. "We have to go."

I kissed Nova's muzzle before wrapping my arms around her neck one last time. "I love you. Ride safe." She turned, but it was only after I patted her flank firmly that she trotted off, pausing for one last look over her shoulder. Suddenly I was overwhelmed with feelings that were not my own. Neither did they belong to the Darkness. I gazed into the dark wells of Nova's eyes and understood: There were no human words to describe her sadness. I nodded, swallowing my tears as she turned and disappeared into the woods.

Behind me, Luka had begun to form a portal. He whispered to the tree in a tone too low for me to understand the words, touching the trunk in a pattern that looked a lot like the rune I'd seen before when my cousin had smuggled me out of Aythia. Only this one had more flourish.

"It's like a password," Luka said over his shoulder. "Some pathways are carved for folks who don't have one of the Fae with them, those you have to travel by foot. This one has my signature in it, so we can harness energy from the Twilight Realm and get there faster." He paused to look at me, his hand hovering over the tree. "That's what makes it so dangerous. It basically announces my presence to the whole Realm."

With that he pressed his palm against the bark, which lit up in response before expanding along the width of the tree. The light dimmed and an image of the castle garden rippled before me. My eyes grew wide. The last time we'd traveled I'd been unconscious. Knowing Luka's power and seeing it in person were two different experiences.

Luka took me by the hand, ignoring my sweaty palms. "S'alright," he said. "I've got you."

I held my breath as he pulled me through the portal.

Chapter Fourteen

A T FIRST THERE WAS DARKNESS. But from that darkness bled other colors from deep purples to fiery oranges. They flowed into one another and out again, never retaining the hues of the others, almost as if they were separate, sentient beings. It was beautiful and terrifying at the same time. Voices began whispering from all around us, their sources hidden. Then one voice broke out above the rest.

"You've returned to us, my lovely," the Fairy Queen's voice was soft and silky as it fell on my ears. I knew I should be afraid, but instead I felt myself drawn in her direction. A swift yank on my arm snapped me out of it.

"OW! Easy!" I complained.

"Wasn't me!" Luka said defensively, "You were tryin' to wander off all on yer own!"

"Did not! It was you who was moving away from me!"

The voices tittered to each other in a way that sounded suspiciously like laughter. I held Luka's hand a little tighter, only to have it pull away again.

I grabbed his hand between mine and planted my feet. "You can't have him!"

"Oh but my lovely, we already do."

Pain shot through my body, causing my knees to buckle. Even as they hit the ground, I kept ahold of Luka. *No*, I thought, *Not again*. Anhedonia was fighting to break free of me, lashing out with a power beyond what my body would hold. The pain amplified my panic, and I did the only thing I could think of. I opened my mouth, filling my lungs until I thought they would burst, and screamed.

It took me awhile to regain my bearings before I realized my forehead was pressed against the ground. I coughed and choked, fighting to find my breath. Luka's hand rested on my shoulder. "It's okay, we made it," he said.

I sat up but regretted it instantly as my body responded by dry heaving.

"It's all right, here." Luka pressed a flask of water against my lips.

"What happened?" I sputtered.

"She had me," Luka said. "She had me right-quick and she was pulling me back to her realm! And then." His face went white. "This dark cloud just burst out of you!"

I rubbed my head. "It hurt."

"Yeah." He nodded. "It looked like it. The Darkness came right out of your throat and wrapped around the Fairy Queen's wrist and pulled us apart! It saved us!"

I had no doubts that it had been for selfish purposes. Though it had taken root in my own being, Anhedonia was trapped. It couldn't escape the Twilight Realm without me, and when it because clear I wasn't leaving without Luka, the Darkness had no other choice but to save him too.

"Anhedonia saved itself," I corrected. "We were just tools it used to do so."

"Yeah, well." Luka rubbed the back of his head awkwardly. "At any rate, I'm glad we're safe now."

"I wouldn't necessarily say safe," a voice behind us made me jump. I spun around to find Luka's Pa stepping from behind a nearby bush. Luka raced to his Pa, wrapping his arms around him. A sight I had seen many times before, only this time the man who had towered over him the last time we'd seen one another came nearly to the man's shoulder.

"Son," he said.

"I have so much to tell you!" Luka's tone was like that of an excited child. Robert took him by the shoulders, looking him over.

"Aye, I bet ya do. But not now, not yet. Soon, when we're all safe."

Luka nodded stoically, but I wondered whether his Pa noticed the way his lip trembled slightly the moment before. *Men are funny about their feelings,* I thought to myself.

"I hate that this burden must lay with you," Robert continued, looking at each of us in turn. "But it is truly our last hope."

"'Lana's grandad, Brian told us what needed to be done," Luka said. "We're ready."

"I don't doubt you are, son. I just wish it was someone else's hide on the line besides my boy's. I'd do it myself, but—"

"You'd be recognized," I inserted. "From your time as a scribe."

Luka's Pa was taken aback. "So the old man told ya everything, did he?" He handed Luka a rolled-up piece of parchment. "A map of the castle tunnels. Secret pathways not even the King knows exist. They were once used to smuggle out the King's captives. Escaped through 'em myself, years ago."

Luka surveyed the map, running his finger along the lines, tracing our path before we began, "Aye, I can see it here," he said. "Won't even have to travel through the main hall for most of it, by the looks of things." He looked up. "Good thing I've always been good with maps."

"You were good at lots of other things," his Pa replied. A shudder ran down my spine as I realized what was happening. Why Robert was being so heartfelt with Luka.

"*He doesn't think you'll come out of this alive,*" the Darkness' voice was so strong the words almost came out of my own mouth. I looked at Robert's posture. He held himself like a man in mourning.

No, I argued. *That can't be it. He's just reunited with the son he's lost. Or maybe he knows about Luka's Ma.*

"*They're sending you on a suicide mission, and they know it!*"

"The Amasai were imprisoned in enchanted jewels," Robert explained. "Avardi and Metuza are fused into Ludlum's crown. He keeps them close to him at all times, safe upon his head all his waking hours."

298

"How are we supposed to get our hands on it, then?" Luka complained. "Just walk up to his Majesty and swipe it off his head?"

"All his waking hours," I mumbled. "Where does he keep it when he sleeps?"

"There's a smart lass," Robert commented, pressing his finger to his nose and winking in my direction. "Word is he places it on a silken pillow at his side. You'll have to sneak into his chambers after dark. See that spot on the map?" He pointed to an area near the center which was marked with the same rune Luka had used to create the portal.

"It marks a path," I mumbled.

"The Rune?" Luka's Pa nodded. "Aye, it was used by Mystics during the first war. Not many humans recognize it when they see it. Kind of like a secret code, if you will. This one marks a secret door to the King's chambers."

"If you've had a way in all this time, why has no one taken the Amasai until now?"

"You mean why has no one succeeded?" Robert's face became solemn. "Don't be foolish enough to think that no one before you has tried."

"What happened to them?" Luka asked the question I was too afraid to voice.

Robert's silence told me all I needed to know. There had been no survivors before us.

"This way has never been done before," Robert tried to comfort me. "The entry to the King's chambers was a recent discovery." He paused.

"And why is that?" Luka was quickly learning to be suspicious.

"See these markings here?" Robert pointed to places on the map where the quill had paused, and then been traced over. "We sent scouts to test the old maps and make changes where needed. These spots where the ink stops and starts again are where some of those scouts picked up the work where one left off."

"Left off as in?" I already knew the answer. I was hoping I was wrong.

"Fallen. As if by some outside force. None of us ever figured out why."

I surveyed the splotches on the parchment. They became frequent and closer together close to the King's chambers.

"It's the Amasai," I said with an unknown certainty. "My grandfather said you were working with the Dark Breeds." I held his gaze. "The fallen scouts, were they—"

"Dark Breeds. Some of them were half, maybe. Not many full-bloods would venture beyond the city's boundary. "

"That means we should be safe, then!" Luka looked relieved.

"Don't let a false sense of security make you a fool," his father cautioned. "We don't know for sure that's what caused it. And even if we did..." His eyes fell to the chain around my neck. "We don't know what affect *that* thing will have on the others."

So there it was, then. The reason he didn't think we'd make it out alive.

"Why me, then?" I demanded, "I didn't want any of this! I didn't ask for it! If you're certain the burden I carry will be our end, why send me?"

"It is because you've carried Anhedonia so long that we have any hope you can retrieve it," he said, a hint of regret in his voice. "One Amasai is powerful enough on its own, but to hold three? That is a feat not many can accomplish."

"But what about the other guardians?" Even though I knew it was too late to change my fate, an unexpected panic welled up in my chest, drowning me.

Robert suppressed a chuckle. "Well, I hardly think a dragon would go unnoticed in the castle," he replied.

"And Eoma has no idea about your treaty with the Dark Breeds," I finished, hoping that putting the realization to voice would calm the lump in my chest that threatened to steal my breath.

The three of us fell silent, mulling over the task before us. Luka was the first to speak.

"Well, that's all there is to it then," he said, squaring his shoulders. "We'd better get goin'."

Robert clenched his jaw and looked Luka in the eye. "You look after her, ya hear? And when you get your hands on that crown, you run. I don't care what else happens, you run, and you get far away from the castle, ya hear?" His voice gave out at the end.

"Yeah. Yeah, I understand," Luka managed. They embraced, and Robert seemed to hold on a little longer than usual, burying his face in Luka's hair. The sight made my heart ache for my own family. What knowledge, if any, would they have of my last hours? Were they still searching for me, or had they ceased their search, assuming the worst? I didn't have the answers. I probably never would. I swallowed the tears that threatened to end my quest and made my way to Luka's side.

"I'm ready," I lied.

CHAPTER FIFTEEN

LUKA'S PA LED US TO A CISTERN on the far side of the castle wall. It was large and wide, and blocked by a set of iron bars. Robert tapped the top of one bar, then another, eliciting a flat thunk from each. On the third one down the sound was different. More of a tink than a thunk. This was exactly what he was looking for.

"Ah, there it is," he said, and he wiggled the bar loose. Two more followed until there was enough room for Luka and I to squeeze in sideways. Robert replaced the bars behind us before he slipped back into the shadows, pausing only long enough to clasp hands with his son one last time.

"Gods be with you." he said. And then he was gone.

It didn't take long for the light to fade behind us. Unlike the last tunnel I'd been in, there was no light here for my half elven eyes to absorb, making my elf sight all but useless as we traveled through the ankle-deep water.

The first time I'd been taken through a tunnel, my whole life had changed. How fitting, I thought, that this time I might very well be marching to my doom. No wonder elves hated being trapped underground. The darkness brought me nothing but sorrow.

The tunnel grew narrower, and soon Luka and I had to walk single file rather than side by side, forcing our hands apart. My hand felt cold and exposed without his fingers threaded through mine, and suddenly I felt even more uneasy.

The water subsided as we came to an incline that wove us up and around a corner so tight that Luka nearly scraped his nose as he went around it. It was no wonder they didn't try to sneak a dragon through the tunnels. The two of us barely fit! I felt myself begin to panic as the walls closed around us, brushing against my shoulders as I followed Luka, my hand on his shoulder.

From time to time we heard echoes of the goings on in the castle. Soldiers standing guard, the gossip of one maid to another about who in the royal court was caught making eyes with one of the servers. The thought occurred to me that if we could hear them, perhaps they could hear us. Even more reason to move quickly and quietly.

You learn a lot about a castle when you're creeping through its hidden crevices. For example, did you know that the protective wall around the castle was two meters thick? Or that, no matter how well the servants clean, there are most certainly rats scurrying about in high beams and behind walls. That last bit of information I could have done without, especially since it was learnt by having one of the vile creatures scurry across my boot.

I suppressed the scream that threatened to give us away, but even still Luka had spun around, covering my mouth. The smell of his skin against mine was a welcome distraction. When the urge to yell had passed and he stepped away, I found my knees weak. Whether it was from the fright of the rat, or Luka's touch I was uncertain. I decided it was best not to mention it, just in case.

I have no idea how Luka managed to lead us through the tunnels with only the memory of his father's map, but he did it. Just as the map said, we hit a dead end. Luka and I ran our hands along the wall, searching for a latch. It didn't take long to find it. Slowly, cautiously, we slid it to the side and opened the door just enough to peek through a crack. We were met with more darkness, but this one was not as complete. Somewhere beyond our enclosure was a light source. I pushed the door open just a bit more, reaching my hand out to confirm my suspicion. My fingers came in contact with something soft, like silk. I was right! The tunnel opened up to the back of the King's wardrobe. I wondered at how those before us had accomplished such a feat. It must have taken both stealth and creativity. I eased the door shut again, and slid the latch closed. Then we waited.

The hours passed too quickly and dragged by at the same time. We were in a state of limbo. It was an odd feeling, to be waiting for our fate together, and yet be isolated by an inability to speak. Until Luka had the bright idea to trace letters on each other's hands. I had never been more thankful to Mother for insisting I learn to read than I was in those few hours, possibly our last. We reminisced over our childhoods, laughing quietly at the things we'd been sure were so important when we were tots, like who learned to lace up their boots first. It was like we'd been apart for an entire lifetime, and for no time at all.

CHAPTER SIXTEEN

THE SOUND OF SOMEONE FUMBLING WITH A DOORKNOB made me go silent. The muffled sound of boisterous laughter cut through the air, making the hairs on my arm stand up in alarm. Then followed clamoring footsteps, and a curse as a crash sounded. It sounded like the King had been celebrating something and indulged in a little too much mead. After a few more mild bumps and clamoring we heard a sigh, and the sound of a body falling firmly onto a soft surface.

Not long after, King Ludlum's snores began to vibrate off the walls. Even behind the cover of the wall behind the wardrobe, the sound was staggering. From time to time he would cough and sputter, usually right as Luka and I were about to make our way out of the wardrobe. The sound would cause us to freeze on the spot, and for a while I was sure we'd spend our last night alive in this constant limbo state.

Finally, Luka tapped my shoulder. I took his hand, letting him lead me through the wardrobe. In the dimly lit room he looked like no more than a shadow, and it was only when I looked down at my own hand that I realized that was part of his illusion. The affect made its way up and over my shoulder, shrouding me in shadows.

We tiptoed across the room, holding our breath in hopes of making our bodies lighter. One squeaky board could mean the end of us, our mission. The end of the Alliance. Funny how such small moments can cause a chain reaction, whether for better or worse.

In the center of the room was a four-post bed, and on it a man was strewn, disheveled and still in day clothes. The sight would have been repelling even if I hadn't known who he was. My eyes traced the lines of his face, which looked like it was meant to belong to a much younger man. How could this one person have caused so much suffering?

Because he wasn't just any man, I realized. He was a powerful man, fueled by grief and illogical fear. Yet there was nothing unduly special about him, save for the fact he'd stumbled into a place of power and ruled over a people who were content enough in their ignorance to allow themselves to grow complacent.

But not us, I reminded myself. Not me. It took more than one person to make this mess, and it took more than one to remedy it, if I was being honest. I wasn't fool enough to think I was the only one with a hand in the shift that was about to happen.

On the other hand, what if I'd refused? I was one person in a chain pulling society toward change, but a chain is only as strong as its weakest link. What if I turned around right now, decided it wasn't worth it. That this wasn't my fight. What if I took Luka and ran, far from here. What if I saved us both?

"You'd be sacrificing everyone else," Anhedonia answered for me. It had been silent for so long I'd almost forgotten its presence. And now it was urging me forward in my quest. The realization made my stomach tie in knots. If the Darkness was pushing me toward the other Amasai, that meant it had a plan. A dangerous plan.

No use fighting it, the Darkness smirked. *What choice do you have?*

It was right.

A sharp corner thumped into my shin, almost taking me down. Luka spun to adjust, but I'd knocked him off balance too and we tumbled to the ground.

"Harumph! Who's there?!" A disgruntled voice shouted. Luka squeezed my hand and motioned for me to be silent, pressing himself against the floor. The fade wavered, then intensified as he struggled to hide us. I pressed my face against the floor, breathing in the smell of dust and oak as I prayed that the fade would hold.

There was a knock at the door. "Your Majesty?" a voice from the other side called, but the King had already rolled over and resumed snoring. I let my breath out slowly, relieved that the standing guard hadn't burst in and trampled us. I was pretty sure the fade was a visual illusion. Being trampled would have given us away for sure. After a minute or so had passed, we pulled ourselves up from the ground and made our way to the King's bedside, where Ludlum's crown sat upon a red silken pillow.

The crown was cast in rose gold, a strange choice for a ruler of such cruelty, I thought to myself. It was decorated with ornate carvings that spiraled up to the peaks of every point, of which there were eight.

Upon the crown, front and center, was the King's emblem, a two headed serpent meant to symbolize a basilisk, with a sword running through it at the middle. There were four settings for four stones, though only two were set. I wondered, looking at the design, at how long Ludlum had been planning to get his hands on the other Amasai. When the ships from the Old World set sail, did he intend to conquer the native people? Or was his perversion progressive, something that grew over time as he acquired power? It wasn't unusual in my mother's people's history, for those with the best of intentions to face corruption over time. Perhaps it was the human condition.

The thought made me pause, and for a moment I recoiled, reluctant to take the crown in my hand. I was half human, and therefore vulnerable to the same corruptions. What if this was what the Amasai wanted? To be taken by another who would fall victim to the burden of their power.

"No choice, silly girl," Anhedonia's voice cooed softly in my head. I don't know what I'd expected from it in this moment, but the silky, whispering voice wasn't it. *"More flies with honey, my pet,"* the Darkness answered my question. It wanted me to move forward and knew that forcing my hand would only lessen my chance of following through.

Still, I could feel the draw of the other Amasai, Avadari and Metuza.

Greed and Fear. I felt them pulling me in their direction. They wanted to unite with their brothers. To multiply their influence. As my hand grasped the cold metal of the King's crown, images flashed to the forefront of my mind, the faces of their past victims, the battles they'd set into motion. Laughter welled up in my mind, not the kind that comes from joy, but the kind that is propelled by triumph. The voice was joined by others, causing my chest to swell with the force of it. It would not be long, I knew, until it made its way up my throat and out my mouth. I knew my voice would echo their triumph. I shot a desperate look in Luka's direction. He took the hint and pulled me toward the door in a panic.

No, I thought. *Not the main hall.* But the words wouldn't make their way out of my mouth. I no longer had full control of my senses. Luka squished his eyes shut, concentrating until the shadowy outline of his body began to flicker as he went deeper into his fade, taking me with him. Beads of sweat collected on his brow as he struggled to concentrate.

By the time we reached the main door we were nearly invisible. Luka threw the door open, pulling me out in such a hurry that we breezed past the standing guards before I'd had a chance to protest. It would have felt like a rush of wind had blown the door open, had the sound of our footprints not given us away.

"What was that?" one guard shouted, as the other made his way into the room to check on the King.

We didn't wait for them to figure it out. Luka dragged me down the hall, nearly yanking my arm out of the socket. My muscles ached with the effort of trying to keep up. As we ran through the dimly lit corridors, I noticed Luka's outline wavering. The fade was failing.

"SOUND THE ALARM!" a voice bellowed behind us. "THE CROWN HAS BEEN STOLEN"

Great, just what we need, I thought. *This will be the end of us.*

"Not if you get them before they get you," a voice like the Darkness offered. I glanced over my shoulder, surprised to see we'd not put as much distance between ourselves and the King's Chambers as I had hoped. My heart leaped into my throat, and I stifled a yelp. We had to get out. We had to go faster, we had to—

Luka gave my hand a squeeze, bringing me back to my senses. Now I knew who the new voice belonged to: Metuza. Fear.

Fear is a funny thing. It is necessary for survival. Fear is what makes us wary of predators. Fear of illness leads to new ways to prepare food or build shelter. But too much fear can be distracting, and misplaced fears can be deadly.

"Almost there," Luka puffed between hard breaths. I had no idea where "there" was, but I felt a wave of relief knowing this would all be over soon.

"*Aye, but it would be over sooner if he gave you a head start,*" another voice joined the fray. This one I knew immediately. It was Avadari. Greed. Another way Mother Nature propelled our minds toward survival. But at what cost?

I'm not sacrificing Luka, I thought to myself. *No matter what. Nothing is worth that cost.*

"*But isn't it, though?*" Metuza chimed in again. "*Imagine what they'll do, once they catch you.*"

Images of the execution circle at the center of Aythia were forced to the forefront of my consciousness. These memories didn't belong to me, and yet they felt like mine. Memories from the past, forced from the dormant parts of my mind by the Amasai. The effect was painful in layers, both psychological and physical. The wave of pain made me start, causing the tip of my foot to catch against the floor and send me tumbling to the ground, taking Luka with me.

Luka was up in a flash, ready to run, but I remained sprawled on the floor. I looked around, trying to make sense of my surroundings. We'd made it to the main balcony of the castle, the one Ludlum stood on when he addressed his people. The one he had stood on countless times, as he gave the final order at executions.

Beneath me, the cool marble was a welcome distraction. I pressed my forehead against it, hoping to cool the fiery ache in my head. It felt like my brain was boiling in my skull.

"Come on," Luka's voice urged me up. "I know it's hard. We're almost there, but you have to get up." He reached around me, lifting me under my arms until I was standing again.

Luka moved toward the balcony doors, pushing them open. A cold breeze invited itself in, filling the corridor.

"Just jump," Anhedonia urged.

"No, it's too far, you'll never make it," Metuza replied. Each utterance was like shards of glass being pressed deeper into my mind. The world began to spin and go dark, and I was sure this was how I would meet my end.

"Run." My mouth had gone dry, making my warning no more than a hoarse whisper. "Save yourself."

Luka shook his head, tears welling up in his eyes. "No. No, you're not giving up now. I won't let you." He reached for the crown and I recoiled, shaking my head.

The Amasai were too strong.

"If you can't walk, I'll carry you," he insisted, but I balked at his touch, tears running down my cheeks. Their power coursed through me like electricity. I was sure any contact I made would cause them to lash out, injuring, if not killing him. I moved toward the balcony, gazing over the city I had once called home. In the distance the faintest bit of pink sky crept upward through the darkness.

"Stupid girl," Anhedonia chided. *"Can't even make it out of the Castle. Time's up."*

"This is it." Metuza added, *"The Dark Breeds will never come now."*

"For the best," Avadari chimed in. *"There's barely land to go around as it is. The last thing we need is their like spreading outside their boundary."*

It was too much at once. I couldn't think straight. How could I signal that we had the Amasai?

"LET US GO," they chimed in unison, and I realized what was happening. They were vying for control, taking turns tearing me down until I was too weak to fight them. What would they do with my body, once they'd shredded my mind? Destroy it, most likely.

"Or you could save everyone time and do it yourself," Anhedonia coaxed me to the edge of the balcony.

Yes, I thought. *Yes, that would be good. I could end it all now. All the suffering.*

310

The Amasai would be gone, Luka could make it to safety—

"STOP," a commanding voice pulled me back to the present. Unlike the Amasai, this voice came from outside of me. It was one I hadn't heard in a long time.

"Stop, child," Eoma spoke cautiously, but with authority.

Luka put himself between us, an act that any other day would have elicited a mocking laugh from the High Priestess. Instead she smiled sadly.

"Move aside, boy. I'm not going to hurt her." Her eyes darted in my direction. "But if you're not careful you'll be party to her hurting herself."

The look of horror on Luka's face as he turned in my direction made my heart shatter. I wanted to deny it. To tell him I would never ... but finding myself poised at the edge of the balcony, its marble railing pressed against my back, I couldn't even convince myself.

Footsteps from around the corner stole her attention momentarily as two guards raced toward us. With a flick of her wrist, Eoma tossed them like ragdolls, rendering them unconscious. She returned her attention to me.

"I know you're confused." Eoma inched toward me, her hand held out in a gesture of peace. "I know you're frightened. But this is not the answer."

"What do you know about anything?" I shouted back. "What do you know about pain or loss or ... or sacrifice!" Fear backed me into a corner, pelting me with every emotion I'd repressed for the sake of my quest.

Eoma didn't take the bait, and instead remained calm. "I know you think this is the only way to save everyone, but you have to believe me, it will only make things worse." She continued to move toward me slowly as she spoke. "You have to control it. To see the thoughts for what they are. Not yours. Not real."

Now I knew she was lying. "It feels real enough," I snapped back. "You don't want to save me, you just want this." I waved the crown in her direction. "This power. You want it for yourself."

"Oh, child." Her face softened beyond any expression I'd seen from her before. "I'm so sorry. I should have known. I should have seen~"

"But you didn't!" I choked back a sob. "You didn't and now here we are! The sun is rising, the Kingdom is at stake. And you want what? For me to come back with you? To be your pawn?"

"All I want right now is for you to back away from the ledge, Azlana."

"And why should I?"

"Because if you end your life you will set them free!" Her frustration had finally gotten the best of her, and she raised her voice.

My breath caught in my throat. Was it true?

"The witch lies," Metuza accused. *"She just wants us for herself. Look how she flaunts our brother's prison."*

My eyes darted quickly to the jewel encased upon her headdress. It burned a brilliant red as she grew closer. I looked down and saw that the other jewels responded, pulsing with light. They wanted to be united.

"Well," I mumbled to myself. "If that's what you want." I braced myself as if to jump the railing. The act propelled the priestess forward in an attempt to stop me. Just what I'd hoped for. I reached out my hand as she flung herself forward, pleased when my fingers raked against her forehead, breaking Imari's prison free of its encasement. Together we tumbled to the ground.

I didn't stay down long. My body almost seemed to move of its own accord as I pulled myself up in triumph. I had it. The last Amasai. All of their power was tied to me now. Their laughter welled up inside of me and the world spun, kicking up a whirlwind that caused my hair around my face and stung my eyes until tears collected in their corners. I turned one way and another in alarm, trying to find the wind's source before I realized: It was me. I was doing this.

In the distance a rooster crowed as the first day's light crept over the horizon. A shadow rose in the distance.

A dragon-shaped shadow.

"I've come for your King!" Fiora roared before letting loose a stream of fire from her belly. The blaze ignited the long grass that divided Ludlum's kingdom from the Mystic's land, effectively cutting us off from any hope of aid.

We were out of time.

Eoma looked up at me from the ground in horror. She had no power here.

"*No need to fret,*" Anhedonia whispered. "*You can end it all here.*"

"Don't listen to them!" Luka called out to me. I'd almost forgotten about him. "You're in charge of your own fate, 'Lana. Not them. Not me." He gestured toward Eoma. "And not her either! Don't let your story end here."

"What right does he have to tell you what to do," Imari purred as it settled into my mind like a cat at the hearth, stretching itself out to touch the last bits of my mind that I still considered mine. A fiery rage welled up in me. My face must have reflected it, for Luka's face went white as a sheet.

"She's not here anymore," the chorus of voices came from my body, but it was not of my free will. The Amasai were in control now. Their essences molded together within me, a shrill buzz that grew in discord along with their power.

The last thing I felt was the warm trace of a tear that ran down my cheek as I looked at Luka's pained expression.

As I turned to step back onto the railing several things happened.

First, Luka's body crashed into mine. At first I thought he meant to stop me, but as we fell, his arms wrapped tightly around my waist. It wasn't until my body made contact with the dragon's back that I realized he'd taken us both over the edge on purpose.

"Fight it, half-breed," Fiora urged as her wings sliced through the air, raising us higher than castle's tallest peak. I sat up, resisting the urge to vomit.

"I can't!" A cyclone of wind rushed over my face, stealing my voice.

"Yes you can!" Luka tightened his grip around me as Fiora banked left. "You have to!"

Fiora blasted another stream of fire upon the city as the King's archers assumed their stations on the battlements. In the far distance an army of specks marched through the flames surrounding the city. The Dark Breeds were coming.

"If you let the Amasai win, we're done for," Fiora warned. "All of us."

Pain coursed through my body. I clenched my jaw, bracing against it. "I don't know how," I cried.

If this was how I was going to die, I was glad   was here. He took my hand in his, squeezing gently. The act sent a rush of warmth up my arm like nothing I had felt before. A sense of calm washed over me. I knew what had to happen.

"I'm so sorry I dragged you into this," I whimpered

"It's okay," he said, even though I knew it wasn't.

"I don't want it to end like this," I sobbed. "I tried so hard."

Luka took my face in his hands, brushing the sweat-plastered hair from my face. His thumb caressed my cheek, wiping away a tear.

He pressed his lips against mine as the world ended.

At first there was nothing. I was floating in an endless sea of darkness. Then I began to drift downward until my feet made contact with solid ground. I spun one way, and then the other, looking for a sign that anyone else survived. I was alone.

Until I wasn't.

Colors pulsed in alternating hues of green, red, and yellow, each casting itself across all of eternity. My hands flew up over me, shieling my eyes against their terrible glory.

"Where am I?" I called to the nothingness.

The pulsing paused, almost as if it were thinking to itself. *"In between,"* a chorus of voices answered.

"What do you you want from me?"

"Freedom."

"I can't give that to you. You know that." I tried to keep my voice steady. To give the illusion of composure, but to my chagrin my voice quivered with every word.

The lights grew brighter. They didn't like my answer. *"You dare defy the Amasai?"*

I fell to my knees from the force of their response. My ear drums felt as if they would burst under the pressure. The feeling spread throughout my body, crushing me.

"Let. Us. Go."

"No!" I felt myself being torn in different directions. My joints strained against the tug of the Amasai until they ached.

And then another voice called in the distance, faintly at first. Then again, stronger with every repetition.

"'Azlana!" The voice was familiar, and yet I couldn't place it. "You have to fight it."

"She's been out too long," another voice murmured. This one drew me toward it. It sounded like home.

I'd made it only a few steps when a gust of wind took my feet out from under me, dragging me back into the abyss.

"Nooooo!" I screamed, clawing at the floor in vain as the force pulled me further and further from my freedom.

"Give up," the Amasai chanted. "They don't want you. They'll strip you of your power."

Doubt crept into the corners of my mind as the darkness took root. What if it was right? What if they didn't want me?

"You're just a pawn," Metuza mocked me. "Poor little naive girl. Don't you see? They only want to use you."

An image of Eoma appeared before me. One of the lights moved down, circling it.

"This one is familiar," it said. "I have known her a long time. So much power in that one, to feed on her would have been lovely."

The light turned to me. "Pity she sent you in her stead. A measly sacrifice, at best. Still, you'll do."

"No," it came out a whisper at first. I wet my lips, took a deep breath, and tried again. "NO! I won't be fooled by your trickery. Not this time. You'll never be free!"

The darkness around me wavered, and the scene changed. I was home. My real home. The smell of soup on the stove invaded my nostrils, making my stomach growl.

I ran to my room, then out again, searching for signs of Mother, but I found none. A knock on the door startled me.

"'Lana!" The voice was Luka's. "'Lana, let me in!" He was pounding on the door now, his cries growing more urgent. I ran to open it, recoiling as my hand made contact with the brass doorknob. It was blazing hot.

"Not so fast," Anhedonia teased. Images appeared out of nowhere, surrounding me. At first they were arranged neatly in a circle, suspended in darkness. They played back like memories, though not all of them belonged to me.

There was the time when I was five and I snuck sweets from one of the merchant's carts, even though I knew I wasn't supposed to.

Another where I lied for Luka after he snipped the braids off a girl who had been picking on me.

Me, yelling at Mother and storming to my room.

And lastly, me pulling the hood of my cloak over my head as I snuck away from the Safehold.

Greed.

Fear.

Anger.

"*And me,*" Anhedonia's voice was almost soothing compared to the others. Familiar, almost like it came from me. Almost like it *was* me.

The images began to spin around me with increasing speed, pausing only a moment as I focused on them individually, each a memory of a time in my life touched by one of the four burdens.

"*We've always been here,*" one of them said.

"*We always will,*" another picked up where its brother left off.

"*Might as well accept it...*" they joined in unison

They were right. They had always been there. Somehow their influence had been branded upon my ancestors, bleeding into their offspring for generations.

We hadn't imprisoned them. We hadn't beaten them. We had become them. What use was it, then, to keep fighting?

"*Yes, yes that's it,*" Anhedonia cooed. "*Just give in. It will be so much easier if you stop caring. Stop feeling."*

Stop feeling? The images came to a halt, on a memory that was not my own. A young girl sat beside an elf. She had the same raven hair as I, and he looked oddly familiar, almost as if he were related.

"It is okay to feel sorrow, and it is okay to weep. It does not make you any less of a respectable person. It does not change my perception of you."

The voice wasn't speaking to me, and yet it was meant for me. For this moment. Suddenly the images changed course, fading one at a time. Each one of them had one thing in common: Luka

The time I'd mended his best tunic when he tore it jumping a fence before his dad could find out he'd tattered it.

Fishing at the pond near our home.

Memory after memory of Luka climbing in my window when the other children had shunned me.

I knew what I had to do.

I had never felt secure in myself, so fighting off the Amasai on my own wasn't going to work.

I had to look at things from outside of the burden I carried. And I had to let them be what they were: a part of who I was.

The images faded into smoke and I faced the door once again. This time when I reached for the doorknob it was cool to the touch. As I opened it, light poured around me, warming my face. I sighed.

It felt like home.

EPILOGUE

ONE YEAR LATER...

The room smelled of oak and incense as Eoma declared an end to the meeting of the Three Lands. I watched in silence as ambassadors from different realms rose and filed out the door, paying their respects with a bow to me as they did so.

It still felt odd, to be seated at the head of the table where my grandfather should have been. I had listened intently to each ambassador's advice regarding Cain's fate. I refused execution, as he had done me no actual harm. Eoma's advice was to hold him captive, but that seemed too harsh a punishment as well. Perhaps it was because I knew the Darkness he had faced. Where I had succeeded he had fallen, and to me that was worse than any punishment I could imagine.

It was his wife, Thana, who suggested banishment. He would live out the rest of his days in the uncharted territories—what was known to me as the Darklands, and to her was simply home. What they would do with him once he was transferred to their care was left unsaid.

One by one, members of what had once been the Alliance took leave to the dining hall, where a grand feast was planned to honor the unity of the humans, mystics, and dark breeds. Only Eoma stayed behind, unrolling a parchment which listed the day's order of events, checking to make sure everything was in order.

"Will you stay awhile?" I asked her.

She raised an eyebrow. "If it is the Queen's wish."

I wondered if I'd ever get used to her calling me that. Queen. In my mind I was little more than a child, even now.

"Your student wishes," I said, wanting to clarify the role I was asking of her. I motioned for her to take a seat at my side.

"Something troubles you?" She could have ventured into my mind for the answer if she'd wanted. I was sure she had better things to do with her time than to reassure my qualms. Still, I appreciated the courtesy of a spoken question.

"Does it ever get easier?" I motioned to the air. "Not this. Not the laws or the taxes or the ruling, but ... this?" I was doing a poor job of getting my point across, and it showed on the Priestess' face. "This feeling. Does it ever go away?"

Her eyes fell to the sword on my hip. Luka's Pa had made it for me as a coronation gift. Set into the hilt were four jewels: All that was left of the Amasai. Well, almost all.

"Oh, child, no." She spoke softly, placing her hand over mine. "No, it doesn't go away. Not really. Not forever. You can't go back to the way things were. None of us, not a single one who has been touched by the Amasai will ever be the same as we were. That is our curse. And our blessing."

"Blessing? In what way could this ever be considered a blessing? To be separate from all of them in a way none of them can truly understand?"

"The demons you have faced, the ones that were only ever really a part of your deeper potential. The ones you accepted as part of yourself, they bring with them something more than just a deep sorrow. And yet it is something only deep sorrow can bring."

"And what is that?"

"Empathy. Patience. A way of connecting with those around us whether their situation mirrors ours or not. It is how we connect with one another. It is how we survive. The pain might feel as if it breaks us, but it is within the space of our broken pieces that we find room for growth."

I mulled over her words, absorbing them the way plants absorb light from the sun. A warmth washed over me, feeding my soul.

"Very well, then," I said. "What's next on the agenda?"

"Your tasks are done for the evening. You're free to dine with your family."

"Thank you, my friend." I stood, clasping her hand in both of mine in gratitude. I made my way down the corridor and out to the garden where Luka and Nova waited to begin the next adventure in this, our beautiful chaos.

BOOK FOUR

RING OF FIRE

AN AMASAI RISING PREQUEL

PROLOGUE

YSTICS AND HUMANS HAVE BEEN ALWAYS BEEN ENEMIES. Since the explorers of the Old World migrated from across the sea. Our leader, Irvin Ludlum, fled with his wife Allana and a handful of Old World misfits to build a new life; however there was a conflict between peoples.

Those who had first inhabited the continent-the elves, faeries, imps, and other mystical creatures that my people had never encountered– were reluctant to surrender their land to these new foreigners. Even the elves, originally our allies, turned against my people as Ludlum's greed transformed the colony into a vast and intrusive kingdom. Outnumbered by the Mystics, my people prepared to take to the seas once again in search of a new home.

The tides turned when one of our soldiers made a discovery while searching the unclaimed territories at the edge of Ludlum's kingdom. It was the journal of an ancient elven ruler; a journal that held the secret weaknesses of many of the mystic breeds. The battle that followed became a legend among my people. Many of the innocent lost their lives in the fray. Three generations later, the grasslands where the battle took place are stained red, as if the land still mourns.

In the end, my people were victorious. Ludlum built the crown city of his kingdom, Aythia, in the center of the newly-claimed land, expanding his kingdom outward in all directions. The Mystics retreated into the forest, but never forgot their loss, or their hatred.

After the war, Ludlum enacted a system of laws forbidding contact with each species listed in the elven king's journal. Violation of the law was considered treason, and the punishment was death.

To enforce his laws, the king and his descendants trained an Elite force of soldiers loyal to his cause to patrol the boundaries of his kingdom.

Over the years they tracked, captured, and killed not only Mystics but their human allies as well. An execution circle was erected in front of the castle. It was designed to draw in spectators, instilling fear and from that: loyalty. It was an effective deterrent to most citizens.

I am not most citizens.

Chapter One

M Y NAME IS KALA. At the beginning of my story, I was just nearing the age of 16. It would have been a story beautiful in its simplicity had it not been intertwined with other, more complicated stories.

But that is the nature of all our fates: stories and lives weaving in and out of one-another. Touching briefly, or knotting together in an untangleable chaos. We are both masters of our own fates and victims of others'.

I was born to a woman named Gwen, a descendant of royalty in the Old World. She and her brother John had been cast aside by their jealous aunt and guardian when the New Kingdom was established.

My mother was a wild young thing who preferred men's clothing to long gowns and wasn't afraid to get her hands dirty. She shared the same raven hair as I, though she wore it short and angled by her chin as opposed to the waist-length plaited braids my generation found fashionable. It was from her that I inherited my pale freckled skin and dark eyes as well. Both of which were an anomaly amongst her kin.

Her brother John, in contrast, had sandy blonde hair and hazel eyes. He lived the life of a farmer. Though he was still mostly a child himself, he provided for my mother. When the war was settled, John married and joined the king's army. In times of trouble, he would leave his sister in charge of the homestead responsibilities, one of which was the trading of wares.

That was how she met my father. A tall merchant's apprentice with sandy hair, brooding eyes and the tongue of a poet, he won my mother's heart easily. It was not long after that they were married, and I came along.

My early childhood was typical. My parents were kindly, though they were often away on important trips. While they were away I spent time with my uncle and his family. My cousin Audri was two years my senior. She had honey-colored hair, icy blue eyes, and a sweet disposition; though after her mother abandoned them her spirit withered, and she became more frigid.

I was 6 when my parents were killed. Uncle John had been summoned early in the afternoon on a scouting mission— a once rare occurrence had become more frequent since my aunt had run off. Audri, only 8 herself, wove intricate tales of her capture and subsequent rescue by her father. (Surely that was the reason for his increasingly frequent absences!)

It was all very romantic and fantastical in her imagination; a charade she maintained for years even after word had spread that her mother had left of her own free will to tour the Old World with a musician she had been courting behind my uncle's back. She may have made light of it during the day, but in the evenings when she thought I was asleep, I would hear her crying softly into her pillow.

On the night my parents died I remember sitting by the hearth with Audri. Outside, the rain beat against the roof and the wind whistled harshly, making the house creak. The two of us were playing with a pair of rag dolls we had fashioned from two burlap dish cloths, sticks, and twine.

The game was a mock battle between a soldier of our kind and one of the Mystic priestesses (though we knew them only as witches). It was one we played often, as I imagine most children of our time did. The story of the War and Ludlum's Laws were the first (and in many cases only) education many of us on the outer limits of the kingdom received. Formal education was reserved for children of more affluent families.

"Eat steel, you Mystic wench!" Audri declared. She had claimed seniority between the two of us. Her character was always the soldier and I was always some mystical creature in these make-believe stories.

"Never!" I replied, waving my rag doll in the air dramatically. "Whoosh!" I thrust my hand from the chest of the doll mimicking what I imagined was a great act of magic. "Curses on you ahahahaha!" I cackled in my best crusty old witch voice.

I wrapped my hands around her doll and tossed it about for added effect. Just then the front door flew open and lightning crashed. In lumbered Uncle John, his uniform disheveled and soaked through from the rain. His hair was plastered to his face, which carried a pained expression. His eyes were red. I did not realize it at the time, but he had been crying.

He was winded, and when he exhaled his breath hung icy in the air, as if his body were trying to expel an evil it could not escape. He closed the door behind him with a heavy THUD.

Immediately our play ceased. Audri ran to him. "Father! Father, look at the dolls we made today! Mine is a soldier. He is strong like you! Kala's is a nasty witch! We tied them with string, Father, see? SEE?!!" She bounced around excitedly.

John held out his hand, motioning for her to stop, "Hush Audri."

She fell silent. It was not like him to speak to her in such a manner, nor to dismiss her narratives. He had always been a doting father who hung on her every word. He pushed past her and sat in his chair, gazing at the fire as if in a trance before lowering his head in his hands and sighing. An eerie silence hung in the air before I gathered up enough courage to speak.

"Uncle," I started softly, "what's the matter?" His eyes met my own, and for a moment I could almost hear his heart shatter.

"Kala-," his voice broke. It was weak and raspy. It reminded me of my own that time I was scolded and sent to time-out for tattering Audri's favorite dress. Sent to my room unjustly, I'd cried and screamed myself hoarse. Suddenly I was afraid of what he would say next.

"Kala...your mom...Oh, Gods Gwen!"

A wretched sound escaped him and I realized he had choked back a sob. Gwen? What had Mom done? Perhaps my parents' trip had been extended? But that did not explain why he was so distraught.

"Are they delayed on the road, Uncle?" I ventured cautiously.

"Delayed," he repeated. His eyes fell again to the fire. His focus was distant and his voice seemed far away. "Kala, your parents will not be coming home."

He rose before I could ask for clarification and walked down the hall to his room, leaving a trail of muddy footprints and sorrow behind him as his tears mingled with rainwater and fell upon the wooden floor.

I stood there a moment as my little brain tried to process his words. "Your parents will not be coming home."

Audri fidgeted nervously beside me, twisting her reclaimed doll in her fists. Those few years between us suddenly seemed amplified as I looked to her. She suddenly became very wise in my small, frightened eyes. I knew she had understood her father's words.

"What does that mean?" I asked.

Her eyes darted down the hall at her father's door and back to me, making a connection that my mind was too young to process. Her mouth opened but was void of sound. She closed it again. I felt myself grow angry. Why wasn't anyone telling me what was going on?

"Audri!" I stomped and tugged at her dress with my free hand, somehow wrestling her doll from her in the process. I clenched a doll in each hand now. The pressure of my palms against the sticks and cloth felt somehow soothing.

"They are not coming home," Audri echoed her father's words, "Kala.... your parents were killed. That's why the King has been summoning Father. It had to be Mystics"

I shook my head. "No!" my voice squeaked. Audri stood where she was. I swung at her. "NO! You're lying! You're a LIAR!" She stared at me in shock. "You're just saying that to be mean! You are jealous because you don't have a mother!"

Audri slapped me hard across the face. Never before had she struck me.

"I HATE YOU!" I screeched as I chucked both of our ragdolls into the hearth. I listened briefly to the crackling sound the previously waning fire made as it came back to life, before darting down the hall to the room we shared and slamming the door behind me. The force of it jarred my arm and I clutched it as I sank to the floor, wailing.

When I had finally quieted and laid down on my bed it was long past dark. I heard the door creak as Audri crept in and laid down in her own bed across the room. We were both silent. When I was sure she was asleep I rolled over and saw her clutching the ashy remains of a burlap cloth. I closed my eyes and waited to wake up from what I hoped was a nightmare.

We never spoke of what happened between us. Though we seemed to remain close, my cousin's and my relationship was permanently marked by the events of that night.

There was no funeral for my parents.

After the death of his sister, my uncle changed. Though he maintained his work ethic, he went about his duties with a heavy heart and little enthusiasm, as if the weight of the world rested solely on his shoulders. He was silent for weeks and hardly ate. When he did start speaking again, it was in short bursts to give a direction or command.

The change, which impacted my then very-young-brain most dramatically, was that instead of the usual bedtime tales of his own childhood and the Old World, or what it was like to work so closely under the King in his court—Uncle John began to quiz us on the various Mystic races. Their history, their habits, and most importantly: their weaknesses.

He drilled us over and over, impressing on us that we needed to be able to recall the information at a moment's notice. He would stand in our room, a coin resting in his hand and say, "You need to retrieve and recite their weakness before this coin hits the floor, girls. Do that, and you are safe. If the coin hits the floor, you are dead. It happens that quickly out there."

While at first it was terrifying to think of, over time this became a game to Audri and me. A sort of competition between us to see who could recall the information most quickly. I was always more skilled in rote memorization than she was, though she seemed to take her father's lessons much more seriously as time went on. Sometimes I would have to stall and let her win just to avoid a pouting fit on her part, but inside my head, I recited the answer to each question.

"Imps," he would say tossing the coin in the air.

"Related to faeries. Weakness: Speaking their native name" Just in time. The coin clattered on the floor.

"Dragons."

Audri spoke out before I did, "Drowning."

Mentally I corrected her. Drowning or poison.

CLANG!

"Trolls."

We spoke out together, "Sunlight!"

CLANG!

"Faeries," and the coin was in the air again

This time I beat Audri, "Silver."

CLANG!

It was the same every night. The knowledge was so deeply embedded into our minds that I would often find myself whispering them back to no one in particular as I drifted off to sleep.

CHAPTER TWO

O VER THE YEARS THE LOSS OF MY PARENTS BECAME MORE BEARABLE, though I would always carry a hole in my heart where they should have been. Because there were no formal laws regarding orphans, my uncle's custody over me remained unchallenged. The sun continued to rise and fall; the seasons changed, and Audri and I grew from wild-haired youths who played with rag dolls into young ladies who attended to farm chores.

Of the two of us, Audri was more reserved. A rule-follower. Her demeanor was curt and sometimes cold, but she rarely lost her temper; and at this point in our lives, there had never been another time that I saw her raise her hand to anyone.

I was the adventurous one. The joker. The dreamer. It was not uncommon to see me giggling with the chickens while collecting their eggs. Or telling jokes and having conversations as if they had the capacity to understand. Other days I could be found gazing at the sky, picking at the end of my braid as I contemplated the cosmos instead of cleaning the stables as I'd been told.

On a particularly wild day, I might even be caught rolling down the hill behind our farm, my hands covering my face, just like we had done as children. My antics were an annoyance to my cousin and a worry to my uncle who was certain he could never convince a decent young man to take my hand. Never mind that at eighteen his own daughter had no suitors of her own.

In spite of our differences, my cousin and I developed a strange bond, mostly out of necessity. It was a sort of hot and cold sisterhood. One moment we were best friends, and the next, sour enemies. The changes in polarity became more subtle as we grew older; so that I was never quite sure where I stood with her. Still, we often found that we were all that the other one had. There were no other girls our age this far in the country, and mingling between genders was forbidden past a certain age.

Her father was often away, either trading with other farmers or training new soldiers. He had retired from active duty due to a leg injury a few years after the death of my parents. Especially in the colder months, I would see him rubbing his bad knee and muttering to himself softly. While his leg pained him, it was the death of my mother that crippled him. Though he remained a steadfast caretaker, he retreated further and further within himself as the years passed.

And so, with only one another as cohorts, Audri and I grew to become very much like sisters. Sharing our hopes, dreams, and our worst fears. For this, we had created a special place in the back of the farm property, way atop the hill that I was often chastised for rolling down. Our tree house was a sanctuary and a secret, even from my uncle. It was hidden from outside eyes by the vast tangled branches of a long-neglected and overgrown tree whose leaves never withered.

We'd built the shelter ourselves when she was nearing ten years old and I was eight. It was primitive, built from rough but hardy wood planks from the crates Uncle used to transport produce when he would venture into the market to trade.

The roof was once flat and not suitable for the rainy season. We had been forced to replace it the following year when it collapsed under the pressure of heavy rains, flooding our sanctuary and nearly washing away the entire thing. When we rebuilt it we also cut a hole on the side facing the boundary we were forbidden to cross, lining it with large pebbles secured with clay, partly for aesthetics and partly because it was more pleasant to lean against the cool, smooth rocks during the summer season. The window seemed a tiny rebellion against an otherwise strict upbringing, and we were pleased with ourselves.

The tree sat at the top of the hill, on the edge of my uncle's property, just yards from the kingdom's border. Indeed our proximity to the Uncharted Territories was likely the main motivator for the King to recruit my uncle into his army in the first place. Who better to guard the border than he who had already settled there?

From our tree you could see the crimson field, which wrapped its way all around the back end of our farm and, further out, the woods. The field was said to have been cursed and was excluded from Ludlum's claim based on that superstition. The woods, being outside the boundary of his reign as well, had never been named by my people.

Looking back, there must have been whispers in the town about the propriety of bringing up two young girls so close to the enemy's land, but Audri and I neither heard nor saw any signs of danger as we went about our simple childhoods.

The first time I saw it I was alone. It was nearing dusk and I was supposed to be ushering the chickens into their coop for the night. Instead, I had crept up the hill and sat in the grass to watch the sun setting. It was one of the few memories I had of my parents-sitting outside and watching the daylight fade.

"Well there it is, the end of another day," my father would say, right as the last sliver of the sun was fading from our view. He tried to sound exhausted, but if you looked, you would see a playful smirk run across his face as he glanced at my mother. She would slap his arm playfully as darkness overtook us. Then she would lean down to me and whisper in my ear.

"The fools who see it as an end, my lovely, are blinded by their own limited realities. What is the end of one day, if not the beginning of another?"

She would look out of the corner of her eye at my father and smile as if they were sharing in some secret that I was too young to understand. Then, standing they would lock hands with each other, their fingers intertwining as they started across the yard to the house. I always stayed a moment longer to look up where the sky had exploded into thousands of tiny flickering lights surrounded by the darkness. I'd always imagined those lights were where the next day began.

I was jarred back to reality by a loud squawk. I was on my back. The grass beneath me was cold and damp. The sky was dark. Around me, the hens were in a tizzy. I must have fallen asleep! In a panic I stood and began to round up the chickens, counting them as I went along. The rooster was missing.

I ushered the hens into their coop and locked it, then turned to the house. Uncle John was away again, so my only worry was that Audri might still be awake. The windows were dark. I breathed a sigh of relief and trudged back up the hill to look for the rooster; or his remains.

While I was sure that I'd have awoken at the sound of a struggle, it would not be the first time we had lost livestock to local wildlife. Raccoons, foxes, even coyotes would sneak in from time to time if we weren't careful, but, despite the lack of fencing on our property, we had never had an animal escape.

I scanned the area where I'd collected the hens. The grass where I had been lying was bent, a telltale sign of my diversion from my daily work. I was in so much trouble. Briefly, I tried to rustle the land up with my feet, hoping to destroy the evidence. I was mildly successful. I turned, hoping to have a halfway decent view of the property, but I was out of luck. It was overcast, and the light from the moon was barely seeping through the clouds.

There was a rustling sound in the distance behind me. I spun around. The air was still. No explanation for the noise. I thought I detected movement in the tall grass that covered the land between territories. I squinted. Nothing. Then another noise:

"Kukelekuuu!"

The rooster! I dashed toward the sound, stopping just below the tree house. My hand rested on the rough trunk of the tree as I listened again. For a long time there was silence, and then:

"Kukelekuuu!"

But this time the sound was different. I could not explain how, but it sounded almost hollow. Like an imitation. Then a rustling again and I saw the tall grass moving. The path it was creating was big, too big to be a rooster. It was coming my way!

I took a step back, hesitating. If it were a coyote or wild-cat climbing in the tree house might be wiser than running. I did not think I could outrun a large predator. My blood pounded in my ears as my brain worked in overdrive trying to commit to a plan of action, but my body stood frozen. Whatever was coming seemed to be taking its time, moving not in a straight line, but more in a swaying side-to-side pattern. Then it stopped.

"Kukelekuuu!"

Again, a false crow, followed by a pause, as if whatever was down there was waiting to see if I would walk down to investigate. A shadow rose from the grass. I could not quite make out its shape in the darkness, but it stood upright like a man, though its stature was not quite as tall. Then I saw two yellow lights hanging parallel to each other, reflecting the dim moonlight that shone down through a break in the clouds. he phenomenon reminded me again of the wildcat. No man's eyes reflect like that.

I ran.

The windows were still dark when I reached the house. I flew in, slamming the latch on the door as soon as it closed behind me, and held my breath. My pulse was still pounding in my ears, making it hard to hear, but I was fairly certain I hadn't woken Audri. I looked out the window. No sign of whatever had been in the field.

I fumbled around the kitchen for a match and lit a candle, then scanned the area for something I could use as a weapon. Uncle John kept a shotgun in his room, a relic he had carried with him from the Old World. Both Audri and I had been taught to shoot at a young age, being that we were often left alone, but it was kept locked in his closet for safety, and Audri was the one who held the key. Waking her would mean admitting that I had screwed up and I had no doubts that she would find a way to use that to her advantage.

I looked out the window again. Still nothing. Finally, I pulled the fire-poker from the hearth and settled on the floor in front of the door.

When I awoke again, the morning's first light had just begun to creep over the windowsill. I rubbed the sleep from my eyes and put the fire-poker in its proper place. Audri must have still been sleeping. I peered out the window. No sign of any disturbance. I smoothed the wrinkles in my dress with my hands, washed up, and started breakfast, trying to decide what to do next.

"You were up late," a voice from behind startled me. Audri stood, still in her night clothes. Her pale hair was braided tightly, but a few wisps had broken loose while she slept. I shuffled the warm skillet on the stove and cracked in two eggs, avoiding eye contact.

"I don't remember hearing you come to bed last night," she continued. "Is that the dress you wore yesterday?"

"I couldn't sleep," I mumbled.

Audi stretched, extending her arms above her head as she let out a yawn. "The house is too quiet with Father gone," she said matter-of-factly. "I shall be glad when he returns. Anyway, don't think it will get you out of any work today. I am going to get dressed. Another day of chores. I will feed the chickens if you want to take care of milking the goats."

I tried not to cringe. It seemed my mistake would be found out after all, and then I would have a lot of explaining to do. But then, as if my thoughts had cued it, I heard a crow.

"Kukelekuuu!"

I dashed to the window, forgetting myself for a moment and looked out to the pen. There was the rooster, standing proud on his perch as always, his chest puffed up prominently as he announced the start of a new day.

"Kala, what is wrong with you today?"

I looked at my cousin who was staring at me with a puzzled expression.

"Oh...uh," I fumbled for something that would not give me away. "Nothing. Just startled me is all. I must be tired."

She held my gaze a moment longer, then shrugged and started down the hall to our room.

"I'm getting dressed. Breakfast smells amazing. Don't burn it!" And with that, she closed the door.

CHAPTER THREE

THE NEXT FEW DAYS went about without any sign of...whatever it was I had encountered. Where the rooster had been and how he had gotten back in the coop remained a mystery. I said nothing to my cousin about my concerns, but I often felt the hairs on the back of my neck standing on end. I would go about my chores glancing over my shoulder with the most eerie feeling that someone was watching me.

But whoever or whatever it was remained hidden so long that I began to believe it had all been a figment of my own imagination. A silly dream. I fell back into a rhythm and regained most of my confidence. Still, I never let myself be caught alone after sunset.

Uncle John returned from his trip looking weary and dissatisfied. He had grown older since I had first come to live with him, but this was something more. It seemed that every journey he made to Aythia aged him beyond his years.

"'Tis those ruddy young soldiers, egos as big as a horse's rear. Spoiled too. Think they know everything. Will suck the life right out of you," his voice was gruff but he wore a half-grin. Though he was trying to make a joke; his eyes did not smile with him and his attempt at jest left me uneasy. Something was afoot. Something more than just the routine schooling of the King's army. Occasionally I would pry for more information, but my uncle was steadfast. He would say no more.

Time went on and the season neared its change. It was not long before Uncle was saddling up the horse to its cart and preparing to take the season's crops in for the market. The trip itself was short, but it would be at least a week before he'd made enough profit to justify what the trip there and back would cost him. On bountiful years he might bring one of us with him, but this year the fruits of our labor were lacking and my uncle could hardly afford to house himself in an inn. He would be staying with an old friend and fellow soldier. It was well enough, as we still had our livestock to tend to, and it had been years since we could afford to hire a farmhand to stay in our stead.

Last season he had taken Audri out for a couple of days, but recently he had become more tense and paranoid. He did not want to leave either of us to tend to things alone. I did not say it, but I was glad I would not be left behind on my own.

My trepidation was further validated when my uncle pulled something down from the front of his cart. It was a wooden box with the King's emblem scorched into the cover. When he opened it I gasped. Cradled in the red velvet interior were two large hunting knives. They had matching hilts made from carved bone and were sheathed in dark leather with straps on the back meant for fastening around one's ankle. He handed one to Audri who looked it over in awe, then turned and handed me its twin. He closed the box and placed it back in the cart, then addressed us both solemnly.

"Keep these on you at all times. Do not take them off to sleep, and do not leave the property. Be in the house before the sun sets, and keep the door bolted—even in the daytime."

"But, Father..." Audri trailed off. She was not sure what to make of the situation. Fumbling for something to say, she continued, "We have the shotgun."

My uncle shook his head. "A gun is for killing animals." He took the knife that Audri held and unsheathed it. The early morning sun reflected in the blade and for a moment I was blinded. When my sight returned I noticed a line of thin, strange characters engraved in the metal, near the hilt. They indicated the quality of the materials used to forge the weapon. It took a moment, but when I had deciphered their meaning I felt my jaw slacken

"These are forged from silver." I stood aghast. Silver was one of the only materials known to be lethal to the majority of Mystic creatures. Once a commodity, it had been used heavily during the Great War. The mines on our side of the boundary had since been stripped of their resources, and it was now considered a precious metal. Precious and rare meant expensive. Where had he come across them? What did he expect we'd encounter? I did not venture to ask. He climbed into the cart, said a final goodbye, and started off.

Audri did not say a word as she watched her father's cart fade in the distance, kicking up dust behind it until it was just a cloudy dot on the horizon. My cousin bent down and lifted the hem of her dress, tying the leather threads of the knife's sheath at mid-calf before slipping the whole thing under her high-topped work boots. The weapon was completely concealed.

She righted herself and looked over, waiting for me to follow her lead. I stared at my knife for a long while. Audri sighed, growing impatient but remained otherwise silent. I thought of the shadow in the field and a shudder ran down my spine. I glanced over my shoulder toward the boundary before fastening the knife around my leg and slipping it into my boot as I'd seen Audri do. She seemed to have noticed my gaze but had mistaken its intent.

"No time to be rolling down the hills like a child, Kala," she scolded. "There is work to be done this day."

I was irritated by her tone, but thankful for her misinterpretation. I was not ready to explain to her my odd encounter. I was not sure I ever would be ready. I nodded and we turned back to the farm to begin our chores.

My uncle had been gone nearly a week's time before anything seemed out of the ordinary. Audri and I followed his instructions meticulously. Our knives stayed tethered under our boots at all times. We were in the house; door bolted before night fell each evening, and did not open it again until after the rising of the sun.

Sometimes at night, I thought I could hear a strange whistling and my body would freeze beneath my blankets as I strained to decipher the noise. It was a stealthy and soft sound, only slightly different from the familiar whooshing of the wind in the trees.

After a while, I would convince myself that it had been my imagination. I was certain that the livestock would have reacted to a stranger on our land. Something would have been found awry on the property if there had been any intrusion. Content with that thought, I would drift off to sleep.

We went about tending to the livestock and preparing the field for the next growing season, falling into a comforting monotony. Though our work was executed adamantly, mentally and emotionally we began to let our guard down.

One afternoon when we had finished the morning chores, Audri and I decided to have lunch in the tree house. We sat facing each other on a blanket on the floor. My back rested against the wall with the window as we talked about the usual things: what we had accomplished, what matters still needed our attention. Eventually, the conversation drifted to her father.

"Where do you think he is staying?" I asked.

"He said he would be with an old friend. Someone he served with before he retired. I hope he is eating okay. I hope he has a cot and is not sleeping on the floor with that leg of his," she sighed. "I wish we had been able to go with him."

"I know...I wish we could have too...but the farm" I shrugged.

Audri looked down at her leg where the knife was strapped and then back at me.

"I think he could have hired a farm hand," she trailed off as if lost in a serious thought, then shook herself back to reality and smirked. "Like that blonde-haired fellow he used last time? Remember him?"

I felt myself blush as I shook my head, "Which one was that again?"

"Oh you know," she drew the words out in a sing-song voice. "The one you fancied."

She tore a piece of bread from her plate and tossed it at me. I tried to block it but it landed on my shoulder and caught in a piece of hair that had fallen from my braid.

I flicked it back-right at her face.

"Did not!"

"Oh don't deny it, Kala," she goaded me. "We could all see you looking at him with dreamy eyes. It is not like it is anything to be ashamed of – you are almost of marrying age."

She was starting to get on my nerves, "You are the eldest, Audri," I reminded her. "Why don't you marry him instead?"

She opened her mouth to respond but something caught her eye over my shoulder. She ducked down, putting her finger to her mouth, motioning for me to be silent. I turned myself toward the window, keeping my body low, and peered over the edge.

There was a figure in the distance at the edge of the woods. It was moving stealthily, one way, and then the other; as if it were unsure it could leave the shade of the trees safely. It stood near the same height as the figure that had approached me from the grasslands. In the mid-day sun, there were no glowing eyes. From this distance, I could not determine race, but the outline looked humanoid.

My mind raced trying to narrow down the possibilities. Nymphs are female, and this figure was clearly too broad-shouldered. A wizard would not have to hesitate but could incinerate us and our entire homestead from that distance with just a flick of the wrist. Hopefully, it was not a wizard.

The figure was too tall to be a goblin, too short to be a troll. Vampires could only walk the earth at night, and could only leave their territory during Samhain. The same was true of ghosts, and their female counterpart, ghouls. My mind went blank. I could hear my pulse roaring in my ears as I struggled to access the information fear had stolen from me. I swore under my breath.

The figure stopped pacing and crouched down. It leaned to one side, and then the other, turning its head in a manner that I knew meant it was scanning the property. Was it looking for us? Then it stood and darted back into the forest. I turned to Audri, my back falling once again against the wall next to the window, and let out a sigh of relief.

"What was that?" I asked, keeping my voice low as a precaution. Audri's hand drifted again to where her knife was hidden.

"Trouble," she replied. We sat in silence for a while, our food still laid out, unfinished. I folded mine up in my napkin and tied the top. Audri did the same. We had both lost our appetites.

We climbed down from the tree house cautiously, making sure to climb down the side facing the farm, out of sight from whatever had been watching us from the woods. I crouched against the base of the trunk and drew up the hem of my dress, drawing my knife from inside my boot. I leaned to get a better view of the land beyond our property.

"What are you doing, Kala?!" hissed my cousin.

"I'm going after it," I whispered back as if the answer should have been obvious. In reality, I had made the motions automatically and was uncertain of them myself.

"Father said not to leave the property," she reminded me in her best 'I'm older than you so I am the enforcer of rules' tone.

"What are we supposed to do, Audri? Bolt ourselves in and wait for it to come to us? We're as good as dead anyway if it ventures to come after us"

"You saw it hesitate. Maybe it can't leave the forest?" she offered uncertainly. I thought of the thing I'd seen in the field weeks before, and the rooster who had returned to the coop, as if by magic. It already had.

I scanned my brain for other, less foolish options. Uncle had taken our only horse and the nearest homestead was more than a day's walk by foot. There was no way to get word to anyone without the risk of being overtaken, should the strange figure choose to pursue us.

"No," I answered myself out loud. "No, there are no other options, Audri. I will not sit in fear and wait for it to come after us."

I felt a sudden fire in my chest. It wasn't quite what I expected bravery to feel like. Fear, mixed with anger maybe? And loyalty. "Go to the house yourself, bolt the doors, and wait for me." And with that, I dashed out into the open.

I cringed as I hit the high grass of the field. There was no point in seeking shelter from it, as it reached only a hand or two higher than my waist. Even at a crawl, the sway of the long, crimson blades would have given away my position. I do not know why, but I had expected the grass to be painful to touch. It felt like any other plant of its type that I'd encountered, though perhaps less lush.

The dry crimson blades made a crunching sound as I attempted to jog through them, pushing them aside as best I could. For a moment I considered using my knife to clear a trail, but that seemed irreverent given the land's history. Human blood had been spilled here, and one should never disrespect the dead.

I trudged through as swiftly as I could manage. The field had looked much shorter from a distance than it did once I was in the thick of it. Finally, I reached the end and took shelter behind one of the trees at the edge of the woods. For a moment I felt my gut tug at me, urging me to look back and check on Audri, but I ignored it. I was sure if I looked back I would lose my resolve and retreat back to the illusion of safety I had created inside my home. I took a deep breath, clutching my knife tightly, and plunged into the forest.

I was not prepared to be met with darkness. The tree limbs above me had become so interwoven that only a few specks of light were able to break through their cover. Looking up at them gave the illusion of stars in the sky.

I staggered briefly while my eyes adjusted, but even then I could hardly make out more than vague shapes and shadows. I again began to doubt my mission. Still, I stepped forward carefully, my knife clutched in my right hand, and my left thrust out in front of me as I groped my way through the dense woods.

I was about thirty feet in when I saw it. A figure darting from one tree to another without making so much as a sound. I was suddenly aware of how loud I must have been, lumbering through the woods like a fool. I froze.

Whatever it was, it did not give any indication that it knew I was there, but I ducked behind the nearest tree as a precaution. All of a sudden whatever it was darted behind a tree and seemingly disappeared. Kneeling with my left hand down to maintain balance and my knife hand raised and on alert, I crept forward willing my feet to be silent against the forest floor.

No sooner had I done so than I felt a hand against the wrist on my knife-hand. Before I could react a boot between my shoulder blades forced me to the ground. I could smell the musty scent of earth as the dust kicked up by my impact invaded my nostrils. The twigs beneath me prodded my tender face. My assailant clenched my wrist tight.

"Drop it," a male voice commanded.

Although I knew it was futile, I resisted, clutching the hilt tighter. He squeezed my wrist until holding on became painful and I was forced to loosen my grip. I heard my weapon fall to the ground, muffled slightly by the mixture of moss and soft dirt. My arms were then twisted behind my back and bound tightly with a material I wasn't familiar with.

It was cool and smooth against my skin, but when I struggled stung me and pulled tighter around my wrists. My captor picked up my knife, yanking me upward by my arm with an unnecessary amount of force, and brushed the cold flat side of the blade down my arm as a warning. He shoved me forward roughly.

"Walk."

We trudged through the forest awkwardly. Whoever held me captive remained behind me with his hand firmly around my right arm just above my bindings, prodding me now and again to encourage me to walk faster. I did not dare to attempt a glance back at him; not that it would have made any difference as the further we delved into the woods, the darker it became. I was as good as blind. This made navigating more difficult, and I often found myself stumbling on stray roots.

He did not seem to share my handicap and moved about surefootedly. He grew more agitated each time I faltered, and his handling of me became more brutal. My shoulders began to ache from the way he swung me about. I did not waste my time plotting an escape. I was certain I would not make it out of this scenario alive.

I was so wrapped up in the thought of my own death that I did not stop to wonder why he had not simply killed me when he had the chance. There would be a time in the not so distant future when he would wish that he had.

About the time that I was sure my legs would give out from under me, we approached a clearing. It was small, perhaps as far across one way as our barn. As we stepped into it I filled my lungs with fresh air. I hadn't realized how stale the air in the woods had been until we were free of it. My eyes struggled again to adjust to the change in lighting. It wasn't much. Night had fallen as we walked. There was a small fire near the center of the clearing, and a figure stood beside it.

He was tall with honey colored hair that might easily have fallen to his shoulders were it not pulled back. He was clothed in fancy garments that were foreign to me. From his left ear hung a green diamond shaped earring dangling on a short chain.

At his hip sat a jewel encrusted sword, and on his back was a quiver of arrows. He leaned slightly on the bow with both hands as he stared at the fire. Even in the fire's orange glow, his skin was pale; as were his eyes. He was gazing into the flames, lost in thought. When the light caught his eye just right they glowed. I thought of the night in the field and shivered. Elves.

When I was younger, my uncle would recount the tales that they would tell in the Old World. Children's stories of tiny little men who dressed in pointy hats and mended shoes. These were no such creatures. Elves were possibly the smartest of the Mystic breeds and had advanced further than almost any other species, not only in the realm of magic but in technologies. They were stealthy, strong hunters and their aim with a bow was near infallible. Not all of their game was of the four-legged variety.

I searched my memory for more information. Elves had always been the hardest for me to remember. They had extended life spans and were nearly immortal. In times of peace, they had acted as diplomats.

Methods of execution included decapitation, fire, and piercing of the heart; the same methods used against vampires. It made sense, as the two were distantly related.

He looked up, suddenly aware of our presence and his face furrowed in anger. He rushed toward us yelling in a language I did not understand. I flinched, but his anger was aimed not at me, but at my captor. I was shoved aside, as the two faced each other, and fell to my knees. When I looked up, I saw that my abductor was almost a mirror-image of the aggressor, save that his hair was cropped shorter-similar to the style of my people. His eyes were a few shades lighter, and he was smaller in stature, but they shared roughly the same facial features. I guessed them to be related.

They quarreled a long time, slipping in and out of a foreign language. The one who had been waiting in the clearing stepped up so that he was toe-to-toe with the smaller one.

"....their own free-will" was all I caught from him before he slipped back into the foreign tongue.

"She crossed the boundary on her own!" The one who had captured me motioned my way with one hand. "You are a fool Azlyn!"

My captor shoved the other as if to accentuate his point. My eyes darted back and forth between them trying to put together the pieces. I was not supposed to be here, I knew that much. The quarrel continued and my abductor thrust forward the knife he had taken from me as if it were some damning piece of evidence. The other one fell silent, inspecting the blade closely and then looking at me.

The look on his face was a mixture of confusion and... something else. Betrayal? But that didn't make any sense. He shook his head and returned to his conversation. His words seemed to further infuriate his companion, who threw his hands up in the air and turned away. The other one spoke, and this time I could understand him.

"It is not supposed to be this way." He clutched my knife to his side and moved toward me. I recoiled and he paused, maintaining a space equal to about 5 feet between us, and held up his empty hand in an attempt to look less threatening.

"Tis alright," he said, leaning in closer. "I'm not going to hurt you."

He motioned behind me before moving around me. My gaze was drawn to the blade in his hand. I closed my eyes, choking back a sob. I was familiar with this scenario, as many of my kind had been killed in this manner. The executioner stood behind the bound, kneeling victim and severed their spinal cord with the weapon of their choice. It was said to be a painless death, but my uncle referred to it as more cowardly than merciful.

"If you see fit to kill a man, you should have enough respect to look him in the eye," he would say.

I felt the sting of tears in my eyes as I thought of him. How would my family remember me? Would they ever even find out what fate had befallen me? How foolish I had been to dart off on my own. My tears fell softly on the ground below me as I hung my head, waiting to die.

Then something strange happened. I felt a pressure on my wrists where they were tied and heard a sound that reminded me much of the rending of flesh from a deer when you clean it. Suddenly my hands were free. My shoulders ached as I pulled them forward, falling into a crouching position.

I scrambled away from my captors and turned. The one who freed me was kneeling in the grass wiping the flat of the knife which was coated in a black, tarry substance. The grass made a sizzling sound and smoked slightly. There was a foul stench. Next to him on the ground was a shriveled up coil of scaled flesh that reminded me of a discarded snake skin.

"From the tail of a dragon," he stated as if that should make perfect sense to me. I must have looked puzzled, because he elaborated, "It carries some life to it still. It will tighten around an organic object; squeeze the life out of it if it is allowed. The scales expose themselves when its victims struggle, cutting into the skin."

He motioned to my wrists which carried various shallow gashes. "It was not meant to be used on you." His eyes narrowed as he looked in the direction of his companion, "My brother, Cain. You'll have to excuse him. He is not himself..." his voice trailed off, but I wasn't really paying attention. My mind was still stuck on what he'd said about the restraints.

"But...dragons are Mystics," I mumbled, mostly to myself. It was the first time I had spoken since being captured and I realized my voice was hoarse and dry from the journey. I was thirsty. For a while, I was not sure he had heard me.

"Not all creatures are on our side, Kala," he said in a tired voice. What did that mean 'on our side'? More importantly, how had he known my name? My thoughts jumped again to the field, and the rooster. They must have been watching us more closely than I'd thought. I shuddered.

He held out a flask, "Thirsty?" I made no move to take it. "It is just water," he promised. When I still did not move to take it he rolled his eyes "Oh for goodness sake," he took a swig from the flask, swallowing dramatically, and offered it again. This time I took hold of it cautiously.

"We shall take you home in the morning. Try and get some rest. It is not an easy journey," he said absently as if I had not already walked it in half a day's time.

"Oh and Kala," he added, "I would not try to run off if I were you. There are things in these woods much less friendly than a pair of elves."

The thought was terrifying. I nodded obediently. He hesitated. "That was not a threat," he added, his eyes lingering on my face with an expression I could not make sense of. "Go to sleep. I must go talk to my brother." He turned and walked toward the one he had called Cain.

I took a sip from the flask. The water was crisp and cool. I detected nothing out of the ordinary. I gulped down the rest in a rather uncivilized fashion and set it aside. Cain and... what was it he'd called his brother? Azlyn stood face to face by the fire, leaning in and whispering in what I assumed was their native tongue. I would gain no knowledge from eavesdropping.

I looked up at the sky, considering my options. The stars seemed brighter here in the clearing than they had at home. My life did not seem to be in immediate danger, and though I was wary of the Elves, one of them had shown some semblance of kindness toward me...or at least pretended to. I was weaponless and would not last long on my own, blind as I was in the forest.

Elven eyes absorb every bit of light; much the same way as a cat's. It would not be long until they overtook me, should I try to run. I decided my best chance was to be patient, waiting for one of them to let their guard down. I laid my head down on an overgrown patch of moss and willed myself to sleep.

My dreams were a mixture of memory and fantasy. Flashes from my childhood haunted my subconscious. My mother's face, laughing as she listened to me recount the story of my capture as if it were a jest I'd created. Audri, slapping my face as our rag dolls burned. And stars, hundreds and hundreds of stars spinning in the night sky.

When I opened my eyes I was met with sunlight. The ground around me was cold, and the fire had fizzled out. At some point in the night, someone had laid a blanket over me. I sat up and looked around. Cain was nowhere to be seen.

Azlyn was sitting off to my right as if he had stayed up the whole night keeping watch. He was still holding my knife, but in his other hand, he held a strange looking fruit. It was perfectly round, bright red, and the size of your average apple. The outer skin, which he was using my knife to peel, looked velvety. The meat of the fruit was orange. When he cut it down the middle I saw no seeds. He offered half to me.

"Eat."

"What is it?" I asked as he placed it in my hands. I was starving but not about to ingest something I had never encountered.

He rolled his eyes at me again, "It is food. It grows in my homeland. Do you not have food where you live?"

Well, that was a ridiculous question! I did not care for his tone much either. I sat in silent rebellion and used every ounce of willpower I had to hold the fruit out toward him.

"Eat it," he insisted. "We won't have time to stop for food again, and this should keep you satisfied for the majority of the journey."

"So there is some magic to it then?" I eyed the fruit suspiciously. As I pulled it closer to inspect it, its sweet aroma caught in the wind and invaded my nostrils. My stomach rumbled.

"If such a word settles your mind then that is what you may call it, yes." He took a bite of his half.

Realizing that was the only explanation I would receive, I ate. I was surprised, not only at the sweetness of the fruit but the warm feeling it gave me. I felt my muscles energize, the soreness from the previous day gone.

"Where is the other one? Cain?" I asked. There was absolutely no trace of him in the clearing.

"He has...other business," Azlyn replied as if the question had pained him.

We sat in silence for a while. The clearing was still. If there were any signs of life in the forest my ears could not detect them. After a while, Azlyn rose to clean out the fire pit. He rolled the rocks that had contained it outward, scattering them across the clearing. Then he raked at the ashes with his sword and finally, mumbling again in his native language, brushed his boot against the ground where it had been.

He took the blanket I had been using and packed it away in a bag I hadn't noticed the night before. Soon there was no sign that we had ever been in the clearing. He rose and indicated that it was time to leave. I stood, smoothing out my dress awkwardly, "Where are we going?"

He looked at me as if the answer should be obvious, "I'm taking you back." He leaned over and offered me my knife, hilt first. I paused as my brain tried to process the awkward scene. Why would he arm me? He must be an idiot. It must be a trap. For a moment, I contemplated taking the knife and wounding him before making my escape. I looked into the woods and remembered his words the night before.

"There are things in these woods much less friendly than a pair of Elves." When I looked back at his face he was smiling.

"You can try it if you want, but you would not make it far." His voice was not malicious. He said it as if the idea that I might ponder escape amused him. My face flushed. That *he* thought me amusing infuriated me.

"I am capable of more than you think," I said defiantly, but I took the knife and sheathed it beneath my boot.

"I am sure you are full of surprises, Kala," he said solemnly, "but now is not the time to test them." He looked up, noting the position of the sun, "We need to get you home before night falls." He took me by the hand and took the lead. I had only a moment to gaze out at the sunlight one last time before I was plunged into darkness.

My trek through the forest with Azlyn, in contrast to the journey with Cain, was not entirely unpleasant. He kept hold of my hand so as to lead me through the darkness. His grasp was not firm or forceful, but a matter of practicality.

The obstacles I had encountered before, tree roots and the uneven terrain one would typically expect in a wooded area, seemed to move in his wake as if the forest were creating a path just for him. Whether the path had always been there, or if he was using some sort of magic, I did not think to ask, but I had no trouble navigating with him in the lead. Our pace was steady and I could sense urgency from him, even in the dark, that I did not quite understand. He was silent for the greater part of the trip.

Eventually, my fatigue caught up with me. Even on smoother terrain, the journey was tedious. My wrists were tender where they had been scratched, and the soreness had returned to my shoulders. I felt my legs buckle more than once, and I nearly fell. Unlike his brother, Azlyn did not force me onward but slowed the pace to accommodate me.

Finally, he spoke, "My brother should not have been so rough with you."

I said nothing in response. I was not even sure what a proper response would be. I thought of my cousin. She would likely have jeered at his apology, distrusting him. Or spat in his direction. Strangely, I did not harbor any resentment toward him, or any real fear. I knew that I should have both hated and feared him, this sworn enemy to my people, to my family, to my survival. Anything else was treason, and a betrayal to my king.

And yet, he carried about him this essence, this sense of forlorn wisdom that made it hard to feel any ill-will toward him. Quite the contrary, I felt drawn to him. He seemed so...human. It sparked something, my sense of adventure I suppose, and my curiosity. So, conflicted, I remained silent. Azlyn must have interpreted the silence as bitterness because he continued.

"He is not normally so...unreasonable," he seemed to be choosing his words carefully. "His son, Cazlyn, was wounded. He has fallen ill."

I pondered this a while. It had never crossed my mind that a Mystic might care for their young. My life had been built around the idea that they were savage, heartless beings; incapable of relating to other creatures, let alone caring for them. And yet one was guiding me gently by the hand. One who had fed me and tended to me while I slept. My brain screamed at me that it was a charade-a trap of some sort, but my gut churned, torn in another direction.

"What happened?" I asked. Surely there was no harm in a question.

"He was careless. He took off ahead of us in the middle of the night. His position was compromised. He was hit with an arrow."

"His heart?" I asked. Almost any other injury would have been relatively superficial to his kind.

"*Venifyre*," he said, slipping into his native tongue. "Poison. The tip was coated in hydra's blood."

I stopped in my tracks and pulled my hand from his. I could not see him, but I felt the air around me shift as he turned to face my direction.

Hydra's blood was toxic to many of the Mystic creatures; but not in the same way as it was for Elves. When mixed with the blood of an elven immortal it takes on an identity of its own-one that holds both the properties of endless life, and the evil poison of the hydra.

In the days before my birth, it was said that many of my kind sought out this concoction, ingesting it willingly; giving themselves to what they called the Change. It was said to be painful, and dangerous.

The price of immortality was crueler than death. They would roam the earth in endless hunger, shunned by all other creatures. Damned.

For one whose blood was mixed against his will? The Change would happen whether they consented or not. They would suffer the same cruel fate.

The methods of execution for an elf are the same as a vampire. It makes sense, as the two are distantly related.

Sometimes the relationship isn't so distant.

CHAPTER FOUR

W e began walking again. Azlyn had fallen silent, lost in thought. I allowed my own thoughts to turn inward as well, trying to work through the emotions that seemed to be battling inside of me. I thought of the game my cousin and I played years ago with our homemade dolls. It seemed so simple then. Us, them. Good, evil. The line was firmly drawn. My parents were dead because of 'them', and now one of their own kin would suffer because of my people.

One could reason that in some way things had come full circle. A life for a life. And yet, it felt wrong to me. Who was to say that the one paying the price was not also an innocent? Had he struck down my parents with his own hand? Had he even been there? If he had, would I think twice about his fate? I did not know, and the not knowing made it all the worse.

I thought of the one who had captured me, Cain. My anger flared again. Regardless of his intentions, the way he had treated me was vile and unnecessary. It was true that I had been the one to pursue him, but he could not have seen me as a real threat, could he? And if his son was so ill, why was he wasting his time spying on us? Indeed, what business did any of them have gallivanting along the boundary? The fate that befell them was their own doing.

"We are almost there," Azlyn announced. I had been so deep in my own thoughts that I had not noticed the dim light breaking through the trees ahead of us. From here I guessed there was an hour or so left before sunset. The light crept into the forest, and I could finally see my feet again. Azlyn released my hand, no longer needing to guide me. After traveling the better part of the day with a companion, my hand felt cold and oddly light without his.

Azlyn halted just before the woods broke into meadow. The crimson field looked ominous in the low light. I could see my home in the distance. The animals were all put away for the night. Smoke was billowing from the chimney. Audri must be inside feeding the fire, likely preparing for the evening meal.

Azlyn stepped aside, extending his hand toward the clearing, urging me on. "Your freedom, Kala."

I should have been elated. I should have torn through the field, filling my lungs with fresh air and thanking the Gods that I was free. Instead, my feet felt like lead beneath me. Though I willed them to move, they would not.

Azlyn noted my hesitation, but misinterpreted it, "It is alright Kala. We will not come after you. Your family is safe, for now." Somehow that was not reassuring.

I scoffed, "Safe? Safe he says!" I threw my arms in the air, "You, sir, are a walking contradiction! How can we feel safe with you lurking at our border? You come spying; you kidnap me, and now what? What elaborate trap have you planned for us? It is my Uncle, isn't it?" suddenly it all made sense.

"You think he has some high placement among the guards? You wish to use him as a bartering tool against the King?" I laughed and continued without waiting for a response, "Well, you are a fool. He has been retired for a long time. He is no more than a teacher of young warriors now. He knows no secrets, he has no power. He is useless to you."

Azlyn stood a moment, his jaw slack, and then a smile crept across his face, "You underestimate your kin, Kala. Your uncle has more secrets than you would care to know, maybe more than he can keep...but he is not our target. We were not here to kidnap anyone. Cain would not have taken you had you not been foolish enough to cross into our land. It was you who pursued us."

I opened my mouth to argue, then closed it again. Technically he was right. I had crossed the boundary into their land.

"I was protecting my home," I stammered, but it sounded foolish. I felt my cheeks flush, but the embarrassment only rekindled my anger. "Your brother was spying on us!"

At this Azlyn's face grew serious. I had insulted him. "He would not have wasted his time concerning himself with the actions of two silly girls while his son lay wounded."

"Then why was he here at the boundary? He was watching us, there in our tree house." I motioned toward where Audri and I had been having lunch, but Azlyn held a hand up, cutting me off.

"Fool!" he exclaimed, at no one in particular. For a moment his eyes seemed far away, "Of course that is what he was after." He turned again to me, "A tree house?" he shook his head, and began to pace. "You have no idea what you are desecrating."

"What?" I asked, perplexed.

"Menohathi," he said, reverently. "That is a holy tree. Few are left in this world since the war. Ludlum, of course, has one hidden away, for those among your people who were crazy enough to seek out The Change on their own. But the others, those trees he felled. There are none left on our side of the boundary...." he trailed off, "She would have planted one, of course... but how could it have remained a secret for so long? Surely, he knows. Why did he not tell me?" He was speaking to himself now, and his words made absolutely no sense to me.

"Who would have planted it? Why does it matter? It's just a tree." I could tell I had said something wrong because an angry expression flashed across his face briefly before it fell again into an expression of pain and... pleading?

"Kala, Cain was not after you. He was here because of the tree. Did you not ever wonder why its leaves never change seasons? It is a tree of eternal life, a healing tree." He studied my face. Seeing my confusion, he continued, "Very few species know of its medicinal value. It holds the power of goodness and light. Properly prepared, it can fight the dark impulses brought on by The Change. Kala, it can heal my brother's son." His eyes assessed the remaining light. "He is running out of time."

My internal clock was jumbled from spending so much time in the dark shadow of the forest, but I reasoned that I'd been gone about a day and a half. The Change peaked when the moon was at its highest point in the sky, though the number of days required for the cycle to complete itself depended partially on the strength of the poison. Thinking that he held the only means of healing, Ludlum would likely have diluted the Hydra's blood, drawing out the process and making it more painful. Knowing that the victim would either be banished from his land or, if his people were merciful, put to death before The Change could take on its full course.

"How long?" I asked

"Tonight. My brother is with him now. If I do not make it in time, he will do what needs to be done."

I shuddered and looked back into the darkness behind us. "You'll never cover that much ground in time."

He smiled wryly again, "Not at your pace, no. Your people are painfully slow."

In spite of myself, I laughed. My eyes fell again upon the tree, and then my home, and then my...captor? Companion? There did not seem to be a label that fit him appropriately.

"Well, I suppose you had better hurry," I said. "My return will keep Audri busy enough. If you can manage to keep yourself hidden for a while longer, I will keep her attention."

He nodded. As I was darting out of the woods he said something I was not expecting, "Your mother would be proud."

I did not have time to process his last words to me as I tore through the field. This time I felt no fear approaching the high grass. Rather than running a straight line, toward the tree house, I cut across the field at an angle, near the front of the house. I hoped that my arrival would prove enough of a distraction to give Azlyn the time he needed. The early evening air was cold and jolted my lungs. My heart was pounding, more from fear than I would have liked to admit. Just before I turned the corner to the front of the house, I turned back to see Azlyn slinking out of the trees. "NOT YET" my mind screamed, willing him to wait. It was too late.

I turned the corner. There was no sign of my uncle's return. I reached the front door. It was locked. I pounded on it, hoping to catch my cousin's attention in time. The door flew open.

"Kala!" My cousin's arms flew around my neck and I almost toppled over. It was not the reaction I had anticipated. I expected her to scold me for running off, to question where I had been, but I was met with none of that. When she finally pulled away I could see she had been crying.

"Kala, I was sure you were dead! What happened? Where were you? Look at you— you're a mess!"

I glanced down at myself. I had not thought about it, but I must have been in a miserable state. My dress was covered in dirt and tattered at the bottom. It was stained red where the grass had come in contact with me as I ran through the field. I ran my fingers through my hair, just noticing the pine needles and moss that had become entangled in it. The motion brought to light the marks on my wrists where I had been bound.

Audri gasped, "What happened to you? Oh, Kala!" If I'd wanted to create a distraction I seemed to have succeeded. Unfortunately, I had not come up with an explanation for my injuries, my absence, or my appearance.

"I-I...I was lost," I stammered.

My cousin misinterpreted my anxiety and hugged me again, "Shhh. It is okay. Come, let's get you cleaned up." She ushered me gently down the hall toward the washroom, her arm around my shoulder. I breathed a sigh of relief. There were no windows in that part of the house.

By the time I was bathed and in my night clothes, the sun had long set. We sat in our room and Audri combed my long hair out by candlelight— a chore that was quite the undertaking on a good day. I leaned back as she worked through the knots as gently as possible, looking out our window and taking note of the moon's position. I found myself wondering where

Azlyn was, whether he had made it in time. I wondered what he had meant when he said my mother would be proud of me. Audri's voice cut into my thoughts.

"Father sent word," she said softly. "It was this morning. Conner, the courier from the King's court."

I pulled away and turned toward her, confused. He had never sent word while trading before. One of the King's couriers? I thought of how strange he had acted before he'd left, the increased amount of training he had been doing lately. Azlyn's nephew had been overtaken by soldiers at the boundary. I shuddered. Audri mistook the reason for my response, handing me a blanket before she continued. "I sent word back that you had gone missing."

My eyes went wide. I did not understand why, but the thought of him coming home early on my account terrified me. Surely, he would be angry that I had disobeyed him, but he had never acted toward me in a way that was less than kind. He had never even raised his voice to me, let alone his hand. I knew other children raised by distant kin were not so lucky. So my fear surprised me.

"We have to send word out that it was a mistake," I said hastily. Then, as an afterthought, I added, "We cannot afford for him to come home before his wares have sold."

Audri nodded "This winter is supposed to be a harsh one," she agreed, "but, Kala; we have no way to intercept the messenger. We will simply have to hope for the best." She finished braiding my hair and blew out the candle. As an afterthought, she added, "I am sure he won't be too cross, Kala. Try and get some sleep."

I laid down, thankful for the soft pillow beneath my head, and suddenly the fatigue of the past two days caught up with me. I slept a long, deep sleep. I did not dream.

Looking back on that evening, I still do not know how much my cousin suspected. For her to have sent word to my uncle was to be expected, I suppose, but her reaction when she found me on the doorstep had been shocking, to say the least. Not that I believe my cousin would not mourn my death, should that have been the case; but we had not been so close as to warrant the way she tended to me once I was home. It had been almost as if she was cleansing me of some perceived evil. The way she had washed and combed the forest from my hair was almost reverent. I awoke in the morning to find that she had burned the dress. I said nothing about it.

The following day was awkwardly monotonous. We went about our chores as if nothing had been amiss. I fretted silently to myself about the message that Audri had sent her father, wondering at the time it would take the messenger to deliver it, and calculating from there how long it might take my uncle to travel home.

I figured it would be at least another 4 days, assuming that he was trading in the market nearest to our property. More if he were further out, as I suspected to be the case given that the King had sent a messenger from his own court. What was that all about?

I mulled over the possibilities as I swept the kitchen floor that morning, but whatever conspiracy I concocted in my head would eventually fade into the memory of Azlyn's face. The way he had smirked when he thought me naive, the feel of his hand in mine as he guided me through the woods. More than that, I thought of the last words he had spoken to me as I raced my way across the boundary.

"Your mother would be proud."

In truth, it had been a long time since I had thought about my parents. Perhaps the pain had simply dulled over time. Now it felt like it was simply a pain I had been pushing to the side, hoping that by ignoring it I could bury it deep enough so that it seemed it had never happened.

Azlyn's words ignited a curiosity in me, but it also felt a lot like tearing open an old scar. I became so absorbed in these thoughts that I forgot myself, losing track of the chore at hand and tripping over the broom I was holding. I managed to catch myself, but the broom fell from my grasp and clattered on the stone floor. My cousin looked up from the kitchen sink.

"Is everything alright?" she asked.

"Oh. Yes, it is fine. I just..." how could I explain to her what I had been thinking? I would have to admit to her first that I had lied about where I had been. That I had helped a Mystic, committed treason.

"I must still be tired," I lied. And then I ventured to ask something that was close enough to the truth without being dangerous, "Audri, do you ever miss your mother?"

The clattering of the dishes in the sink stopped. Neither of us had spoken in this manner since the night my parents had died. She was quiet for a long time before answering.

"Yes, Kala. I miss her very much, and very often. But it is not the same as you miss your mother."

I tilted my head and waited for her to continue, but she had gone silent again, returning to her work. We finished our morning chores as if the conversation had never happened.

That afternoon I went for a walk along the property. Audri was hesitant to let me go out on my own, but I promised I would stay within the boundary. I wanted some time to think.

I found myself by the creek behind the apple orchard where Audri and I used to play when we were children. There was a crude makeshift bridge that we had built one afternoon. The water was shallow on this part of the property, but we fancied ourselves quite the builders and had spent the better part of a day constructing it from uneven logs and wood scraps we had found in the barn.

By the time we were done, our dresses were soaked through and soiled so badly they were beyond repair. Uncle John had been furious and had given us both extra chores for a week. It was the first time we had shared a punishment. The memory made me smile.

I approached the bridge, wondering if it would hold my weight. I put a foot on it and leaned in, testing its composition. It gave way slightly, and the wood creaked, but I was pretty sure if I was fast enough I could cross it. I braced myself, backed up a few steps and darted across.

Just before my feet touched the opposite bank, the bridge gave way and

I fell. I landed with half of my body in the grass, and the other in the sand. The tips of my toes rested in the cool running water. So much for staying out of trouble. I looked back at the remains of the structure Audri and I had built. Now I could see that the lower beams had become rotten, worn away by the gentle current over the years. I would have to wade through the water to get back. Damn.

I pushed myself up to my knees to assess the damage done to my dress. It seemed superficial. I could easily wash it out. I brushed the dirt from my hands and was just about to stand when something caught my eye. It was a simple stone, the size of my fist and unremarkable, save for the markings scrawled across the top in ash.

Gwen

My mother's name. Who would have written such a thing here? I picked up the stone. It was still warm. I brushed my hand across the letters. The act smeared the ash until her name was no longer legible, and covered my hand in the warm sotot. I looked out in the distance, searching for whoever had left it here. Were they still watching us? What purpose did this serve? I dropped the rock and rinsed my hands in the water, reluctantly turning my back on the boundary.

"It did not take you long to get adventurous again." His voice made me jump; he had crept up so silently. I turned about and fumbled for my knife but the skirt of my dress made the attempt awkward. He laughed, "Your choice of clothing is so impractical, Kala. I will never understand your people's obsession with wrapping their women in garments that disable them so." He maintained his distance and held his hands up as if to prove he was no threat.

It was an odd choice, given the situation, to let his words bear enough weight to be insulted, but I was, "It is not about practicality. It is about what is proper."

"Says the girl who goes traipsing through a creek," he retorted. "A lot of good it does you looking proper when you ruin every outfit."

I scoffed.

"I never saw your mother wear such a ridiculous outfit," he added, "and she was a hundred times more proper than any other lady of her kind."

I wanted to slap the smug look off of his face. All the curiosity and fond thoughts I'd had of him that morning drained from my body and were replaced by a childish fury. I felt my nails dig into my hands as I balled them into fists.

"You have no right-" I hissed through my teeth. "No right to speak of my mother." I didn't care that his words had been kind. In fact, that may have made it worse. His expression changed to one of confusion.

"I apologize. I thought you would have been glad to hear stories of her," his tone was sincere. "If our roles were reversed I would have wanted to know more about her. I did not mean to insult you, or cause you any pain."

"Would you?" I asked between clenched teeth. "If it were you in my place, would you be so anxious to hear from the mouth of her murderer's kin, what she was like in their eyes? Your words are poison."

He stumbled, taken aback. His face showed genuine shock before his expression softened, "Kala...is that really what you think happened? Is that what they told you?"

I met his gaze silently, knowing that if I spoke my voice would break. Refusing to cry in front of him, I turned to go and he reached his hand out to stop me.

"The sun is setting. Audri is expecting me." It was both an excuse and a warning.

"Kala, I..." He seemed unsure of himself all of a sudden, the cheeky faux arrogance he had displayed earlier was completely gone.

"Her death was an accident. A tragedy for all of us. She was well loved, revered even, among my people. There was a danger involved in what we were doing, but if we had known... Kala, if I had known I would have prevented it. I can't believe your uncle never told you..."

His words made no sense to me. What was there for my uncle to say? He had lost his sister, the only true family he had ever known, and been saddled with the responsibility of another mouth to feed. He owed me no explanation. For this stranger, this outsider, this enemy to imply otherwise infuriated me. I pulled away from him defiantly.

"No, you could not have known her. You are too young. You know nothing about her," I said, wanting to wrap myself in the denial.

"My people are ageless, Kala, you know that...and I did know her, very well. She was a dear friend." His voice was soft and flat. It was the kind of voice you use when you are stating facts to someone who is being illogical. The way my uncle's had been when Audri and I were little and he was trying to reason with us during a tantrum. He was not trying to coax or convince me.

"I am sorry if I have caused you any pain. That was not my intention. I wanted to show my gratitude, for helping me to save my nephew's life. I simply meant to offer you something I thought that you wanted." He released my hand and looked out at the horizon, "I will not keep you any longer, Kala, but I would urge you to be careful who you trust. Not all is as you have been made to believe. We will be here, waiting, if you decide you are ready for the truth."

And there it was again, the way he could shroud himself in mystery with his own words, drawing me in. I was sure that he was doing this on purpose.

"What do you mean?" I asked, knowing I would likely regret my question.

"Did you ever wonder why there was no funeral for your mother?" he asked. I did not want to admit it to him, but I had always assumed there was some shame related to her marriage that prevented a proper ritual. Even if their bodies could not be recovered (this thought made me cringe), there were still traditional funeral rites that could have been performed as a matter of respect.

Even as a child I had known that my uncle and my father did not always see eye to eye. He had not been good enough for my mother in her brother's eyes. My uncle's silence when they had died, the way he had drawn into himself, I had interpreted as a mixture of shame and regret. It turned out that I was right about his feelings, but so very, very wrong about their origin.

"Your mother was a member of the Alliance."

When our people were victorious over the Mystic breeds, groups began to form among my people. You see, not everyone believed that good had been done in the conquering of the land. There were those that sympathized with the other side. They formed a secret society, dedicated to overturning Ludlum and restoring peace between the Mystics and our kingdom. They called themselves The Alliance.

It was a pipe dream, according to my uncle. The damage had already been done, and no Mystic would look upon our people with anything but contempt for generations beyond my children and my children's children.

And yet, some of them believed. They sent messages to other races in the woods. They held secret meetings. During the time that I was very small, Uncle John would often be away, patrolling the borders and revealing those on our side who were guilty of treason. Mystic sympathizers were sentenced to death.

No. It was not possible. My mother, a traitor? I thought of the way her hands had run through my hair at night when I was lying down for bed, her soft voice singing me to sleep. I tried to recall the song, but in my memory, it seemed to be in a language I did not recognize.

I thought back to her frequent trips with my father, and the way my uncle would mope, forlorn when she went away. I had always assumed it was the burden of my presence that caused his foul mood. Could it have been something else? A personal betrayal?

I shook my head, not wanting to believe it. And yet, here I was speaking with the enemy; having aided in the saving of one of their lives.

"I can prove it to you," Azlyn said, interrupting my thoughts. "I have something to show you. It is about a day's journey from here at your pace. Will you come?"

I looked at the sun setting in the sky and thought of the message that would soon reach my uncle. How much time did I have? Where did my loyalty lie? I longed so much to know more about my parents. Azlyn had not mentioned my father. Was he part of the Alliance as well? Or did he side with my uncle?

What had happened the night of their death? Had he gone with his brother-in-law to retrieve his wife from across enemy lines? Had he fallen trying to save her from the charge of treason? I looked up at him. His blue eyes stared right back at me. He almost seemed to be reading my thoughts. I wondered if he actually could. If that was some Mystic power we had not been warned about.

He said nothing. For a moment we just stood there, looking at each other, both of us trying to dissect the thoughts of the other.

"What is it you would like to show me?" I asked.

"The resting place of your mother."

Just then Audri's voice called for me, bellowing across the landscape. The sun had nearly set. I was late. I looked again at Azlyn before taking off toward the house.

"Tomorrow night!" he called after me. "I will be waiting here tomorrow night if you decide to come."

He waited for a response, then added, "I will wait every night after that if you do not."

For some reason the last part made my heart flutter. I pushed the feeling away and ran.

I ran straight through the creek, forgetting myself for a moment as the cold water washed over my legs. I felt my dress snag on part of the demolished bridge and tear. How would I explain that one to Audri?

She was waiting at the back door impatiently when I sauntered up. Her arms entwined across her chest in the same way that her father's did when he was angry with us.

"Kala, what on earth! Your dress! What have you been up to? I thought you were just going on a walk!"

I was surprised by the sudden catch in my throat when I opened my mouth to explain. I did not want to tell her where I had really been. The sun was low enough on the horizon that I was pretty certain she had not been able to track the direction I had come from. So I lied.

"It must have snagged rolling down the hill," I offered lamely. While it would make her cross, the lie was truer to the personality of the cousin she knew. It would not draw the same suspicion that being out by the river would. Not only that, but I did not want to alert her to Azlyn's and my meeting place.

She sighed, rolled her eyes at me, and stepped back from the door. "Come in and get cleaned up, cousin. We still have work to get done before bed.

CHAPTER FIVE

I DID NOT MEET HIM THE NEXT NIGHT, nor the one after that. I told myself that it was for fear of raising Audri's suspicions. I told myself it was to keep both of us safe. The truth was that I was scared. I would tell myself over and over that it was not denial, that it was not a fear of knowing the truth about my parents. Instead, I would make-believe it was the consequence of treason that held me back.

In a lot of ways those things were true; but, looking back on it now, it was none of those things that kept me from meeting him. It was the fear of what I'd felt, running back toward the house that night. That little flutter in my chest. I was afraid to find out what that really meant.

Two days I spent mulling over my options. Would I sneak out in the night? See what the Mystic had to show me? Would I wait for my uncle to come home and confess my treason to him?

Honestly, I am surprised that I did not confess everything to my cousin during that time. A few times I opened my mouth to try, but something in my gut tugged at me, and I would sigh and return to my work instead. She seemed distant, lost in thought. Perhaps she was wondering what would happen when her father came home, or what the true motivation for his absence was. By this point, I think we had both decided that whatever his mission was, selling the years' crops was only a ruse.

On the third afternoon, I packed Audri and I lunch.

"I thought we could eat in the tree house today," I tried to make my voice sound cheerful and nonchalant.

Her response stung and surprised me, "Don't you think we are getting a little bit old for those kinds of games, Kala?" Her voice was cold and authoritative, "Honestly, will you ever grow up?" She walked down the hall, slamming the door as she closed herself in our room.

I flinched, and left the lunch I had packed her on the table. Determined not to let her attitude ruin my afternoon, I collected mine and ventured out to the tree house myself. It was cool, but sunny outside. While the leaves in the orchard had long since fallen, the leaves concealing the tree house remained the same.

There was no sign that Azlyn had been there. Whatever part of the tree he had harvested to save his nephew left no evidence visible, to my eyes at least. I climbed up into my sanctuary and began to eat. Soon I was lost in my own thoughts as I relaxed to the sound of a light wind blowing through the branches. Azlyn had mentioned someone planting this tree here as if it were a surprise to him.

"She would have planted one." His voice echoed in my mind. Did he mean my mother? That seemed the most logical if she had really been a part of the Alliance. It made sense also, that her brother would have left it standing in her memory. Did he know of its origin? Of its power? If he did, he must have kept it a secret, else it would have been felled years ago.

Something below me clamored noisily, disrupting my thoughts. The sound made me think of what one might hear if a dog attempted to climb a tree. Suddenly a head popped up over the edge of the tree house.

"Azlyn!" my voice squeaked, "What on earth are you doing here, and why are you making such a racket?"

He pulled himself up until he was sitting beside me. A piece of his hair had come loose of its binding and he brushed it away from his face, tucking it behind his ear, "Truthfully," he said between breaths, "it was not intentional."

Not intentional? I laughed.

"And you make fun of my kind for being so noisy, oh sure-footed Prince of the Forest!"

He shot me a look like daggers, but it was all in jest, and he could not keep up the farce for long before breaking into another beautiful smile.

"My people are quite adept in the forest. It is the man-made structures we struggle with. They are too silent."

I cocked my head to the side curiously, "Silent? The trees are silent as well, save for when the wind blows through their boughs. And besides," I rapped my knuckles on the tree house floor, "this structure is wood just the same."

He shook his head. "It's not the same. And the woods are not silent. I am not sure I can explain it in a way that you would understand." Seeing my posture change as I prepared to argue on the offense he added, "That is not an insult, Kala. It is just that the experience in many ways transcends words in your language. Your tongue, like your perceptions of the world that lives around you, is limited in many ways."

"When we move through the trees, they speak to us. Their spirits guide our footing. We know where each handhold lies before our feet are firmly on the branch we have only just reached. When I led you through the forest...it is true that my eyes are more adapted to see with the limited light. But more than that, I can hear and feel the pulse of the life around me. It whispers to me constantly. It whispers to you as well, though your people do not tend to listen."

I took a moment to process what he was trying to tell me, "So you are saying that trees have souls?" I was skeptical.

"All things that grow, and some that do not, have souls Kala. Every moment the earth pulsates with life all around you. It saddens me that you cannot feel it."

"So you are saying that this tree, this one that we sit in right now...the Menohathi," I made a poor attempt to pronounce its name in his tongue, but failed miserably.

"She has a soul; though it is not quite as strong as the others. She was born sprouted from the ground. Still, she is strong, and sacred. Descended from the First Wave and one of the last of her kind," he said reverently.

"Sprouted from the ground? But how else would a tree grow?"

Azlyn looked taken aback. Of course, he knew that I would not have been educated on this matter. As this species, in particular, was not a threat, its history would not have been part of my education.

"They were not always trees, Kala. There was a time when the Green Children roamed the earth as free-footed as you and I. It was long before my time that they were rooted. Their tale is very sad."

"Tell it to me?" I asked, drawn in by the mystery and the magic of it all. I leaned against the wall and drew my knees in toward myself as he began his tale.

"It happened long before the humans sailed to this continent before there were enough Mystic breeds living in conflict. Before war, poverty, hunger or hate. All living creatures were in harmony, working for the betterment of the greater community. The meadows were lush and green, the skies endlessly blue, and the water pure. Crops thrived without struggle, as did many species that are now, sadly, extinct.

The mountains, now silent, sounded their wisdom across the land. Their children, what you call trees, thrived. Of course, their forms were quite different from what you see now. They stood significantly smaller in comparison, about twice my height.

They could run and bound across the grasslands and dwell indoors with the rest of us. Their skin was not coarse as it is now, but soft and gentle. Dark like the soil where their roots rest. Their faces were soft and angelic, reflecting the same innocence as a child. Indeed, they never seemed to age. Their laughter rang out like bells and carried on the wind for miles and miles, filling the land with mirth.

"One day one of the Green Children (their native name, given as a reference to the color of their hair) was chasing a butterfly. She traveled too far west, into the uncharted territories. Night came and she was lost, and afraid. She cried to the Wind God for direction, but he could not hear her in this strange land. Instead, an unknown element answered her call.

"She trusted him instantly. Such was the innocence of her people. The element was called Svetly, known now as the Lightning God. He used her innocent mind to his advantage and learned from her the location of his old Rival: The Earth God Prilehvat— father to the mountains. He traveled with the Green Child back to her homeland, where he laid waste to everything he saw.

Many died, and the mountains, in terror and shame, fled southwest away from their children...where they later became the guardians of my people. For it was our leader and Mage, King Kyrolie, who defeated Svetly and banished him inside of a great cloud. Now, wherever he goes, a great roaring sound follows him, warning the land of his wrath.

"Prilehvat, pained by the cries of his perishing people, turned his anger on the Green Children. He took away their ability to move, rooting them to the ground so that they would forever be dependent on him for life. He turned their skin coarse to deter the softer humanoid species from seeking their touch. He forbade the wind to carry their voices so that now only those with patience and still tongues may hear them. Lastly, he made their arms twist upward toward the sky as if reaching for the God that caused their condemnation.

"To this day, Svetly searches for ways to thwart the Earth God. Occasionally in times of conflict, he will reach down through the trees to strike Prilehvat, killing the tree in the process. He has, in the past, been able to extend his sky fire to one of the Free Peoples, reminding us of the Green Child's betrayal, and adding to their contention. And so they are forever condemned."

Azlyn's gaze lifted and he added, "But not all of us thrive on hatred. The Elves have long been friends of the Green Children."

The story was both sad and beautiful, and I found that ending it felt a lot like coming out of a deep sleep. I blinked a few times before I noticed Azlyn staring at me. I blushed and looked down at my lunch. Suddenly I did not feel much like eating.

"Come with me," he said, climbing down from the tree house before I could respond. I hesitated a moment before following him down. As I reached the ground I noticed his shadow slinking into the woods. I was torn between a fear of the unknown and the feeling that my heart was on a string being tugged in his direction. I glanced back at the house only once, to be sure that Audri was nowhere in sight, before darting off after him.

The path we walked through the forest was different from the place I had been captured. Here the trees were not so dense, and my eyes could clearly discern our surroundings. Though I did not need him to guide me, I found my hand reaching for his. I told myself it was from habit but felt my face flush in spite of myself. I hoped he did not notice.

The woods around us were lush and thriving, not at all sinister. Though it should not have been possible this deep into the woods, I felt a soft, cool breeze catch my hair and rustle through my gown, accompanied by a sound almost like chimes, and then a slight murmur. On impulse I twirled to the music, letting my gown billow out around me. My braid swept behind me with the motion, coming loose at the top before resting over my right shoulder. The act was satisfying, and the wind seemed to respond to my movement, so I continued until I had spun so many circles that I made myself dizzy. I stopped, nearly toppling over and giggling to myself.

Azlyn stood still watching me, a large smile across his face. I could not tell whether he was mocking me.

"Impractical as that gown may be, it certainly does look joyful when you spin in such a way," he said. "The forest approves."

The world had stopped spinning around me, but my stomach was still fluttery.

"And you?" I asked, pulling my hair out of its bindings in an attempt to reset my braid. I avoided making direct eye contact.

Azlyn chuckled to himself, "I too, approve," he said, taking my hand in his again and guiding me deeper into the forest.

We walked in silence from that point on. It seemed irreverent to do otherwise. At times we would come across creatures that I had never seen before, and I would pause, in complete awe. A phoenix nested on a low perch. A fairy zipping from one flower to the other appeared as a tiny green-colored light.

In one clearing we spotted a unicorn grazing. It looked up as we passed, its body tense as if it were about to bolt, but then it made eye contact with Azlyn, who nodded, and its body relaxed. He seemed to have this effect on most of the forest, even those who had seemingly no magical properties.

At one point he had a following of tiny chipmunks tittering as they followed in his footsteps. He had laughed softly before making a clicking sound with his tongue and motioning for them to be on their way. They scattered and scurried outward about 50 feet before turning back to watch us. I could not be sure, but it sounded almost as if they were laughing.

Azlyn clicked once more and they took off into the trees, but all the way I could feel little eyes on me. I wanted to ask him what they had said. I knew he must have been well versed in many modes of communication. It was the standard of his people to be fluent in many languages: which made them valuable as ambassadors before the first war.

I saw him glancing at me from the corner of his eye but remained silent. He seemed almost able to read my thoughts. (It was not until much later that I learned this is a skill only effective amongst those who are closely bonded in his culture and has more to do with interpreting body language than it does actual telepathy.)

"They think that you are beautiful," he said, still facing forward. "You are creating quite the stir."

"Did my mother create this much of a ruckus?" I asked.

"It was different then," he answered. "But yes, the forest did take note. It was a crucial time in our history. It was the point at which we felt there might be hope of peace."

"Surely my presence must pale in comparison," I stated.

"It is not you in particular that they find amusing," he clarified. "It is the sight of us together that causes such a stir."

I tilted my head curiously, but he said no more as we continued our journey.

We walked silently for a while, and Azlyn seemed lost in thought. I scanned the trees around us and took note of a nymph darting from tree to tree hiding from her satyr. She had the deep emerald skin that was the token of her people and long, stark-white hair that framed her body wildly. Unlike most nymphs, who wandered the forest in only their bare skin, she was clad in a flimsy two-piece outfit that concealed her most delicate features.

I tried to approach her, but she darted up her host tree, her red eyes blazing back at me. She tilted her head and I felt her gaze blaze through me. I had always been told that Nymphs were dull in the head, but the eyes of this one reflected something else. A curiosity about me that implied a deeper intelligence.

I was startled when she spoke.

"Be careful with this one, Azlyn," she crooked her head toward him. "You know from what line she branches." It was a riddle to me, but Azlyn seemed to understand, for he nodded.

"I am aware of the risk, thank you, Sapphire," he said curtly, his lips forming a thin straight line. Then he added, "Nykolas sends his regards."

The Nymph blinked rapidly and tilted her head the opposite direction, as if waiting to form some sort of reaction to his words. Then she shrugged and darted the rest of the way up her tree, disappearing into its boughs.

"What was that all about?" I asked as Azlyn took my hand again, resuming our walk.

"An old friend with a reminder," he answered, then. "Nothing that you need to concern yourself with." He squeezed my hand in reassurance. I wanted to let it drop, but my curiosity was buzzing in my head too loudly not to inquire further.

"I did not know that Nymphs could speak in such a manner," I pretended to be nonchalant; hoping my feigning disinterest would lure him into revealing something more. "Why does she dress in that manner?"

"Sapphire is in many ways extraordinary for her kind." The way he said it was innocent, but I felt a twinge of jealousy regardless. "It is believed that there may have been mortal kin in her bloodline somewhere."

"Human?" I asked.

"It seems unlikely it is true, but the Nymphs were here long before any of us, and mingled over many continents after their fall."

I nodded. The history of the Nymph race was not new to me. It was said that they were concubines to the God Pykoboth before his marriage to Hannah. A jealous Goddess, she had cast them out and scattered them across the continents, fating them to be forever plagued by the Satyrs. Their presence in the Old World was no more, though none could account for the origin of their disappearance. Still, the intermingling of the two species was possible.

"Who is Nykolas?"

"Her son." Azlyn started to say more, then thought better of it and fell silent again.

No wonder the Nymph had receded so swiftly into her tree. Nymphs were not known for their maternal instincts, leaving their young to sprout independently. However, the lack of affection was generally reciprocated as the young formed their own grove. Furthermore, Nymphs were all female.

"He is a half-breed of course," Azlyn continued as I pieced my thoughts together. "You will meet him in due course."

I wanted to ask more, but it was then that we stepped into the next clearing, and I felt my heart sink.

It had been years since the last time I had cried over the loss of my parents, but sitting here at the grave of my mother I felt a wave of anguish rush over me. I ran my hand over the stone that marked her resting place.

It was beautiful, with intricate characters from Azlyn's language carved along the center, and her native name below it. Stars adorned the top of the gravestone, etched in emerald dust. I ran my hand over it, my fingers lingering on her name. The stone was warm, having been bathed in the day's sun.

"It was late in the day," Azlyn said softly behind me. "A team of 5 was escorting your parents to the border after a meeting with the Council leaders. It began to rain." He paused, taking a deep breath.

"We were in good spirits. The meeting had gone well. Gwen had proposed a new idea to our King. She would recreate the lost journal from the information used to educate your people's children, giving us the power to force the dark breeds to rejoin the Alliance.

"It was not fool-proof. Your people are not given the full text; merely taught enough for your leader to maintain control by instilling fear. Still, she had been an apt student, and the time had come to begin your education. She was confident that she could recreate enough for us to present to the other tribes and convince them to join the Alliance."

I glanced over my shoulder. Azlyn's head was bowed reverently, his eyes cast to the ground as he spoke. It was obvious that he and my mother had been close. Seeing his pain intensified my own.

"We were foolish to travel in such a large group so close to the border. There was an ambush. The Elite..." his voice faltered and for a moment he fell silent, lost in the memory. "In the fading light, with the weather...Kala... he couldn't have known it was her."

I felt the air rush out of my lungs.

"No," I whispered as I struggled to inhale. My body refused to obey as memories of that night flashed before my eyes. The flash of lightning as my uncle's silhouette stood in the doorway. The smell of the rain as it fell from his clothes. The sound of his voice as he lamented the death of his sister. Fear rushed over me as my mind raced and my body seemed to go numb. Azlyn had stopped talking. I didn't want know. I couldn't stand not knowing. I already knew.

"What happened?"

"A soldier attacked from behind. There were so many... we were outnumbered. Your father turned to warn her, but he was too late." Azlyn closed his eyes and shook his head, as if doing so would shake the memory from his mind.

"The attacker struck her with his sword, but his aim was off. The injury would have been disabling, not fatal for an elf, but for a human..." he trailed off and was silent a moment.

"The soldier fell to his knees beside her. Your father soon had his sword firmly against his throat. It was only then we realized who her attacker was." I felt my body go stiff as I waited for him to finish the story.

"Your uncle commanded the soldier's retreat. We retrieved our wounded and fled."

It's hard to describe what it feels like to have your world turned completely upside down. My head swam as I pieced together Azlyn's story with my own memories. I understood now, why my uncle had never talked about that night. Why I had never been given a proper explanation of my parents' deaths. Why there was no funeral.

Years of sadness I had restrained welled up inside of me. My stomach churned and I felt like I might throw up. And then I was on the ground, the cold earth of my mother's resting place gave way under me and my knees sank in. An inhuman wail broke the silence. Buried in the fog of my own despair, I didn't realize that the sound had come from me. I felt Azlyn's hand rest firmly on my shoulder, giving silent reassurance as my tears mixed with the soil. He said nothing more, but knelt beside me in silence, allowing me to grieve.

CHAPTER SIX

AZLYN WALKED WITH ME MOST OF THE WAY HOME, stopping at the orchard. I insisted on going the rest of the way myself. I said it was for his own safety. In truth, I really wanted to be alone with my thoughts.

I walked with my arms wrapped around me, guarding myself against my own vulnerability as much as the cold. My eyes ached from crying, and my face felt dry and irritated. I rubbed them briefly as I walked through the orchard and tried to make sense of my own emotions.

I had always looked up to my Uncle. His actions may not have been the most affectionate, but I had never wondered whether he truly loved me. He spoke often of the greater good and of sacrifice and nobility. He said the greatest honor you could do for your people was to find a way to better the world. His way was educating the young soldiers who came after him. He believed in education as a cornerstone in the foundation of a full life and dreamed of a time when an efficient education system would become available to those who were not of royal descent.

In the Old World, he had told us, education was doled out freely to all people, noble or not. I could tell, during these stories, that he missed the world he had been born into, and often wondered if he had resented that he and my mother had been brought across the seas. I never asked him.

He was a hard worker. A farmer had to be. His voice could be stern, but his hand was always gentle. In many ways, he treated me as his own daughter. I knew him better than I ever had my own father. I knew who he was. He was not a murderer.

And so, the thought that my mother's life had been taken by her own brother-my uncle...the man who had raised me— it was crippling. My mind created the scene over and over again and still could not make sense of all the anguish.

How could a man who repeatedly preached honesty have spent so many years lying to me? How could he withhold from me the knowledge that my father was still alive? It felt as if my entire existence had been a lie. I began to dissect every fond memory I had of him. Every hug, every word of encouragement and praise. Had it all been a farce? Perhaps he had hoped to mold me into something like him as some sort of twisted revenge on my father. Surely he knew that someday I would find out the truth?

My head spun with questions unanswered, and my heart ached as if it had been taken into his very hands and smothered. I walked slowly, wrapped in a blanket of overwhelming dread. I had hoped to leave all traces of my journey behind as I approached our property, but I could not shake the dismal feeling. It followed me home.

There was no light coming from the house as I made my way. For a brief moment, I worried that the door had already been bolted shut as the sun had long since set. I breathed a sigh of relief as it gave way when I pushed on it. There was no sign of Audri. At least I would not have to explain myself.

I entered our room and found that she had packed up her bed clothes. A note was left saying she had decided to take her father's room in his absence. I donned my nightgown and sat on my bed, wrapping my arms around my knees in an attempt to ward off the loneliness I felt when I heard a soft tapping on my window. It was Azlyn. I didn't know whether to be annoyed or relieved that he had followed me. I bolted the door to my room and opened the window for him to climb in. He did not say a word, but sat by me and wrapped me in his arms while I cried softly into his shoulder. I do not know how much time passed with us that way, but eventually, I fell asleep.

When I awoke I was surprised to find him sitting cross-legged on the floor, eyes closed, seemingly in a trance. Sunlight streamed through the open window and fell lightly around him, making him appear quite angelic. I did not stir, afraid to disrupt his rest. I lay quietly a while, thinking. My hair was still down, and I wanted to leave it that way, but I knew that Audri would protest. I sat up; pushing aside the blanket Azlyn had covered me with and pulled my hair back with a piece of blue lace. I did not braid it.

I felt a hand on my shoulder and nearly jumped out of my skin. Azlyn had snuck up on me while I was lost in thought.

"You have got to stop doing that," I said, letting the tension leave my body.

"Sorry," He apologized, but his eyes were dancing and I knew he wanted to laugh.

"What time is it?"

He glanced out the window "Nearly mid-day."

"Mid-day??!" Why had Audri not come for me? I rarely slept this late. Wasn't she worried?

"She is not here," he said as if reading my mind.

"What?"

"She and a young male left this morning."

"Conner," I sighed. "He must have brought news of my uncle."

"From what I can tell she is still on your property, somewhere near the river," he said. I furrowed my brow, confused and he placed a finger gently on my forehead, dragging it down the bridge of my nose and causing me to smile.

"Do not dwell on it," he said. "I am sure it is nothing."

I wrinkled my nose playfully, and he removed his finger

"Perhaps," I said, "but I am still worried."

"How did you sleep?" he changed the subject.

I looked down at my knees, slightly embarrassed, and pretended to be busy smoothing the wrinkles from my skirt.

"I slept well enough I guess," I said awkwardly. "I apologize, for last night. I don't normally behave in that way."

"In what way?" Glancing up I saw he had moved to the window. His eyes scanned the horizon once before turning back to me.

I found myself at a loss for words. I'd spent so many years mourning silently that I wasn't even sure what to call my reaction. Azlyn knelt down until his face was level with my own.

"It is okay to feel sorrow and it is okay to weep. It does not make you any less of a respectable person. It does not change my perception of you."

I looked at him, a bit embarrassed, "And how do you perceive me?"

"Strong, and beautiful. Compassionate. Joyful. A dreamer."

I blushed, "You think too highly of me."

"You think too little of yourself."

I changed the subject, uncomfortable with his praise, "Why are you here?"

"I wanted to apologize, Kala. I did not think how deeply the truth of your mother's death would affect you. Indeed I have been rash in all my interaction with you. I fear my judgment has been clouded."

"I don't understand," I looked away, unable to meet his gaze, though I didn't know why.

"The Alliance is growing, Kala." he began to pace a bit nervously, careful to stay away from the window. "It has not gone unnoticed by your King. The Elite are on to us. I fear my carelessness has drawn their attention. They are preparing to wage war on my people, and your uncle's soldiers are everywhere, crawling through the forest. I myself was nearly discovered on my way to see you last night."

Now I was frightened, "What does this mean?"

He did not answer my question but instead continued, "There is strife, also, within my family. My brother Cain has been against the efforts of The Alliance since the beginning. He felt that gathering in such numbers would simply make us a target. And now...now he thinks me a traitor."

"But you saved his son!" I declared, mortified.

"True," he nodded, "But it was because of our mission that his son was injured in the first place. And besides that," he hesitated as if struggling to find the right words, "I have also broken one of our people's most sacred laws."

"How?" I could not think of anything aside from his position in The Alliance that could cause so much trouble in his family. And yet, were his family, the King even, not themselves contributing to the efforts of The Alliance?

"What law have you broken?" I inquired again.

He stopped pacing and looked me in the eye intensely, "Kala, I'm falling in love with you."

I sat in shock as his words sank in. My heart fluttered, but words escaped me.

"What?" It was a stupid reply, which I chastised myself for later.

"It is forbidden for my kind to court a mortal," he stated. "My family, save for my brother and his son, do not know." He paused. "If my King were to find out..." he left the rest unsaid.

"Why is such a law still in place, if the cause of the Alliance is to unite our people?"

He opened his mouth to answer, then thought better of it and raised his hands submissively, a deep sorrow in his eyes, "Does it matter? Law is law."

I felt my face flush again, this time in anger, "And your mere presence in my home breaks my kingdom's laws." I pointed out, my voice harsh. "What will your people do?"

"I do not know. No one has ever broken this law."

"The penalty of my people is death," I reminded him.

He shook his head, "We do not kill our own as punishment. Death comes at the hand of your kin only out of mercy."

"So what do we do now?"

It was a while before he spoke. For a moment I thought I saw fear in his eyes, then he blinked and it was gone.

"I can ask naught of you, Kala. Tell me that you feel nothing and I will not come again."

"I can't do that," I exhaled as I spoke. I hadn't realized I had been holding my breath. The way he looked at me sent shivers up my spine. His fingers tracing a path softly across my forehead and down my face as he brushed my hair to the side was electric, and I felt the hair on the back of my neck stand on end.

I found myself swept up in the moment, overwhelmed by an emotion I had never experienced before. I felt as if I was flying and drowning at the same time. My entire body screamed at me to breathe, but his gaze left me breathless. My heart was beating so hard I thought it would burst from my chest.

It was excitement and terror at war with each other inside my head. By the laws of my people, it was wrong. By the laws of my heart, it was right. My uncle would be devastated if I stayed. My soul would be shattered if I walked away.

His eyes locked with mine, darting back and forth swiftly as he observed my inner conflict. His lips turned upward in a subtle, crooked smile.

And then he leaned down and his lips touched mine and my mind went blank.

I wanted to laugh, but I did not want to lose the sacredness of this moment. Cradled in his arms I felt the most complete I had ever been. Like there had been no loss, no loneliness, no struggle. As if it had all been a misperception of my heart's ardent search for him.

The euphoria was short-lived. It seemed like only moments had passed before I heard the front door slam shut. Audri had returned!

"Kala! Kala, wake up you lazy thing! Father is coming home!"

I did not need to tell Azlyn to hide. Before I had even moved from my bed he was out the window and on the roof. I unbolted the door just in time for my cousin to burst through it. She danced about the room gleefully. She wore brown sandals and a plain gray gown with long sleeves neatly cuffed at the wrists, the skirt disheveled. Her face was flushed from running and she had flowers woven into her golden hair.

She came to a halt inches away from me, breathless. I stared at her in shock.

"What is in your hair?" I asked, motioning to her hair. She had never been one to adorn herself in such a way and had always thought it childish when I had done so in the past.

She cast her eyes askance, avoiding the question, "Conner rode in this morning with a message."

That explained my cousin's appearance. I had long thought she was sweet on the King's messenger.

"We are going to war."

I thought the news to be grim, but if she shared my sentiment there was no trace of it on her face.

"Does that not mean your father will do battle?" I reminded her.

For a moment her face fell, but then it brightened once more. "He will not fight," she said, raising her head as if to convince herself that such an action was somehow below him. "His rank is too high. He has already been injured in battle, defending his country. He will oversee the development of battle strategy. With him at the King's side, the war will be over in no time, and my father will return home."

I stared at her, speechless. I could feel my lips move, but it was as if my voice had fled, so much was my astonishment. She studied my expression critically, then satisfied, excused herself from my presence.

In a trance, I closed the door slowly and locked the deadbolt. I heard the soft sound of Azlyn's boots hitting the floor as he climbed back through my window, and I vaguely sensed his presence behind me. When I turned, he wrapped his arms around me, drawing me into his comforting embrace, and kissed the top of my head lightly.

"He will not stay long," Azlyn said as if he had seen what was to come. "I will be back for you."

Azlyn slipped back out the window. I watched him for only a moment before he seemed to disappear into the landscape.

CHAPTER SEVEN

AZLYN WAS RIGHT. My uncle returned home only to gather supplies. Ludlum had called the men to war and my uncle, despite his injury and his past service, had been drafted.

Though he was angry that I had disobeyed him and left the property against his instructions, I noticed his chest puff up slightly as Audri recounted the tale from her perspective. He was proud that I had taken off to protect our homestead. Still, I was not above his reprimand.

"It was foolish, Kala, and could have proven deadly," he said, almost wistfully. "Gods help me; you have your mother's spirit...and that same fire, that reckless abandon." His tone turned sour. "That kind of impulsivity is what killed her."

I felt my face grow warm with shame. Uncle John assumed it was the result of his lecture. Only I knew the truth. It was not reckless abandon, but foolish whimsy that would put me in harm's way again and again. And it was not only my own life that I was risking.

My uncle's face softened. He never could stay mad at me for long. He put an arm around me.

"She was a lot like you. Optimistic, a dreamer. Her head was always in the clouds."

That sounded like me alright.

"It does no harm for your head to be in the clouds," he said. "As long as you are sure to keep your feet on the ground."

He squeezed my shoulders and kissed the top of my head as a father does to a young child and then released me. "Keep your wits about you. Tend to the fields— where there is war there can easily be famine. Keep to yourselves and look after each other. I will send Conner with word when I can."

And like that he was gone again, this time leaving behind our mare in favor of one the King's steeds. Audri stood outside and watched him depart, leaving me to my own thoughts.

They say that attraction is survival based. A man may be attracted to a woman because her frame is well suited for children, or her face is particularly appealing. A woman is attracted to a man because his chiseled jaw and broad shoulders portray that he would be an adequate hunter.

In more socially developed times, one might choose a partner to wed for social standing, or property. The very basis of attraction is to further a species.

And yet here I was, attracted to someone that could easily mean my death. In what way would this further my species? I tried to argue myself against it. I willed myself to feel nothing, but it was useless.

The door slammed, sending a jolt of fear through my body. I tried to hide my nervousness and busied myself by clearing the morning dishes from the table. My hands were shaking so much that the cup I was washing slipped from my hands. I swore softly to myself as it shattered. My response did not go unnoticed.

"You think you have it bad?" Audri chastised me as I bent down to collect the shards of the cup that had shattered against the kitchen floor. "Kala, you have no idea how lucky you are."

I lashed out at her mentally; angered that she would assume that anything about my existence in that moment would be considered lucky.

"My father has given you everything. Every opportunity to be successful; and with little to no recourse for your careless actions. Do you have any idea how different it would have been if I had been the one to take off like that? He would have been livid. And yet you get a pat on the head and sent on your way. He favors you."

I realized then that my cousin was jealous. It was true that my uncle's affections toward me were less scrutinizing than they were toward her. I had always assumed that was because he expected more from her than from the poor orphan girl he had taken into his care.

"No matter what wrong you do he will always see your mother," she spat as if she had known what I was thinking. "He loved her greatly, Kala. He practically raised her. You can do no wrong in his eyes because he sees her spirit in your face. Whereas I..."

She trailed off but I knew what she was thinking. Her presence reminded him of his estranged wife. The woman who had left him rather than idolizing him and putting him on a pedestal in her heart as my mother had. I had never thought that my uncle might give anything but unconditional love.

Perhaps my perception was tainted by my own experience. Perhaps I did not see things for what they really were.

"I would rather she had died, like your parents," Audri admitted, her voice quivering as her hands balled into fists at her side. I realized she was holding back tears, "Than taint me with the legacy of her betrayal."

It was the first time I had ever heard her admit to anyone that her mother had left of her own free will. With that, she stormed off to her father's room. I did not see her again that day.

Audri and I spoke little in the days following her confession. I assumed that she was ashamed of what she had confided in me, and I...well I had no idea how to approach her. She had always been a well-behaved child, eager to please. Not only a strict follower of the rules, but a fierce enforcer of them when we were alone together.

Growing up, her role was more that of the militant big sister than an older cousin. I suppose my uncle must have thought the discipline would be good for me, wild as I was, because he rarely stepped in when Audri became power hungry. It was not that there was no love between us, but it was a complicated mix of emotions.

At this point in my life, I found my nights to be increasingly sleepless. I would lie awake, tossing this way and that and then back again; full of anxiety about what the next days would bring. Sorting out all the emotions that seemed to be swimming around inside of me. Little whispers in my mind tore my conscience one way and then another. Dividing my loyalty; placing it all on one side, then again on the opposing side. Trying to work out a solution that would best serve everyone I loved. If such a solution existed I never became aware of it.

And so I would rise the next day with all the worries of the previous evening still heavy on my heart, and go about my duties as stoically as possible. Only to repeat the same scenario over and over again until I felt that my bones would simply collapse under the weight of my exhaustion; leaving me in an ambiguous heap of girlish despair.

Audri and I avoided each other where we could, working in silence when avoidance was not possible. The combination of her father's absence and the impending war put a strain on our livelihood. There would be no more trips to the market to trade and sell our crops, and there were many tools and materials we could not produce on our own. This forced us to trade with other homesteads individually. Audri took up the task of negotiations, and I was relieved when she demanded I stay and look after things at home.

Azlyn took advantage of my cousin's absences, though I never thought to ask how he knew she would be gone. His presence seemed to chase away my inner conflict and with it all reason. Such is the peril of young love.

Bright with new hope I would skitter across the grass, feeling as if my feet were almost floating. Bathed in pure inebriated joy I took note of the wonder around me. I could smell the cold new morning dew on the crisp grass beneath my feet. I could taste the sweet texture of autumn as the wind brushed my face gently, whipping up the loose pieces of my hair and making them dance around my face. The whole world seemed to echo my elation.

He told me tales of my mother when she was young. These stories stirred within me a sense of duty, and a longing to follow in her footsteps, as if that could somehow bring her back to me.

"Kala, this isn't a decision you are ready to make," he argued as we sat in beneath the shade of the Menohathi. Blossoms from the tree floated to the ground as he leaned against its trunk and whispered in a language I didn't recognize. This was the way in which his people procured the healing properties of the tree. It was something to be granted, not taken by force. I turned my eyes away, feeling like an intruder to this reverent ritual.

His visits had increased, I believed in part because of this resource. Knowing the purpose of the blossoms he packed neatly in his pouch made the war more real, and again I insisted I go with him. Still, he refused, arguing that it was too dangerous, or that my mind was too clouded to appreciate the consequences of siding with his people. He brushed my hair from my face and kissed my forehead before darting back into the woods.

Our next meeting he was distant. He mumbled to himself as we traipsed through the foliage near the creek. If there was an explanation for his foul mood, he did not offer it. I remained silent as we sat to eat and watched the sun dance on the water.

My mind wandered to the time he and I had attempted to cross a deeper section of the creek before eating. We had fumbled for a bit before deciding to bind our supplies in twine and ferry across on a large piece of driftwood. The practice proved to be clumsier than the theory, however, and neither of us escaped from the venture with dry shoes. The sight of our disarray made him laugh explicitly.

I was jarred from my thoughts by the sound of Cain's voice. His son Cazlyn strode behind him. It was not unusual to see the latter. He occasionally accompanied his uncle during our visits and was deeply curious about the customs of my people.

As they approached I could tell this would not be a social visit. It was obvious by Cazlyn's body language that he wished to stay out of whatever argument was about to unfold.

"Mynderward!" Cain hissed through his teeth.

The word is derived from an ancient rune in the mountains. The origin of the cave writings is unknown even to the oldest Mystic species in the land, but the root word which sprung from it is known to be derogatory, and I felt a sense of indignation at having it used toward me.

Azlyn stood to meet his brother. The emotional contrast between them was chilling. I stood to the side, my eyes darting between the two brothers, both of which looked as if they were poised to strike at any moment. Azlyn's face was contorted in an expression I had never seen before. It was one of rage. It was he who spoke first.

"You would do well to remember your place, brother."

"You need not remind me, oh cherished firstborn," he spat back. "I have resigned myself to living forever in your shadow."

"So that is what this is about? You would endanger our mission and her life over a petty jealousy?"

Cain cackled, "You are a fool if you believe it is so simple, brother. Though I will not deny that there does exist a certain...contempt for the fact that I was not born first in your place. This is about what is best for our people. Consorting with a foolish girl-"

But Azlyn cut him off, "Watch your tongue, brother," he threatened. "I need not remind you to choose your words carefully in this matter."

"Is her hold on you that potent already? Clever vixen," he smirked. Azlyn stepped closer so that his face was but inches from his brother's.

"I said watch your tongue."

"Very well," he conceded, but his smile did not disappear. This seemed almost a game to him. "What will your people think? Or your King? That you would run out into the wilderness after the daughter of a con-man. You risk the very mission you pretend to preserve."

I could see that the accusation cut Azlyn to the core. His nostrils flared and his jaw set, but he did not argue otherwise.

"Tell them before I do," Cain threatened. His son and I stared on in disbelief at the conflict that was unfolding before us.

Azlyn shifted his weight back and forth, enraged but not wanting to give his brother the satisfaction of seeing him truly lose his cool.

"It is not as simple as that and you know it. Why must you make this so difficult?"

"Because I believe our people deserve to know the full truth before committing themselves to a cause that will almost definitely end in the extinction of our race!"

"Our race will fall into extinction just as well without anyone's help if we stand by and do nothing." His rebuttal was powerfully projected, but Cain did not so much as flinch.

"Take her to the Alliance then, if you are so certain," Cain mistook his brother's silence as stubborn disagreement. "See how well they take it." His eyes darted to me, "See if they welcome her with open arms...or if they decide perhaps the golden child is a less capable leader than everyone has come to believe. Shall you break the news to them, or should I?"

"Do not force my hand, Cain." Azlyn's tone made it hard to determine whether this was a plea or a threat.

"You speak as if I am not even here," I interrupted. "Do I have no say in this?"

Azlyn shot me a look of shock. Cain's smirk grew wider.

"See brother? She wants to go. Who are you to stand in her way?"

Azlyn sighed, "Kala, you have no idea~"

"It was all well and good for my mother to join the Alliance. Why would I be any different?"

Azlyn opened his mouth to answer, but the sound of a horse whinnying in the distance cut him off.

Audri was home!

Cain motioned silently for his brother to follow before he and his son darted into the woods. Azlyn lingered a moment longer.

"You're impossibly stubborn, Kala."

"That's why you love me," I tried to make light of our argument.

"You have no idea the danger you put yourself in," he retorted.

"Stop treating me like I'm a child," I said indignantly. "What danger do you put yourself in by coming here? And your brother? You think that he will hold his tongue? What will be, will be."

Azlyn sighed and kissed my forehead, "Very well. Make yourself ready for travel. I will be back in a fortnight."

I watched his silhouette disappear into the trees before making my way home. On the way, I was hit with an overwhelming sense of dread. I cannot explain how I knew in that moment, but I had felt...a shift in the balance around me.

It was not only a shift in myself, my internal sense of right and wrong, but a shift in the air, in the trees, in the ground beneath me. Change was coming, and I was afraid of what that meant for my family, my people. Myself. And yes, I was worried what that would mean for my relationship with Azlyn as well.

Audri was sitting at the dinner table when I finally made my way back to the house. She locked eyes with me as if expecting an explanation for my absence. I offered no excuses for my behavior this time, but simply walked past my cousin and prepared for the evening chores as if nothing was amiss.

I could tell that she wanted to push me for information, but to my surprise, she made no inquiry. To this day I don't know whether it was the fear of harming our already fragile relationship; or of having her growing suspicions confirmed that held her tongue that night.

CHAPTER EIGHT

MY RELATIONSHIP WITH AUDRI IN THE FOLLOWING WEEKS was a lot like a needle: a necessary and valuable tool. Something I could hold in my hand and use to bind the two worlds I was living in together. But it was also sharp and elusive. I spent much of my time feeling as if I was struggling to thread it in vain.

Though our relationship had always been a mix of fierce loyalty and intense competition, Audri's confession about her mother had made me see her in a different light. My first reaction was one of anger and the need to close myself to her out of self-preservation, but I realized my anger was only a mask I made to hide my sadness. By all accounts, we had lived a lonely childhood, both motherless and essentially cut off from the outside world.

Most of our lives all we'd had was one another, but that had changed now. At the time I don't think either of us knew how or why, but the growing rift in our relationship with each other was rivaled only by her growing isolation. Still, we went through the intricate dance of interaction; both of us seeming to have two left feet. When I tried to reach out she seemed to pull away self-righteously. In retrospect, I suppose I did the same.

The night before I expected Azlyn to return, Audri knocked on our bedroom door. Being half-asleep, the sound made my heart jump into my throat.

"Come in," I yawned, sitting up in my bed.

Audri came in and sat across from me hesitantly. The moonlight shone through the window, bouncing off her feathery blonde hair. There were dark circles under her eyes and her face was taut. At first, I thought it was the dim lighting, but looking more closely I could tell she had lost weight. How wrapped up in myself had I been, to have let such a thing escape notice?

"I know," she said so quietly that I wondered if I had imagined it.

I felt my body tense without permission. What did she think she knew? More importantly, how much was I willing to admit to? So much damage could be done to our already fragile relationship if I admitted to the truth; but how much damage would a lie do if she knew more than I was hoping? She was harsh and stubborn and a million other things that made becoming vulnerable to her a terrifying thought, but she was also my kin, and I did not think for a moment that she would betray me in a way that could cause my death. I felt the strain of the symbolic seam I had sewn pulling apart.

"I know that you've been sneaking off," she said, leaning in toward me. Her tone wasn't quite accusatory, though it wasn't friendly either. It reminded me of the time we had coaxed a stubborn hen off her nest with a slice of melon, cooing sweetly only to swipe away the eggs she had been hoarding once she let her guard down. I held my tongue.

"I haven't told anyone, if that is what you're worried about, Kala." Her shoulders slumped and she leaned back in exasperation. "What is going on with you?"

I inhaled deeply, mostly to stall. I didn't think that she knew more than she was letting on but I couldn't be certain. Maybe this would be the moment that finally brought all our disjointed attempts at reaching each other come together. Maybe this would bring us closer.

"I've....met someone," I offered. Easing her in seemed like the safest approach.

"Met someone?" she echoed, "As in~"

"I'm in love, Audri." A huge weight lifted off of my shoulders while my hands shook with fear. It was a glorious and chaotic contradiction.

"Oh thank the Gods, Kala, you silly girl!" she laughed, visibly relieved. "You've been off with a boy! And here I thought— well never mind all that! Who is it? It's the old farm-hand isn't it?"

"He's not exactly a boy," I answered. I hadn't really planned what I would say beyond that I felt my resolve starting to diminish. "Well, not like one of us would be. He's still fairly young, I think, for one of them."

"One of them?!"

"An elf," I didn't give her much time to respond before continuing, "I know what you're thinking Audri but please....they're not like we were made to believe. At least, not all of them."

For a long while, she stared at me, trying to grasp the magnitude of the situation. Her eyes darted across the room in such a way as to express how rapidly her thoughts were forming in her mind. She shook her head in disbelief, opening her mouth to say something and then closing it again, her words escaping her.

"Are you mad??" she stood with her mouth agape a moment waiting for my response. I had none. At least, not any that would satisfy her in this moment. All of the excuses I had practiced fell short of satisfactory in this moment. So I simply stood there, lamely, under her critical gaze.

"Kala...just...I am not even sure what to say to you! What were you thinking?! Do you want to get us all killed? This is treason at the very least! What would my father say? What would your parents think?"

"My parents were part of the Alliance, Audri..." I trailed off. I wanted so desperately to have someone to confide in, to share the pain and the joy of all that I had discovered; but doing so meant telling her the truth about her own father. I looked closely at my proud cousin.

Her once beautiful hair had thinned and hung, sorrowfully on either side of her face. Her clothes were tattered, but I could see she still carried the knife her father had given her. No, I had to protect her from that truth.

She rambled on as if she had lost control of her own utterances, pacing back and forth in front of the window. And still, I stood silent. What could I say? And I was certain she would crawl right out of her skin at the first suggestion that she meet him before casting judgment.

"I have to go somewhere tomorrow." I had to force the words past the lump in my throat. "I don't know when...or if...I will be back. Audri, I don't want the last time we speak to be like this."

I was on the verge of tears as she sneered down her nose at me.

"To think that my father wasted so much of his life on trying to pick up the mess your filthy, traitor parents left behind." She spat in my face. "What a bloody waste that was. A lot of good it did him! Betrayed by the very girl he took in."

If it was not so sad it would have been comical, the way her face contorted in anger. She looked down her nose at me with disgust, as if I were somehow inferior to her.

My response was a mixture of outrage and heartbreak. I swallowed both, pretending to be too tired to argue with her, and pulled the covers back from my bedding, turning my back to her silently.

After what felt like an eternity of silence I heard the hinge on the door creak.

"Take the horse," she said before shutting the door behind her. I waited until the echo of her footsteps down the hall faded away before letting myself cry.

The next morning I loaded my pack onto my uncle's horse. I had packed lightly-a bed roll, change of clothes, a day's worth of food and water. I had traded in my gown for a pair of slacks and a red tunic that had been packed away in my mother's old hope chest. The fabric was faded but soft. It smelled a bit musty but would be more practical for the journey ahead.

I untied the knife my uncle had given me from my ankle and unsheathed the blade, cradling it in my hands. I had no need for it where I was going, but leaving it behind felt like ripping a piece of my heart out.

I stared at the silver blade as it caught the reflection of my face. It had changed somehow, since the last time I had seen it. The child-like innocence was gone, replaced with a mix of stern sadness and idealistic hope. I sighed.

The night before I had told my cousin that I did not know if I would return; but the truth was, I hadn't really decided if I would really leave until this moment. Sighing, I sheathed the blade and shoved it into my pack. I wasn't ready to let go. I took hold of the reins and began walking. Horses see better in the dark than humans do, but their eyes also take longer to adjust. I didn't want to chance being thrown when we entered the forest. I paused to look back for only a moment before stepping into the cover of the woods.

I paused a moment in the darkness, blinking and waiting for my eyes to adjust. I could see the shadows of the great trees surrounding me, but not much else. Looking up I saw the familiar specks of sunlight fighting to break through the leaves. My fear of the forest had long since left me, having walked through it so many times with Azlyn. Still, I remained alert.

Beside me, the horse whinnied and I felt a rush of air as a figure dropped down from the tree in front of us. For a moment my heart raced and I found myself reaching for my knife, forgetting it was no longer tied to my ankle.

"Peace, Kala," said a familiar voice. I sighed in relief. It was Azlyn. Two more shadows fell from the trees silently. Cain and his son Cazlyn. Azlyn hugged me briefly in greeting. The weight of his arms around me was a welcome comfort. The smaller of the two shadows behind him moved forward and placed a hand on my horse's muzzle, whispering softly in his native tongue. Cain remained still as if refusing to acknowledge me.

"We will cover more ground if she rides, Uncle," Cazlyn said. "Sienna fears the forest, but will carry Kala willingly."

"Sienna?" I asked.

"Do you not know the name of your own horse?" Cazlyn seemed taken aback.

"Names are for pets," I said awkwardly. "She is a working animal. We don't name them."

Cain scoffed in disgust, "Arrogance! I don't know how you can bear it, brother."

"I meant no offense," I apologized. "I'm not sure I understand."

"Who gave you your name?" Even in the darkness, I could see Cazlyn's head tilt curiously.

"My parents. More my mother, I suppose."

"Why should it not be the same for your horse?"

"Well," I paused, knowing my answer was bound to make things worse, "I guess we don't consider them that aware of themselves."

The horse snorted loudly and Cazlyn laughed.

"What's so funny?" I asked.

"Nothing," Azlyn said sternly. His answer was directed more at his nephew than myself.

"She called you an idiot," Cain offered. I felt myself blush. Azlyn took my hand and squeezed it.

"Enough you two," Azlyn said. "Kala can't help her upbringing. Enlightenment is a journey. We are all on the same path. Do not fault her for being further behind."

He turned to Sienna, then again to me, "Will your cousin not be alarmed to find her father's horse missing?"

I bit my lip. This was a conversation I had been dreading all morning.

"Azlyn, she knows."

Cain hissed through his teeth and moved in closer but his brother stepped between us. They argued in their native tongue while I fought to get their attention to no avail.

"She told me to take the horse!" I finally yelled over them. "She's not a threat! She won't betray my trust." I hoped I was telling the truth.

Cain's hands flew up in the air in frustration. His brother growled something in response and everyone was silent.

Azlyn held out his arm to help me onto the horse and took hold of the reins. We journeyed in silence for most of the day. Around nightfall, we arrived in the same clearing where I had first met Azlyn. I climbed down from the saddle shakily as my eyes adjusted to the light, glad for the opportunity to stretch my legs. Cazlyn tended to Sienna, whispering joyfully to her while Cain and Azlyn made a fire. I pulled my bedroll from my bag as well as a loaf of bread I'd taken from the hearth that morning and sat by the fire. After a short while, Cazlyn sat down beside me.

"What is that?" he asked, pointing at my bedroll.

"It's a bed, of sorts," I replied, thinking it an odd question.

"Why do you not sleep on the grass?" I looked at him, confused. In the light, he did not look as young as I had expected. Then again, age is hard to determine when it comes to elves.

"This is more comfortable. The ground is hard and cold."

Cazlyn's perplexed expression remained, "The ground is not hard and cold. It is warm and full of life. How do you survive when you insist on separating yourselves from the earth? Your people are strange, Kala."

I shrugged, not having a good answer, and finished my meal.

It was decided that Azlyn would scout the perimeter during the first watch. The knowledge that I had told Audri about Azlyn put everyone on edge. I wished that he would stay behind with me, but I accepted that he was the more levelheaded of my travel companions. Cain was too quick to act out of anger and would likely strike before asking questions had Audri followed us. I tried to push the thought from my mind.

I was certain I would fall asleep before my head even hit the bedroll, but my body ached with exhaustion and my mind was at war with itself. I closed my eyes and focused on the sound of the breeze blowing through the blades of grass and the crackle of the dying fire.

Cazlyn stirred briefly beside me, then settled his breathing full and steady as one who is in a deep sleep.

"It was your father who insisted we come for you," Cain said, tossing a twig he had been fiddling with into the fire. "Coward though he was after your mother died. He fought with the King's court to approve our mission.... years too late I might add."

"My father is alive?" I bolted upright, facing him. I could not form any more words than that, though I felt an anger rush through me at the thought of my father being called a coward.

Cain almost seemed to smirk, "Did Azlyn not tell you?"

I shook my head.

"Well. That information would not necessarily have been to his benefit, would it?"

"What do you mean?"

Cain leaned in and looked at me solemnly, "Kala, you are a pawn, in a long line of pawns. The Alliance is looking for leverage. Someone strong on the side of the humans who might have a claim to the crown once Ludlum is overthrown. It could have been either of you. You or the other one...your cousin,"

"Audri," I filled in the blank for him.

"Audri," he nodded. "Both of you have royal blood on your shared side of the family. It is not much, but in the ruins of war and with no leader it may be enough. That is what the Alliance is striving for. My father was skeptical at first. The mission was very risky. Your father spoke up for you, reminding him of the price he had paid for his loyalty to the cause and," he swept his hands outward over his crossed legs, "here we are."

"I don't understand," I said, "You meant to kidnap me and take me to your people...in hopes of using me against them when my King was overthrown?" Though I held no residual loyalty to the government I had been raised under, the idea of being used against them without my consent enraged me.

"It was not supposed to be that way, no," he admitted. "Actually, if you are being quite technical, it was not supposed to be at all. You see, though your father pleaded with the King, ultimately our quest was rejected."

"But I thought you said-"

"Let me finish," he cut me off. "It was initially and officially rejected. And that is why your father came to us. War is imminent, Kala, and he was concerned for your safety. He was willing to circumvent the proper channels to be reunited with you. He knew my brother had a soft spot for your people in general and your family in particular." His eyes met mine. "He took the death of your mother very personally and spent a time in his own dark place. It is for this reason I believe he took pity on your father.

"The agreement they was that there would be no force. You would come of your own free will, or not at all. My brother had planned to come alone and scout the area so we could form a plan. Your father pushed to go with him but..." for a moment his eyes danced in jest, much like his brothers, "well your kind is not exactly known for their graceful travel. He agreed to make contact with us on a later journey. Still, he would not let Azlyn travel alone, and so I took up the journey with him. Reluctantly, I might add."

He glanced at his son who was still sleeping. It boggled my mind that the two could be related. First of all, they looked almost the same age, though there was a significant height difference. I reminded myself that the lifespan of elves was not the same as with humans.

"My son is stubborn. It is the disability of youth. He insisted on following. By the time we had discovered him it was too late to send him back. His heart is full of fire and a desire to see justice. I fear it will not be long before he gives his official Oath." For a moment Cain was no longer talking to me, but seemingly someone whom he wished I was. Our eyes met again and he snapped back to reality.

"It was he who tried to lure you into the woods that night. So determined he was that you would follow. Technically, it would not have been against your will, and he was certain that once he had a chance to explain himself, you would join us. But he was found out sometime after you fled. As you know, he was injured that night. It was then that we realized your home was being carefully guarded. In my anger, I chanced being discovered. I knew your mother was a smart woman. She must have left some sort of healing spell or the like behind for you. But I was found out, and followed...and well you know most of the rest."

"Most of it?" I pried.

Cain looked at me very seriously, then glanced over his shoulder as if afraid to be overheard.

"Any affection that he shows you is a farce. A means to an end, Kala. You do not know his standing among our people. If he can secure one of your people whose lineage is royal as a mate it would not only seal the alliance between our people but secure his placement in power."

I was shocked at his nerve and angry at his accusation. If I am being honest, I did also feel a twinge of panic that he may be right. That I had fallen for an elaborate trick somehow. I pushed the thought away and replaced it with a memory of his hand in mine. I was silent a long time, tracing one of my hands with the other where his had so often been.

"But to court a mortal is against your people's law," I said, my voice only a little shaky.

"Has he really not told you?" Cain's expression was convincingly astonished, except for his eyes. His eyes reflected a sick sense of satisfaction in what he was about to say. "Who makes the laws in your kingdom, Kala?"

"Well, at least the larger decrees, they come from our King..." I answered, not sure where he was leading me with this.

"And what do you suppose would happen if someone were to break one of that magnitude?"

"They would be punished...perhaps executed... although Azlyn said that your people do not do that."

"Would anyone be punished?" Cain continued, drawing me along with his words like a boy with a string taunting a cat.

"Ludlum shows mercy to no one," I reasoned. "I imagine it would be the same for your King."

"Mercy comes more naturally to my people." Cain smirked. "Especially for the King's son."

He could not have shocked me more if he had hit me with a sack full of rocks. I felt the air rush out of my lungs.

I had not just fallen in love with an elf....I had fallen in love with an elven Prince.

I pretended to brush the comment off, but I felt the words Cain had said creep along the edges of my mind, planting little seeds of doubt.

"A farce. A means to an end."

Chapter Nine

SITTING WITH MY OWN THOUGHTS only made me fidget more so I decided to get up and take a walk around the camp. Cain did not move to stop me, though we both knew that Azlyn would object to me wandering off on my own.

The sun had set and the air was crisp and cool. I could see my own breath expelled in icy tendrils as I stomped across the wooded landscape, trying to will my anger outward through my extremities. It did not work. I was as agitated as ever.

Why would he withhold his standing from me? Was he afraid my affections toward him would change with the knowledge of his social status? Or was it truly as Cain said, with me merely a pawn in this game he played with the Alliance? Would my father truly have sent him to me for the sole purpose of deceiving me? I wanted to believe that the answer was no, but I realized that the belief was more of a wishful thinking, tied to the memory of a man that likely no longer existed.

I heard a rustling sound behind me and rolled my eyes. I knew that he was making the noise on purpose. Whether to warn me of his presence, or in hopes that it would startle me into remembering how foolish I was to take off on my own I was not sure; nor did I really care. I sighed and turned around.

"What do you want?" I asked pointedly.

"You should not be out here alone," he ignored my question. I rolled my eyes again.

"I needed some time alone."

He looked concerned, and confused when I pulled away as he moved toward me.

"Kala, what on earth is going on?"

I looked up at him, a grave mistake as I found myself lost in his eyes. For a second I was mesmerized. The distraction took the edge off my anger, which only irritated me more as I broke eye contact.

"Why did you lie to me?" I retaliated, answering his question with a question. He was visibly taken aback.

"I have not lied to you."

"You told me it was against the laws of your people to court a mortal. You made this big production of being forbidden to be with me. Drug me out into the middle of the wilderness, away from my family, against the laws of my people for which, I will remind you, the penalty is death..." I was forced to pause for breath," And you did not think to mention to me that you just happen to be the son of the King you pretend to fear."

I stopped. He was speechless; visibly confused by the flood of words I had thrown at him.

"Maybe," I started, my rage fueled by his lack of a response, "Maybe he is right and it is all a ruse. Maybe you are just in this to gain my trust. Maybe this is all a grand scheme to win me over and convince me to betray my people~" I was rambling now, speaking more to myself than to him, but he cut me off.

"I see my brother is at it again. Damn him." His body language tensed in a way that I was not accustomed to seeing. "What did he say that would so easily turn you against me?"

I wanted to tell him that what was said did not matter, that he had fooled me into this mission and that I would go no further. I wanted to dart off into the woods, back to my home and hide beneath the soft comfort of my blankets and pretend that it was all just some freakish nightmare. But my feet were made of lead. Though I willed them to carry me far from this moment, they remained rooted to the ground. I wanted to hear it from him. I wanted his confession, so that I could hate him properly. So that I could escape a lifetime of looking back on this moment with regret.

"Why did you come for me Azlyn? Not in this moment, but in the beginning. Why did you come?"

"Does it really matter so much, Kala, the why? Or does it simply matter that I am here?"

"It matters," I insisted stubbornly. "Did you come here thinking you could use me as a means to unite our people? Was I simply some conquest you took on out of a warped moral obligation?"

He waited a moment before answering me. It was not long, but it felt like an eternity. Like years of having my heart ripped to shreds, my pulse pounding in my ears waiting for him to say something, anything that would convince me that what his brother had said was not true.

"Your father approached mine. He was concerned for your safety. He wanted you on our side where you could be better protected. I cannot say that he did not mention such an arrangement. I can tell you it did not go over well with my own father."

He looked at me, desperation in his eyes.

"When he came to me...I helped him because I understood how his heart ached for you. Because I knew your mother, and I loved her dearly; and I knew that if it had been her asking my father he would have consented. Did I hope that your cooperation could somehow tilt the scales in our favor? I will not lie to you and say that I did not."

He moved toward me, even as I recoiled from him in disgust and betrayal.

"But, Kala, when I say that I love you, it is because it is the truth. Not for any political gain, because the truth is, it is likely our union would have the opposite effect. It could tear asunder the treaty we are hoping to form, just as easily as it could solidify it."

"Then what is the point?" I hissed at him. "What is the point of loving me at all?"

He blinked, searching for an answer that would satisfy me.

"There is no point, Kala. It just is. Love defies all reason, all logic. It does not exist to make one's life easier, or harder. It simply exists."

I woke the next morning to find Cain and his son missing. Azlyn was brooding, sitting by what remained of the fire. I guessed that there had been some argument between the two brothers, but Azlyn would not elaborate. We packed our supplies in silence and continued our journey with me riding Sienna and Azlyn guiding her through the forest. As we journeyed deeper into the woods the light broke more easily through the treetops. I mentioned my observation to Azlyn, and he grinned mischievously.

"Those who journey this far are rarely a threat to our people. The trees have no need to hide the light from friends."

Near midday, we stopped to rest by a stream. The water was still, unlike anything I'd seen before. I stood there in awe of its incandescence, brushing my fingers lightly over the top of the water. It hardly stirred. I assessed its obvious traits. It was warm, lush, and obviously liquid. Was it safe to drink? I was afraid to be the first to test it.

Neither Azlyn nor Sienna seemed to share my trepidation, both drinking freely. I splashed the water on my face, letting droplets pool in the corners of my mouth. It was light and refreshing, and I cupped more in my hands to drink. Azlyn looked at me and smiled.

"Different from what you are used to?" he asked.

I nodded.

"'Tis amazing what nature will provide when left unadulterated."

I said nothing in response but wondered what my people might have been able to learn from the natives of this land had we not insisted on conquering it with brute force.

CHAPTER TEN

WE JOURNEYED UPSTREAM FOR MOST OF THE DAY as its twists and turns took us further from my home. The terrain was often rough, scattered with ancient roots that rose from the ground, but it all seemed to smooth out in front of Azlyn as he guided my horse. I could not be certain, but it almost seemed as if the trees bowed in greeting.

As the sun was sinking below the tree tops we reached an immense clearing covered in sand and rock. Ahead of us the water pooled beneath a massive waterfall before flowing into the stream that would eventually reach my home. Though the origin of the waterfall was too high to see clearly, I took note of how gracefully the water was greeted by the ground below it. Though it roared against the rocks of the cliff from which it fell, it hardly made a sound as it met with the calm waters below it, simply pooling and creating gentle ripples as it pushed onward. Tendrils of blue mist wafted outward from the base of the waterfall, twirling at the water's surface and dancing up and out.

As we crept closer I could see there was a path hidden up against the wall of the cliff. It was too rocky for my horse to navigate, so I dismounted. Azlyn did not bother tethering her, but whispered something in her ear as he ran his hand affectionately down her muzzle. He patted her neck and motioned for me to take his hand.

My eyes were drawn again to the mist. So captivating were its movements that I almost expected it to come to life. I paused a moment before stepping into it, thinking that it might have some solid form. Azlyn nudged me forward and I held my breath, afraid to inhale it. I could not be certain in the dim light, but I thought I saw him chuckle. I experienced a brief moment of terror as we stepped into the darkness. The crashing sound of the waterfall overwhelmed my ears, roaring as if in warning.

And then we were through it. I blinked several times, trying to adjust to the change in light. The cavern was cast in a dim green light, the source of which I could not locate. I took the scene in slowly.

Near our feet, the water from the falls formed a small pool. In it was a woman...no... when I looked closer I saw that she was half fish. A mermaid! Her skin was a deep caramel colored and her hair was done up in intricate blue dreads, pinned back with star shaped crustaceans. Her top half was clad in seaweed that contoured perfectly around her form in a way that was almost immodest.

Her tail, the same powdery blue color as her hair, was adorned with shimmering scales that caught the light when it twitched. She was beautiful, and I felt a twinge of guilt when the memory of my uncle's voice echoed in my head

"Their livelihood is intertwined with their well-being. Taint their waters and they will perish."

Her eyes locked with mine and for a moment I was afraid that she could read my thoughts. To my relief, she smiled at me as she leaned her elbows against the stony floor. I scanned the room. Cain sat secluded in a far corner, clad in shadow so that I could not see his face. I could tell from his posture that he was brooding over something.

A handful of dwarves were whispering to one another as we entered. Nearby a faerie fluttered over their heads, darting this way and that. Her flight pattern reminded me of a hummingbird in the spring.

Across the cavern, a four legged creature was pacing. From a distance, in the dim light I thought it to be a lion, but when I squinted and leaned in closer I saw that it was no lion, but a sphinx. My heart jumped into my throat and the air rushed out of my lungs. I noted a small squeak escaped my lips and hoped that no one noticed. Azlyn squeezed my hand in reassurance and approached another of his kind.

He was visibly older, though his age did not seem to instill in him the same physical disabilities that often come with age. He stood tall, almost regal; his wheat colored hair was paler than the younger men of his kind. He wore it short and cradled in a sterling headdress that almost resembled vines, interwoven into four points around his head. His eyes were a deep blue and wrinkled in the corners. Something about them seemed unusual. As if he were gazing off into the distance.

"Father," Azlyn's voice interrupted my thoughts. He bowed at the waist slightly, greeting his King. I attempted to curtsey but my efforts were awkward at best. The King tilted his head in acknowledgment, but said nothing.

At his side stood a woman who nearly matched him in height. Her skin was pale like the elves, and her ears pointed slightly. In contrast, her hair was a deep auburn, and red stone hung from a thin silver string, resting in the center of her forehead. Her eyes were rounder and a deep gray. She smiled at me and I thought I saw her eyes change color, first red, then blue, finally settling on a honey color. Their shape seemed to have changed as well, more cat– like. Though quiet, her voice echoed off the stone walls when she spoke, and I almost jumped out of my skin from the shock of it.

"So this is the one you have chosen, young prince?" She was addressing Azlyn.

"High priestess Eoma," he bowed in greeting, ignoring her question.

"*So this is a witch,*" I thought to myself. She certainly did not look anything like my cousin and I had imagined in our make believe games.

"*Be more careful with your tongue than you are with your mind young one,*" The same voice that had echoed across the cave interrupted my thoughts. I stared into the eyes of their owner. Her lips had not taken part in her warning; I realized she must have been reading my thoughts and blushed, hoping that the message was one she had given to me alone. I was not sure how to respond, but bowed my head as I had seen Azlyn do and greeted her with her proper title, "High Priestess."

This seemed to satisfy her and she looked me up and down once before smiling and shifting her gaze back to Azlyn, "She is a quick learner. This will do nicely." She dipped her head pleasantly and excused herself to greet others.

Azlyn and his father began to exchange pleasantries with one another, something I found to be intriguing and almost petty given the circumstances. Admittedly I grew bored, not comprehending much of their conversation, and let my eyes wander around the cavern. The mermaid was conversing with a dwarf using a series of clicks and whistles. Whether he understood her I was not certain, as he never seemed to reply, simply nodding as she continued her tale.

The Priestess Eoma seemed to be speaking with the Sphinx. How this was possible I was not exactly certain, as Sphinx only ever respond in riddles. I pondered this for a moment before deciding to ask Azlyn about it later. My eyes moved on. Everyone seemed to know everyone else, and though they had all certainly seen my entrance with Azlyn, few seemed to be paying us much attention.

Except for a man in the back, opposite of Cain. I was sure that he had not been there when we entered and wondered if he had snuck in behind Azlyn and I. The two were crouched over a makeshift table, each leaning in closely to each other, but not necessarily in a way that was friendly. They were muttering something, one seemingly speaking over the other and then becoming silent again. Cain was visibly agitated with the mystery man. His jaw set and his shoulders scrunched up so high they nearly covered his ears. His head jerked subtly in our direction and his companion glanced my way.

The first thing I noticed about him were his bright red eyes. They stood out like a sore thumb in the dark cavern, even amongst so many other Mystical creatures.

The second thing that I noticed was that, aside from his appearance, he felt oddly familiar. Not looked, but felt. He rose to his feet with Cain still in the middle of an utterance and turned away from him, making his way toward us in the crowd.

"Azlyn," he greeted him with a slight nod of his head, as seemed to be typical of many of the prince's close friends.

"Nykolas," Azlyn returned the nod and extended his hand in greeting. The two shook, grasping each other's forearms.

So this was the son of the Nymph Sapphire. He turned then to me, a wide grin spreading across his face. As unsettling as his eyes were, I was relieved to find he had inherited the teeth of his human father, rather than the pointed ones of his mother.

"Kala, I have long been waiting to meet you."

This seemed an odd thing for him to say. To the best of my knowledge, Azlyn had not shared with anyone that he had conceded to my father's wishes. No one should have even known that I existed, let alone been waiting for me.

"Kala, this is Nykolas, son of Sapphire. Sired of Brian."

I felt the blood leave my face. He was my half-brother.

CHAPTER ELEVEN

M Y VOICE FAILED ME. I looked at him awkwardly, trying to decide how I felt about this stranger, now that I knew we were kin. He looked to be my age, perhaps older...which would mean that he had been with the Nymph at the same time that he was married to my mother. This automatically made me want to hate him. He must have sensed my tension, or seen the anger reflecting in my eyes because he spoke up.

"It was after your mother died," he said simply. He did not seem to be offended by my standoffishness toward him.

After she died? But that made no sense...it would have made him a boy of no older than ten! He seemed to predict my line of thinking.

"Technically I am closer to 9, by the measure of your people's years. Nymphs, however, age quite differently. I am by all accounts an adult, in both body and mind," he assured me.

"But..."I stammered. I was not exactly sure what I had intended to ask. I had always assumed that my father would have been true to my mother, even after her passing.

This time it was Azlyn who spoke, "Kala, when your mother died your father was lost. He made...a lot of unsavory choices. No offense, Nykolas"

"None taken your highness. It is no secret to me that the act is viewed as a blasphemy to many."

I was confused by this comment also and turned to Azlyn for an explanation.

"Nymphs were the concubine to the god Pykobeth before his marriage to the Goddess Hannah. Out of jealousy his wife cast them down onto the earth and burdened them with the affections of the satyr. It is said that the nymphs still hold the God's affections and consorting with them in such a way that would produce offspring is considered to be both an insult and an ill omen."

"So no one has ever..." I trailed off.

"I am the first and only of my kind," Nykolas confirmed.

"My...our father...Is he here?"

Nykolas shook his head, "He is not generally welcome among...most people."

"Is it that bad? What he did?" My heart sank. I had been hoping when I found out that he was still alive...well I was not sure what I was hoping for, but this was not it. There was a void I had felt my whole life, even with the love and guidance of my uncle, which I had hoped could be filled by reuniting with my father. It did not appear likely to happen.

"Do you ever see him?" I asked, surprised by the resentment I felt at the thought that my father had left me behind only to start a new family. He had replaced me.

"He runs in a rough circle," Nykolas explained. "He is here and there, usually showing up when he wants something. But if you are wondering, he did not raise me. Not really."

I felt a wave of relief, and then immediately on its heels a twinge of guilt. Nykolas seemed nice enough, and if he was a friend of Azlyn he must have been of stout character. There was no reason for me to wish him ill other than petty jealousy.

"Do you...Do you wish that it was different?" My questions were becoming more personal, an odd and socially inappropriate series of inquiries I was aware. But in that moment I did not care much about social niceties. I was grasping for a missing link.

"I hold no ill will toward him if that is what you are asking," he said. It was not. He continued, "In many ways, I have acquired the apathy of my mother's side, I think. And it has been a great tool when it comes to self-preservation. Matters of the heart can be...messy." I got the feeling that he was hinting something to Azlyn but I ignored it.

"Do you feel any emotions?" I pried.

"I feel them, yes. I am capable of anger, or sorrow, or joy. Of love. I do not crave the family bonds as much, I suspect, as my human relatives do." Thinking twice about his wording he added, "Which is not to say that I do not wish to have those bonds. Just that they are harder to develop. I have, however, been anticipating your arrival for quite some time. I am glad that Azlyn was able to convince you to come."

I was not sure how to reply.

Suddenly I was aware of Cain's glare from across the way; so intense it felt as if he could burn a hole through me.

"What were the two of you talking about?" I asked, turning my attention back to Nykolas

"We have...a difference of opinion on the matters the Alliance will be voting on today," he said delicately. "He does not share the same sentiments as I in regards to your presence here."

This was no surprise. I could not understand why it was that Cain seemed to hate me so fiercely, especially considering the part that I had played in the rescue of his only son. "Why does he hate me so?" I asked, to no one in particular.

"He has a long standing wound in regards to your people," Nykolas said. "One that is best not discussed at this time. He also harbors a great jealousy, having lived in the shadow of his kingdom's heir," he looked at Azlyn, "Through no fault of your own, of course, Your Highness. You have always been more than kind to him."

"It is no secret to me that my brother harbors ill feelings. I cannot say that I would not feel the same in his position. I have tried, again and again, to reach out to him and help him see reason. My efforts, unfortunately, have fallen short in the case of my brother."

"But not in the case of his son, thankfully," Nykolas added.

Their conversation was obviously based on background information that I was not privy to, and I found myself both confused and intrigued. What had happened to turn Cain's heart so sour? I was not certain that I wanted to know; but seeing the look on Azlyn's face as he discussed it, I felt my heart soften slightly in regards to his brother.

I was just about to inquire more when Eoma stepped on to the platform and called the meeting of The Alliance to order. Looking around at this cluster of strangers, I was met with somber expressions. Where just minutes ago they had been exchanging pleasantries and victories, their faces had all fallen into dubious expressions.

Beside her stood the King, his eyes gazing off into the distance. As Eoma scanned the crowd, preparing to address them I wondered why he did not do the same. Again his gaze was far-away as if his mind was reflecting on something else. Eoma lightly placed her hand on his arm and I could have sworn I saw him startle.

The King was blind! I suddenly found myself wondering what I had gotten myself into. How could a group of Mystic bandits hope to overthrow a kingdom that their leader could not see?

Suddenly a series of images flashed before my eyes as vivid as if I were living them myself. Save for one difference: they were completely silent. I saw children dashing gleefully down the brick streets of a great city. A little girl in a brown dress with her golden hair woven into two side-braids chasing after a boy with a red balloon.

Flash

The same pair, but older stood at an altar, her hands clasped tenderly in his. She wore an elegant silver gown, and he a green silken suit. There was a great crowd gathered to watch. They rose to their feet in joy as he leaned in to kiss her.

Flash

They sat at a throne, the King with his chin resting dismally in one hand, the other clasping tightly on the hand of his wife. His brow furrowed, concerned as he received some news from what looked like an elven soldier.

The Queen gasped, covering her mouth with her hand and they both turned their attention to the right, where two young boys played on the floor before them.

Azlyn and Cain, I realized.

Flash

An older elf knelt at the foot of the King. His face contorted with pain and his skin clung tightly to his cheekbones. He writhed in agony, reaching out a hand to the boy who stood behind the King. He was taken away by two guards. And the scenes began to change more rapidly.

Flash

A private guillotine in what looked like a dungeon.

Flash

A young Azlyn in tears, his hand tracing the emblem on a silver casket as his father stood at his side.

Flash

The King was face to face with Ludlum. They appeared to be arguing. The King stormed away.

Flash

The same city from my first vision went up in flames. Soldiers of all different breeds bore down on them from ground, water, and sky.

Flash.

A small group emerged from the wreckage. Tattered, injured, their spirits broken. The King was among the survivors, his face badly burnt.

Flash

The group of outcasts traveled through the forest.

And then a voice:

"Blindness has nothing to do with physical sight. A man who is missing his eyes can still clearly perceive the world around him. True blindness is a blindness of the mind. A man unable to see outside of his own experiences."

Chapter Twelve

I WAS BACK IN THE CAVERN, Azlyn's hand in mine. It seemed as if no time at all has passed. I heard the voice of Eoma echo in my mind, *"Do not be so quick to judge him, child."*

It was her second warning. I did not get the feeling that I would survive the third.

"I believe we all know why we were asked to meet here today," Eoma's voice filled the cavern as she addressed the crowd. Her announcement was met with silent nods from several. Only one voice spoke out:

"Excuse me, Priestess, but I do not believe I understand the meaning behind this meeting," It was Cain.

A hush fell over the cavern. Though no one dared to say it, I got the impression that his comment was treading on dangerous territory. Tension hung in the air.

Eoma's face was a blank slate, though if you looked carefully you could see the straight line of her lips tense.

"We are here to vote on our next action." She addressed the crowd, "Long have our people waited for this moment. A time when the tables would turn in our favor. A generation ago we believed that time to be upon us."

She looked at me and I thought I saw a trace of sorrow flash across her eyes, "We remember the loss of our great friend and ally. Gwen's death was a tragedy to all of our communities. Her work, and our hope died with her that day."

She paused for a moment and the room was silent. Heads bowed slightly in an act of respectful remembrance.

"Before us today shines a new light," Eoma continued, "Kala, daughter of Gwen has come, of her own free will, to pledge her allegiance to the Alliance. She holds within her mind the knowledge which was long ago written by the great elven king Charlezon."

"How do we know she holds such knowledge?" Cain interrupted, "We know that their people study us, but how can we be sure what she has retained."

Eoma's jaw set. It was obvious that she did not like to be questioned. I felt something in my mind tingle and got the feeling that Eoma was prodding the outskirts of my mind. The feeling was not invasive, but it was also not welcome. I wanted to will her out of my head, but knew that I could not force her from my consciousness.

Instead, I focused my thoughts on something she would not want to see. I turned my mind to the execution circle in the crown city. I had seen it only a handful of times, as a child when my uncle would take us with him on his travels. Even as then the sight of it had filled me with dread.

I imagined the mermaid, chained to the walls of the makeshift aquarium as soldiers poured poison into it, tainting the water.

My eyes grazed the crowd and met the gaze of my half-brother. I imagined felling his mother's tree, forcing her to wander the woods alone in despair. I met Eoma's gaze and projected the image of her bound in the throes of a funeral pyre, being burned alive.

Her eyes widened slightly. She had expected to find the information she sought, but I do not think she expected to have it given to her in such a manner.

Her eyes remained on mine, and she looked slightly shaken.

"She knows."

The crowd turned their attention on Cain, waiting to see if he would interject.

He said nothing. Eoma continued, "With this information in our possession, we can once again force a treaty with the dark breeds. With their numbers, we can reclaim our land."

"How do we know we can trust her?" I could not identify who had spoken.

Eoma tilted her head in response and then turned her gaze to Azlyn.

"I will vouch for her," he said.

A hush once again fell over the crowd. Suddenly all eyes were on the two of us. Many who had not seemed concerned with the sight of us together took note of his hand in mine.

I felt my face grow warm, both from embarrassment at the thought of their criticism, but also from anger that I would be doubted. What did they think I came all this way for? Could they not appreciate the risk that I was taking? Their lack of appreciation left me feeling indignant, and their critical gazes made me feel insignificant.

This time it was Azlyn's father who spoke up for me. I wondered if he would have done so if he could see that his son's hand was intertwined with mine.

"Friends," he started, "it is wise to be cautious during such a pivotal time. All of our peoples have suffered at the hands of Kala's kin. This is true. But she comes from a line of good blood. She has her mother's heart.

"I will remind you that of all of us, it is my people who have dealt most closely with her kind. Indeed, I had many encounters with the earliest settlers. I am familiar with the minds of her people. If she was of ill intent, believe that we would have known by now." He turned in our direction, and though his eyes were seemingly blank, I got the impression that he could see more clearly than anyone else in the room.

"There have been, no doubt, many opportunities for Kala to betray us. Indeed, she could have been followed here today. But she was not. I have faith that her loyalty will hold steadfast."

This time, there was no argument from the audience. The King bowed slightly, conceding the platform once again to Eoma.

"And now," said the High Priestess, "all that is left is the matter of logistics. The transferring of knowledge in a manner that would elude our enemies. One of the dead languages should do." She turned to the King, "Your people are the most versed in those I believe."

No one challenged the suggestion that an elf should be the one to transcribe the document. I supposed that was because it was an elven ruler who had given his life to accumulate the knowledge to begin with. They had a long running history with all other Mystic breeds and seemed to be the ultimate authority figures when it came down to needing a leader.

"I volunteer," said the King. Heads nodded in agreement. It was then that the Sphinx leaped onto the pulpit, his voice booming. The crowd gasped.

"Brothers and sisters, I have none but this man's father is my father's son. Who is the man?"

I did not understand the riddle, but it was clear that he was addressing Azlyn's father. It was contesting his bid as transcriber.

The King did not so much as flinch, "The man is my son."

The crowd again broke out into nervous chatter.

"Of which son do you speak, Sphinx?"

Cain stood from his dark corner, sending a seething look his brother's way before interjecting, "The Sphinx speaks of me, Father. Of course, our people cannot afford to risk the heir to your throne. But I decline the nomination. I will no longer take part in this foolishness. We should be preparing our people for war! Take back what is ours with force! Surely all these great minds together can form a plan without wasting countless more years trying to recruit the dark breeds!"

The Sphinx roared and Cain's voice fell silent. The King spoke again.

"No one is asking that you take on any part in this that you do not see fit, my youngest son." The king's voice was even and unemotional, but by the look on Cain's face, I gathered that the 'youngest' remark had been added to remind him of his station in life. He was not in line for the throne, and therefore had no authority.

"The Sphinx does speak of me," Azlyn spoke up, releasing my hand and making his way through the crowd to his father. The Sphinx was silent now, eyeing the young prince as its tail twitched this way and that in a manner that communicated tension. I could not be certain from a distance, but it looked like it may have been smiling.

It was the King's turn to be surprised, "Azlyn? The heir to my throne? You are suggesting that he take this on his shoulders? Why?"

The Sphinx took its time before answering, pausing to lift a large front paw, licking it and grooming his face.

"If you have me, you want to share me. If you share me, you haven't got me. What am I?"

The answer eluded me again. Azlyn addressed the Sphinx as if he had foreseen this, "A secret."

"Secret?" The King piped in again, "What is a secret? Are you saying that you cannot tell me why you are nominating him?"

Eoma placed a hand on the King's arm, "He is saying that it is because of a secret that your son carries that he is being nominated." She spoke delicately. It was likely not a secret to any of us who had seen us enter together, but the King had not seen that.

"What secret would my son keep from his father, from his king, which would qualify him for this task?" he asked.

"Feed me and I live, yet give me a drink and I die."

This was a riddle I knew the answer to, and I wondered why the Sphinx would have chosen fire to describe love. I wondered if a proper word for love even existed in the Sphinx's language. Seeing as how they themselves did not procreate, it did not seem likely. Out of context, I wondered if the King would understand what the Sphinx was referencing. The wide eyed look on his face suggested that he did. Eoma leaned in toward him, again placing a hand on his arm. Though she did not cast her voice out to the masses this time, nor did she whisper. I could hear her clearly from my position.

"They seem to be bonded, Your Highness."

The King turned his head to Eoma, his eyes looking through her. She squeezed his arm gently, the way that one does to reassure a good friend.

Everyone else had gone quiet again, but the air was abuzz with anticipation. I could feel the hair stand up on the back of my neck as we all waited to see how the King would respond.

He turned in the direction of Azlyn, "Is this true?" He tried to keep his voice even, but it wavered ever so slightly. I wondered how he could react with anything other than absolute acceptance after the speech he had given to the rest of the Alliance. Anything else would seem hypocritical. The crowd would lose faith, not only in the mission but in their leader's judgment.

"I do not deny it," he said from his spot beside me. Hearing this, Cain's breath hissed through his teeth so sharply that I could hear it from across the cavern. Of everyone around us, only Eoma and the Sphinx seemed unconcerned by what was transpiring.

For a long time, the King was silent. His face was stoic, and he seemed to be weighing his options.

"Very well." he said, choosing his words carefully, "And you are prepared to take on this task, knowing full well the risks involved?"

"They have already begun the transfer of knowledge," Eoma said mystically. It seemed funny to me that she would word it in such a way. Certainly, I had shared much of the information I had been taught with him during our time together, but it had not had the magical air to it that Eoma's voice implied. Certainly, nothing had been written down.

Obviously, what she had said had a deeper meaning to the King, and to Azlyn as well. The tension in the room shifted to a sort of solemn form of cautious acceptance. His father stood on the pulpit, deep in thought.

"So be it. Azlyn. Bring the girl forth." Azlyn's hand tightened around mine, giving it a reassuring squeeze before leading me up to the pulpit. The crowd parted before us as if each creature we passed was afraid to touch either of us.

Azlyn climbed onto the pulpit, foregoing the steps on the far end, and turned to help me up. Standing before the King and Eoma, in front of such a large crowd, I suddenly felt my head swim with anxiety. My palms became sweaty and my heart raced. Azlyn gave my hand another squeeze and smiled at me brightly.

Despite his lack of sight, the King did not need to be informed of my presence before him. I remembered hearing of a boy in one of the towns near my home who had lost his sight at a young age. It was said that his body had compensated by increasing his awareness of his other senses. Hearing, smell, touch. Elves' senses were already amplified in comparison to ours, but I wondered if the King had experienced something similar. The thought made me slightly uneasy, though I was not sure why.

"Kala, daughter of Gwen," The King's voice carried across the cavern once again, emanating authority and commanding a sense of reverence as he spoke.

"Do you accept the task requested of you, swearing your allegiance to the Alliance and the peoples represented within it; forsaking the laws of your people, committing to the ultimate goal of peace?"

I was suddenly aware that I had no idea what their customs required regards to my response. I was pretty sure that a simple 'yes' would not do, so I replied in the most respectful way that I could think of, willing my voice to come evenly and hide my anxiety.

"I do, Your Highness."

"And you accept this role, with absolute knowledge of the risks that you take. That you face the possibility of capture, torture, and even death?"

Of course, I had known that from the start, but hearing it now from the voice of the leader of my King's enemies suddenly made it feel more real. My mouth went and I cleared my throat quietly before responding. Terrified as I was, my resolve was still strong.

"I accept the burden asked of me with full knowledge," I confirmed.

With a wink, the Sphinx bounded on to one of the higher walls of the cavern. He paced in a circle the same way as I had seen our barn cats do in the past, before settling down in a tightly curled circle. His wings folded tightly against him. It was an odd sight; the combination of fur, feathers, and human features. His tail twitched back and forth a moment longer before relaxing. Although he seemed to be asleep, I could see him peer out from under a small slit in his eyelids; keeping watch over the goings on of the rest of the races.

As I marveled at the Sphinx, Cain had made his way through the crowd.

"I see you did not heed my warning," he said to me. He turned to his brother.

"Your Majesty," he bowed at the waist obscenely, a gesture that felt as if it may have been at least half-mockery. Around us some shifted nervously, not wanting to acknowledge the disrespect.

"That is enough, Cain," It was the King himself who spoke up, his voice echoing with a stern implication of chastisement.

"I was merely paying my respects," Cain scowled.

The King waved him off, "I may be blind my son, but I am not a fool. Your insolence is thinly veiled at best."

"Very well, Father," Cain replied, "I will speak plainly: I do not approve of Kala's initiation."

The King raised an eyebrow.

"Shocking. Your disapproval of our efforts to reform an alliance is no secret. Indeed, many have expressed concern about your presence here this day. Why come?"

"To warn you against this. She is a danger to our people, whether she intends so or not. You welcome the wolf into your den, Father. Though you are too blind to see so."

The King's jaw tensed and he drew himself up taller as Eoma stepped between the two of them.

"You would do well to remember your place." the Priestess warned. "Larger powers are at work here."

Cain became visibly agitated, "Then it is even more dire than I feared. You would use her as your pawn? Does she even understand, Priestess, what you have committed her to? You speak of acting with full knowledge, but she doesn't know yet, does she?"

I shifted awkwardly as Cain's gaze turned to me. Hearing them speak about my lot as if I wasn't present made my skin crawl. I looked away.

"She has no idea," Cain reiterated.

"Hold your tongue!" Eoma growled. "Her fate will reveal itself at the appropriate time."

She turned to Azlyn, "For now it is best to see her on her way," she cautioned. "Lest your brother's careless tongue put us all in jeopardy."

It was clear the matter was not up for discussion.

"Very well, Priestess," Azlyn bowed and ushered me back through the mouth of the cave.

Chapter Thirteen

W E WALKED ALONG THE RIVERBANK HAND IN HAND. Sienna followed closely behind us. She seemed to have taken a liking to Azlyn, and did not need to be restrained while in his presence. I was lost in thought and started when Azlyn spoke.

"Could you be happy here with me?" He asked, his eyes turned toward the ground watching our feet move in sync with one another across the sandy bank. The question caught me off guard. I had not considered what would become of us beyond this moment that we were living in. I thought of Audri and my uncle. A life with Azlyn meant a life in exile. What would become of the family I was leaving behind if I simply disappeared into this new world? They would mourn, I was sure. But they would pick up the pieces over time.

Could I stand to be cut off from them completely? And what of the impending war? What would it be like, with the lines drawn firmly between the Mystics and my people, if peace never happened? Could I stand on the front line and face my uncle from the opposing side? I worried that I had been silent too long, but Azlyn did not press me for an answer.

"In time," I chose my words carefully but looking at the way the corners of his eyes crinkled as my response made him cringe ever so slightly indicated that perhaps I had not chosen them carefully enough.

"It is not as simple as that, Azlyn," I tried to explain myself. "With you, I am happy. Every moment in your presence is a moment of joy." I squeezed his hand, "But sometimes that joy is bittersweet. I would miss my people, and my family."

"You have family here." His response surprised me. It was not like him to argue so selfishly.

"My father and Nykolas you mean?"

He nodded.

"They are as good as strangers to me. At least right now," I pointed out.

"But perhaps, over time..." he let the question hang unfinished in the air.

"I love you," I stopped and pulled on his arm pulling him to face me. He looked over my shoulder, at the waterfall behind us, avoiding eye contact. The words exchanged between Cain and Eoma had obviously shaken him up. I wondered if he, too, knew more than he was letting on.

"I love you, Azlyn. And I love my family. I love my people... And I am afraid." I admitted. "I am afraid that we will forever be in conflict with one another. I am afraid we may never see peace. That terrifies me. I do not know how it would feel, to spend the rest of our days this way. I do not know if I would ever truly be happy."

My lecture left him looking crestfallen. His pained expression made it feel as if a hundred tiny daggers were lodged in my heart. I tried to swallow the lump that had settled in my throat, to no avail. My eyes stung, tears forming in the corners.

"Please do not ask me to choose between you."

He stared, aghast, "Kala, I never meant-" he stopped as if words escaped him.

"I would never ask you to choose a side for my sake. It is not you against us, or us against them. The Alliance is made up of those among us who would strive for peace, though we know the cost will be high." He drew me in his arms and held me tight, kissing the top of my head, "I did not mean to make you think that you must choose."

I felt the tension melt away from me as my body rested against his.

"I am happy with you now. I will always be happy with you," I said. My answer seemed to satisfy him, if only for a moment. We continued walking. The woods around us were bright and full of life; the air crisp and fresh. It was hard to imagine the land home to a kingdom fraught with war.

"Do you ever wonder what it was like before all of this?" I asked. It was a silly question. He was born with the knowledge of his forefathers. I wondered what it must be like to bear the weight of the memory of peace, without ever having lived it. The thought made my heart ache.

"Years before your people came to our land this continent was wild and untamed— in more ways than one. Your people group us together into one community. Mystics, you call us. But that is not an accurate portrayal of the way our peoples lived. There were those of us, it is true, who lived in peace. The griffon prides, intelligent and noble. The dwarves, merfolk, fairies, werewolves, and imps generally cooperated with one-another.

Species like the nymphs, satyrs, shape shifters, unicorns, pegasi, and Sphinx kept to their own people and were not concerned with the goings on of other breeds.

But the dark breeds— the trolls, basilisks, manticores, chimeras, dragons, hydras, harpies," he paused, "and vampires...not only did they not care for the survival of other clans, they actively sought to destroy us.

"There were lulls in the fighting of course, but for many generations before me we were a land at war, fighting to keep some semblance of balance. It was my grandfather who put a stop to the endless bloodshed between species."

He paused to check in with me and make sure I was following his story. I nodded for him to keep going.

"He was a great king, wise and timeless. He was also a great scholar. He began by sending ambassadors to those who were our allies. They were hesitant at first. To put into writing the complete history of one's people, their strengths, their weaknesses. It was a gamble and the stakes were quite high. It took a decade for him to gain their trust.

"Then he sent word out to the neutral species. The Sphinx and the

Griffins were the hardest to convince. They are proud warriors skeptical and wise. A high-stakes gamble is not their style.

"Convincing them took a decade and a half." He smirked at me playfully. "Of course, my people have the benefit of time. While many other Mystic breeds have extended life spans in comparison with your people, few of them compare with the lifespan of an elf. Eventually, our patience won out. Both our allies and the neutral species were in compliance.

"My grandfather kept the records separately at this time, for fear of them falling into the wrong hands before it was complete. Then it was time to collect information from the dark breeds."

I interrupted, "But surely they would not comply?" I said. He held up his hand, motioning for me to be patient.

"Of course they would not," he answered solemnly, "and thus this tale ends in tragedy for my kingdom. My grandfather sent out scouts— two men to each species— to spy on them. Some returned unscathed. Others fell during their service. Prisoners were taken...much of our information for their breeds came about as the result of unsavory methods."

"Torture?"

He nodded, "This part of my people's history is dark. But it was a necessary evil, to ultimately achieve peace."

He took a breath, "I was a young boy during this time. My grandfather was well respected-revered by our people. But to nowhere did he stand as tall as he did in my eyes."

His eyes were distant for a moment before he continued, "The journal was nearing completion. Only one species had not been investigated. The one most closely related to our kind...."

"Vampires," I said it for him as he trailed off. I could see I had struck a sore spot because he flinched.

"No one was willing to take on that mission." He looked me in the eye, suddenly defensive.

"It was not from fear-" he added. "Not the kind of fear you would think, at any rate. They shirked from the idea out of pain. Many men and women of their kind were once close kin. The idea of seeing them as they were after the Change was too painful." He paused again, gathering the strength to finish his tale.

"My grandfather went alone, into their territory. It was not long before he was found out." Azlyn swallowed hard, pained by the memory of what came next.

"I was with my father when my grandfather returned. He made it as far as the city wall before The Change overtook him. With the knowledge, he had acquired tainted by the evil that now coursed through his veins. My people had no choice but to execute their King.

I leaned over and grasped his hand in mine, not knowing what to say. For a long time, no words passed between us.

"My father took his father's life's work and compiled it into one document. He used the information to force a treaty among all the Mystic breeds on the continent. The journal was kept safely guarded for a long time, deep in a cavern outside of the city. Over time, the mere knowledge of its existence became enough to deter even the vilest of the species from laying an attack on another. Boundaries were firmly drawn between people and there was peace. Until –

"Until my people showed up," I finished for him.

"Yes," he stopped there and his eyes were distant, lost in thought. "When your people landed, there was a meeting of the Council-the eldest and wisest among my people. We consulted with those races that had been loyal to us before the treaty, as well as some of the neutral breeds, before making contact. Initially, the consensus was that we should go in armed.

Since we knew nothing of your kind-what your powers or weaknesses might be, the decision was made to approach in peace. My people, being the most physically similar and therefore the least threatening, were the first sent. Your King was arrogant and we saw evil in his heart. Many of the Mystics wanted to wipe your kind from our home from the beginning."

I shuddered at the thought, "What changed their minds?"

"My father advocated for the settlers." His eyes were distant again, "I remember his plea to the council as if it were yesterday:

"'*It is true there is much evil among them,*' he said.

There was a murmuring from the crowd. A wave of panic whispered through them. He did not motion for it to cease but waited patiently for them to fall silent before he continued, '*There are also innocents. Families struggling for a brighter future. Women and children. Their eyes reflect much pain and much hope. There are many among them that would be our allies. Their race is weak, but their weakness is a testament to their resilience. They are not born with the knowledge inherent to many of us. Each generation must start over again. And yet their race continues. Perhaps they will be a benefit. Perhaps there is something they can teach us.*'"

Azlyn stopped there, his eyes returning to the present.

"Why did he advocate so strongly, for a people he knew nothing about?" I inquired, though I was glad that he had.

"I do not know," Azlyn admitted. "My father, like his father, was a scholar. A seeker of knowledge. In a lot of ways, I think your people fascinated him. We had never encountered a people whose time on this Earth was so brief, and the things that humans choose to do with their time fascinated him.

He found it particularly tragic that the knowledge of one generation was often snuffed out when your elder's lives were over. The idea that each of your young had to start as a clean slate was both inspiring and heartbreaking to him. He was greatly intrigued by the youth of your people. He loved children. He spent much of his time among them."

My heart skipped a beat. My mother would have been a child at this time, and her brother just teetering on the edge of manhood. "Did he know my mother?" I asked.

Azlyn nodded, "We all did. She was his favorite." He smiled. "He loved her tenacity. No matter what the fates threw at her, she rushed her destiny head on. Many children would lose their compassion for the world in her position-orphaned, alone in a land she knew nothing about. Your mother seemed exhilarated. She had an unrivaled sense of adventure." He smiled, and leaned in toward me, kissing my forehead. "You are very much like her."

"It was her idea to build their homestead so close to the boundary after the war," he continued. "Your uncle resisted but she would not concede. Though their loyalties laid on opposing sides, he loved her dearly. He would have taken down the stars for her if he could. He faced a true internal battle when he was drafted. It broke her heart. Many times when we met she would express her doubts. She did not like to see him so conflicted: Knowing his loyalty was to his king; yet loving his sister enough to turn a blind eye as he did."

She had confided in Azlyn? I felt a sting of jealousy. Though I knew it was ridiculous to feel in such a way, "Were you two..?" I started hesitantly.

He laughed out loud, "Us? No, Kala, your mother and I were never more than very dear friends. Cain though, he was sweet on her. When she wed your father you would have thought he had been mortally wounded, the way he carried on."

"Is that why he looks so unfavorably on me?" I asked.

Azlyn pursed his lips together as if he was unsure how to put it into words.

"Her death hung heavily on his heart, Kala. On all of us. He went into a rage after; wanting to hunt down your uncle himself. At first, your father was the only one who stood between your uncle and the world beyond. It enraged him that your mother's mate would stand in defense of her murderer."

I flinched at the reminder that my mother had perished at the hand of the man who had raised me.

"I'm sorry. It is not a story that is easy to hear. Neither is it one that is easy to tell." I nodded for him to continue.

"Your father stood in the rain, his mate slain at his feet, and argued in favor of your uncle. He knew he could not go back to retrieve you. Your uncle would be lost in his guilt, his grief. The protection that extended to your father while your mother lived was no more. Furthermore, a life on the run from Ludlum's soldiers was not fit for a child. In the midst of mourning, he defended the only person who had a chance at offering you a proper upbringing."

"And Cain?"

"Had they been the only two present I have no doubts that my brother would have struck your father down right then and there; and your uncle shortly after. Instead, he darted into the forest and mourned privately. We buried your mother, though her proper funeral rites were not performed until much later.

"As for your father...my brother had stirred up enough trouble within the Alliance to keep him away a good while. It was over a year later when he returned, this time with a red eyed boy who appeared to be close to the age of five, though he had only just been sprouted on his mother's side."

"Nykolas," I finished for him. "My half-brother."

He nodded. For a while, we walked in silence.

"If your people are born with the ability to carry on the information of their ancestors, why could your father not simply recreate the records himself?"

"It does not quite work that way," he explained. "It is not some mystical passing on of knowledge. It is a genetic phenomenon, rather than magical. The link is something naturally inherited from previous generations. The knowledge we acquire throughout our lifetime becomes, quite literally, a part of us. There is a permanent imprint on our biological make up.

"It is one that we pass on to our young, though it does not usually blossom before the age of ten when the brain is developed enough to receive the wisdom without being overwhelmed. Even then it is a gradual awakening." He stopped a moment to check in with me and make sure I was absorbing what he was saying. I nodded for him to continue.

"This genetic memory is passed on at conception. It grows and develops during gestation...but Kala; the link is severed at birth. From that time on there is no inherent wisdom from the previous generations. Only that which is passed down through...more traditional means. When my grandfather sought to unite our people, his son was already grown. His grandchildren already born. There would have been no way to retain the information unless he chose to share it with someone."

"And he told no one?" I inquired. Azlyn shook his head.

"Not a soul, not even as his death was shown to be imminent. It was not a burden he wanted on his family, and he knew that passing the information to his people would put a metaphorical target on their backs and put the peace he had worked so hard for at risk. No race was to have the upper hand. The journal was only ever meant to exist – a form of insurance if you will. It was never meant to be read."

It finally dawned on me, "That is why it remained hidden."

He continued as if I had not spoken, "It is not known for certain who tipped off your king to its whereabouts. Each of the breeds has blamed another at some point after the war. We had all but pushed the King's soldiers into a retreat when it was discovered to be missing. I am sure your history lessons have told you the rest," he said, sweeping his hand in the air dismissively.

"We are taught that your kind were banished. The boundary was drawn. All Mystics and their human sympathizers were executed." I tried to keep my part of the story short, as it was unpleasant and I lacked the skillful narration that Azlyn seemed to have. "But, on your side of the boundary, what happened?"

"It was chaos," he said. "So many fallen to mourn, so many injured to tend to. Blame was cast this way and that between species that had long been allies. To say nothing of the dark breeds who had been waiting for an opportunity to seize control. For the first time in a millennia the land was torn with unadulterated violence, the rules of battle cast aside. Mystic species were nearing extinction at an alarming rate. Many of them targeted my people as the cause for their suffering. In truth, we are not entirely out of hiding."

"How many are currently in the Alliance?" I asked.

"Our support suffered greatly after the death of your mother," he admitted. "To many of us, she was the last beacon of hope. A hope that perished with her. The representatives you saw today are all who remain loyal to our efforts."

"And my father?" I asked. "Could he not have helped?" Surely, he would have known enough of the King's Code to garner aid from the other races.

Azlyn shook his head, "Your father was once a man of honor and charity. The death of your mother changed him. He became concerned only for his own survival, moving among the darker corners of each territory looking for someone who would fall for his latest con. He had no interest in our efforts until it suited his desire."

He must have seen that his words had pained me because he quickly changed his tone. "I know he is not the man that you were expecting. I know he cannot undo the hurt he has caused, but deep down he is as much a victim as anyone."

I realized that he pitied my father and that perhaps he mourned the man he had hoped he would be just as I did. I remembered that Azlyn had known my father before he had fallen from the Alliance's graces. What kind of a man had he been then?

"Besides," Azlyn added, shifting the conversation, "presenting an incomplete record would have proven disastrous. We must, all of us, be equal in our weakness to avoid the rise to power of any one race over another."

"And you believe I can finish it?"

I saw a new expression cross his face briefly. One I didn't recognize.

"Yes," he said. "In time, you will."

Chapter Fourteen

AZLYN AND I PARTED WAYS NEAR THE BORDER. He had wanted to escort me all the way home, fearing that Audri's reaction to my return might be less than warm; but I stood firm in my faith that she would be glad to see me. To this day I am not sure which one of us was right.

Audri did not welcome me with open arms, but she did not shun me either. She treated my return as if it were commonplace; like I had simply been out tending to a mundane chore and not gallivanting across the uncharted territory with the enemy. She didn't ask where I had gone or whether I was alright, but simply went about business as usual.

Though it caused me great pain, I drew away from my cousin and kept my silence where Azlyn was concerned. At times I would feel I might burst at the seams from withholding all of the emotion that was churning inside of me. Such is the way of life sometimes.

I continued to see Azlyn. I severed my relationship with Audri. For what felt like an eternity, I receded into myself, leading a double life.

And then one day it all changed.

Conner came one afternoon with an official message. But this one was not written down on paper. Written correspondence was too risky in times of war. He rode up beaming, the sun bouncing off his chestnut hair and his eyes full of joy. Audri invited him into the house for a drink as she had recently grown accustomed to doing. (My suspicion that she fancied him seemed to be justified, and lately he seemed to return her affection. I hoped that that affection would soften her heart some, but it was not to be.)

He politely declined the offer, explaining that his orders prevented him from delay.

"But I shall hold a reservation with you for the next time I journey to this part of the kingdom," he added with a wink.

I was pleased that he would not be staying. His unnaturally perfect smile, flawless posture, and booming voice made me sick to my stomach. In my mind, there was nothing more revolting. He was a member of the Elite, and my newly-awakened-self recognized him as the enemy.

Conner was proud of his newfound rank. Having worked his way up from a mere messenger boy, I suppose pride was within his rights. He would sit at our kitchen table recounting story after story of his triumphs over what he referred to as the "Mystic scum" while Audri smiled sweetly, waiting on him hand and foot.

If I could not escape these rancid tales, I would pace about the kitchen. I hoped that occupying myself with menial chores would help to conceal my contempt. If Audri or Conner noticed my hostility they paid it no heed.

This time I had decided to be civil. I stood next to my cousin. She was gazing up at Conner as he looked first to her, and then to me, and back to her again, that perfectly disgusting smile creeping across his face again.

"Your father has been given three weeks of leave. He is coming home."

I watched Audri fight the urge to squeal with delight. She looked to me and I forced what I hoped was a convincing smile. I loved my uncle and missed him greatly, but my heart was torn. How could I look my uncle in the eye, knowing all that I knew now? Could I maintain the illusion of innocence? I was afraid for him to come home.

Conner bid us farewell, declaring that he must return to his post. He did not bother to mention where that was. I should have paid more attention. Audri hardly noticed his departure, as she was walking on a cloud.

And I...well I was busy thinking of how to sneak away so I could tell

Azlyn.

The following days were uneventful. Audri spent them cleaning and decorating to prepare for her father's return.

I paced the house in between my duties. Like a ghost, my face expressionless. I was in agony as I pondered the decisions ahead of me. I couldn't continue to dart between identities. I must either resolve myself to a life of exile from my own race or end things with Azlyn and betray his people.

I planned to meet him for the last time at our traditional place by the river.

What I did not know was that Conner's report to us had been false. My uncle was not coming home on leave. My actions had been monitored from the beginning, and he had been sent to take care of things. To follow me, and use the information I had acquired about the Alliance against the Mystics.

Azlyn was also followed that day. His brother, whose hatred for my people had been fanned by the blow to his pride at the Alliance meeting, had finally decided to take matters into his own hands.

Hatred feeds off ignorance, and ignorance off of hatred. Our inability to accept each other is often the source of our own demise. Both ignorance and hatred ran rampant that day, which led to the beginning of many ends.

I got up early, washed my face and plaited my hair. Audri was busy preparing the house and did not notice me leave. I reached the river before the sun rose above the forest. I sat in the sand, dipping my toes into the cool water, and rehearsed in my head what I would say to him. How could I explain myself, this far into things? Secretly, I was searching for a way out of doing what I knew to be right. There was no way to protect those I loved without severing the hold I had on his heart.

I am not sure what I had expected to happen. I was young and truly naïve. My uncle was no fool, and to think that I had gotten away with as much as I had was asinine. Love had blinded me to all logic, wrapping me in my own denial.

He had known about the Mystic sightings even before he had been called out of retirement. He had no doubt gotten reports of my frequent absences. I was not aware at the time, but it was he, my own kin, who was responsible for the wounding of Cain's son.

Putting two and two together he could have a pretty accurate, if not entirely complete, idea of what had been going on beneath his very nose. But he was family, and loved me dearly. Much like he had with my mother, my uncle had turned a blind eye.

On this day he had set aside his kinship. On this day he was a soldier; first and foremost a servant to his king. And he was armed.

Of course, none of Azlyn's people, save for his brother, had questioned his actions or his absences. They seemed a more permissive race when it came to acts of treason, though I didn't fully understand their motive until the end.

Azlyn and his brother had gotten into a fight. While blowing off steam Cain had decided to follow him. By the time Azlyn reached the river, his brother's anger was raging. One would think that such a long journey would give him time to cool off, but each step had only amplified his hatred. He, too, was armed.

If we had only known, it may have ended differently.

Azlyn jogged gleefully in my direction just before midday. His grace, his smile, and the way his hair flew behind him as he did so made him seem so much like a child. It was hard, even then to believe that he had lived generations before me. Seeing him I found myself smiling in spite of myself. I rose as he approached and took my hand, kissing me lightly.

"Hello, my love," he greeted me.

My voice failed me, as it often did when I found myself captivated by his presence. I looked away, trying to recover the words that his gaze had wiped from my mind.

Azlyn placed a finger under my chin, gently directing my gaze back to him. He looked concerned.

"Kala, what is wrong?"

I sighed, tears forming in my eyes, "Azlyn, I can't do this."

He looked hurt. I opened my mouth, wanting to console him. Wanting to explain. Wanting to tell him I still loved him. He put a finger to my lips, silencing me, and glanced over my shoulder.

I heard a twig snap where Azlyn had been looking and spun around. Our pursuers had both stayed on the opposite side of the river, where the ruins of the bridge that Audri and I had once built lay, concealing themselves in the shade of the orchard. My uncle had crept closer to get a clearer view of Azlyn.

Meanwhile, Cain was doing the same, trying to get a clearer view of me. Eventually, their paths had crossed, and caught off guard, they attacked.

My uncle never stood a chance. He fell to the ground, dead before any of us could react, an arrow protruding from his chest.

The rest is all a blur. One minute I was standing barefoot in the sand, the next I was kneeling at my uncle's side, nearly in hysterics, lost in my grief. Azlyn had disappeared into the forest in pursuit of his brother.

I don't know how long I sat there, but it must have been hours. The sun had set by the time that Azlyn returned for me.

He knelt by me, putting a hand on my shoulder. My hands were covered in my uncle's blood, long since dried, and my gown was stained at the knees from kneeling so long in the blood stained grass. I did not respond to Azlyn's touch.

Finally, he spoke,

"I followed him –" he paused, breathless. I had never seen him winded before. "– all the way to the boundaries of the lands untraveled even by my people." He did not name the territory, but I knew he meant his brother had gone into the land of the darker breeds.

"I could not follow." It was an apology.

It was also a lie. Had he wanted, he could have chased his brother to the very ends of the earth; though it would have been perilous, maybe even fatal. He had chosen instead, to come back for me.

"Why?" My voice cracked, "Why was he a target? Why him and not me?"

Azlyn started to speak, then stopped, gesturing toward the shoulder of my uncle's uniform. His jacket bore the King's emblem. I understood. In a rage, Cain had discovered our meeting place and had been surveying the situation when he and my uncle had stumbled upon each other. In a panic, he had forgotten his plot against me to fight a more dangerous enemy.

Azlyn drew me closer to him as I wept.

We buried my uncle under his favorite apple tree on the outskirts of the orchard that was closer to our home. Azlyn offered to help, but I did not want to risk Audri connecting him to her father's death. I cleaned, wrapped, and carried his body myself. I dug his grave. The entire process lasted through the evening and into the next morning.

Audri wept inconsolably and knelt by his grave for almost two days, refusing both food and water. I do not know that she even slept. I didn't know what to do to comfort her, and she would not speak to me. I was overcome with guilt. I made excuses to myself, trying to reassure my conscience. Deep down I knew that his death was on my hands.

I tried to keep things together, to keep them the same as they were before. Before Uncle John. Before Azlyn. Before anything.

Above all things, I missed Azlyn. I knew it was selfish. I knew it was wrong. But my heart ached so much and I longed for his reassuring touch.

I tried to keep myself busy and not think about all the trouble I had caused. The lives I had ruined. I went to sleep that night still wondering about Audri. She had been acting odd, there was no doubt about that, but she was grieving. Grief does strange things to people. Uncle John had been the only family she had left, save for me, and I had betrayed her.

Though Audri refused both food and drink I continued to set her place at the table. On the third night, she finally joined me. I had been sitting for only a moment when I heard her come around the corner. My back was turned to her. For some reason, this made me nervous. I did not dare turn around. She walked slowly about me and then sat down facing me, reaching for the cup of tea I had poured moments earlier. She held the cup gingerly and peered into it as if doing so would unravel the greatest mysteries of the universe.

Her hair was unkempt and her skin was pale from lack of nourishment. Her tan dress, once so tight that she had to struggle to button it, draped around her like a tent. But there was something else about her. A smell I could not place and the tint of her skin was unusual.

"*She's in mourning,*" I reminded myself. The process was not one of beauty. I let it pass. I should have paid more attention. Her eyes were cold and broken, and she bared her teeth as she spoke.

"Tell me," she commanded. Her voice was weak and raspy.

"Tell me," she repeated.

"Tell you what?"

"Tell me how it happened," she spat the words at me.

I took a deep breath, holding it and thinking. And then I told her. I told her everything. Everything I could remember from the past months, ending with the death of her father. When I had finished the floor was stained with tears, both hers and mine.

She shattered the glass against the wall before turning toward me, her eyes ablaze with an anger that can only be born of intense grief

"You still love him."

I turned away, ashamed.

"You miss him."

"It matters not, Audri. It is over." I glanced up to see her expression. It was unchanged. She shook her head.

"It has only begun. Leave me."

I was startled and confused, but I did as she said.

By the time I had finished my chores it was nearly dark. I walked back to the house, exhausted. I saw no sign of my cousin and I assumed that she had gone to bed. I decided to follow her example. I was asleep before I even hit the mattress.

The next morning I still had not heard Audri stir, and I began to worry. I knocked on her bedroom door. There was no answer. I opened the door.

Her window was open and a light breeze wafted through the room. On the floor lay the dress she had worn the night before. It was caked in dirt. Propped against her nightstand was an ax.

She had played me like a harp, plucking at my emotions as if they were chords that would create a great symphony. I did not see the truth until it was too late.

I flew from the room, out the back door, hoping against hope that what I feared was not true. I felt the air leave my lungs as I stared at a blank spot on the horizon where the *Menohathi* had once stood.

I ran.

Chapter Fifteen

I found Cazlyn crouched beside the fallen tree, whispering a blessing as he collected its leaves. "What are you doing here?" I asked. He looked up at me only briefly before continuing his work.

"An army is coming," he said. "I was sent ahead to warn you but..." he motioned to the tree.

"Audri is gone," I said. This was my fault. If I hadn't been so self-absorbed I would have seen this coming. Cazlyn simply nodded, refusing to look up.

"We have to go," I said. "She could be anywhere by now."

As if in response to my words, I heard the sound of hoof beats in the distance. Cazlyn and I stood to run, but were overtaken before we even reached the bottom of the hill. My hands were twisted painfully so far up my back that I had to lean forward to avoid having my shoulder dislocated.

I tried to lift my head and was met with a sharp blow between my shoulder blades that knocked the wind out of me. I fell to my knees. My hands were tightly bound. I heard a thud as Cazlyn was forced to follow suit. Keeping my head down, I could see his knees hit the dirt.

"Not a move, traitor," I recognized the voice. Conner's feet hardly made a sound as he stepped down from his steed and approached us proudly.

I chanced a quick glance upward, cringing as I anticipated another blow. None came.

"They were exactly where she said they would be, Sir," the voice of the soldier holding me addressed him.

Conner bore the uniform of an Elite soldier. It was not the usual royal blue, but a dark, murky green. This uniform was not merely a matter of status-it was designed for camouflage. For war. On his chest was the emblem of the King, and on his left shoulder, the rank that had once belonged to my uncle.

"They wasted no time in replacing him," I thought to myself. I found myself wondering if Audri knew.

"Kala, Kala, Kala," Conner chided as my gaze met his. "What would your uncle think? You bring shame upon your bloodline. Your poor cousin-" For a moment his voice faltered but he cleared his throat and came back strongly, "It was wise of her to consult with me."

My heart shattered. I had, of course, suspected that Audri, misguided and drowning in grief, would make her way into the arms of someone familiar. I had guessed, even, that she would betray us to the enemy; but suspicion was easy to push aside. It was easy to give way to denial. To have it confirmed by an Elite was as if Audri had personally shoved a dagger into my chest.

"What should we do with them, Sir?" The voice behind me inquired.

"I have half a mind to fell this creature right here and now," added the soldier restraining Cazlyn.

Conner held a hand up to silence them, "The King will want to deal with them personally," he smiled sinisterly and put a finger under my chin, turning my head one way and then another as if he was inspecting a trinket he might purchase at the market. "A shame you shall lose your pretty little head, Kala. More tragic that your cousin will not have the satisfaction of witnessing it."

"What do you mean?" I had assumed she would be with them.

Conner struck me for speaking out. My lip stung and I tasted copper. Bracing myself with one knee against the unforgiving landscape, I glanced up at him willfully. I longed for nothing more than to feel his jaw bone rake against my knuckles in that moment. Blood pooled in my mouth. I spat at his feet, narrowly missing the toe of his perfectly polished boot. He laughed and struck me again for my insolence. The hands that restrained me squeezed my wrist as if in warning.

"Enough." Conner snarled, and then looked at his henchmen, "Tie them to the back of the carriage. They can walk from here."

"But, Sir," the one behind me spoke up, "the girl will never make it that far on foot."

Conner's eyes flashed in anger, "Soft on her are you? Sympathizing with the enemy is as good as treason." It was a warning.

"I only meant, Sir," the soldier chose his words carefully, "that it would be a sore lot for you to run the King's trophy to death before he has had the chance to make an example of her."

Conner thought on that a moment, "Fair enough, soldier. The lady can have your horse then. Tie it to the cart." He stepped over to Cazlyn and spared no strength, kicking him harshly in the ribs before turning about and mounting his horse.

And so we were marched through woods until we encountered a pathway where the rest of the camp was waiting. I was set atop and bound to the soldier's horse, which was then tied to the back of a small military supplies cart. Cazlyn was bound on the opposite side. The soldier, whose horse I had taken, was nowhere to be seen.

The troop was larger than I had anticipated given how quickly they had snuck up on us. They had no qualms riding through the woods at night. They carried torches-one to every third soldier, to light the way. I could feel the forest cringe and the trees seemed to lean almost outward from the path, hoping to escape the tongues of fire my people brandished so irreverently.

Heavily guarded as we were, there was not much opportunity for Cazlyn and I to communicate, and almost no hope of escape. Both of our weapons had been stripped from us. My knife brought particular joy to the soldiers who took turns testing it lightly against the skin on Cazlyn's left arm. Though the cuts they made were superficial his skin would bear scars from the silver for the rest of his life – however long that was to be.

I tried to shake the sense of imminent doom and instead let my mind wander to the information we had at our disposal. The Alliance had known the King's soldiers were coming. Cazlyn had been sent to retrieve me.

Audri was...well it did not even seem that Conner knew, though I got a sick feeling that she would not miss my execution. I pushed the thought from my mind as we came to a break in the trees. I did not recognize the land that lay out before us; but as the tall grass brushed up against the side of my horse I knew we had made our way back to the King's side of the boundary.

When we'd cleared the grasslands, the soldiers set up camp for the night. Cazlyn remained tied to the back of the cart. I was secured on the opposite side in the front to prevent us from communicating with each other. I could barely lie down with the length of rope allotted to me, but if I turned my head slightly and leaned to one side I could just make out Cazlyn's outline from underneath the cart. Despite the uncomfortable arrangements, I was exhausted and fell asleep quickly.

I awoke in the night to see a figure hovering over me. It was the soldier who had given up his horse. Assuming his intentions were less than favorable, I opened my mouth to scream, but his hand was over my mouth so swiftly that the air was forced out my nose instead, making a pitiful high pitched sound that would hardly serve as an alert to anyone. I do not know why I even thought to scream. It was not as if I was surrounded by friends here. Likely waking the other soldiers would have only resulted in a more unsavory fate.

The soldier put a finger to his lips, indicating that I should be silent. There was no surprise there.

"I am going to remove my hand, Kala. I need you to be silent and trust me. I am not here to hurt you."

My eyes darted over to where Cazlyn was laying, hoping that my protest had at least fallen on his sensitive ears, but I could not make out his form in the darkness. A lot of good it would have done me to have him as a witness. He was bound tightly, just as I was.

The soldier pulled a knife from his belt and I felt my blood run cold. I had broken out into a nervous sweat. I closed my eyes, unsure of what fate would befall me as the knife drew closer....

And tore through my bindings, freeing my hands.

"There is no time to waste," the soldier whispered. "Run for the woods. Do not look back. Go now."

I froze for just a moment, expecting a trap. Farce or not, this was my best opportunity at gaining my own freedom. I obeyed his word and darted for the forest.

I did not make it very far before being intercepted by Cazlyn whose arms darted down from a tree, pulling me up into its boughs. Startled at first, I tried again to cry out, but found myself breathless from the shock of it all. We sat on a high up branch while I tried to gather my composure.

"What? I... how?" I gasped in between breaths.

"Shhh," he urged me to remain silent, nodding out toward the soldier's camp which he no doubt could see clearly from here. I remained almost completely blind, barely able to make out his outline. The only feature I could see clearly were his eyes as they caught the moonlight, reflecting a honey colored glow.

For a while there seemed to be no movement at the soldier's camp. Then I saw the shadow of a figure make its way across the boundary towards us. Cazlyn leaned in, squinting, then nodded and began climbing down the tree. I opened my mouth in protest, but he simply shook his head and motioned for me to follow.

The soldier who had released me was waiting at the base of the tree. As my feet touched the ground, I saw him nod slightly in greeting.

"Cazlyn," he acknowledged my traveling partner. I wondered how he knew his name. None of this made sense, until Cazlyn returned the greeting.

"Brian. You certainly took long enough."

I staggered a moment, and knew that even in the dim light Cazlyn could probably see the look on my face. My father?

"You hit me," I said flatly. Why those were the first words I could say to a man I had once thought dead, I do not know.

"Conner is a bull-headed man," my father replied solemnly. "He is stubborn, but he is not stupid. Any sign of sympathy and our mission would have been compromised."

"So you are working with the Alliance then?" I asked.

"When it suits my own need, yes."

"How brave of you," I replied, wryly. Perhaps my response was unfair. I am sure he had expected a warmer welcome from his long-lost daughter; but the truth was I had not yet sorted out my feelings in regards to him. While I was grateful for the rescue, I still carried a great deal of resentment where he was concerned.

"Bravery is not something I have ever been accused of," he said, attempting a joke. His tone was sour in my ears. "It was your mother who was the adventurous one. I was simply along for the ride." His eyes were almost far away as he looked me over. "You seem to take after her."

"So I am told," my reply was cold and unsteady.

"He has been good to you then? Your uncle?" my father pried. I wanted to slap him across the face. I did not move a muscle for fear I would lose track of my wits and instead responded flatly.

"My uncle is dead."

My father staggered a moment, taken aback. I guess in all of his unsavory travels he had missed the news of his brother-in-law's passing.

"How? When?" I was stunned by the emotion in his reaction. I had not thought that the two of them had ever gotten on with each other.

"Recently. It was Cain." I offered him no details.

He looked to Cazlyn, studying the son of the murderer with a suspicious eye. Cazlyn cringed under his cryptic gaze and looked to me for help.

"And this one?" Brian asked roughly.

I was determined to keep my answers short and void of any emotion. "He is on our side."

Brian's eyes darted between us as he ran his hand across his scraggly beard as if he was lost in some deep internal debate.

"Alright," he muttered. "That is good enough for me then." He brushed his hands together and righted his sword, which had shifted on its belt slightly.

He said nothing more, but started deeper into the woods. I looked at Cazlyn who simply shrugged and motioned for me to follow. I fell in line between them. Cazlyn placed a hand gently on my arm, guiding me in the darkness. My father did not seem to struggle with the same night blindness. Indeed he moved more like a Mystic than a man. It made sense, as he had spent so many years among them.

An hour into our walk Brian broke the silence. "What of your cousin, Audri?"

I was taken aback. I had assumed that, traveling with the Elite, he would know more about her whereabouts.

"She is gone," I said.

"And the elf? The one who killed her father?" he knelt, examining the ground as one would if tracking an animal.

"He escaped. Azlyn followed him"

"I was afraid it may be so. Likely he has taken refuge with the dark breeds," he said. I cringed visibly hoping my father's choice of words would not upset Cazlyn too badly. If it did, he showed no outward sign.

"But why? What would make him go there?" I asked. My father did not seem to have an answer, not one he wanted to give at any rate. It was Cazlyn who spoke

"To be with my mother," he said flatly.

My father avoided eye contact with the young elf as he continued.

"She is one of The Changed...it was years ago," he struggled to form the words.

"As you know, if the Change overtakes one who is unwilling, it is considered merciful by my people to end their suffering. My father...when it came down to it, he could not stand the thought of losing her. He could not admit that he already had. Any fool could look upon her suffering and know that it was the right choice, but my father...when it comes to matters of the heart his resolve has always been rather weak. He would not let it be done. He snuck her out in the night, and released her into the uncharted territories. To her new people."

"But would not she have..?" he cut me off before I could finish my question.

"Their love was strong, and my mother...she knew the end was coming for her. She knew it was risky. She wanted to be put to rest. But she could not stand to leave my father in such agony. She went willingly, and staved off her hunger as long as possible, trying to protect him...I think," he faltered.

"I think sometimes, that perhaps it had been his hope, secretly, that she would change him as well. That they could build a life together that way; but she would not. My father returned, a broken man."

He was silent for a moment before looking at me, "Thus was the beginning of the conflict between him and my uncle. Did you know that they were once very close?"

I shook my head, unsure of what to say.

"So much so, that my father named me after him," He continued. I hadn't realized it before, but Cazlyn's name was indeed a melding of Cain and Azlyn's. "When my father returned, Azlyn would not even look at him, he was so ashamed," Cazlyn's brow creased, deep in thought, as if coming to a new realization.

"They had lost their grandfather in the same way. He was just a child then. I suppose, to see my father succumb to that weakness as an adult was too painful for him to acknowledge. When they did begin speaking again, neither of them mentioned my mother, or the fate my father had sought out for himself."

"And so now..." My voice trailed off.

Cazlyn picked it up with, "I believe he is going to be changed with or without her consent.

My father broke back into the conversation, "It is my fear that Audri is in pursuit of him.

The three of us were silent as we mulled this over. The idea that my cousin, delicate, rule following Audri, would not only be slinking into the dangers of a land she knew nothing about...but that she would do so in pursuit of an armed and dangerous murderer was almost asinine. My mind could not process it. And yet, in some strange way, it almost made sense.

In her eyes I had betrayed her. Cain had killed her father. If it were me in her shoes, I cannot say that I would not be seeking revenge, by any means necessary. I remembered the crazed look in her eyes in the days before she left, and wished that I had not been so blind to the path she was choosing. What would happen when the two of them crossed paths? I shuddered at the thought. There was no way that would end well for either of them.

"What do we do?" I asked my father. Why I expected him to have the answers, I do not know. Perhaps there was still some subtle paternal force pulling on my heart, willing him to be the wise and honorable man that I had held so long in my memory.

"There is naught, for now." He rose from the crouching stance he had maintained. "We have larger troubles afoot, I am afraid. But keep this knowledge in the back of your mind, both of you. I do not think we have seen the end of either of them yet."

Once we had put enough distance between ourselves and Conner's men, we turned East. Brian explained as we walked that he had been part of an undercover effort meant to gather intel for the Alliance. The King, it turned out, had spies of his own in their midst, and was planning an attack on their stronghold. It was then that my father learned of Conner's intent to capture me. He abandoned his post to intercept their efforts.

"I couldn't just let them take you," he said. It felt less like he was reaching out to me and more like he was seeking absolution for the lives that may be lost because of his decision.

The landscape was changing. Though we were still surrounded by trees, the forest had thinned significantly. The rising sun cast a shadow of red all around us. Crimson skies do not bode well for the day ahead. Looking at the sky, I feared it was a reflection of the blood that would be spilled this day. I shuddered, and tried to push the thought from my mind.

"Conner said Audri was wise to confide in him," I said, changing the subject. "How much does the King know of me?" It shouldn't have mattered to me. There was truly no going back, I knew that. My old life, my family, it was all gone.

"Nothing, as far as I can tell. Conner would have reveled in the glory of his capture much more if it had been a surprise." Brian paused, choosing his words carefully, "Whatever knowledge John had before his passing he kept to himself."

I held onto his last words, and they stung my heart. Even as I was a wolf in sheep's clothing, my uncle had protected me with his silence.

A scream in the distance jolted me from my self-pity. Though we were all exhausted, Cazlyn and Brian both jolted alert. I crouched behind a tree and Brian motioned for me to stay put. He and Cazlyn crept ahead, disappearing from my view within seconds.

CHAPTER SIXTEEN

KNELT BY THE TREE UNTIL MY KNEES ACHED, leaning on its trunk for support. It felt like an eternity with no sign of either of them. What if they had been captured? Killed? How long was I to sit here and await the same fate? I stood, allowing my legs to regain feeling before starting off in the direction I had seen them go.

I was foolish.

The thinning woods did not offer much cover. I'd walked only a few hundred yards before encountering a steep drop-off. At the bottom marched the King's army. Far in the distance the army appeared to be nothing but a swarm of ants, but I knew it would not be long before they overtook us. I looked around for signs of Cazlyn or my father, but there were none.

A hand was on my wrist before my mind could process what was happening. It pulled me away into the cover of the forest just as an arrow lodged itself into the tree I had been standing by-right at the level of my head. It was silver. My stomach flopped as I contemplated what might have happened if Azlyn had not shown up right when he did.

I did not know from where he had come, but I was certainly glad to see him. I wrapped my arms around him briefly as we took cover behind a large rock, surveying the situation that was approaching.

The approaching army was larger than I had expected. Hundreds of men marched steadily in our direction. Beside me, my father and Cazlyn found cover. The forest was abuzz with murmurs of disbelief. I looked behind me to find a handful of members of the Alliance, no doubt a rescue party for Cazlyn and myself, standing in shock at the sheer force of what lay before us.

Azlyn called out in his native tongue, snapping them out of their stupor. He pointed to one of them, a young centaur.

"You. Go. Summon the others." His voice shook. "NOW!" So stunned was he at what we were about to face that he was unable conceal his own fear.

Calling for reinforcements seemed pointless. I gathered that the army would overtake us before the messenger could reach enough of our allies to create a formidable army. Who would come our aide? And yet it was also obvious to me that we would not be retreating. The young centaur galloped off into the forest, blowing a horn that had hung on a strap across his chest as he disappeared in the woods.

"Everyone scatter!" Azlyn yelled. "Keep hidden until I give the command to attack. No one moves until I make the call!"

And just like that they darted off in a million directions, disappearing in the cracks and crevices of rocks, and among the boughs of the trees. Cazlyn, my father, and I remained.

"You heard me, out of here, all of you," Azlyn turned to face us. His eyes met mine and lingered a moment before he turned to his nephew.

"You know what is at stake here. Take her and go. Do not look behind you. Do not come back, no matter what you hear. Do you understand?"

He turned to me, kissing me on the lips firmly before I could protest, "Go. I love you."

I opened my mouth to argue, but before I could speak Cazlyn had hoisted me over his shoulder and ran.

The earth was a blur beneath us as Cazlyn rushed deeper into the forest. The sight made my head swim and I closed my eyes, struggling to still my insides so that I could voice my protest. I took a breath and tensed my muscles, preparing for the inevitable impact with the ground that I would experience when I struggled against his grip on me.

Before I could act we had stopped and Cazlyn sat me upright, holding both of my shoulders to steady me. It was a good thing he did. I felt my knees buckle and my body sway as I tried to regain my bearings. When he was certain my legs would support me, Cazlyn released his hold.

"We should be safe here," he said, looking over my shoulder.

I turned around. We stood at the mouth of a cave. I stepped forward carefully despite Cazlyn's reassurance, afraid to intrude on the dwelling of something with which I may not be familiar. I did not desire to venture into the home of a creature I was not prepared to do battle with. A dragon for instance, would have made for a rather unfortunate and premature ending to my story.

Luckily the cavern appeared vacant, though it was dimly lit. I could not seem to find the source of the light, which puzzled me briefly before I remembered that I had other more important things to worry about.

"Why are we here?" I demanded. "We should be out fighting with the others." I was surprised by the tears welling up in my eyes. I was terrified. For Azlyn. For my father. For myself. I wiped the tears away angrily and moved toward the entrance of the cave.

Cazlyn stood in my path, "Kala, don't. Please."

"I won't hide here like some coward!" I flung my hands in the air in frustration as I tried to skirt around him. He was relentless, refusing to let me pass.

"Self-preservation for the greater good is not cowardice," his voice was shaky. His expression was pained. I was taken aback. He wanted to be out there fighting too, not stuck guarding me. In my frustration I had forgotten myself. I sighed.

"How can it be for the greater good?" I pressed. "What good am I if none from the Alliance are left standing? What good are either of us?"

"What help would you be on the battlefield?" he shot back. "Your presence would serve only to distract those you wish to defend. There is more at stake here than you know."

I balked at his response. He was right. I was no coward, but I was also no soldier. I growled in frustration and turned away, not wanting him to see me cry.

"It just seems so hopeless," I whispered to no one in particular.

"It feels helpless. Helpless is not the same as hopeless." It almost seemed like he was trying to reassure himself as much as me. I looked at him. He seemed to have aged significantly since we'd first met. No longer was it obvious that he was younger than Azlyn. Whether it was due to the anomaly of elven aging, or the burden of experience I was not certain.

"Get some rest," he suggested. "It will make the waiting go by faster."

There was no point in arguing, and I was physically and emotionally drained. I laid down on the cave floor. The coolness of the stone felt good against my face. In moments I drifted out of consciousness.

I slept fitfully, tossing and turning until finally I couldn't take it anymore. I opened my eyes to a hazy darkness. Cazlyn laid an arm's length from me, his chest rising and falling steadily. I stood and paced by the mouth of the cave. I could see a sliver of light in the distance, though I couldn't tell if it was the sun rising or setting. How long had I been asleep? Was I truly going to stay here and hide while the others fought?

Not likely.

I stepped out from my cover and ran. Before long I found myself surrounded by the chaos of war. I heard the clash of iron on iron as a battle raged all around me. I spun around, trying to make sense of my surroundings. How much time had passed? How had the battle made it this far into the border? For a moment I thought that I must have gotten stuck in some sort of time warp.

The scene around me was lit as if it were midday. It was only after I smelled the smoke that I realized the source of the light came from a fire blazing all around us. I didn't have to go far to find the cause. A group of Elite soldiers surrounded a large ruby-colored figure wrapped in chains. A dragon. The King had a dragon.

The dragon thrashed against her captors, letting out a blood-curdling screech before belching a sea of flames up into the air. It was clear she was not a willing participant.

"Hold her steady!" someone yelled in the distance. "HOLD HER!" But it was too late. The creature had already come loose from her tether, throwing her captors this way and that as she reared and set the scenery aflame.

"Kala!" I heard Azlyn in the distance. I ran blindly in the direction of his voice. The thick, smoky air burned my lungs as I darted through the chaos in search of him.

"Azlyn!" I shouted. I could see his silhouette in the distance. His sword was locked with one of the Elite soldiers'. He spun so suddenly my eye almost couldn't follow, and felled his enemy before turning to me. His face lit up with relief and joy and he ran in my direction.

The hair on the back of my neck stood up as he approached me. Though it was impossible, one sound stood out to my mortal ears among the battle cries and swords clashing. It was the creak of wood and twine of a bow being drawn.

The arrow was loosed before I could shout out a warning. I felt the rush of wind rustle my hair as the arrow sailed over my shoulder and struck Azlyn in the chest. He hit the ground seconds before I would have reached him.

My grief was greater than fire in that moment. It consumed me, burning from the depths of my soul and billowing outward. In the distance I was aware of a shrill howling sound echoing across the valley as my knees hit the ground. It took me a long time to realize that the sound was coming from me.

The possibility of a future together, of uniting our people...it all vanished in that moment. I felt a rage build up inside of me at the injustice of it all, and a desire for reconciliation.

I bellowed my rage upward at the Gods, my hands digging into the earth, but my voice was lost in the chaos of battle. A wind picked up around me, blowing my hair to one side, and I hoped that it was a sign that the Wind God had taken pity on me and decided to carry my expression of grief and hatred across the valley.

I heard Eoma's voice

You cannot stay. They are coming.

My vision panned upwards and suddenly it was as if I was viewing the battle from above. The army became mere specks as the ground seemed to fly out from under me and the battle waged on surrounded by a ring of fire.

Then came the pain. It was cold and sharp, and it was the most pain I had ever felt in my life. I struggled to breath under the weight of the agony I was feeling.

In a panic I realized that, though I seemed to be drawing in an endless breath, none of it was registering in my lungs. In that moment I was certain that I was doomed to death. My vision went dark.

My eyes flew open. I was still in the cave. I bolted upright and looked up to see Cazlyn do the same. His wide-eyed stare told me all I needed to know. It hadn't been a dream.

"We can't stay," he said reaching out a hand to help me up. "They're coming."

EPILOGUE

THE ELVEN PEOPLE CARRY WITHIN THEM A GENETIC LINK. The knowledge of their ancestors is passed on through their bloodline. All prior learning, all their people's wisdom is passed down their bloodline. Everything that was known at the time of their gestation lives on in their offspring, growing with them, in the same way that one might inherit hair or eye color. Blossoming and flowing through their very being from the time of their first heartbeat, lying dormant until the age at which their brain has developed enough to handle the burden of the knowledge they are born with. It was a phenomenon his people referred to as the transfer of knowledge.

It was not long after the death of Azlyn when I learned that which Eoma had known when I stood before her and the rest of the Alliance. I was with child.

It seemed, at first, a cruel twist of fate that I would carry and raise the child alone; but it was also a ray of hope in a time of darkness. The Alliance, having been forced into battle before they were fully prepared, had been sorely beaten. Forced, once again, to retreat into the recesses of the forest. The death toll was high, and I was not the only one to lose a loved one that day.

Upon admitting their defeat, they sent me only one message: Stay. Hide. My treason had been known only to my cousin and the soldiers she had sent after me on her way to the uncharted territories.

My uncle had used his position in the army to keep the knowledge of my betrayal hidden well enough that it had not made it all the way up to the king. If I kept my head down, there was a chance that I could still have a life within the borders of my kingdom.

It would be dangerous, yes, but with the death of their prince, the affections of his people had turned sour, blaming me for his fate and accusing me of being compromised from the start. The Elders had deemed that my own kingdom was the safest option for my child.

But the promise of the new life that I carried represented a brighter future. The first ever of her kind; a perfect blend of human and elf. My daughter would be the key to the future of both Kingdoms. In time she would have at her disposal all of the knowledge of the lost journal that I had passed on to her father, and enough royal blood and standing to do something about it. Over time, Ludlum would age, and without an heir, his reign would come to an end. It was not much, but there was hope.

In those first days alone with her, it felt sometimes as if she felt it too.

About The Author

Stevie Rae Causey resides in the Pacific Northwest with her family, a dog, and a handful of quail. She enjoys adventure and can often be found searching for magic in the forests of Washington. She is currently working on her second series—A YA retelling of Rumpelstiltskin.

If you enjoyed the Amasai Rising series, please consider leaving a review on Amazon.

To keep up to date on scheduled events, signings, and new releases, you can join Between the Lines, a monthly newsletter by emailing stevieraecausey@gmail.com

Printed in Great Britain
by Amazon